FORTUNE'S WHEEL

BOOKS BY CAROLYN HUGHES

THE MEONBRIDGE CHRONICLES

Fortune's Wheel

A Woman's Lot

De Bohun's Destiny

THE FIRST MEONBRIDGE CHRONICLE

Fortune's Wheel

CAROLYN HUGHES

Riverdown

Published in 2019 by Riverdown Books

Riverdown Books
Southampton, SO32 3QG, United Kingdom
www.riverdownbooks.co.uk

ISBN 978-1-9160598-2-5 (paperback)
ISBN 978-1-9160598-3-2 (eBook)

British Library Cataloguing in Publication Data
A CIP catalogue record for this book is available from the British
Library

Cover design by Avalon Graphics www.avalongraphics.org

CAST OF CHARACTERS

ALICE ATTE WODE, a villein
John, Matthew and Agnes, her children
Stephen, her husband, dead in the plague
Geoffrey, her son, dead in the plague
Jack Sawyer, carpenter

ELEANOR TITHERIGE, a freewoman
Edward, her father
Roger Stronge, her stepbrother
Walter Nash, her shepherd
Cecily, Walter's aunt, a healer
Alysoun Greene, a friend of Eleanor

LADY MARGARET DE BOHUN, mistress of Meonbridge manor
Sir Richard, lord of Meonbridge, her husband
Philip and Johanna, their children
Alexander, their seneschal
Agatha, Lady Margaret's maid
Sir Giles Fitzpeyne, suitor to Johanna

Robert Tyler, the bailiff
Margery and Matilda, his daughters
Nathan and Hawisa, their servants
Gilbert Fletcher, a freeman

Thomas Miller, Meonbridge's miller
Joan, his wife
Peter and Maud, their children
Henry, Thomas's brother
Tom, Henry's son

Master Hugo Garret, priest
Simon Hogge, the butcher-barber-surgeon
Geoffrey Dyer, the constable
Martin Foreman, the hayward

Adam Wragge, a prosperous villein
Nicholas Cook, a prosperous villein
Thomas Rolfe, a prosperous villein
Ellen, Thomas's sister, brewster

Emma Coupar, a cottar
Bartholomew (Bart), her wastrel husband
Beatrix and Amice, their children
Ralph Ward, a cottar
Alys, his mother
Ann Webb, a cottar
William Cole, a cottar
William Mannering, a cottar
Harry, William Mannering's son
Susanna Bigge, a cottar and widow
Francis, her husband, dead in the plague

Nicholas Ashdown, a Winchester labourer
Kit Chapman, a pedlar
Edmund le Bowyer, an elderly soldier

PROLOGUE

Little Peter Miller ran down the path to the mill, his bare feet squelching and skidding in the mud, his arms clasping the bundle that contained his father's dinner. Pa was too busy to eat his dinner at home, because tomorrow was Midsummer's Eve, and he'd got his orders from the manor. And bread and pies for the whole village needed a lot of flour, and he was racing against time to grind it all.

So Ma wrapped a hunk of coarse bread, a lump of cheese and a flask of ale in a cloth, and bade Peter run to the mill and give the bundle to his father.

'But mind you hurry home again,' she said. 'The mill's no place for a lad to linger.'

Peter loved going to the mill: the noise and power of the rushing water made his heart beat faster, and the huge wheel as tall as a barn filled him with wonder. He knew he'd find his father upstairs in the loft, perhaps with Uncle Henry, feeding the grain into the hopper, from where it slithered down the tube to be ground between the two great millstones.

Peter climbed the narrow wooden stairs. The air in the loft was full of flying debris, motes of grain escaping from the hopper and clouds of dust rising from the millstones. It was hard to see beyond the floury fog.

Pa'd always warned him to be careful in the loft.

'Keep away from the stones,' he said whenever Peter ventured up there. 'And don't you get too close to the shaft.' His bushy eyebrows knit together in a frown.

So Peter stopped at the top of the stairs and called out. But the din of the great wheel driven by the torrent of the millrace just beyond the outer wall, and the grain whooshing through the hopper, and the huge stones grinding one against the other, drowned out his little voice. His father didn't hear him.

A few moments later, Peter realised he could just see his Pa on the other side of the hopper: he was red-faced and hot looking. But he wasn't looking his way, so Peter stepped a little further forward, still cautious but not wanting to make Ma cross by taking too long with his errand.

'I've brought your dinner, Pa!' he called again, waving the bundle in the air. But then his heart lurched, his head reeling, as he found himself teetering on the edge of the wide, open hatch in the floor, through which the full sacks of flour were hoisted up from below to the floor above for storage. He rocked slightly then, regaining his balance, stepped quickly back, his heart thumping, like the little throbbing hearts of rabbits just before he broke their necks.

Suddenly his father looked up and saw him. 'Stay there,' he shouted, his eyebrows meeting, and Peter didn't move. He held up the bundle again to show his father, who smiled and started forward to collect his dinner.

Thomas Miller's love for his son was so great that sometimes he thought his heart might burst: the very sight of the boy filled him with joy. He was a careful man: he knew his mill, and well understood its hazards. But his love, and anxiety for Peter's safety, made him hasty and, as he lunged forward, his foot caught on a beam in the floor, and he was falling towards his little boy.

He yelled 'Peter!' but the speed of his fall was too swift for the child's reactions and Thomas slammed into him, knocking him over, and down through the open hatch. Thomas cried out as he landed heavily face down at the hatch's edge. He looked down, praying that a pile of flour sacks had broken Peter's fall. But there were no sacks today: Peter's beloved little body was lying still, his slender legs crooked and awry, a trickle of blood oozing from his head, carving a bright red shiny trail through the floor's dusty coating.

Alice atte Wode, the Millers' closest neighbour, was feeding her hens when she heard Joan's first terrible anguished cries. Dropping her basket of seed, she ran to the Millers' cottage. She wanted to cry out too at what she found there: Thomas and Joan both on their knees, clasped together, with Peter's twisted body between them, sobbing as if the dam of their long pent-up emotions had burst. Alice breathed deeply to steady her nerves, for she didn't know how to offer any solace for the Millers' loss.

Not this time.

It was common enough for parents to lose children. It didn't mean you ever got used to their loss, or that you loved them any less than if they'd lived. Few lost five children in as many months. But the Millers had. The prosperous family Alice knew only six months ago, with its noisy brood of six happy, healthy children, had been swiftly and brutally slaughtered by the great mortality.

Every family in Meonbridge had lost someone to the plague's vile grip – a father, a mother, a child – but no other family had lost *five*.

The great mortality, sent by God, it was said, to punish the world for its sins, had torn the village apart. It had struck at random, at the old and the young, the rich and the poor, the innocent and the guilty. Some of its victims died coughing up blood, some with suppurating boils under their arms or next to their privy parts, some covered in dark, blackish pustules. A few recovered, but most did not and, after two or three days of fear and suffering, died in agony and despair, often alone and unshriven for the lack of a priest, when their loved ones abandoned them. After five months of terror, half of Meonbridge's people were dead.

When the foul sickness at last moved on, leaving the villagers to pick up the pieces of their shattered lives, Thomas and Joan Miller went to church daily, to pray for their five dead children's souls, and give thanks to God for sparing Peter. Then the arrival of baby Maud just a few days ago had brought the Millers a bright ray of hope in the long-drawn-out darkness of their despair.

But Peter hadn't been spared after all.

Alice crouched down in front of his weeping parents, kneeling together on the path that led to their cottage door, muddy from last night's rain. She intended to withdraw the child's body from between them and take him to be washed and prepared for burial. But Joan screamed and beat her off, grabbing at the still-warm little corpse. Clasping the limp husk of her son to her breast, she rocked back and forth, keening piteously. Thomas looked up at Alice, his dirty, floury face almost washed clean by tears, his eyes imploring her for an answer.

Alice eased herself to her feet, and stretched her painful back. Her once sturdy body ached a lot these days, perhaps from advancing age, but also from having so much to do since she had lost Stephen, and their dear son Geoffrey, to the plague. She brushed the worst of the mud from the skirt of her brown woollen kirtle, and pushed an escaped strand of greying hair back inside her wimple.

Alice shrugged at Thomas, not knowing what to say. She wanted answers for herself.

Why had the Millers been singled out for such particular anguish? And why, once their prolonged suffering had seemingly come to an end, along with everyone else's in the village, had this latest torment been inflicted upon them? It was hard to understand where God's love was in all this desolation.

Perhaps He had abandoned Meonbridge after all?

1

JUNE 1349

A lice atte Wode gazed around the vast high space of the manor's great hall. It was only six months ago that Meonbridge had come together here for the Christmas celebration. Then, everyone was full of dread; fearful of the news they'd heard about a terrible sickness sweeping across the world and already at England's shores. But at least they were then still all together.

Alice's beloved Stephen had still been alive, and their sweet boy Geoffrey, both now lying cold in the common grave that Stephen himself had ordered to be dug, as more and more folk died and the churchyard no longer had space for them all.

And it was Agnes's last evening before she disappeared, only the Good Lord Himself knew where. The girl had seemed uninterested in the celebrations, sitting silent and distracted, with none of her usual vivacity. She had not even bothered with her appearance, neither begging her father for a new kirtle, as she often did for Christmas, nor taking any trouble to decorate her hair, but letting her yellow curls hang plain and loose.

Tonight was Midsummer's Eve, usually a time of revelry and merrymaking, with games and mummers, and a great feast held on the village green. But this year, the new priest, Master Hugo Garret, decreed the festival would be one of thanksgiving, not merriment. At church the other Sunday, he mounted his platform on the chancel steps and glared at his flock standing together in the nave.

'This Midsummer Eve,' he said, 'all must come here to church, to pray and thank God and Our Lady for delivering Meonbridge from the evil that has stalked our lanes and byways since last Christmastide.' A few among the congregation murmured discontent, but Master Hugo glared again and coughed. 'Only then will it be fitting for the village to come together for a communal dinner.'

But, after months of constant rain, the green was too muddy for the dinner to be held in the usual place just beyond the church door, so, after prayers, everyone trooped up to the manor.

The hall was festooned with the Midsummer decorations of birch boughs, fennel and orpine, and garlands of flowers, and a hundred candles lit up the shadows. Despite the priest's avowal that this should not be a merry feast, it seemed Lady de Bohun had worked hard to bring some cheer to the occasion: a cheer most guests scarcely felt, despite doing their best to smile and wish each other good fortune.

But it was hard for them all; Alice was not alone in her grieving.

Alice's sons, John and little Matthew, were sitting on her right, and on her other side sat Simon Hogge, the butcher, and his wife Ann, still mourning the loss of their only child. They were young enough to have more children, but knowing this didn't make up for the ghastly death of their darling Elizabeth, a child of three with a mop of fair curls, a sunny smile and a perpetually dirty face. She was naughty but sweet-natured, the apple of her parents' eye. Yet no more so than the three small children of Agnes and Alexander Baker, or the grown up daughters of Margery Watson, or the two young sons of Robert Tyler, the bailiff, who had also lost his wife. Or, of course, Peter, the last surviving son of Joan and Thomas Miller. The Millers hadn't come this evening: Thomas was still in shock, and Joan had taken to her bed and wouldn't be coaxed out of it. And who could blame her? No-one here.

The parish clerk had drawn up a list of the dead, and Alice went to see it. Although she could not read the names, she could see the list was very long. Alice knew everyone who had died. She knew all their stories. It became her business to know, not because she was a gossip but because all the village families were her friends and neighbours, and she made a point of visiting them all and they were only too happy to pour out their hearts to her.

This was of course the job of the parish priest, but Master Hugo had come only recently to Meonbridge, given the post just a month ago, eight long, worrying weeks after dear Master Aelwyn finally gave up his soul to God. Hugo knew no-one in the village and was finding it hard to become accepted. Many folk no longer trusted the Church: angry that Meonbridge was left without a priest for two whole months, they didn't understand why God's ministers on earth couldn't prevent the mortality's terrible spread. They were aghast when God's wrath struck down two of His own, Aelwyn himself, and Alice's own son Geoffrey, apprenticed to Aelwyn and taking his first steps to training as a priest. It seemed the Church was no longer the rock of safety they had imagined it to be.

Sir Richard de Bohun banged on the table and rose to his feet. He looked thin and haggard, the neat rufous beard of his youth now grey and shaggy. The lord of Meonbridge was a man of action, not fashionable but careful with his dress and appearance. But, despite seeming to work hard at his smile, it was clear he too had been shaken by the horrors of the past six months.

'My friends,' he said, raising his voice and holding his goblet in the air. 'Let us raise our cups and give good cheer to one another. And let us give thanks to God that He has delivered us from the great mortality that has laid waste to Meonbridge, and taken so many of our loved ones from us.'

A small commotion rippled around the hall as everyone lifted high their cups, brimming with Sir Richard's good ale, and calls of 'Thanks be to God!' rose up into the rafters.

Alice lifted her best pewter goblet and, turning to her sons John and Matthew, bade them knock their wooden cups together. 'May we have good fortune.'

'Good fortune, Ma,' said John, forcing a smile, then wrapped a great arm around her shoulder and crushed her to his chest. A tear escaped from his eye, and he wiped it roughly away on the sleeve of his

river just beyond, for it was slippery from the rain. It was a bright, cool evening. The rain had stopped, the moon broken through the clouds, but, even though it was June, she found herself shivering and wrapped Stephen's best woollen cloak tightly round herself. They stopped for a moment on the bridge to look down into the river, shimmering in the moonlight, and rushing noisily downstream towards the mill, full from the torrents of rain that had fallen for so many weeks. Then Alice took Matthew's hand in her free one and the three of them marched briskly the short distance to their cottage.

Eleanor Titherige couldn't sleep. Bubbles of excitement kept welling up inside her as she recalled how John atte Wode had smiled at her this evening after the Midsummer feast.

She had been dreading going to the feast, because she'd be alone, without her father or her little brothers. In the end, she went with her stepbrother Roger, although when they arrived they separated and sat with their own groups of friends. Eleanor was disappointed that her best friend, Matilda Tyler, wasn't among her group but sitting on the lord's high table with her father, Robert, the bailiff, a big, dark-faced glowering man. Robert's position as Sir Richard's chief manor official gave him the privilege of eating with his lord every day if he so wished, and today the privilege extended to his daughters, Matilda and Margery. The scowl on Matilda's face suggested she'd not accepted the honour with much grace. Eleanor regretted she couldn't speak to Matilda: she particularly wanted to know who the man was sitting between her and her father. But Alysoun Greene, who knew all the gossip, was sitting opposite Eleanor.

'Oh, that's Matty's betrothed,' said Alysoun, her eyes alight with mischief. 'Gilbert Fletcher. Don't you know him? He's got a big house, very near yours, Elly, and two whole virgates. Quite a prize.'

Eleanor eyed the so-called prize. She realised she had seen him before, but he'd only lately come to Meonbridge. His long hair was straggling and lank, and his face was thin and gaunt, its expression unvaryingly sullen.

'He looks horrible,' she whispered to Alysoun, who giggled.

10

'Yes, doesn't he. He's so old too – nearly forty. And I've heard he's got a nasty temper.'

Poor Matty, thought Eleanor, wondering if Gilbert was really Matilda's choice, or if her father was making her marry him for his own advantage. It was true Matilda was rather vain and often said she'd have to marry a man who could keep her in fine clothes, so perhaps the marriage would give her what she wanted. But the more Eleanor stared at Gilbert, the more she thought Matilda must be an unwilling bride. After all, didn't she have her eyes on John atte Wode? But John was neither heir to a great estate nor a freeman, so no doubt Matilda's father would consider him an unsuitable match for his daughter.

Eleanor missed her own father greatly: her mother Christina had died in childbirth four years ago and since then she herself had been mother to her three young brothers and helper to her father, until he had married Roger's mother, Sarah, just over a year ago. She blinked away tears as the memory of the hideous and long-drawn-out deaths of her little brothers wormed its way back into her thoughts. Her father's death had at least been quick: weakened by the futile agony of nursing and then burying all three of his sons, at last the mortality seized him too in its vile grip and finished him off in hours. Eleanor was left alone with her stepmother and stepbrother, for whom she felt little affection and had received none in return. But it was not long before Sarah too died, and Eleanor and Roger had to fend for themselves. She couldn't understand why neither she nor Roger got sick, with the mortality in the house for weeks and everywhere in the village for months. But nobody understood how it spread or whom it would kill: in a few families everyone died, in most one or two, in a fortunate few no-one at all.

Roger inherited his mother's cottage, and chose to continue living there after his mother died. And, as no love was lost between the two stepsiblings, Eleanor was content with his decision.

So here she was alone in this great house, one of the best in the village, with a chimney in the hall and a large croft filled with fruit trees. Edward Titherige was already a prosperous merchant when he moved from busy Winchester to the quieter life of the village, on his marriage to Christina, the daughter of a wealthy Meonbridge family. Her father had promised her a substantial property when she married, and so Edward Titherige became a farmer as well as a merchant, and proved to be as successful in his new profession as in his former.

Eleanor lay in the big, canopied oak bed that once had been her parents'. It comforted her to sleep there: she felt closer to them, lying in the spaces where they had lain happily together for so many years, despite the fact that more recently it was Sarah who shared the bed with her father. Not that Sarah was a bad woman: Edward married her a year after her first husband Nicholas, the blacksmith, died, believing it right to provide a mother for his daughter and three young sons. But Eleanor resented the older woman's intrusion, and found her new stepbrother, at fourteen, four years her junior and on the cusp of manhood, yet still acting like a spoilt child, an unwelcome invasion into the household that for three years had been her own domain.

She pulled the blanket up around her chin and closed her eyes firmly, craving sleep. Tomorrow was Midsummer's Day, a holiday for most folk in the village: they'd tend to what animals had survived, but most would do no other work. Yesterday evening the customary Midsummer bonfires were set around the village, for the flames to ward off evil spirits and the smoke to purify the air.

As she lay in the dark, Eleanor could not help thinking once again of how last night had ended: Mistress atte Wode was bidding farewell to Lady de Bohun, her two sons John and Matthew standing politely by. Nearly everyone had gone home, but Eleanor lingered, hoping to speak to Matilda. But then Robert Tyler suddenly hurried his daughters away, and Eleanor had no chance to see her friend. So she made her way to the porch to thank Lady de Bohun, according to the courtesies her mother had taught her. But she found herself having to wait while Mistress atte Wode and her ladyship exchanged farewells, and she felt awkward and gauche with John standing nearby. Eleanor cast a sly glance in his direction, not wanting to be caught staring. But at that very moment John looked her way, noticed her glance and smiled broadly. She quickly looked away, sure that the pale skin of her cheeks was flaming, despite the coolness of the manor porch. Then Mistress atte Wode was wrapping her cloak around herself, and John came forward with his little brother to accompany his mother home and, as he did so, he came close to Eleanor and whispered 'Fare thee well, Mistress Titherige' in her ear. She turned in surprise and found him grinning playfully. Feeling both charmed and foolish, she bobbed a brief curtsey and managed to stumble out 'Master atte Wode'. He nodded his head to her, then bowed more formally to Lady de Bohun before taking his mother's arm, and the atte Wode family went out into the night.

To Eleanor's deep humiliation, it seemed Lady de Bohun had noticed the little exchange for, as Roger finally arrived to escort her home, the lady took her hand and squeezed it warmly. She smiled at her. 'It seems that the future may bring you good fortune, Eleanor. You deserve some happiness.' Eleanor was astonished: she couldn't remember Lady de Bohun ever speaking to her before. But she thanked her for her kindness, then pulled her hood close about her head, and she and Roger also stepped out into the cool starlit night.

For the past two months, Eleanor's grief had been so profound she'd hardly begun to think about how difficult life was going to be for her and Roger now they were alone, with no parents, yet with so many and such great responsibilities. If she thought too hard about it, she'd be too afraid to leave her bed and wish she were a child again. It had occurred to her that she needed a husband to manage her property for her, but with so many of Moonbridge's eligible men dead, it seemed likely she'd have to look outside the village, and that prospect frightened her dreadfully. But maybe all the eligible men *weren't* dead after all? Of course a smile was hardly a proposal of marriage, but it gave Eleanor some small grounds for hope.

Margaret de Bohun was alone at last, in her private room up in the solar. It was very welcome, this time to herself. She had left Richard, their son Philip and their cronies still carousing in the hall. They would drink and tell bawdy stories all night long, as was their custom on Midsummer's Eve. Good luck to them. She had no wish to join in with their drunken revelry; not that women were invited. All the wives had gone home to their beds or dispersed to their quarters around the manor house. She hoped Alexander would keep a watchful eye on his master and his friends, and not let them fall into the fire.

Margaret removed her elegant headdress and veil, and unplaited her hair, the colour of a mouse's fur Richard had often said, though now it was streaked with grey and even white. Wrapping her heavy blue woollen cloak around her, she slumped down a little heavily into the great oaken chair that stood next to the hearth. She closed her eyes and drank in the quiet of her chamber. She could just catch the sound of laughter and cheering drifting up from the men in the great hall below but the thick walls and floor muffled the noise so well that it would scarcely disturb her.

She breathed out a long sigh of relief. The Midsummer feast had been a success, despite her concerns that there might be insufficient food. There was of course more than enough of everything, because this time the company was much smaller than at the Christmas feast. Not only had so many people died but, of those who had survived, many had declined to come, saying they had little to celebrate. But for those who came, there was adequate ale and Richard was more generous than usual with his wine, so the tenants drank their fill, and, despite everyone's gloomy mood at the beginning of the evening, by its end a good deal of laughter and song were ringing round the hall.

Johanna had come upstairs too; she was still tired from her long journey from Surrey. Margaret was glad to have her daughter home again: she had missed her so much at Christmas. Richard had not understood how good a companion Johanna was to her mother. When he sent Johanna away to the de Courtenays, he said it was for her benefit and education, and who was she, her mother, to argue? Anyway, he did not ask for her opinion.

'Isabella will be a perfect substitute for our own daughter,' he said. What a fool he was to think such a thing. Isabella de Courtenay, who was living with them then, prior to her marriage to their son Philip, was a silly, vain girl, not at all, in Margaret's view, a good match for her son, despite the undoubted wealth and influence of her father. Isabella was most certainly *not* a substitute for Johanna, even though Margaret was the first to admit that her daughter had become most difficult and withdrawn in the weeks before she went away. Perhaps with good reason? Margaret wished she knew.

She was sure that Alice atte Wode would like to know too.

Poor Alice. She was three years Margaret's junior, yet her once cheerful face somehow looked much older than it did six months ago, or maybe it was just the melancholy of losing her beloved Stephen? But when Alice took her hand this evening to say farewell, her grip was still firm enough. Margaret returned the gesture and tried to show her heartfelt warmth in her smile, and offered her deep condolences for Stephen's death, and Geoffrey's. But she was not sure that Alice realised how very much she wanted to heal the rift between them. Margaret would not blame Alice if she did not want to, but her hand suggested otherwise. Margaret's heart grieved sorely for Alice, for her daughter Agnes had still not returned. And of course, since the mortality had struck down so many, in every town and village in the land, Alice did not know if her beloved Agnes was even alive.

Agnes had been such a pretty lively girl, so different in spirit from her own daughter Johanna. But, the day after the Christmas celebration, Agnes just disappeared from the village. No-one knew why, or where, she had gone. Perhaps she had found her way to a place spared the worst of the terrible sickness? But in the past two months Robert Tyler had brought back dreadful tales of even greater loss of life than here in Meonbridge. In Winchester, he said, many *more* than half the people died, and, in some places, whole populations perished, the villages left deserted.

Alice's misery must be all the more desperate for her not knowing if Agnes had found a safe haven. Or if she had even survived her flight, or had perished somewhere on the road, alone...

2

E leanor stood at the threshold to the forge, watching: Roger was doing his best to beat out the iron to make shoes for the priest's fine new chestnut mare. The boy was stripped to the waist, his skin red from the heat of the fire and black from the charcoal he was burning, and glistening with sweat from his exertions. She watched him for a while, then retreated to the small room behind the forge where they lived during the working day. In the middle of the floor was a small hearth, where she kept a fire going and cooked dinner for them both. She wondered whether it had been fair of her to encourage Roger to take on the forge. Yet it hadn't been entirely her persuading.

Several days ago, Sir Richard de Bohun had sent his son Philip to speak to Roger, who was summoned by Sir Richard's messenger to meet the young knight at the forge. Eleanor went with him, wishing to support her young stepbrother, and was listening from just behind the doorway, thinking she shouldn't interfere in men's business. Sir Richard was keen (or perhaps anxious) for Roger to continue the work. The forge was well sited, right in the centre of the village, and Roger's father, Nicholas, and then Edward le Smith, had built up a good reputation.

'My father has bid me encourage you to continue, Master Strong,' said Philip. 'The village must have a forge. It needs a good blacksmith.'

Roger shuffled his feet. 'But I'm not sure I can be a good smith, Sir Philip. I've been 'prenticed a bare two years. How can that be enough?'

'These are difficult times,' said the young de Bohun, 'And there is no-one else to do the work.' Surprisingly, then, he turned to where Eleanor was standing.

'What think you of this matter, Mistress Titherige?'

Astonished to have her view sought by such a man, she emerged from the doorway, blushing, and stammered a little in her answer.

'Sir, my stepbrother's young and perhaps lacking in confidence. He'll find it hard, especially if he has to work alone...'

'So you think he should refuse it?'

Eleanor shook her head. 'Indeed I do not, sir His father, Nicholas, was a fine blacksmith, and it was a great misfortune he died before his son was old enough to inherit. But my father told me Edward, who took on the forge, thought Roger a worthy apprentice and would've urged him to continue with his trade. As do I, sir.'

Philip gave a sort of half smile. 'A pretty speech, mistress.'

Eleanor blushed again, and nodded acknowledgement. She'd never been this close to Philip de Bohun before. There'd been much talk about him amongst her friends, especially when he returned from the king's wars in France a celebrated knight. When he came back to Meonbridge two years ago, no-one in the village had seen him since he was a child, for he'd been sent away when he was eight to learn to be a page. As a child, Eleanor recalled, Philip was slight, with dark curly hair and soft grey eyes and, although rather pretty for a boy, wore a permanently petulant expression. When he returned a man, the village girls were eager to set eyes on him, though occasions had been few: he attended the Christmas feasts and village festivities, and sometimes could be seen in the fields at haymaking or harvest. But the de Bohuns didn't generally go amongst their tenants, preferring to keep to themselves and to their own pastimes of hunting and hawking. However, when they at last saw Philip, everyone agreed the sullen boy had grown into a handsome man, no longer thin but tall and strong, with a thick mane of raven hair and his grey eyes now steely bright and piercing. His childish petulance had gone, but was replaced by a fierce solemnity that, for Eleanor, spoilt his undoubted physical attractions. Still, her best friend Matilda thought him perfection, but she always did set her sights very high, so it might have been his noble standing rather than his beauty that was Matilda's chief interest.

Eleanor remembered also that, soon after Philip returned to the manor, gossip flourished about him tumbling lots of the village girls. It was even rumoured he'd been seen with Agnes, John atte Wode's sister, and then *everyone* saw them together at last year's Midsummer celebrations. Eleanor couldn't quite recall what happened next, but two months later, Isabella de Courtenay arrived at the manor, and she and Philip married in November. Agnes vanished from the village around Christmas-time: a search party went out, but no trace of her was found and Agnes's father Stephen came home distraught. Rumours abounded about where and why Agnes had gone. A troupe of travelling entertainers had been in Meonbridge that Christmas, and some said they'd stolen Agnes away, for she was certainly the village beauty, with her yellow curls and pretty figure. But then the mortality struck, people stopped coming and going, and, although the atte Wodes were desperate to keep searching for their daughter, Sir Richard forbade them to leave the village again.

Philip nodded at Roger. 'So, young Stronge, your sister urges you to accept this opportunity. It is wise advice. And my father, Sir Richard, also bids you to accept.' He paused then added, perhaps thinking diplomacy might win the day, 'Though he would not of course demand it.'

Roger looked gloomy. Eleanor realised the boy was feeling cornered and that she'd contributed to his discomfort. In truth her view arose partly from fear of how he, and she, would live if they had no trade between them. Her father had left her a little money, but most of his property was in land – land she was ill equipped to manage. Roger's own inheritance of a cottage and croft included no money. So their joint inheritances would not put food on their table for long, and the half-siblings needed to earn a living.

After Philip's visit they ate their dinner in silence. But the visit did, it seemed, persuade Roger to accept, however unwillingly, that he would try to make a go of the enterprise. In a few days he would go to the hallmote to ask formally for the right to take it on and pay a fee for the privilege. Eleanor planned to attend the hallmote too, as she was now the owner of the Titherige land, and could play her part in the administration of justice in Meonbridge. Not knowing what was required of her, she was anxious: most tenants were certainly men, and she knew well enough that women's opinions were commonly held in low esteem. Still, she had to go, if only to support Roger's claim.

But, if Roger had decided where his future lay, Eleanor remained perplexed. She never expected to have to find work. Six months ago, as the daughter of a wealthy freeman with the prospect, even before her father's death, of a fine inheritance, Eleanor presumed she'd soon be married, perhaps to the son of one of Edward's equally prosperous merchant associates. She knew she was no beauty, with her lightly freckled skin and reddish hair, but she had always made the best of her appearance, and thought herself quite personable. So, when her father found her an eligible young man, already making his way as a wool merchant in Winchester, and heir to another of the more successful merchant houses in the city, she was delighted. And when they met, early last December, he seemed as attracted to her as she was to him. But she didn't meet the young man again, and in February, Edward received news that the merchant's entire family had perished in the mortality. Two weeks later Eleanor's own brothers sickened and she forgot all about her charming suitor.

Now Eleanor had her inheritance but her prospects for finding a husband seemed bleak. Despite her initial excitement at the brief attention shown her by John atte Wode, he'd not repeated his mischievousness towards her, and she wondered if she'd imagined it. But who else was there? And what was she to do about her land? She couldn't farm it on her own and few if any of the labourers left in the village were able or willing to help her. How far her fortunes had changed: despite her family's former prosperity, she was now scarcely any better off than the cottars, perhaps even than Emma Coupar.

Emma had called at Eleanor's house early this morning. Both Emma and her husband, Bartholomew, were constantly looking for paid work; with no land, apart from a tiny croft on which they could hardly do more than keep a pig and a few hens, they relied on their week-work for the manor and whatever other employment they could find to put food on their table.

Eleanor was finishing her small breakfast of bread and weak ale when there came a light knocking on her door. Emma stood outside, holding one grubby child by the hand and balancing a smaller one on her hip. Eleanor's heart melted at the sight of the children: a few months ago Emma had had five children, whom she took with her everywhere. Presumably the other three had perished, but Eleanor didn't have the courage to enquire.

Emma gave a little bob of a curtsey, as best she could with the children. 'God be with you, mistress.'

'And you, Mistress Coupar,' said Eleanor.

'I'm seeking work, mistress,' said Emma. 'Any work, indoors or out. Tending sheep or swine, digging the croft garden, field work...'

Emma looked hopeful but Eleanor couldn't give her work.

'Oh, Emma, I'm so sorry,' she said, 'but I truly can't afford to pay you.'

She thought Emma looked sceptical, but did not complain.

'I'm sure you'll find work, Emma, for there's so much to be done and so few people left.'

'Aye, mistress,' said Emma, pursing her lips, and, bobbing another curtsey, went to try Eleanor's neighbour.

It was true that, with so many dead, more work needed doing than there were hands to do it. But what could Eleanor herself do? She had a little education: her father had taught her her letters and she could read a few words; she could spin and weave, and she was skilled at growing vegetables and fruit and herbs, so she could perhaps earn a living as a weaver or a gardener. But how would she manage all her land if she spent her days toiling for someone else?

The state of her land was a worry in itself. After dinner, Eleanor walked out to look at her field strips. She knew little about farming, but she could see the land was in a sorry state: some strips had been ploughed and sown but in others, where the soil was not yet ploughed, last year's crop remained, rotten and slimy, in the ground. In some of the neighbouring strips, grass had been sown and was growing well, and would soon be ready for haymaking. They presumably belonged to folk with enough energy or family members still alive and able to do the work. The prospect of working her own fields by herself was daunting, not to say impossible.

As the day was unusually still fine, Eleanor decided to go on and look at the rest of her land. She had walked all the Titherige fields and pastures many times with her father, and knew where all the parcels of land were, both on the manor and outside it. On the outskirts of the manor's demesne, well to the south of the common fields, lay a large area of open grazing. The manor and a few individual villagers maintained several small flocks of sheep, all of which ran together there. But her father, having spent most of his merchant career in wool, developed a fancy for breeding sheep, and when he had an opportunity to buy Riverdown, an extensive parcel of uncultivated downland between Meonbridge and the neighbouring manor, he took it and stocked it with a sizeable flock. Eleanor was anxious to know how the sheep were faring: she hadn't seen them for three months. She knew they'd been in good hands: Edward had employed a full-time shepherd, Walter Nash, a young man who lived in an isolated cottage close to the pasture. She prayed he'd not succumbed to the mortality.

It was a beautiful walk up to the pastures, a long gradual pull uphill away from the village, and when you arrived at the top you had a wide view over the surrounding countryside. She thought about the time she last went up there with her father: three weeks before his death, they'd come up together to see Walter and the flock, and it was the last time she walked anywhere with her father.

It had been a wonderful crisp March day, a rare dry sunny day in a wet spring. Both shepherd and sheep looked well: Walter had had no visitors since the start of the mortality. The shepherd was tending to the first of the lambing ewes, doing it alone to avoid coming in to Meonbridge to get the extra help. As they approached, he climbed over the side of the wicker sheepfold to welcome them.

'Good day to you, shepherd,' called Edward Titherige, standing at a distance from Walter. 'I'm glad to find you yet untouched by the mortality. But we'll come no closer.'

'Aye, sir,' said Walter, 'it's as well I'm so far from the village. How is it there?'

'Not good, shepherd, not good at all.'

They talked a little of those lost, and Walter asked after his elderly aunt, Cecily, who lived alone in a small cottage on the outskirts of the village. Eleanor told him she was well.

'It's strange,' she added, 'how few of those who've died from the mortality were old. And many of those few elders who were afflicted got well again.'

'So 'tis the young are dying?' said Walter.

Eleanor nodded. 'Yes, the young and fit.' She thought of the strong young men who'd died, and those of her friends: so many people who'd not marry or have children. Walter was one of relatively few healthy young men left in Meonbridge. She looked at him, standing in front of the sheepfold hurdle, holding his cap respectfully in one hand. He was not handsome and his skin was even darker than the farmers', but his face was kind, and she knew him to be a gentle, thoughtful man, who found peace in his isolation.

'And what of the sheep, Walter?' said Edward, raising his voice a little above the rising wind.

'As you can see, sir, 'tis a fine flock. And the lambs are good this year.'

Edward nodded and Eleanor wished she could clasp one of the new lambs to her, to plunge her fingers into their soft creamy wool. But her father had given her strict instructions not to approach the shepherd or the sheep.

'But I've a worry, sir,' continued Walter. 'Can I take any of the lambs to market?'

Edward thought for a moment, then shook his head. 'I think not, Walter. The mortality's still raging throughout Meonbridge and we hear it's worse in Winchester. Best keep them here until it's passed and we can move about freely again.'

Walter nodded agreement, and Eleanor and her father turned to walk back to the village.

'Fare well, shepherd,' called Edward.

'Fare you well, Sir Edward. You also, mistress,' said Walter, and climbed back into the sheepfold.

Three weeks later Edward was dead, and Eleanor beside herself with grief.

Once she recovered a little from her initial shock and anguish, Eleanor tried hard to take on the responsibility of the farm that Edward had built up, but she found her efforts thwarted. The death of her brothers and her beloved father had not only left her deeply disconsolate, but also burdened her with a disagreeable stepbrother, and a stepmother whose only interest appeared to be her own son's inheritance. Sarah constantly discouraged her stepdaughter from taking an interest in the farm, claiming it was Roger's legacy, although Eleanor knew well enough this was not Edward's wish or intention. But the mortality thwarted Sarah's scheming, for she too was dead by the end of April without having altered Edward's will.

As Eleanor approached Riverdown this bright but cool June day, she found her sheep scattered beyond the Titherige pasture, with several wandering down the hill back towards the village. Dotted amongst the flock were dozens of well-grown lambs, staying close to their mothers. Then she saw a ewe prostrate upon the ground, and when she went to her, she found the animal wild-eyed and panting. Eleanor felt suddenly too hot, and her breathing became short and shallow, for she didn't know what to do if the ewe was sick. She scanned the horizon, searching for Walter. Surely he should be here with the flock? Where *was* he?

She ran the last few hundred yards towards Walter's tiny cottage. As she ran, she continued looking to see if he was out among the sheep, but there was no sign of him, and the sheepfolds in the home pasture were empty. Her heart pounding, Eleanor hurried to the cottage and rapped upon the door. There was no reply, so she knocked again, more loudly. Walter did not come, but Eleanor thought she heard a low sound coming from inside. She tried the door and it opened stiffly. It was pitch black inside and a strong, fetid smell assaulted her nostrils. Eleanor instinctively recoiled: the smell reminded her of the room where her family had died. She spun around and flew in a panic from the cottage, halting her flight by a young oak tree, where she leaned, trembling and breathless. As she took in great gulps of air in an attempt to calm herself, her thoughts thrashed around. If Walter was dead, she had to know and arrange for his burial. If he was sick with the mortality, how could she abandon him?

Steeling herself, Eleanor returned to the cottage. She pushed at the door and went inside, leaving the door open for light, and waiting a few moments until her eyes became accustomed to the dark. She saw then that the straw on the floor was sodden and rank, the fire in the central hearth was dead, and on a small table to one side of the hearth lay a trencher with a single piece of mouldy bread and an empty cup. There was no pallet in this room, so Walter must sleep elsewhere. A low door led to another room, which might have been a storeroom but she guessed was where the shepherd slept.

Cautiously Eleanor approached the door, knocked and called out 'Walter?'

A faint voice responded. 'Mistress Eleanor?' He was alive.

As she pushed open the door, the appalling smell assailed her again, but she drew the edge of her hood across her nose. The windowless room was darker still, though a small beam of light seeped through a gap in the thatch, enabling her just to make out the thin figure of the shepherd lying twisted on a pallet, covered by a coarse blanket. He groaned a little then spoke again, his voice thin and rasping.

'Mistress Eleanor, I'm glad indeed to see you. I thought you'd not come before I'd left this world.'

Eleanor knelt down by the pallet to try to see him better. 'Are you sick, Walter?'

'Nay, not sick, mistress, but near to death if you'd not come.'

'Why, what's happened?'

Walter feebly drew back the blanket and pointed to his leg: even in the gloom, she could see it was a bloody twisted mess wrapped in rags. Nausea rose in her throat at the sight and smell of it.

'Oh, Walter, how did you do that?'

The shepherd answered slowly, in short bursts. 'An accident. Chasing off a tod... foot slipped into a ditch... leg twisted under me... snapped...'

Eleanor gasped. 'How did you get back here?'

'Crawled... Dark when I got back... Been lying here since...'

Eleanor jumped up. 'I must get help.'

But Walter shot out his hand to stay her. 'Aye, but afore you go, get me ale.'

Eleanor darted into the other room to find some ale and, she hoped, something for him to eat apart from the mouldy bread on the table. She found another loaf in a basket hanging from the rafters, which was old and quite hard but not rotten, and a piece of salted meat. The small quantity of ale she found tasted sour, and she thought to try a ewe for a little milk. She was not practised at milking, but had done it once or twice and persuaded one of the mothers to give up a small bowlful. Walter was grateful for her efforts, though she had to stay and help him drink before she could leave, promising to return with someone who could mend his leg.

As she flew back down the hill to Meonbridge, Eleanor chided herself for making such a promise, for in truth she doubted there was anyone in the village who could mend Walter's broken leg. Once, when John the Thatcher fell from a cottage roof, the bailiff sent to Winchester for a surgeon. But with all the deaths in Winchester, it was likely there'd be no surgeon there, and anyway, if Walter was to live, he probably could wait no longer. Then Eleanor remembered that Simon Hogge, the butcher, had served Sir Richard in the king's wars, and was practised in removing limbs that could not be mended and, as she approached the village, it seemed to her that Simon might be Walter's only chance of life.

3

A lice was feeding the last of the few hens that had survived the cold, wet spring, when a messenger arrived from Lady de Bohun, asking Mistress atte Wode to call at the manor that afternoon. Apart from the Midsummer feast, Alice had not been to the manor for more than six months, a few days before the mortality came to Meonbridge. She was glad that Margaret wanted to see her again. She'd been a frequent visitor for many years, weaving cloth and making garments for Margaret, her daughter Johanna, and some of the servants. Alice was a skilled seamstress, but since that terrible day in December when her precious, petulant Agnes disappeared, she'd not practised her trade at the manor, nor even paid Margaret a social visit.

It was true that Alice wanted to heal the rift that arose between her and Margaret then, but now the time had come for the two women to meet again in private, when the matter of the rift, if it came up, could no longer be gainsaid, she was anxious. John said she should still keep away from the manor, as the reason for Agnes's disappearance had never been resolved, despite the rumours that flew about at the time. Everyone knew, he said, that Philip de Bohun was responsible, but Alice was slow to blame, unprepared to believe what "everyone knew" until proof had been established. And it hadn't.

· · ·

Before she went up to the manor, Alice made her daily visit to her neighbours, the Millers. She hadn't seen Thomas on any of her recent visits; it seemed he spent more time than ever at the mill, perhaps finding unremitting labour the only possible distraction from the anguish of losing all his sons. He barely acknowledged little Maud's presence: the death of Peter, his last and favourite son, seemed to have killed his fatherly instincts and he neither touched nor responded to the tiny girl in any way. As for Joan, unable to break free from the despair that confined her to her bed for hours of every day, she was neglecting her only surviving, and probably last, child. The Joan whom Alice had known just six months ago, the cheerful mother of a happy brood of healthy children, had vanished, replaced by a desolate sloven.

Alice always approached the Millers' cottage with caution, never sure if her neighbour would welcome her visit. She called out Joan's name as she came close and, surprisingly, before she had a chance to knock, Joan opened the door. She stood on the threshold, scowling, with the bundle that was Maud balanced precariously on her hip.

'Oh it's you, neighbour,' she said, forcing a weak smile. 'Come in.'

She stood aside to let Alice pass. The room was very dark and it was no warmer indoors than it was outside: Joan had let the fire go out, and not bothered to open the shutter on the single window.

'Shall I help you with the fire?' said Alice, bending down to clear the hearth of debris. 'You must keep the fire going, Joan, for Maud's sake, if not for your own comfort.'

Joan nodded but said nothing, then put Maud gently down in her cradle, and stooped to help Alice.

'I'd fain we'd all died,' she whispered.

Alice shook her head. 'No, Joan, you mustn't say that. Only God decides who lives and dies.'

Joan snorted. 'What do I care for God?'

Alice reeled a little at the blasphemy. Of course she could understand Joan's rejection. She was hardly alone in her bitterness: many people in the village had turned their backs on the Church, blaming it for not preventing the mortality destroying the lives of their children and families. But most did not blame God Himself. Alice couldn't blame Him either, despite watching her beloved husband and gentle son give up their souls in the cruellest agony. But she was

27

bewildered that He would allow His own servants – Geoffrey, and Master Aelwyn – to perish while doing His work. It was very hard to understand. And, not really understanding what she believed or wanted to believe, she decided to put her faith in the Holy Mother.

'Perhaps you could pray to Our Lady?' she ventured. 'She was a mother who watched Her Son die. Surely she could give you comfort in your grief?'

Joan sniffed. 'Maybe. I pray little.' She took a broom and listlessly swept the soiled rushes through the door.

Alice wasn't sure whether to persist, sensing rancour in Joan's resistance, but made one last attempt. 'I do find comfort with Our Blessed Virgin Mary.'

'I know you're trying to help, Alice,' said Joan. 'But I've no need of that sort of help.'

Alice sighed, and nodded acknowledgement of Joan's wishes. Perhaps she'd speak to Master Hugo about Joan. But for now she'd just help her to get a little comfort back into the damp and gloomy cottage.

So far the day had been fine and dry, if not as warm as might be expected for the end of June. Alice wrapped herself in Stephen's good cloak, and put on her best boots, for the short but still difficult walk from her house to the manor. It might be summer, and dry today, but it had been raining on and off for weeks and the gulleys at the sides of the road still ran fast with rainwater. The road itself was muddy and tricky to negotiate, and she picked her way carefully to avoid slipping into the deep ditches. It was not far, but by the time she reached the manor gate, Alice's boots were soaked through to the inside.

The gatekeeper opened the massive oak door to let her in to the manor porch. A servant came to escort her to Margaret's quarters. Standing outside the door to the solar, Alice felt a stranger. She'd come to this room almost every day for fifteen years, but now it seemed as if those happy days when Agnes and Johanna played together had never been.

The servant announced Alice and showed her in. The great room was just as she remembered it, rising high up to the rafters, with a grand fireplace set into one of its long walls and a fine tall window that looked out across Meonbridge. But the richly coloured carpets that adorned the wooden floors were new to Alice, and she fancied the walls had been freshly painted, in bright, warm colours.

Margaret advanced, her hand outstretched, a welcoming smile on her face. 'Alice. Thank you for coming. It is good to see you here after all this time.'

Alice took her hand and bowed her head in greeting. 'Lady de Bohun.'

'"Margaret", please, Alice,' said the lady. 'You know you do not have to be formal with me.'

Alice smiled acknowledgement. 'Margaret.'

The lady bade her sit. 'I have a task for you, Alice,' she said, sitting down in her grand oak chair. 'Johanna has brought home some wonderful cloth from the de Courtenays, and I wish you to make us some gowns.'

Alice smiled acceptance of the commission. It was not like her to be so mute, but it troubled her that Margaret was behaving as if there'd been no disagreement between them. Did she intend simply to forget what had happened? And if she did, could Alice resign herself to that? The pain of Agnes's disappearance never left her: every night she prayed to God and Our Lady that tomorrow Agnes might be delivered back to her, and every day she grieved when her daughter did not return, and she'd no way of knowing if she ever would, or even if she could. Margaret had her daughter back home; how could she fail to recognise Alice's grief that hers was still missing?

'If you show me the cloth?' said Alice.

Margaret signalled to her lady's maid, who came forward with three great bolts, two of fine wool and one of woven silk, all in rich, vibrant hues of blue and green. Alice suppressed a gasp at their beauty. She was not poor, but her own tunic, of good but coarse wool, was grey; as were her surcoat and hood, and as were the clothes of most of her neighbours, grey or perhaps brown, but never blue or green. Except, she thought, for Matilda Tyler, remembering the fine, richly coloured gown she wore at the Christmas feast, a young woman who certainly aspired to the fashions of the gentry.

29

'They're beautiful,' she said, lightly running a finger along the fine wool. 'They'll make fine gowns. For you?'

Margaret nodded. 'Three each, I think, for myself and for Johanna. And perhaps there is enough of the green wool for a tunic for Agatha.' She gestured towards her lady's maid, who bobbed her head and smiled graciously. 'And also for Edith?' Alice had heard Edith was a young girl brought home by Johanna to be her personal maid.

'There's plenty, I'm sure,' murmured Alice, nodding, and could think of nothing more to say, as the likeness of that other young girl, her lovely Agnes, with her yellow curls, floated into her mind. She steeled herself for the conversation she felt she could not evade.

'And how is your daughter, the Lady Johanna?' she said. 'Well?'

Margaret visibly faltered, making Alice think that all this talk of cloth and gowns was, for Margaret too, a distraction from what really must be said. But the lady barely missed a beat as she threw back her head and laughed with joy.

'Oh, Alice, Johanna is quite splendid. Do you know, the mortality missed the de Courtenay castle and manor entirely. Sir Richard and I were so relieved to learn that Johanna was safe.'

'I'm so glad you can rejoice in her return,' said Alice.

A sudden cloud passed across Margaret's face and, unusually, she seemed to struggle a little for what to say.

Margaret rose suddenly from her chair, made a small circuit around the room and then, coming over to Alice, took her hands.

'It has been too long, my dear Alice, that we have been estranged. It must end, do you not agree?'

Alice gave a single nod, not wanting to appear too eager. 'But the reason for it's not been answered.'

Margaret withdrew her hands and turned her face away. 'No, Alice, it has not, and we must resolve it, I do accept that.'

'But?' said Alice, sensing that Margaret was about to say she could not resolve it now or even soon.

Margaret turned around and smiled thinly. 'Oh, Alice. Yes, there is a "but", but only that now the manor, and of course Meonbridge, is still in such turmoil, perhaps it is not the right time to investigate what happened.'

'I don't think John'll let it lie unanswered,' said Alice. 'Now he can travel once again, I'm sure he'll pursue the matter.'

'And is that what you want, Alice?'

Alice almost gasped. 'How could I not? You have Johanna back; can you possibly imagine I don't want my Agnes back too?'

Margaret flushed slightly. 'Of course. How foolish of me to suggest otherwise.'

A short silence filled the space between the women. Then Margaret rose briskly from her chair and, going over to Agatha, bade her go. Agatha curtsied and left the room.

'Alice,' said Margaret, 'I do want you to make some gowns for me, but you will understand, I think, that my real reason for asking you here was so that we could try to heal the rift between us.'

Alice nodded but said nothing.

'It is clear,' Margaret continued, 'that we must speak about the rumours surrounding Agnes's disappearance. It will be difficult for us both, of course, but we cannot allow this estrangement to continue and destroy the friendship that we enjoyed for so long. Do you agree?'

'You know I do.'

Margaret sat down again. 'It has been a long while since Agnes went, and there has been such suffering all that time. I pray she found a place of safety, from the mortality as well as from the world.'

Alice sighed. 'It's not knowing that's so cruel. If I knew she was dead, it'd be a terrible pain, but somehow easier to bear.'

'I do understand. That is why we would hardly hinder John from searching for her.'

'But he doesn't know where to start looking. He needs to talk to those who might know.'

'And so many are dead...'

'But there's at least one who's not dead,' said Alice, looking at Margaret directly.

'Johanna?' said Margaret, anxiety returning to her face, and Alice nodded.

'But Johanna had already gone to the de Courtenays when Agnes disappeared.'

'But Agnes stopped seeing Johanna before she went away. Though she wouldn't say why.'

Margaret nodded. 'Johanna became withdrawn and solitary, yet refused to say what ailed her.'

'It was then, I think, that you sent her away.'

'It was Richard's decision, not mine,' said Margaret, pursing her lips. 'I would have preferred to keep Johanna here with me. Perhaps then I could have discovered why she was so gloomy.' She paused, then added quietly, 'And maybe also why Agnes disappeared.'

4

Eleanor flew back to the village in a panic. Reaching the rough track that entered the village from the south, passing between the wide acres of the common fields, she called out to the men working there, cutting the meagre crop of hay. But her gasping voice did not carry, and she had to stop to catch her breath. Looking over towards the men, she thought she could see John atte Wode among the group of five or six scattered across the nearest field and, jumping over the ditch at the side of the track, she ran towards him. As she got closer, she could see it was indeed John and began to call his name. By the time she reached him, she was breathing hard, and John looked up from his work, concerned.

'What's up, Mistress Titherige? Is something amiss?'

'Oh, Master atte Wode, please come and help me. Our shepherd, Walter Nash, is badly hurt. He needs help.' She gesticulated wildly back up the hill. 'Up there, at his cottage.'

'But how can I help, mistress?' said John, 'I don't know any physic.'

'No, no,' she gasped, still trying to recover her breath, 'I just want help getting him down to the village.'

John called two of the other men to come over, then leapt onto the back of his cart and started spreading out the hay. Bartholomew

Coupar and Ralph Ward threw down their scythes and came running across the field.

'Summat amiss?' said Bartholomew.

'Just help me with this, Bart,' said John. 'We've to take the cart up to the pasture to bring down Walter Nash.'

Eleanor could see they were working as fast as they could to get the cart ready for Walter, but she felt so anxious and agitated, thinking of the shepherd lying in such pain and perhaps near to death, that she had to bite on her fist to stop herself from crying out. But at last the cart was ready and John called to Eleanor to climb up onto the seat beside him, while Bartholomew and Ralph clambered into the back. John took the reins of his two strong plough horses and turned the cart to take it along the track up to the pasture.

It was rough going on the track, for the endless rain had deepened the wheel ruts, and John had to work hard to keep the cart from sliding into the ditches on either side. It was better once they came off the track and started climbing the shallow hill, for the chalky ground was well drained and firm.

They found Walter alive but barely conscious and somewhat out of his wits, though he did give a weak smile when he saw Eleanor had kept her promise.

Not knowing what else to do, Eleanor asked John and the others to take the shepherd to her own house, and once there she quickly laid down a straw pallet in the hall, close to the hearth. Then, as John rekindled the fire, Ralph went to fetch Simon Hogge the butcher, and Bartholomew ran to the parsonage to bring Master Hugo, she unwrapped the filthy, bloody rags from Walter's leg. She soaked them well with water but the blood had dried stiff and sticky and it was hard to remove the cloth without Walter crying out in pain.

As the fire burned stronger, John put a pot of water on to heat, then helped Eleanor to bathe Walter's leg and clean away the congealed blood. Not only was the leg clearly broken and at an unnatural angle, but a great flap of flesh was torn away, exposing the bone beneath. To their inexperienced eyes, it looked bad.

Butcher and priest arrived together: Hugo knelt at Walter's head and prayed, while Simon Hogge crouched by his leg and ran his hands over it. When he first arrived, Eleanor had taken Simon aside and said quietly she thought he'd have to remove the leg, but shortly he looked up at her worried face and smiled.

'I can mend this, Mistress Eleanor. I seen a lot worse 'n this at Crécy.'

'I didn't know you were at Crécy, Master Hogge,' said Hugo. 'Did you attend Sir Richard?'

'I did, sir.'

'I warrant you saw more broken limbs on the battle fields than you'd ever see here in Meonbridge,' said the priest.

'Indeed so, sir. More 'n I care to remember.'

'What do you need to mend the leg, Master Hogge?' said Eleanor, anxious for Walter's misery to be eased as quickly as possible. 'What can we get for you?'

Simon gave instructions for thread and needle, wine for cleaning the wound, wood for splints and cloth for bandages, and John and Eleanor set off in different directions to find them, while he put on another pot of water to heat.

When Eleanor returned, she sat by Walter's side and held his hand. He was a strong young man and, despite his pain and the fear he was going to lose his leg, he seemed determined to remain optimistic and conscious of what was happening to him. But the distress of his accident, the hours of lying alone in the dark with hardly a morsel of food or a sip of water, and the agonising journey back to the village as the hay cart lurched from rut to rut had all weakened his spirit and finally unconsciousness overtook him.

She called Simon over. 'Poor Walter's sleeping at last.'

'It's as well he is,' said Simon. 'If he stays that way, mebbe I can mend his leg the easier.'

It was late afternoon by the time Walter's leg had been cleaned, bones straightened, flesh stitched and the splint tightly bound. The shepherd had not stayed asleep but awoke just as Simon was starting to stitch his torn flesh back together, and he had to be held down and given wine to help him through the ordeal. But it was finally done, and Walter sank back into a fitful sleep. Eleanor thanked Simon effusively and offered to pay him for his skill but the butcher refused payment, saying he was content to have helped a neighbour survive and perhaps continue to make a living. Master Hugo had already bidden them goodnight, saying he'd go to the church and pray for Walter's recovery.

And so Eleanor now found herself alone with John atte Wode.

'It's been a long day,' said John, as they sat quietly together by the hearth, sipping warmed wine.

'Yes, indeed,' said Eleanor, smiling up at him. 'But, thanks to you, a happy outcome.'

John shook his head. 'Thanks to Simon Hogge. I didn't know he could do that.'

Eleanor smiled ruefully. 'No. I thought he'd just hack off poor Walter's leg.'

She looked across at Walter, sleeping but restless and moaning from time to time. 'But at least he's alive.'

John frowned. 'You do know he may not be able to work again, don't you?'

Eleanor gasped. 'Not work? But I thought that, with his mended leg...'

John shook his head sorrowfully. 'I'm sure Simon did a fine job, but the leg'll surely not be the same as it was? You must've seen people with mended legs, Mistress Eleanor?'

Eleanor nodded. 'Of course. It was foolish of me to think otherwise.' She sipped at her wine and a tear ran down her cheek.

John looked at her. 'You care for Walter.'

Eleanor nodded. 'He's a loyal servant. And a good shepherd.'

John breathed out a small sigh. 'He's a very fine shepherd. And perhaps he'll be able to carry on with some of the work.'

'But not all of it,' Eleanor added, and then was working out what to say next.

'Master atte Wode,' she said at length, 'please advise me. D'you think *I* could be a shepherd? I know something of sheep, and my father built up a large flock that I'd not wish to sell. I've been thinking I could turn more of my land to pasture, for sheep are easier to manage than beans and barley. What d'you think?'

John seemed to think for only a moment before agreeing that Eleanor's plan was a good one.

Eleanor thanked him, and then he added, in a low voice: 'I admire you greatly, Mistress Eleanor. You're strong, and kind, giving support to your stepbrother and doing so much for your shepherd.'

Eleanor knew she was blushing, and was glad it was too gloomy in the room for John to see. He leaned across and placed his hand lightly upon hers, then got to his feet.

'I must go home. Ma'll be wondering where I am.'

'Up to no good in a maiden's house,' said Eleanor playfully, then regretted it in case it sounded immodest.

But John just smiled broadly and bade her good evening.

5

It was almost evening by the time Alice took her leave of Lady de Bohun. She nodded farewell to the gatekeeper and stepped out again into another downpour of summer rain. Her boots had dried out during her stay in Margaret's comfortable solar, but by the time she reached home, they were soaked through again, as was her woollen cloak. She'd left Matthew in charge of the fire, so was hopeful it would be cosy in the cottage but, when she pushed opened the door, leaning heavily against it to prise the swollen wood from its frame, she saw to her exasperation that the fire was a feeble thing, and Matthew was nowhere to be seen.

Alice's temper did not rise easily: she was irritated that the boy had not done as she'd asked, but she was so grateful he was still alive when so many children had died that she'd not reprimand him when he came home. She felt fortunate to have two surviving sons. Among all of her friends and neighbours, so many had lost husbands and wives that it seemed few couples now remained. But terrible as it was to lose your partner, it was the loss of children that often caused the cruellest pain, especially when those children had grown almost to adulthood and were on the brink of making their own way in the world. Like Geoffrey, who so long dreamed of becoming a priest that Stephen had asked permission from Sir Richard for him to be educated, and they'd paid the fee so he could train with Master Aelwyn. And like Agnes, a mischievous, almost wayward girl, but the light of their lives.

Alice lit a tallow candle, rekindled the fire and hung a pot of water on the hook. She arranged her sodden cloak and boots around a wooden rack close to the fire, hoping they might dry a little. In winter they invariably found their clothes were permanently damp, for there was never time, or heat, enough for them to dry. Sleeping in them helped a little, but she always longed for spring, when longer days and the promise of some sunshine and less rain meant damp clothes could dry outside. But this spring and summer, as last year, had been almost as wet as winter and brought no respite from the discomfort of wearing clammy clothes.

Alice decided to make a little pottage for their supper: she added oatmeal to the pot, together with a few dried peas she'd already soaked and a scrap of the small piece of salted pork that remained, hung up in the storeroom. She stirred the pottage well, and waited for her sons to return.

But when John returned, he was alone.

'Is Matthew not with you?' she said.

John shrugged. 'I've been haymaking all day, then Mistress Eleanor came and asked me to help her with Walter Nash.'

Alice looked confused. 'Help her do what with Walter Nash?'

'He broke his leg,' said John. 'I'll tell you all about it later, Ma. First, we must find Matt. I thought he was staying here today, to help you.'

Alice sighed. 'He was, but then I went out and I told him to stay home and tend the fire.'

John grinned in understanding of his little brother's wilfulness. 'He didn't, then?'

'No,' said Alice, crossly, 'and now I'm worried. Where is he?'

John put his arm round his mother's shoulder. 'Shall I go and look for him, Ma?'

'I'm sorry to ask you when you've just come in, and it's raining again.'

'It don't matter, Ma, I can't get any wetter, and I think I might know where he is.'

John heaved the door open again and dived out into the downpour.

Alice smiled to herself: he was a good son. And how important he was about to become, if what Margaret told her earlier was true.

It wasn't long before the door of the cottage was shoved open again and John fell into the room with a giggling Matthew close behind him. The boy was surprisingly dry.

'And where've you been all this time, my lad?' said Alice, pretending to scold.

Matthew looked across at his brother and they exchanged grins.

'Go on, tell Ma where you've been,' said John.

'To feed the pigs,' said the boy.

'But why were you so long?'

Matthew looked at his feet and shuffled from side to side. 'Fell asleep,' he said, sheepishly.

Now Alice laughed, and ruffled her son's hair. 'You ninny. It's a wonder the sow didn't trample you. And, anyway, you were supposed to be looking after the fire.'

The boy mumbled an apology and ducked away from his mother's caressing hand.

Alice set out three wooden bowls and spoons upon the table, and put down a jug of ale, as John removed his outer clothes to hang them by the fire next to his mother's cloak, and put on his only dry tunic.

'If only it'd stop raining,' he said. 'Still, most of the day was fine, and we got in all the hay in Long Acre, though it's a poor crop.'

Alice nodded in sympathy. 'Perhaps you'll not have to work the fields much longer.'

'How so?' said John.

'I was up at the manor today with Margaret–' she began, but John interrupted her.

'I thought you'd agreed not to go up to the manor,' he said, frowning.

'No, John, you said I shouldn't, but I didn't agree. It's not my way to go on with a quarrel when I've a chance to heal it.'

John pressed his lips together but said no more.

'Anyway, I was going to tell you what Margaret said,' said Alice. 'It concerns you.'

'Me?'

'I'm surprised you haven't heard. Sir Richard wants you as the new reeve—'

John snorted. 'But I'm too young.'

Alice shrugged. 'You're younger than usual to be chosen for reeve, but these are unusual times.'

'Anyway, reeves have to be tenants, and I'm not.'

Alice did wonder why the usual rules about the appointment of reeves were apparently to be ignored.

'So why does Sir Richard want me for reeve?' John continued. 'Did Lady de Bohun say?'

'She said Richard thinks you're your father's son, and'll be as good a reeve as he was. And, after all, you're well-liked in the village.'

John sat down heavily on a stool, and poured a pot of ale from the jug. 'I'm not sure I want to be reeve. If I'm well-liked now, I soon won't be.'

'But, if you're chosen, surely you won't refuse?'

John shrugged. 'Anyway, it's not for the lord to choose. The tenants elect the reeve.'

'Margaret told me Richard's asked Master Hugo and Robert Tyler to go round the tenants and get them to support you. So at the court you'll be asked to serve, and I think the election'll go your way.'

'Why me?' said John wearily. 'I've our farm to run. D'you want me to leave all the work to you?'

'Remember that as reeve you'll be freed from all the week-work,' said Alice. 'And you'll have more money to buy labour to help us in our fields.'

John snorted again. 'What labour? There isn't any.'

'That's not true. Emma Coupar was here only this morning looking for work.'

John grunted. 'Emma Coupar can't plough. And the men are complaining already there's too much to do and not enough folk to do it. If I'm reeve, it'll be me who has to force them to work the manor fields, when all they want is to farm their own land.'

John's face was dark, all sign of his earlier merriment vanished.

'Will you refuse it, then?' asked Alice.

'Can I refuse?' he said, brightening a little.

Alice shrugged. 'I know men've refused the office in the past, but when Sir Richard's asked for you, do you think you can really say no?'

John shook his head. 'Perhaps not.' Then he pulled a half smile. 'But his lordship might regret his choice. If he thinks I'll be his man, he's wrong. Times've changed. Folk don't want to give the manor week-work anymore. They want to work their own strips. And those who work for money say they should be paid more. Labour's in short supply now, so they'll demand higher wages. And who can blame them? Not me.'

6

Two days after Simon Hogge had set his leg, Walter woke up from a deep sleep. Eleanor had watched over him all that time, not wanting to leave him, in case he needed help. As he opened his eyes and looked around, confused by his surroundings, Eleanor smiled at him, but Walter frowned and tried to rise from his pallet. He immediately sank back down with the effort of raising a body that had lain immobile for so long. He tried to speak but his voice was croaky and Eleanor held a cup of water to his lips and he drank.

He cleared his throat to speak. 'How long've I been here, mistress?'

'Two days since I found you. Simon Hogge mended your broken leg and you've been sleeping ever since.'

Walter looked alarmed.

'But I can't stay here, Mistress Eleanor, it's not fitting.'

Eleanor dismissed any idea of impropriety. 'You're not going home, Walter. You need rest and food, and you'll have that here.'

'But it's not right you should—' began Walter.

But Eleanor held up her hand. 'That's for me to decide. And I have. I need you to get well, Master Nash, for we've a fine flock of sheep to care for.'

Walter looked up in surprise. 'We?'

Eleanor nodded. '"We" indeed. I've decided you and I are going to build the finest flock in Meonbridge, even in the whole of Hampshire.'

Despite the pain in his leg, Walter managed to laugh. 'You've ambitions, mistress.'

Eleanor laughed as well. 'Yes, I have, Master Nash. As I can't plough my land, I'm going to turn it over to pasture and have hundreds of sheep. What do you think of that?'

'I think very well on it, mistress. And, if I may say it, I think Sir Edward'd be proud of your decision. He prized his flock so well.'

Eleanor knelt down by Walter and smiled. 'Yes, he did, and that's why I so much want to continue with it. But I need your help, Walter. I can't do it alone.'

'Then my leg must mend soon,' he said, his eyes twinkling despite his obvious discomfort. 'So I can get back to work.'

'Indeed, and that's why you must stay here until you're strong. Of course I must also attend to my brother Roger, and I'll tend the sheep as best I can. So I've asked Mistress Nash to care for you while I'm out and about. But I'll return during the day to be sure you have whatever you need.'

Walter looked a little abashed. 'I'm obliged to have so kind a mistress. I'll repay your kindness, as soon as I'm well enough to work again.'

A few days ago Eleanor had been wondering how best to earn her living, but now she'd both a plan and plenty to do. First, she had to help her stepbrother, for the boy was trying hard yet struggling a little with his new trade. He needed her moral support, as well as the daily dinners she cooked for him. Then, every day, she took the long walk up to the Riverdown pasture to check her sheep were thriving, though in truth she knew little about sheep husbandry. She did know it was time for the sheep to be shorn, but as she'd no idea how to do it herself, she'd have to use some of her meagre funds to pay someone in the village. She was loath to worry Walter with it, for she was fearful he'd try to go and do it himself. The shepherd was strong and it was clear already he'd survived his accident, though perhaps he'd not walk again without a painful limp. But he needed time to recover and she'd have to manage the flock by herself for some weeks to come.

Often, as she stood on the top of the hill at Riverdown, looking out across the wide panorama of the Hampshire countryside, she thought of those she'd lost: her mother and her brothers, but mostly her father, who'd built up this great flock of sheep that was now her responsibility. She stood and stared, sometimes wondering what other villages and towns she could see and how far away they were. On a clear day she knew she could see as far as the sea, which Edward had told her was a vast expanse of water across which men travelled in boats to go to France. Eleanor couldn't imagine what this mysterious sea must look like and thought how much she'd like to see it. But today, and for the future, her concerns had to be her sheep, her shepherd, and her stepbrother. And also, she thought guiltily, the friend she'd barely spoken to for months, Matilda Tyler. At the Midsummer feast, Matilda had looked melancholy and it seemed her father was deliberately keeping her from her friends. Even so, Eleanor was determined to try to see her.

Matilda Tyler was once Eleanor's best friend. Eleanor's father Edward had disliked Robert Tyler, thinking him a rogue, despite his elevation to the position of bailiff, but he'd not prevented Eleanor from taking up a close friendship with the daughter of Meonbridge's wealthiest and most influential villein. The two girls had played together and whispered together in secret places ever since they had first met, when as little children they accompanied their then less affluent mothers to draw water from the well.

Now the Tylers lived in a large, long house on the western edge of the village, a house that seemed to grow larger and more opulent each year, as Robert's wealth increased and he added another bay or imported another tapestry or table to demonstrate his affluence to his neighbours. Edward Titherige was a merchant and no stranger to exercising his influence to win more business and increase his income, but Eleanor had often heard him say how much he despised Robert's tactics of using his wealth and his power in the village to advance his own position at the expense of his neighbours. He seemed to be

45

plotting the inexorable rise of the Tyler family, to be raising his children to believe their position in life was an exalted one. Yet he was still a tenant of the manor. Edward surmised that one day Robert would buy his freedom, though for now, his close association with the de Bohuns apparently suited his purpose well enough.

As well as his two daughters, Matilda and Margery, Robert had also had two sons, younger than their sisters, whom he had clearly been grooming for a life of privilege. But the mortality halted their progress up the ladder, snatching them cruelly away, along with their mother Anne. Anne had come from a cottar family and never quite adapted to the wealthy yeoman life that her husband was carving out for them. Despite the servants Robert employed to help her in the house and croft, she often did much of the domestic work herself. Margery took after her mother in this respect: a rather plain girl, with seemingly little interest in her appearance, she behaved like any other cottar girl, expecting to dress plainly and work hard.

Matilda, however, was not at all like a cottar girl: she revelled in her father's burgeoning wealth, making every effort to help him demonstrate the family's success by wearing the fashionable clothes of the gentry, not caring that by doing so she was undoubtedly flouting the law. She was handsome rather than pretty, with glossy black hair that was always elaborately dressed, and bright blue eyes that often flashed with haughty defiance. Unlike her sister, Matilda didn't feel driven to domestic working life, and indeed somewhat irked her father by spending most of her time tending to her hair and clothes.

But the past few months had changed Matilda's life, just as they had Eleanor's and everyone else's in the village. Matilda had lost her mother and two little brothers in a way that would make even her heart break, and her father continued to work ceaselessly, in his efforts, Eleanor assumed, to keep the manor's demesne functioning in these most difficult of days. His daughters were left to grieve alone.

Eleanor put on her summer cloak and pulled her hood close about her head, for a brisk northerly breeze was blowing across the manor fields. Eleanor's house, along with two more of Meonbridge's more substantial houses, one of which she now knew belonged to Matilda's betrothed, Gilbert Fletcher, was set between the village and the wide expanse of fields. She felt the full force of the wind as she stepped out of her door onto the narrow, still muddy, road that fronted the three houses, then continued out of Meonbridge, barely a track, towards the tiny, impoverished hamlet of Upper Brooking.

It was not far to the Tylers', but it was difficult to walk quickly. Even the main road through the village remained claggy from the months of rain, the ditches either side treacherous, obliging Eleanor to be careful where she put her feet.

She was relieved when she finally reached the Tylers' house. She banged on the door and it was opened shortly by Margery, Matilda's older sister. Her face was pale and wan, and at first she seemed not to recognise Eleanor.

'Oh, it's you, Mistress Titherige,' she said at last, peering at the visitor through half-closed eyes. 'It's been a long time since you were here.' Her voice was barely audible.

'Indeed,' said Eleanor, 'and I'm sorry for that. It's been a terrible time for us all.'

Margery's mouth twisted into a grimace, and a small sob escaped as she said 'Terrible.'

Eleanor felt uncomfortable: perhaps this was not an appropriate time for a visit? But she did want to see Matilda.

'Is Matilda at home?' she said, trying to keep her tone light.

Margery looked up. 'You know she's about to be married?' Her voice was tinged with bitterness.

Eleanor nodded. 'I'd heard. I've come to wish her well.'

Margery snorted. 'You think good wishes are due?'

Eleanor was dismayed at her tone: Margery had always been a gentle, placid girl, but now she seemed troubled and sour. Eleanor wondered if she was bitter because her younger sister was getting married before her. 'May I see Matilda?' she said.

Margery nodded distractedly, stepping aside to let Eleanor into the porch, and then ushered her through to the hall.

'I'll call my sister,' she said, and shuffled off past the heavy curtain at the back of the hall, which led, Eleanor knew, to the private upper rooms of the house. She looked around the hall she'd not visited for months: it was certainly impressive, with a great tapestry on one wall, pewter plates displayed along the length of the heavy oak table and brass candlesticks on top of the tall cupboard. The room was not furnished as most of the peasants' houses in Meonbridge; its opulence was more like the style of the manor's hall. Master Tyler, thought Eleanor, is undoubtedly eager to impress.

Margery reappeared shortly. 'My sister bids you attend her in the solar. I'll show you.' She gestured to Eleanor to follow her through the curtained doorway. A narrow staircase led up to the room where the family relaxed and slept. It was a long room, with a large wood framed bed at either end of the room each, like hers at home, with heavy curtains and a thin decorated screen between them. Matilda was sitting on the bed at the far end of the room, the bed she undoubtedly shared with her sister. She got up as Eleanor entered with Margery, who promptly withdrew.

'Elly!' said Matilda, holding out her hands. 'It's been so long, I thought maybe you'd given me up.' She gave a rather mirthless chuckle, but as Eleanor reached her and took her hands, she squeezed them warmly.

Although the day was well advanced, Matilda was not yet dressed. Her sister was wearing her tunic and surcoat, as well as an apron, clearly dressed for her daily work, but Matilda was still in her night chemise with a heavy cloak wrapped around her, and her smooth dark hair was loose and unbraided.

'Matty!' Eleanor said, giving a broad, friendly, smile, 'I'm glad to see you again. I'd wanted to speak to you at the Midsummer feast.'

Matilda grimaced. 'My father kept me close. He didn't want me to mingle with my friends.'

'Why not?'

Matilda's face darkened and she seemed unsure how to reply. 'Come,' she said at last, and drew Eleanor across to the bed where they both sat down, still holding hands.

Matilda was silent, and it was clear to Eleanor that her friend was unhappy but didn't know how, or whether, to confess her unhappiness. She'd have to persuade her to speak.

'Is something wrong, Matty?' she said, squeezing one of Matilda's hands as a sign of encouragement.

Matilda withdrew her hands and, pulling her cloak around her again, stood up. She turned away from Eleanor and her shoulders shook a little. Eleanor stood up too and, taking Matilda's shoulders, turned her round to face her.

'What is it, Matty? Please tell me.'

Her face streaked with tears, Matilda wiped her nose on the edge of her cloak and sniffed. She shook her head.

'I can't tell you.'

'Have you told anyone?' said Eleanor. 'Your sister?'

Matilda snorted. 'Oh, Margery knows, without me telling her. But she cares little for my grief.'

'Grief at your mother's death, and your brothers'?'

Matilda looked up at her, and tears cascaded from her eyes. 'My mother? Oh, yes, of course. I miss her so. And my little brothers.'

'But it's not their loss that grieves you so?'

Matilda shook her head. 'You'll think me unfeeling, but, no, it's not that...'

'What then?'

Matilda slumped down again onto the edge of the bed and drew a hand roughly through her uncombed hair. She spoke quietly.

'It's because my father insists I marry that odious Gilbert Fletcher.' She broke again into sobs.

'Do you have to marry *him*?' said Eleanor, aghast at Matilda's misery. 'Will your father not let you choose another husband?'

Matilda shook her head again, with great despondency. 'He insists it's Gilbert. For he's a freeman, and heir to a great deal of land, and not only here in Meonbridge.'

Eleanor tried to lighten the atmosphere. 'You always did want to marry a rich man, Matty.'

Matilda half smiled, and sniffed again to try to dispel her tears. 'Yes, I did, didn't I? But not Gilbert Fletcher. I'd never have chosen him. He's old, and ugly, and ill tempered. And he doesn't care for me at all.'

Eleanor sighed, her heart aching for her friend's distress. Perhaps it was worse, she thought, to be forced to marry a man you didn't like, than to have no prospect of marrying at all?

'I suppose your father's trying to do his best for you?'

49

Matilda snorted. 'No. He isn't,' she said. 'He's doing his best for himself. And I hate him for it.'

Eleanor was shocked to hear her friend speak so ill of her father. She'd loved her own father so dearly, and was sure he'd never have forced her to do anything against her will.

'How can I comfort you, Matty?' she said, putting her arm around her friend's shoulder.

'I don't think you can, Elly. I've no choice. You know my father: he's a hard man. He's strong-willed and determined to get his way. I'm just a girl, and must obey him.'

'But why is it you who's marrying and not your sister? Surely Margery should be married first?'

Matilda shrugged and turned her face away. 'It was me Gilbert wanted,' she said quietly, and tears started to flow again.

'If he truly wants you, maybe he will turn out a better husband than you think?' said Eleanor.

'Maybe,' said Matilda, sighing, 'but I've no faith in it.'

7

A lice took her place in the great manor hall alongside the other tenants and landholders of the village. A few benches were set out in the huge central space and a grand chair stood at the front on a raised platform, a smaller chair with a writing table beside it. Alice felt chilled in the vast, high chamber; she was anxious as well as cold. This was her first time at the manor court. Now she was a widow and about to become the tenant of the atte Wode holding, she had to come and represent herself. Today she would ask formally to take over the tenancy, and pay a fee for the privilege. She must also pay the heriot for Stephen's death, which meant she'd probably have to give up her best cow. It seemed hard that widows should have to part with their best animals just when they'd lost their husbands, but that was how things were done. She'd heard that, on some manors, widows had to give up much more than their animals: carts, ploughs, kitchen utensils, even furniture and clothes. Alice thought poor widows like those might wish they'd died too rather than be reduced to such penury.

Several women were here at the court; many more, Alice imagined, than was customary six months ago. Each of the widows would, like her, have to pay her husband's heriot, as well as the tenancy fee for her family holding. Over there was Elizabeth, the widow of John the Carpenter, who had two young sons not yet old enough to take over their father's carpenter's shop. And standing together were Susanna Bigge and Ann Webb, both cottars who'd been summoned by the bailiff to pay their heriots, but as neither of them had any animals they'd have to pay in goods. And there was the sharp-tongued Alys Ward, whose younger son Henry had been taken by the mortality, along with his wife Edith, and two of their children, and who was now left alone in the Wards' tiny cottage and meagre croft, with three-year-old Robert to care for. Alice knew well enough that Alys had no money to pay for her son's death, nor any goods to surrender, for Henry and his wife were feckless, living constantly on the edge of poverty. Indeed, they'd spent the last few weeks of their lives spending what little money they had left on ale, believing the end of the world was at hand and it was not worth making any effort to feed themselves or their starving children.

But of course not all those who were bereaved were women. Alice knew everyone in the room, and she counted nine men who'd seen their wives die in agony from the mortality, including Ralph Ward, Alys' elder son, William Mannering and Nicholas Cook.

The assembled company was, unsurprisingly, subdued: a few people were talking to each other, but quietly, and no-one's face was smiling. Alice thought how, at the Midsummer feast, only days ago, there'd been a good deal of laughter and merriment, but this court represented real life, when debts and fines must be paid, obligations acknowledged, land reallocated and work shared out. It was obvious to anyone who knew the smallest thing about farming that, from now on, the life of Meonbridge was going to be very different.

There'd been no manor court since Michaelmas, ten months ago, for the usual Lady Day court, in March, had been cancelled, as no-one's heart was in the manor's affairs when so many had died and were still dying and it seemed the whole village might yet perish. But now, with no new cases of the mortality for nearly two months and a new sense of optimism in the village, many felt more confident that for those who had survived there was a future after all.

. . .

Suddenly, the low murmuring of the company stopped, as Robert Tyler, the manor's bailiff and Sir Richard's chief official, entered the hall from behind the ornate screen at the far end of the room. Robert's face bore his usual dark, stern expression and he was wearing a heavy, richly embroidered black tunic, which greatly enhanced his already considerable stature. He was followed by Sir Richard, clad in a cloak trimmed with fur, an elaborate jewelled chain around his neck, and the slight, gloomy figure of George le Clerke, the scribe, who'd not recovered from the death of his wife of twenty years and, being childless, now lived a lonely, melancholy life devoted solely to recording the manor's affairs. Sir Richard took his place in the grand chair; George sat down next to him, took from his satchel parchment rolls, inkpot and quills and, having placed them all carefully on his writing table, began to write. At that moment Philip de Bohun appeared and took up his place just behind his father.

Sir Richard then nodded to the bailiff and the bailiff nodded to another man, who stepped forward and called out in a booming voice:

'Oyez. Let all who have business and owe service to the Lord of Meonbridge draw near. The court of the manor of Meonbridge is in session, this Friday after St Peter and Paul in the twenty-third year of our sovereign Edward the Third, with our lord, Sir Richard de Bohun, presiding. Be silent for Master Robert Tyler.'

The bailiff pulled himself up to his full height and addressed Sir Richard.

'My lord, the first business of this court is to elect new officers to serve your lordship in the business of this manor. First, I call upon the court to elect the office of reeve.'

Alice looked around for John. She'd not seen him this morning, for he rose very early and slipped quietly out of the house. She feared that, despite having been summoned to attend by Robert Tyler himself, he might have decided to stay away, in the hope that he couldn't be elected if he wasn't there to accept the office. At first she couldn't see him, and she was anxious that Robert would make trouble if John didn't do as he'd been commanded. But then she saw her son standing alone to one side of the hall. He looked glum, almost fearful, like a beast knowing it was going for slaughter.

Robert Tyler then made an announcement: 'I have a nomination for John atte Wode to be reeve. What says the court to this?'

Thomas Rolfe stepped forward. 'I've something to say, Master Tyler.' The bailiff nodded for him to speak.

'John atte Wode's too young for the important position of reeve,' said Thomas, and Alice looked across to see John nodding at this. 'He's neither the experience for the task, nor the standing among the tenants.'

Thomas continued at some length, complaining that John was not fit to be reeve for this and that reason, until Sir Richard raised his hand to halt his flow.

'You have another man to put forward for the office, Master Rolfe?'

Thomas looked embarrassed and shook his head.

'Aye, he'll put forward Thomas Rolfe, sir,' someone called out, and Master Tyler scowled at the insolence. But Sir Richard smiled, said 'Ah!', thanked Thomas and waved him away.

Robert asked if anyone wanted to speak for John's nomination, and two men stepped forward in turn to say John was young, but his father's son and a hard-working farmer, and would have their support. Then everyone was asked to show their support in turn for Thomas Rolfe and for John, and there was no doubt John won the day. Alice was delighted, even if John might not be, but she noticed Thomas Rolfe's face was black with anger, or perhaps with shame at being rejected by his neighbours. Poor Thomas, she thought, was not at all liked in the village: quite well-off and a successful husbandman, yet ever complaining about his neighbours, that they'd encroached onto his field strips in their ploughing or their cows had strayed onto his land. No doubt he thought he was the best man for the job of reeve, but she knew his fellow-tenants would not willingly take his orders.

More elections followed. Poor Henry Brooker was manor constable for nearly twenty years but he, together with his wife, was one of the last victims of the mortality in Meonbridge, so a new constable had to be appointed, as well as two new ale-tasters, and six jurors.

Then Sir Richard called his son Philip forward, and announced that henceforth he was appointed steward for all the de Bohun manors, both here and across the south of England. Alice noticed that this declaration seemed to come as a surprise to Robert Tyler, for an expression of shock and even anger briefly crossed his face before he quickly forced a smile and stepped forward to congratulate the young knight on his appointment.

Henry, the miller's brother, and a near neighbour of Alice's, was standing next to her. He too noticed the bailiff's discomfiture, for he whispered in her ear, 'That'll clip Master Tyler's wings. He acts as steward already, and we don't need two.' Then he added, 'Mebbe Sir Richard's giving Philip a job to try and improve his humour.'

Henry's whispering was masked by a good deal of murmuring in the crowd about the appointment, and Alice wondered whether they were murmurs of approval or objection. She knew Philip too was not much liked among her neighbours. After an initial flush of enthusiasm when he returned triumphant from the king's victory at Crécy, most people were dismayed by Philip's unseemly behaviour towards many of the village girls. Then, soon after the arrival of the mortality, the de Bohuns did themselves no favours by choosing to put up barricades around the manor and effectively abandon Meonbridge's villagers to their fate while offering no support or comfort in their anguish. Sir Richard decreed that no-one could leave the manor and go into the village, or enter the manor from the village, and thus it remained for nearly four months, until Philip's new wife, Isabella, secretly sought out the wise woman, Sybil Kemp, for a love potion, and was struck down by the mortality and died, along with her unborn baby. Soon afterwards the family emerged from its self-imposed confinement, but when Philip next appeared in the village, he'd become a morose and angry bear. Alice thought perhaps this change in humour was only to be expected, but John said something more lay behind it.

After the elections came the part that Alice had been dreading, where the heriots were demanded, and the fines paid for taking on tenancies. She was relieved when she saw John making his way through the company to come and stand with her. When her turn came, Robert Tyler called out her name and she pushed forward to stand before Sir Richard. He smiled at her, which gave her some small encouragement that perhaps he'd not be too demanding. She might have hoped that, as she was the widow of his much-respected reeve, the lord would be modest in his demands. But it was a vain hope for, as she knew well enough, Sir Richard was a hard master, always insisting on the full payment of every fine and fee. So she found herself forced to agree to part with her best cow, indeed her favourite cow. Then she made her formal request to take over the tenancy from her dead husband, and knelt before Sir Richard to swear fealty to him and accept the terms of her tenure. Alice wondered if she should've passed the tenancy straight to John after all, but they'd agreed that he should help her run the farm until he found a wife, and only then take over the holding himself. She knew she'd find it hard to manage all the work, especially now John had been appointed reeve. Many widows in her situation would look for a new husband, but Alice wanted to remain a widow, to ensure the family holding remained in atte Wode hands, for if she remarried, the land would belong to her husband and her children could lose their inheritance.

The payments of heriots and fines continued for a long time, for so many tenants had died. Several of the cottar widows, like Susanna Bigge and Ann Webb, were forced to hand over their only worthwhile possessions. Ann Webb wept and begged Sir Richard for pity in her distress, for without her cooking vessels she couldn't provide a meal for herself and her son. Robert Tyler shook his head and declared that it seemed Mistress Webb sought to deny her lord his due, but Sir Richard seemed moved by her tears and agreed to accept a tiny money fine for both the heriot and her succession to the tenancy of her meagre cottage and tiny croft. The bailiff looked astonished at this unusual act of clemency, and Ann threw herself on her knees and poured out her gratitude. Alice viewed this scene with some revulsion, and John, standing by her, was shifting from foot to foot.

'Next court, it'll be *me* forcing folk to give up their miserable chattels!' he whispered, through gritted teeth. 'How can I do that, Ma? How can it be right?'

Alice urged him to be quiet, but she could hardly disagree that it did seem very unjust, even if it had always been the way of things.

Several more people, even a few children, barely adult, asked for the family holdings to be transferred into their names, and one or two individuals proposed taking over land left without either tenant or heir. Sir Richard seemed to be accepting all requests, with an air of resignation.

John whispered again to Alice. 'It's in Sir Richard's interests to encourage folk to take on the vacant holdings, else manor land'll go unfarmed and the harvest will be down.

Then the bailiff called forward young Roger Stronge. Although only fifteen, Roger was a tall, strapping lad, but Alice thought he looked more like a frightened child about to face a scolding. His stepsister, Eleanor Titherige, came forward too to stand just behind him.

'Well, Master Stronge? Speak!' said Robert Tyler, gruffly.

Roger hesitated, and Eleanor gave him a little prod in the back and whispered something to him. Roger spoke at last, stammering a little.

'I've come to ask to take on the forge, m'lord, which was my father's and then Edward le Smith's.'

Sir Richard stroked his beard and looked a little serious.

'And you think, young Master Stronge, that you are fit and able to undertake such arduous work?'

Roger shuffled his feet and half-turned to Eleanor, and she nodded vigorously.

'Yes, m'lord,' he said, sounding less than confident, and then, perhaps thinking he should seem more sure of himself, added, 'Yes, I do think so.'

'Good,' said Sir Richard, smiling, 'Then take it on you shall. My son Philip tells me that you have been working hard to improve your blacksmithing skills, and that your sister, Mistress Titherige, supports your endeavour.'

'Yes, sir,' said Roger.

'Well, then, Master Tyler,' said Sir Richard, 'let Master Stronge be formally assigned the tenancy of the forge.'

So Roger made his mark on a parchment, and paid his fee. As he turned to his sister his expression bore a combination of both achievement and terror.

Finally Robert Tyler presented himself to Sir Richard to ask formally for permission for his daughter Matilda to marry Gilbert Fletcher, which Sir Richard gave with a conspiratorial smile and Robert paid the merchet that the lord demanded. John gave a quiet grunt and said in an undertone to Alice: 'That's much less than usual for merchet. Tyler could afford a lot more.' Alice turned and saw John's face was dark with resentment. She kept her counsel, but could see her son was spoiling for a fight, though who with she wasn't quite sure. Despite her initial enthusiasm for John becoming reeve, she was uneasy now that his new appointment might bring him trouble, though she didn't know from where the trouble might come.

But the final session of the court's business confirmed Alice's sense of foreboding. Sir Richard called his son forward again, announcing that Philip would be consulting the bailiff and the new reeve on the allocations of manor work. A special court would be held the following week, which all tenants must attend. Sir Richard made this statement, then clearly expected to ask Robert Tyler to close the proceedings, but there was some commotion in the company, and suddenly Bartholomew Coupar, the tall, handsome and muscular husband of Emma, pushed his way to the front and asked leave to speak. Robert Tyler scowled and tried to dismiss the cottar, but Philip gestured to Robert to let him speak.

'Well, Master Coupar?' said Philip, 'what do you have to say?'

'Everybody knows,' said Bartholomew, speaking slowly and slurring his words slightly, which made Alice think he'd been drinking ale already this morning, 'there ain't enough men left in Meonbridge to work the fields. So us cottars'll 'ave to work 'arder and longer 'n we're accustomed if you're to get your hay cut, your sheep sheared, and your crops 'arvested.'

Philip's face changed from a condescending smile to what Alice thought looked more like a sneer. 'What exactly are you trying to say, Master Coupar?'

Bartholomew faltered, perhaps not knowing how to continue. Then Ralph Ward stepped forward to support his neighbour.

'I know what he wants to say, sir. That if you wants us to work longer and harder than before, you has to pay us a fair wage.'

Robert Tyler's face turned even darker than before, and Philip's sneer became a deep scowl. But Sir Richard seemed to be controlling his expression, remaining outwardly impassive in the face of this dissension from his tenants. Alice wondered what he was really thinking, and what action he would take. She feared that, if it were left to Philip and the bailiff to react to this small rebellion, they'd act harshly to prevent any further mutiny, and Bartholomew and Ralph might regret speaking out.

She started to worry about Emma Coupar, whom she'd taken on only the other day. Emma was hard working and reliable, but the Coupars struggled to make a decent living, and if Bartholomew was fined for rebellion, it would go hard with them. And if he was marked out as a troublemaker, the bailiff could make their lives very difficult.

Philip and Robert turned away from the company and spoke together in angry-sounding whispers. A low nervous muttering erupted among Alice's neighbours, and Bartholomew and Ralph both looked red-faced and a little scared.

Then suddenly Sir Richard stood up and raised his hand to call for quiet.

'Enough,' he said in a loud voice. 'Enough for now. Go to your homes and your work. Master Tyler, bring this court to a close.'

Robert announced the formal ending of the court, and Sir Richard stepped down from the platform and swept imperiously from the chamber. His son and bailiff did not follow him, and Philip called out to John.

'Master atte Wode. Come here again after dinner. We've matters to discuss.'

John acknowledged the new steward's command, then, as they made their way out of the hall, he spoke very quietly in his mother's ear.

'You see, Ma. I told you there'd be trouble. The cottars know the manor can't do without them. Times have changed, and they're not going to accept the old ways. And I'm going to be caught in the middle of it all.'

8

_____

Margaret eased herself back down into her chair, grateful for the
softness of the velvet-covered cushions. She drew her woollen
cloak around her: she was shivering not from chill but from disquiet.
She was relieved that Richard had left for the morning. He would be
away at least until dinner, so she could compose herself, dress her hair
and perhaps put on the new green gown that Alice had sewn: to please
him; for he needed pleasing. Richard had become as angry as a bull
these last few days, and as blundering. He treated her roughly last
night, as he often did when he was ill tempered, or drunk from a
surfeit of wine. And yesterday, the day of the court, he was both.

After a court, Richard invariably came upstairs to take his dinner
privately with her and tell her of any notable events from the court's
business. Yesterday morning, before the first court for almost a year,
Richard's temper was almost merry: as they shared breakfast, he jested
about the goodly number of rents and heriots that he would be
collecting, and she gently upbraided him for making light of so much
horror and misery. At which he relented, apologising for his
insensitivity and promising her that he would treat with tact and
kindness the grieving souls who came before him to pay their dues. But

when he returned from court later in the morning, he crashed into the solar like a bull breaking free from its byre, his earlier cheerful humour entirely vanished.

Margaret had been reading and was startled by his boisterous entry. She got up quickly from her seat, going over to take his cloak from him.

'My lord?' she said. 'Is something amiss?'

'Indeed there is, madam,' he said, bellowing and striding up and down the room in a fury. 'Rebellion, that's what's amiss, my lady. Rebellion.'

Margaret poured a goblet of wine and gave it to her husband to calm his temper. He took it but did not cease his pacing.

'What has happened, Richard?' said Margaret. 'Tell me.'

Richard continued to pace, fuming.

Then at last he spoke. 'The cottars want more wages.' He laughed out loud. 'I can't believe that's what I heard them say.'

'Who said it?'

'Bartholomew Coupar and Ralph Ward. Bart I can understand; he's a drunk and doesn't always know what he's saying. But Ralph's more prudent, a level-headed fellow. I don't understand why he took Bart's part.'

'Perhaps because he agrees with him?'

Richard spun round, his wine slopping on to his tunic. 'Agrees with him!' He raised his voice again. 'Agrees with him?'

Margaret went to her husband and, taking his arm, led him to a chair. 'Maybe they both want higher wages? Perhaps all the cottars do?'

Richard looked shaken, though Margaret doubted that he could really be surprised.

For most of the five long months in which the mortality raged in Meonbridge, the de Bohun family had shut themselves up in the manor with little contact with the village. Despite their isolation, several of the manor servants perished, but in the village, almost half the population died, including half the men. During those terrible months, Robert Tyler, the bailiff, and Stephen atte Wode, the reeve, had done their best to keep the manor functioning, whipping into line whatever labour was available to work the fields. In March, as the deaths began to mount, the fields awaited the plough, but it became clear that plough teams were in short supply. Master Tyler told Richard that it might not be possible to plough all the manor fields this year. Unusually, Margaret was in the room during this exchange, and she had seen Richard's disquiet turn to anger as he began to comprehend the manor's grim predicament.

'The reeve tells me only five plough teams are left, m'lord,' said the bailiff, looking uncommonly anxious. 'With only five, we can plough but half the manor land.'

'A half!' cried Richard. 'But that's not enough, Robert. You will have to find more teams.'

Robert wrung his hands together and acknowledged that indeed more teams were needed, but he did not know where they could be found.

'The ploughs and oxen must still exist,' said Richard, 'even if their former owners do not. Master atte Wode must find some men to take them on. And quickly.'

Robert agreed that it was the duty of the reeve to provide enough teams to do what was required, but only days later Stephen atte Wode himself succumbed to the mortality, and Robert had to do his best to find plough teams and willing workers. The fields themselves were neglected, for few had the heart for farming when it seemed the world was coming to an end. And many animals were left untended, and ran amok amongst what crops there were, and damaged hedges and fences.

By June, some fields had been ploughed and some crops sown, but not enough to supply the manor's needs, still less the needs of the village as a whole despite the decreasing numbers of mouths to feed. And now it was July and before long what crops there were must be harvested. Richard's fretfulness worsened and the events at the manor court tipped him over into an enduring fury.

Somewhat calmer now that he was no longer pacing the room, Richard drained his goblet and handed it to his wife.

'Let us eat,' she said, gesturing to the servant to bring in the food.

Richard was morose throughout the meal and barely ate, though

Margaret tried to humour him with questions about the other business of the court: who had asked to take on more land, what had been taken in heriot, and whether any merchets or legerwites had been paid. In happier times, he had made merry of this sort of conversation, entertaining her with lurid tales of those loose women forced to pay the legerwite for their adulterous behaviour and bringing her news of who was getting married in the village, willing or not. Sometimes his stories could be amusing, though Margaret disapproved of what she considered his generally harsh treatment of widows. But today, Richard's mood was dour and he had no amusing tales to tell. He would speak only of the rebellious talk of Bart Coupar and Ralph Ward. It rankled with him and he would not let it go. And, though he ate little, he drank a lot of wine and it was not long before he was slumped in his chair, snoring.

But, if her husband was bitter at the attitude of his tenants, Margaret felt some sympathy with their cause.

Margaret had married Richard de Bohun at just sixteen, and spent nearly half of the twenty-three years of her marriage alone, managing the Meonbridge manor, while Richard was away attending to the king's business and fighting in his wars. Richard first went off to war when she was twenty and the mother of a baby boy, her third born. The boy, Philip, seemed to be thriving, but the loss of her first two babies made her anxious, and yet she also had to take on responsibility for running the manor. In those years she learned how to work with her tenants.

Whenever Richard came home from the wars, he took over the running of the manor and Margaret often thought, though she never said it, that much of her effort to establish good relationships with her tenants was set back by Richard's more heartless attitude. With Richard away, she could manage the manor's affairs in her own way, without having to conform to his methods. She worked closely with the bailiff and reeve, and fully understood the manor's business. She presided over the manor court, delivering fair judgements and demanding reasonable fees. She was not weak or over-tolerant in her dealings with her tenants, but Alice, in a somewhat incautious moment, had told her how readily the tenants saw the difference between her way and her husband's, and that they often said amongst themselves that it would suit them well if Sir Richard never did return from France.

Sometimes Margaret herself wished that Richard had never returned home from France but died a chivalrous knight on the battlefield of Crécy. After dinner yesterday, he slept, snoring, in the chair for a while before waking, ill tempered, and storming from the room, shouting for a servant to fetch his son to him and without saying a word of farewell to his wife. When he returned in the evening, again he ate little of the supper they shared with Philip and Johanna, Robert Tyler and a number of the other manor servants. He spoke barely a word to Margaret, turning his back on her to continue an angry-sounding discussion he had clearly been having earlier with Philip and Robert about the so-called "rebellious" tenants. As he drank goblet after goblet of wine, Richard's voice got louder and more agitated, until he was shouting and gesticulating wildly.

Margaret too ate little, distressed by her husband's uncouth behaviour. When she had had enough of his shouting and blatant disregard of her presence, she rose and excused herself and signalled to Johanna to do the same. Mother and daughter silently climbed the narrow staircase to the solar. At the top of the stairs, Margaret smiled weakly to her daughter.

'Your father is troubled. Times have changed in Meonbridge, and the tenants are not so willing to do his bidding.'

Johanna nodded. 'Yes, Philip told me what was said in court today. It's clear that Father is much angered by it.'

'He is,' said Margaret. 'And he cannot, will not, understand the tenants' point of view.'

Johanna looked up, surprised. 'You think he should?'

Margaret nodded. 'Indeed I do, Johanna. The manor cannot survive without its tenants. We have many fewer now than before the mortality, and if we do not show them some compassion, I am fearful what might happen.'

Johanna squeezed her mother's arm. 'I'm sure that Father and Philip will do what is right,' she said, and bade her mother good night.

But Margaret was not at all confident that Richard would do what was right. Nor even what was wise. Her confidence in his judgement had slipped, and she felt no more secure in Master Tyler's counsel.

She was tired of all the argument and longed for sleep. In her room, she dismissed her maid and undressed herself. She could just hear the raucous voices of her husband and son from the hall below, but fatigue overcame her and she fell asleep almost as soon as she lay down on the bed. It must have been much later in the night when she was awoken roughly by Richard, dragging the bedcover off her, then collapsing heavily on to the bed, almost on top of her. He was a physically powerful man, even when drunk, and she did not have the strength to resist him. When the light of dawn began to filter through the shutters, she was lying awake, finally aroused from her fitful dozing since her husband's unwelcome intrusion into her bed. The crumpled folds of her night chemise felt cold against her belly, still damp from Richard's exertions. The chemise was bunched up around her waist and she pulled at it, drawing it down again to cover her naked belly and legs. Richard was naked too, lying with his back towards her, sleeping quietly. She was sore, and fearful that she might also have bruises on her face, remembering the roughness with which he had pressed his whiskered mouth repeatedly against the delicate skin of her lips and cheeks. She slowly swung her legs down from the bed to the floor, and, wincing, got to her feet. Going over to a small coffer, she took out the silver-backed mirror that Richard had bought her soon after they were married, and nervously held it up to her face. She was relieved to see that there were no obvious bruises, even though the skin of her cheeks and mouth felt a little tender. Her arms were also sore, and she could see several bruises there, as well as on her thighs, darkening to purple, but at least they could be covered.

She turned to look at her sleeping husband: she should hate him for his treatment of her, but she couldn't. He was not a cruel man, just so forceful that he did not always recognise when he used his strength to excess. When she married him, it was, unusually among her contemporaries, a love-match. Richard had been a fine-looking man; when he was sober, he still was. As a young man, he was also charming and chivalrous, the perfect knight, and, when her father arranged their first meeting, Margaret knew immediately that she wanted to become his wife. But when Richard inherited the Meonbridge manor, and all the other de Bohun lands, the responsibility of their management weighed heavily on his shoulders. Fighting, not farming, was what he was destined for. In those days, he had taken very seriously his membership of the warrior class, whose role it was to defend his country and its people. In some ways he still did. It was true that, in those periods between the wars, when he was home and overseeing his estates, he did find a certain satisfaction in getting the best from his land and his tenants. But in the two years since he and Philip returned from France, Richard's stern but patriarchal attitude towards his tenants seemed to have changed to one of ruthless self-interest, which blinded him to the needs of those on whom he depended for his livelihood. He seemed not to understand his dependency, nor to recognise that the tenants might not always simply agree to his demands.

And now, Margaret thought, he did not understand at all the change wrought in Meonbridge by the mortality. He needed tenants to take over the acres of spare land, but was not prepared to offer them at low rents. He also insisted that wages should not go up, putting his faith in the government's new ordinance declaring that wages must be kept at the levels of two years before. Only yesterday the envoy of the High Sheriff of the county of Southampton came to Meonbridge, first to tell Richard about the ordinance, and later, standing on the village green, to announce it to the tenants. The envoy's audience was small but the cottars listened to the news with growing resentment. Robert Tyler was in the crowd and reported their reaction back to Sir Richard.

'The mood was ugly, sir,' he said.

Yet Richard seemed unwilling to accept that some of his tenants might simply walk off the manor, declaring that the law expressly forbade it. Margaret realised that the surviving tenants must be nurtured, but Richard refused to agree and she feared that he was set on a course that would unwittingly cause the rebellion to grow.

9

Alice stood on the grassy village green opposite the church entrance, along with a small crowd of her neighbours. They were awaiting the arrival of Matilda Tyler and her father. Gilbert Fletcher, whom Matilda was to marry today, was loitering alone near the church porch, apparently bereft of companions. Alice thought what an unattractive man Master Fletcher was: very tall and thin, with a gaunt face and lank dark hair, and, if he was happy to be getting married, she reflected, you wouldn't think so from his expression, which was morose and gloomy. He paced around, looking restless and impatient, as if anxious to get the ceremony over with.

Alice barely knew Matilda Tyler, even though she'd watched her growing up alongside her own daughter. She'd often imagined the joy of seeing Agnes arrive at the church on Stephen's arm, to marry the man she loved, just as Alice herself had done. But it seemed this day might bring Matilda little joy, for rumour had it that her father Robert was forcing this marriage upon her. Alice knew that at one time Matilda had her eyes on John, and that John had been keen on her. But Robert evidently did not consider him a good enough match for his daughter, as he'd nothing much to bring as dower, whereas Gilbert was not only older but also, as an orphan of the mortality, the new owner of large tracts of good farming land, both in Meonbridge and beyond.

. . .

If Robert Tyler did not deem John a suitable addition to his family, he nonetheless appeared to consider the atte Wode holding a potentially advantageous acquisition. One bright afternoon a short while ago, Robert had knocked on Alice's door. Alice was sewing a new tunic for John, sitting by the window in her hall, with the shutter pinned back to take full advantage of the light. Surprised by the sound of the knock, she dropped her needle onto the floor, and she was muttering under her breath about the likelihood of finding the needle in the strewings as she put down the tunic and went to the door. She was even more taken aback to find Robert Tyler standing there, his hat in his hand and with a rare smile on his face.

'Good day to you, Mistress atte Wode,' he said, inclining his head in a gesture of courtesy.

'Master Tyler,' said Alice, stammering slightly in her astonishment, for the bailiff had never called at her house before, even in all the years when Stephen was reeve.

'I've come to call on you, Mistress atte Wode, because I've something I wish to discuss.'

Alice couldn't imagine what the bailiff might have to discuss with her, but courtesy demanded she should at least hear what he had to say. She opened the door wider and gestured to him to enter the house.

'May I fetch you a pot of ale, Master Tyler?' she said, but he shook his head.

'No, no, mistress, thank you. I'll not keep you long from your work.'

Alice continued standing, uncertain how long he might be staying and if she should ask him to sit down.

'Shall we sit, Mistress atte Wode?' said the bailiff at length, taking command, and she gratefully gestured to him to take the chair, while she perched on a three-legged stool.

'What is it you wish to say, Master Tyler?' she said, a touch of anxiety in her voice.

Robert Tyler leaned forward in the chair and looked very directly at Alice, finding her eyes. Feeling discomfited by the directness of his gaze, Alice couldn't help but look down at her lap.

'Mistress atte Wode,' began Robert, then got up from the chair and took a turn about the room.

'Mistress atte Wode,' he said again, facing her. 'What I've come to say to you is delicate but I'll speak directly.'

Alice was alarmed: what "delicate" matter could the lord's most important official want to speak to her about?

'We're both alone,' he went on, 'each of us torn cruelly from our dearest spouse by the accursed mortality.'

'Indeed,' said Alice simply, not knowing what else to say.

'Mistress atte Wode,' he continued, lunging forward and boldly taking one of her hands in his, 'Alice, I'm but a villein in Meonbridge, although a wealthy one. I've much to offer a wife–'

Alice gasped, as she suddenly understood where this was leading. Aghast, she knew she must divert Master Tyler from his course, but couldn't think how to say it. Her silence allowed him to continue.

'My holdings on the manor are extensive and in addition I've–'

Alice couldn't let him go on and sprang up from her stool, withdrawing her hand from his. 'Master Tyler, please stop. I can't allow you to continue. I understand your intention but I must tell you I'm resolved to stay a widow–'

'But surely–' said Robert, trying to interject, but Alice shook her head.

'No, no, Master Tyler, my mind is set. I can't allow another man to take the place of my beloved Stephen. I've my sons to support me, and with their help I'll run our holding until it's time to pass it on to them.'

The bailiff looked astonished and, Alice thought, irritated. 'But together, Mistress atte Wode, we could run both of our holdings–'

She shook her head again and laid her hand gently upon his arm. 'Robert, I'm honoured you should make me this offer but I'll not change my mind. I'll stay a widow.'

Robert Tyler blustered a little further but at length appeared to accept that his offer had been rejected. He left Alice's house with considerable dignity, but it was clear he was not accustomed to being refused.

After she closed the door, Alice looked through the still unshuttered window to check he was out of earshot before bursting into laughter. She could hardly believe she had said "no" to Robert

Tyler. He was an important man: ordinary folk didn't usually refuse to do anything he asked. But she'd done so. It was true he was wealthy, and that life would be easier as his wife. He was also still an attractive man, despite his years: unusually tall, strong and vigorous, though the burden of his responsibilities seemed to weigh heavily on him these days, for his expression was always dark and inscrutable. She'd known him all her life and, before she married Stephen, Robert had courted her for many months and she thought then she might become his wife, until she found he was spending more time thinking about his own advancement than his marriage plans. But now, even if she'd not resolved to remain a widow, she knew she must refuse him. For he was not well-regarded amongst her neighbours: his prosperity marked him out, for his beginnings were humble, but Stephen always hinted that he'd increased his holdings by means that were less than honest. Alice returned to her sewing with a sigh: she smiled to herself, recognising that she was flattered by Robert's proposal. But her memory of Stephen's judgement on Master Tyler had probably assured her a narrow escape.

While Alice was musing on her encounter with Robert Tyler, the man himself appeared on the green, dressed in his finest clothes, holding tight to the arm of his younger daughter, a small procession of relatives and neighbours following on behind. The small crowd already gathered on the green didn't raise the customary cheer at the appearance of the bride. Instead, Alice could hear comments exchanged about the gloomy expression on Matilda's face, and she had to admit the girl looked no happier today than when she last saw her, at the Midsummer feast.

As Matilda and her father approached the church porch, Gilbert Fletcher came forward to shake his prospective father-in-law by the hand, and he grasped the arm of his bride to take her into the porch, where Master Hugo Garret suddenly appeared, ready to conduct the exchange of marriage vows. Alice fancied she saw Matilda struggle a little against Gilbert's grasp, but he was holding her fast by the elbow and her father stood close behind her. She seemed to have no choice but to stand before the priest.

Matilda turned briefly to look at the small band of neighbours gathered to witness her marriage, and her eyes seemed to beseech them to save her, though she said nothing. At her apparent lack of enthusiasm, Master Hugo looked uncertain whether to proceed, but Robert spoke up and bade him make haste, adding, as if in jest, that he was sure everyone was eager to get to the splendid bride ale he had prepared. Master Hugo frowned a little, perhaps at the lack of reverence of this remark, but he nodded nonetheless and gestured to Gilbert to announce the dower he was providing for his wife. Gilbert's words were few and spoken in so low a voice it was hard to hear him, but "half of all my lands" was clear enough and a murmur of approval hummed around the watching crowd. Hugo then bade Matilda announce her dowry but she remained silent and Robert, looking angry at her defiance, spoke for her, despite the priest's attempt to stop him doing so.

Then Gilbert made his marriage vows, and Hugo turned to Matilda for her to do the same. There was a long pause, and Alice wondered how they could proceed if Matilda continued to refuse to speak, for surely there could be no marriage if she did not consent? But then the girl nodded almost imperceptibly to the priest to continue and, in a small, hesitant voice, she repeated after him the words of her vows: '... for richer, for poorer, in sickness and in health, in bed...' Here Matilda faltered and closed her eyes, and seemed to take a deep breath before continuing. '...and at table, till death us do part, if holy Church ordains it, and thereto I plight thee my troth.'

Hugo blessed the two rings and Gilbert pushed his roughly on to Matilda's finger, then she, trembling, took his bony hand and eased her ring on to his finger, speaking the required words in so quiet a voice that they could not be heard. When she had finished, she bowed her head: she was married. If she didn't wish to be, it was now too late. She and her new husband then followed Master Hugo into the church, all the supporters and watchers trailing along behind.

As Alice moved forward to join those entering the church, she found Eleanor Titherige was walking alongside her. 'Mistress Titherige,' she said, nodding her head and smiling, and Eleanor returned the greeting, a slight flush on her cheeks. Alice had heard John had been seen at the forge several times in the past two months and that it was Eleanor he was speaking to rather than her stepbrother. He'd not mentioned the visits to his mother. Perhaps the girl's flushed cheeks were a sign of her embarrassment at finding herself speaking for the first time to the woman who might become her mother-in-law. If it were so, then Alice was delighted, but she was not so hasty as to assume an outcome for what were, she thought, her son's first steps at serious courtship.

Discomfited though she might be, Eleanor didn't hesitate to whisper to Alice her concerns about what they'd just witnessed. 'Poor Matty. I'd fain she'd married another.'

Alice was surprised. 'Matilda had another prospective husband?'

Eleanor shook her head sadly. 'Oh, no, there was no other. How I wish there had been, and so does Matty. But she told me it had to be Gilbert Fletcher; her father insisted upon it.'

'She doesn't seem much contented with the match,' said Alice.

Eleanor looked as if she was about to weep. 'No, indeed, she isn't. But she had no choice.'

Alice laid a gentle hand on Eleanor's arm. 'It does perhaps seem cruel for a father to choose his daughter's husband, but often these decisions are for the best.'

Eleanor sniffed and wiped away an errant tear. 'Indeed. But, in Matty's case, I'm not sure that's true. She does seem so very gloomy about her marriage to Master Fletcher.'

The two women took their places in the church nave alongside their neighbours, then with everyone assembled, Master Hugo raised his hands to begin the service to sanctify the marriage, and silence descended upon the congregation.

The entire village was invited to the bride ale. After the mass in church, the crowd trooped off in a long line through the grounds of the parsonage, just beyond the churchyard, and on to the bailiff's grand house, by way of the small gate that Robert had constructed between the parsonage croft and his own to give him easy access to the church and the centre of the village. The group was joined there by a few labourers from the fields, allowed time off to celebrate the marriage of the bailiff's daughter, and Alice was pleased to see John was among them. When she and Eleanor arrived at the house, she noticed the same slight flushing of his cheeks she'd seen earlier on Eleanor's when he saw them together, and she was privately amused that these two young people were apparently so shy about their acquaintance. Once she'd greeted her son, she made an excuse that she must go and speak to Emma Coupar and left them together.

Alice moved among her neighbours, quietly passing the time of day, and seeking out Emma, who she knew would be here with her children and her feckless husband, certainly never one to refuse an opportunity for free ale.

It was not until the manor court that Alice had understood how much land was now lying idle and untended, and that Sir Richard needed to find tenants for all the vacant tenements. At the court, several tenants had asked to add this or that parcel of land to their existing holdings and Sir Richard happily agreed, though John grumbled that, as the lord was not making any concessions in the level of rents he was demanding, only those who were already well-off could afford to take the extra land. Later that evening, John had warmed to his complaint.

'D'you realise, Ma, that, for the first time in memory, the poorer folk in Meonbridge could actually get some land of their own, instead of having to survive on wage labouring?'

Alice looked up from the pottage she was stirring over the fire. 'You mean folk such as Bart and Emma Coupar, and Ralph Ward?'

'Yes, just like them. Though I reckon Ralph'd make a better tenant than Bart.' He grinned.

'Emma would make a good tenant,' said Alice. 'Bart may be idle and feckless but she's a good worker.'

'She is, and she deserves a better husband than Bart,' he said, then added, 'much as I like the fellow.'

'But you said Sir Richard's demanding too much rent?'

John nodded. 'That's the problem. If only our noble lord'd agree to let the land for a nominal rent, some of our cottar neighbours could become landowners.'

'Though if Bart and Ralph got their way,' continued Alice, recalling the commotion at the court, 'and were paid higher wages, perhaps they'd prefer to remain free from the burdens of tenancy?'

John laughed. 'I can't see Sir Richard willingly paying higher wages any more than reducing the rents. But you're right, Ma, I'm sure some'd prefer to stay free labourers, and earn their money where they can. But there'll be others who'd welcome the chance to join their landed neighbours – Emma Coupar and Ralph Ward among them – and, though it's not my job, I'm going to try and persuade Sir Richard to give them that chance.'

Alice had not been able to speak to Emma since that evening, for whenever Emma came to carry out her daily work for Alice, she never stopped for a moment to talk. Alice hoped she might find Emma sufficiently unoccupied this afternoon that she could raise with her the possibility of taking on a smallholding. She found her with a group of other cottar women, all in the full flow of strident and vociferous banter.

Seeing Alice approach, Emma smiled. 'Mistress atte Wode, what a fine bride ale the bailiff's laid on.'

'He has,' said Alice, returning the smile, though she imagined Matilda might've wished there'd been no need for any such festivities. 'But, Emma, I'd speak with you. Can you leave the children a short while?'

Emma looked puzzled, then a little alarmed. 'Is summat amiss, mistress? Or is it Bart?'

But Alice laughed. 'No, there's just a matter I'd discuss with you, and we usually have so little time to talk.'

Emma's face relaxed, and turning to her neighbours, she asked them to mind her children, then she and Alice withdrew to a quiet corner of the orchard.

'I'm sorry to take you away from your friends,' said Alice.

'We was talking about the court,' said Emma, but then she bit her lip. 'Oh, mistress, I been so afraid since the court that the constable's going to come for Bart.'

'Surely if Sir Richard wanted him arrested, the bailiff would've already sent Master Dyer to arrest him?' said Alice.

Emma gave a weak smile. 'Perhaps. But I been so afraid.'

'And what does Bart think?'

'I dunno, mistress.' Emma fidgeted with the fabric of her skirt. 'Since the court, he refuses to work 'less he's paid what he says is a fair wage, and he complains without ceasing that the rich folk in the village are greedy and'll become even richer, while we cottars just get poorer. So 'tis just me putting food on the table. And my so-called husband spends half of what I earn at the ale-house.'

Alice patted Emma's hand. 'Bart's not a bad husband,' she said, though she hardly believed her own words.

Emma snorted. 'Would I could believe you, mistress. Bartholomew Coupar's a weak and idle clout. I'd fain I'd heeded my father and married Peter Chapman.'

Alice could hardly disagree. Ten years ago, when Bart was courting Emma, she was not much more than a child, he fifteen years older. Despite his age, he was still strong and handsome, with a shock of curly yellow hair and a constant twinkle in his eyes. But, although he was capable of working hard when well supervised, he'd a reputation for indolence and a love of ale. But Emma was only fourteen and so flattered by Bart's passionate attentions she refused to heed her father's warnings and threats. Then, finding herself with child, she was forced to marry her feckless paramour rather than the more impassive but industrious Peter Chapman, whom her father had intended for her. Since her marriage, Emma had worked ceaselessly, bringing up their five children and taking them with her wherever she had to go to earn her labourer's wage, while her husband worked only when coerced by a persevering employer and spent much of his time carousing with his fellow cottars in one or other of Meonbridge's ale-houses. But despite his fecklessness, as John often said, Bart was a likeable fellow and by no means reviled by his neighbours. When he made his feeble and faltering plea for higher wages in court, whereas his fellow labourers might have laughed at him for claiming more when he was so idle, in fact they supported him, almost to a man, and when Ralph Ward stepped forward to assert the justice of their claim, hardly any dissenting voice was raised.

Of course it was obvious at the court that neither Sir Richard and Philip de Bohun, nor the bailiff, shared the tenants' affectionate opinion of Bart Coupar. Though she'd not said so to Emma, Alice feared, as she did, that Bart would suffer for his outburst in court.

But no action had been taken, so perhaps Sir Richard had decided to overlook the mutiny as an act born out of the suffering of the previous months, for the mortality took three of the Coupars' five children, including all their sons. In one of her gloomier moods of late, Emma told Alice she thought He was a cruel God who allowed the mortality to take the lives of her innocent children but spare that of her sinful husband. And although Alice denied to Emma that Bart was truly sinful, he was undoubtedly slothful, and she couldn't help but wonder how far that counted in God's estimation of men's sins.

She remembered how, months before the mortality struck Meonbridge, Master Aelwyn read out in church, in English so that all might understand, a letter from the Bishop, which told of the approach of some dread disease and declared it was God's punishment for the terrible sins of humankind. The Bishop urged everyone to repent of their sins and do all in their power to turn from transgression, praying unceasingly for God's mercy. Only then, said the Bishop, might we stay God's hand and avert his terrible retribution. Yet, when she questioned her pious son Geoffrey, she found even he didn't understand what terrible sins the people of Meonbridge might have committed to call down such fearful wrath from God.

'Oh, Ma,' he said, wringing his hands in anguish, 'nor does Master Aelwyn comprehend it. We've racked our brains to list our neighbours' sins.'

'And are there many?' cried Alice, though Stephen laughed and said 'A thousand for sure.'

But Geoffrey sought to calm his mother's fears and said, in all honesty, the sins that he and Master Aelwyn had been able to think of seemed few and trivial, and hardly worthy of such punishment as the Bishop had declared would strike them down.

'There've been no murders, or robberies. No adultery or children born out of wedlock—'

'As far as we know,' said Stephen, obviously jesting, though his son looked at him with some vexation.

'It's not a matter for mockery, Pa.'

Stephen pursed his lips and apologised to his earnest, saintly son, but said he could think of many folk in Meonbridge who'd been deceitful or selfish, greedy or careless, and, even if they were not evil, perhaps in God's eyes they were sinners.

'Maybe,' said Alice, still fretful, 'God sees sins in us that we can't see ourselves?'

Which thought frightened her more than ever, and she sought consolation daily in church, as did scores of her neighbours, many of whom were not as frequent churchgoers as she, and some had not been shriven for years. She spoke daily to Master Aelwyn, wanting to understand what was to befall them, but though he tried to comfort her and all his flock, she sensed this looming disaster was beyond even his understanding, for he had no satisfactory answers to her questions.

When the mortality finally did strike Meonbridge, and it was clear it made no distinction between those who might be considered sinful and those who were entirely innocent, and especially when it took even God's own servants, Aelwyn and Geoffrey, while they were ministering to their flock, it was beyond anyone's comprehension why God reviled his people so much that he would allow, or even demand, such suffering.

But Alice never said any of this to Emma: it would only add to her misery if Alice implied Bart's sins might have been the cause of their three sons' agonising deaths. Instead, her intention was to try to lighten Emma's gloom by suggesting how she, and Bart, might raise their remaining family out of poverty. When she explained about the possibility of taking over some land, Emma looked by turns excited and gloomy: the thought of the Coupars having the chance to become real farmers, instead of scraping a living from their tiny croft and whatever day work they could obtain, immediately seemed a thrilling prospect to Emma. But almost at once she put forward a number of objections to the scheme, all of which Alice had already considered.

'How could we pay for it, mistress?' she said. 'We've no money – Bart drinks it all.'

Alice told her she was prepared to help her with both the entry fine and the rent, as a gift or a loan, as Emma wished. She'd already agreed with John that they could afford to be generous.

Emma then raised the problem of tools and equipment, none of which they owned, but Alice reminded her that plenty of spare equipment was lying idle in empty barns, and she was sure that neighbours would loan or give what was needed. But then of course came the most serious objection to the proposal: Bart.

'I think it's a fine idea, mistress,' said Emma, 'but I reckon Bart'll not agree. It'd need too much work, and you know well enough how lazy he is.'

Alice agreed this was a problem. 'Do you not think he'd see this as a chance to provide a better life for his family?'

Emma shook her head. 'I'm not sure he would. Since the court, he's been saying how we're going to make more money labouring when the wages go up–'

'But there's no guarantee they will.'

'That's what I told him, but he says if he can't get more money here in Meonbridge, he's going to take us away to some foreign place where folk'll pay us more.'

Emma's lips began to tremble, and Alice laid her hand on Emma's arm. 'But you don't want to leave Meonbridge?'

Emma shook her head vigorously. 'Why would I? For what might become of us if I follow that idle husband of mine to a place where no-one knows or cares about us?'

10

At Matilda's bride ale, Eleanor had spent only a few moments alone with John. She'd hoped he might come to see her at the forge after supper, as he often did. But the evening was advanced and the sun set by the time she and Roger finished their meal, and still John had not come. Disappointed but resigned, she decided to go home, and bade Roger good night.

It was a warm evening but a light drizzle left a fine mist on the curls of red-brown hair escaping from her hood. She hurried across the green, away from the forge, then along the main road through Meonbridge towards the turning to her house, just across the way from the atte Wodes' croft. Her head was down, her hood obscuring her view, so she was taken by surprise when a figure suddenly stepped into her path, and let out a little scream of alarm before looking up to find John standing in front of her, a broad grin on his face.

'Sorry to startle you, Mistress Eleanor. I called out but you were hurrying along so fast.'

'Oh, Master atte Wode, how stupid of me to scream. I was so intent on getting out of this drizzle, I didn't hear you.'

'Would you care to come to the house for a while?' he said.

Eleanor bit her lip, uncertain if she should accept his invitation, but he seemed to notice her hesitation. 'Ma's in the house. I'm sure she'd be pleased if you'd sit and talk with us a while.'

Eleanor felt foolishly pleased to be invited to sit with his mother, and was glad the light was fading so John couldn't see the colour of her cheeks.

'I'd like that,' she said, and he took her gently by the elbow as they walked together to the door of his house.

The hall in the atte Wodes' house was smaller than her own, and Eleanor could see there was only one chair and little other furniture except a table, a few three-legged stools and a small cupboard. John invited her to sit in the chair but she refused politely, saying surely Alice should take it, and that she would be perfectly comfortable on one of the stools. Alice offered her a cup of ale, then they all sat together with the door open to let in both the warmth of the evening and the pallid light of the moon, which was shining directly through the doorway. The drizzle eased a little and a slight breeze kept it away from the door. Eleanor thought how pleasant it was to feel warm and dry, and to be in good company.

They were all silent for a while, sipping their ale, then John said, 'Did you speak to Emma Coupar earlier, Ma?'

'I did,' said Alice. 'About Bart taking on some of the spare tenant land—'

'Can cottars take on land?' said Eleanor, surprised.

'If they've the money for the entry fine and rent,' said John. 'And of course if they can convince the court they'd be able to manage it properly.'

'Which I suppose, in the Coupars' case, is doubtful,' said Alice, sadly.

'Bart does have a reputation for being rather idle, doesn't he?' said Eleanor, hoping she wasn't speaking out of turn. 'Which is a pity, as Emma's such a hard worker.'

'Emma's very keen on the idea,' said Alice. 'But she told me that, ever since the last court, Bart's been complaining about his wages and how hard it is for the cottars, and has been talking about leaving Meonbridge—'

'He can't do that, can he? Surely he's tied to the manor?'

John nodded. 'He is, but times are changing. He's not the only one talking about leaving to look for better-paid work.'

Getting up, he fetched the jug of ale and poured a little more into each cup, then sat down again.

'At the bride ale, there was a group of them, sat together. They'd all drunk too much and were saying things they'd have been wiser not to speak of, especially in the bailiff's house.'

'Talking of leaving?' said Alice.

'Yes, Ma. That, and complaining the lord and his bailiff demand a lot more work from them but aren't prepared to pay them any more. They were even carping about me, or at least they were 'til they realised I was listening.'

Alice laughed. 'Did they stop their carping then?'

'Oh yes,' said John, grinning. 'Bart got up and staggered over to me, heaved his great arm around my shoulder and, breathing ale all over me, said, "Ah, Master atte Wode, it ain't really you we're blaming, but the bailiff." "Then I wouldn't say it too loudly in his house, if I were you, Bart Coupar." I said. Then everyone suddenly looked a bit sheepish.'

'Bart Coupar certainly isn't known for his good judgement,' said Alice, laughing again. 'But I shouldn't laugh, for, surely, Bart and the others'll find themselves in trouble if they talk like that?'

'I'm sure Master Tyler could find a way to stop the tenants leaving,' said John, grimacing. 'We need every available man and woman, villein and cottar, to stay on the manor.'

'Then surely they should pay them more to make them stay?' said Alice.

'I agree, Ma, as you know. But Sir Richard says the price of grain'll fall, because there are fewer folk around to buy it. So if he makes less money himself, he can't pay higher wages.'

Eleanor gave a little grunt. 'But surely if he doesn't have enough workers to bring in his crops, he'll make even less money.'

'You're right, Elly,' John said, and she blushed in the dark as he used her nickname for the first time. 'Sir Richard's caught between two stools: if he doesn't pay higher wages, the cottars'll leave; if he does pay more, then his profits'll be lower.'

'I don't think he's much choice,' said Eleanor.

'You're right, but perhaps not in the way you think. The bailiff told me this morning the king's passed a new law that wages must be kept at the same level as before the mortality. The sheriff's messenger came a few days ago and made a proclamation about it. And he said Sir Richard'll use that law to support his case against Bart Coupar and his cronies.'

'So Sir Richard'll do what he wants, and not pay any more.'

'But, even if Bart did leave Meonbridge, he can't be sure he'd get more money anywhere else,' said Alice. 'So it seems as if it's the cottars who're caught between stools, rather than our lord.'

Eleanor found it difficult to convince any cottars to shear her sheep at wages she wanted to pay. She even resorted to entering Mistress Rolfe's ale-house to find someone willing to be employed, but the men she saw there were not ones she could trust with her flock. So she was forced to go back to William Cole, who'd been willing enough to do her work but only for the wages he thought fit. When she'd mentioned the king's ordinance, which had been the talk of the ale-houses all week, William was unbowed.

'I'll work for 'ee, mistress,' he said, 'but you know my price. The king's a hundred mile away and he'll not bother us here in Me'nbridge.'

Eleanor knew well enough it was Sir Richard rather than the king himself who'd insist on the letter of the law, but felt herself in no position to argue: her sheep were staggering under the weight of their wool. She made a further weak attempt at negotiation but William was in a persuasive mood and in the end she agreed to his demands.

She also decided to swallow her pride and knock on Emma Coupar's door.

'Yes, mistress?' said Emma, looking rather less cowed than when she'd come seeking work a few weeks ago. She'd already agreed to work for Alice atte Wode but seemed willing enough to help Eleanor with the shearing.

'I'm a good shearer, mistress,' she said, and Eleanor feared she too would demand a high wage for her labour. But despite her new self-confidence, Emma said she'd accept the usual rate for the job, and Eleanor was relieved not to have to haggle for a second time.

William and Emma both lived in the cottars' crofts to the south of Meonbridge on the road that led to the common fields and eventually on up to Riverdown. Eleanor agreed to meet them there on her way up to the pasture. It was not long after first light when she knocked on Emma's door again.

'Won't be long, mistress,' said Emma. 'Bart's not lifting a finger as usual, and the little ones aren't quite ready. Step inside a moment?'

Inside the cottage, Eleanor was struck by its damp darkness. It was much like Walter's, with just two rooms and low ceilings. As her eyes became accustomed to the gloom, she could see the little room was sparsely furnished, with just a straw pallet in one corner, a rough-hewn table and two stools. But the dirt floor was swept and the room tidy: Emma clearly tried her best to make the hovel a home. There was no sign of Bart, though Eleanor thought she could hear his snores coming from the loft. She smiled weakly at Emma.

'Bart's not started his day yet?'

Emma snorted in disgust. 'No, mistress. Bart Coupar's day'll start sometime after dinner, if I'm lucky. He does naught, mistress, naught but argue and stir up trouble.' She seemed on the brink of tears.

Eleanor put a hand on Emma's arm to comfort her. 'Don't fret about him. You've your children to fend for, and you're doing a good job yourself.'

Emma pulled a wry smile. 'Thank you, mistress. I try my best.'

Then she gathered up the two children and hurried off to a cottage just down the road. When the door was opened Eleanor could see it was Susanna Bigge who took the children inside.

'Susanna'll have the children till dinner time,' said Emma, running back and picking up her shearing scissors from just inside the cottage door. 'I hope that's enough time.'

Eleanor nodded. 'It should be, if William comes soon.' And just as she spoke, William Cole emerged from his cottage just opposite Susanna's, still struggling into his surcoat, made more difficult by the hat and shearing scissors he was grasping in one hand. He hurried towards the two women, slightly pink-faced and harassed.

'Sorry, mistress,' he gasped. 'Overslept.'

Eleanor smiled. 'No matter, Master Cole. But let's make haste now.' And she set off towards Riverdown at a brisk pace.

As they approached the point in the road where the track led up to Riverdown and the road bent left to go down to Nether Brooking, a man on horseback suddenly emerged from behind the trees that thickly lined the road, coming towards them at a steady walking pace.

'I've not seen him before,' said Emma.

'What does 'e want in Me'nbridge, a man like that?' said William.

He was clearly neither pedlar nor pardoner, for, as he came closer, Eleanor could see his horse was a fine animal and his clothing that of a prosperous man. 'What indeed,' she said quietly.

As the rider passed the three walkers, he raised his hat and bowed his head, smiling. 'Good day to you, mistresses and master. 'Tis a fine morning.'

Eleanor made an effort to remember his face without appearing to be staring. He was a plain-featured man, perhaps in his thirties, with a well-trimmed beard but a skin dark enough to show he spent a good deal of his time out of doors. She bobbed a slight curtsey.

'Good day to you, sir,' she said. 'Are you seeking someone particular in Meonbridge? Can I direct you?'

The man seemed briefly disconcerted by her question but quickly recovered his composure.

'Thank you kindly, mistress, but I know Meonbridge well enough and'll have no trouble finding the one I seek.'

'Many have died, sir,' said Eleanor.

'Indeed,' said the man, and made the sign of the cross on his chest. 'As they have throughout England, I warrant.' He replaced his hat and bowed his head again. It was plain he did not intend to continue this conversation. 'Good day to you all,' he said, kicking the horse's flanks with his heels, and moved past them, this time at a trot, down the road towards Meonbridge, while Eleanor and her shearers climbed the shallow hill up to Riverdown.

The next day, John called at the forge not, for once, to catch a few moments with Eleanor, but to ask Roger to make a new axle for his cart. Eleanor was just returning to the forge from her regular morning visit to her flocks, when she saw young Matthew atte Wode, looking despondent and holding the reins of his brother's carthorse, which was cropping the grass on the village green. She slipped unseen into the kitchen behind the forge, hoping to be able to observe John in secret. She crept up to the door that led into the forge and, hiding herself behind it, listened to the conversation.

John was clearly annoyed about the need for a new axle: it seemed he'd allowed young Matthew to drive the cart the short distance between two areas of their holding, and the boy had lost control of the mare. She'd bucked, toppling the back end of the cart into a ditch, damaging both the axle and one of the wheels.

'Ma'll chide me if she finds out I let my brother drive,' John said gloomily to Roger, 'But I reckon the boy's old enough to try, don't you? The sooner he learns, the sooner he'll be of some use to me on the farm.'

Roger agreed. 'Look at me. I'd not have reckoned to be a blacksmith at my age, but I am. I had to learn.'

'Anyway, I've told Matt to promise not to tell Ma about the accident. If she asks about the cart, I'll say it was my fault.'

Eleanor peeped around the door at the two young men, and could see them exchange a conspiratorial wink. She was a little shocked that John should be planning to deceive his mother, but supposed it was wise not to alarm her.

John had brought the broken axle to show Roger, so he could copy it. 'It must have been hard work removing that,' said Roger, and John grinned ruefully.

'Yes, with just my little brother to help me. And it's so warm I was already sweating from working in the fields, and then I had to set to with the axle. I don't know how you put up with the heat in here all day long.'

'Oh, you get used to it. When I was first 'prenticed, I told Ma I couldn't stand the forge's heat, and I didn't want to learn to be a blacksmith after all. But she just clipped me round the ear and told me to get on with it.'

John laughed.

'What's more,' said Roger, laughing too, 'she said, as the forge had been my father's, it was my birth right to be a blacksmith, so I'd no choice but to take it on.'

'And now you're a happy blacksmith?'

Roger gave rather a rueful smile. 'Happy enough. I can still only do the simple jobs, but folk seem willing enough to employ me, so I'll never be short of work.'

'You're right, though in truth few folk are short of work these days. Every farmer and labourer could work day and night seven days a week and still all the work'd not get done. But we all have to do our best—'

'I'm sure you always do your best, Master atte Wode,' said Eleanor, smiling broadly as she emerged from her hiding place.

John quickly raised his arm and wiped his sweaty face upon his sleeve. 'Mistress Eleanor,' he said, his ears suddenly bright red. 'I'd not expected to see you here.'

'And now you have, d'you wish you hadn't?' she teased.

'No, of course not. I'm always glad to see you, you know that. But I'd rather be cleaner when I do.'

Now Eleanor felt a little ashamed. 'It doesn't matter to me, Master atte Wode,' she said, giving a nervous little laugh.

Roger seemed to be trying to ignore the conversation, leaning over his anvil and banging energetically at a strip of iron. Having finished his hammering, he stood up straight again and turned to his sister.

'Elly, it must be time for dinner, eh?'

'Soon, brother,' said Eleanor. 'I've not long returned from Riverdown.' She turned back to the kitchen and continued with her preparations, but then a thought occurred to her.

Going back to the door of the forge, she said to John, 'Would you and your brother care to have dinner with us? There's plenty.'

'Have you heard anything of the stranger come to Meonbridge?' said Roger, still chewing as he spoke.

John looked alarmed at the question. 'What stranger?'

Roger finished the mouthful of pottage and took a swig of ale before replying.

'In the ale-house last evening—' he said.

Eleanor gasped. 'In the ale-house?' she said, shocked. 'I'd rather you'd not spend your time there, brother.'

John laughed. 'To be sure, Mistress Eleanor, you can't deny your brother a draught of ale after a hard day's work at the anvil.'

'But he's too young to mix with the folk who go there.'

Roger spluttered with indignation but John held up his hand.

'Mistress Eleanor, don't be so prim,' he said, looking solemn. 'Your brother's working as a man and is entitled to live a man's life. Surely it's not for you to deny him that freedom?'

Roger looked smug at John's support and Eleanor felt a little aggrieved that John should take her brother's part against her. But John did throw her a smile as he urged Roger to continue with his story.

'Tom Carpenter and me were sat in a corner at Ellen Rolfe's,' said Roger. 'The room was pretty full, and noisy, with everyone arguing and shouting. Most people were talking about Bart and Ralph and what they'd said at the court. There was quite an uproar. Some were saying it were only right that labourers' wages should go up, and others said they'd be better off trying to get hold of some of the spare land and not rely on wages.'

John nodded. 'There's a lot of land available. If the cottars can find the money, they could become tenants.'

'But they don't all want to. Some say they just won't work unless they get higher wages, and Sir Richard'll soon be forced to pay them more.'

'I'm not sure he will. Sir Richard's a hard man to shift. He might just get his labour elsewhere.'

'But could he?' said Eleanor, surprised. 'Surely there's a shortage of labourers everywhere?'

John shrugged his shoulders. 'You're probably right. But I doubt Sir Richard'll give in easily to the cottars' demands. And Sir Philip and Master Tyler certainly won't.'

'Anyway,' said Roger, eager to continue with his story. 'There was all this uproar going on, when the door of Mistress Rolfe's opened and a stranger stood on the threshold. She bade him come in, but it was funny how the noise just stopped, and everyone turned to stare at this man.'

'What sort of man was he?' said Eleanor. 'A pedlar? A pardoner?'

'No, no-one like that. This was a respectable, upright man. He looked like a bailiff or a constable. He was of middle age, with a fine wool travelling cloak and a good pair of boots.'

'I saw a man just like that early yesterday morning, riding into the village,' said Eleanor. 'He seemed respectable, so I thought little of it. But it's strange such a man should just walk into a Meonbridge ale-house.'

John frowned. 'Worrying as well as strange. Why would a man of that sort come here? And I wonder what he'd been doing here all day.'

'You think he'd some sinister purpose?' Eleanor said.

'Maybe. Did the man talk to anyone, Roger?'

Roger nodded. 'Not at first. He just got a pot of ale and went and sat at the one empty table. Then Mistress Rolfe brought him a pie and he ate that, keeping himself to himself. And everyone went back to their talk, though now we all kept our voices low.'

Roger scraped the last of the pottage from his bowl with a piece of coarse bread, and emptied his pot of ale before continuing.

'But then, as it got later, and everyone'd had quite a lot to drink, he moved round from table to table, just passing the time of day it seemed. And because most folk were pretty relaxed by then, they seemed content enough to talk to him.'

'Did he talk to you and Tom?'

'Yes, but when he heard I was the blacksmith and Tom the wheelwright, he didn't seem to want to talk to us anymore.'

'So who did he want to talk to?'

'Farm workers: both labourers and tenants.'

'And did you hear what he said to them?'

'No, I couldn't hear. But when we left the ale-house, I walked for a while with Will Mannering and Nick Cook, and they said the man was just making conversation, asking about how many people had died in the village and how it was faring now the mortality had gone. It didn't seem suspicious, but you have to wonder why a man like that should want to gossip with labouring folk.'

John nodded. 'I agree. Why would he? D'you know if he spent the night at Mistress Rolfe's?'

'I don't, but I reckon he must've, for early this morning he came to the forge wanting a new shoe for his horse.'

'Did he say anything to you?' asked Eleanor.

'Not much. He asked how long I'd been at the forge, just chatting. And we talked about the shoe. Then I fixed it and he went on his way.'

Eleanor got up and cleared away the pottage bowls, casting a sideways glance at John, who'd gone a bit quiet.

'He didn't go far,' he said, after a while. 'Before Matt put the cart into the ditch, we'd been working the fields up at Long Acre. You can see a long way from those fields and there was a moment when I stood up and looked across towards the Commons and I could see a man leading his horse and talking to some of the men tending to their beasts. I reckon it was him.'

11

Margaret was becoming increasingly concerned about the turn of events on the manor, and neither her husband nor her son was doing much to help the situation. Richard continued to bluster about his "rebellious" tenants, and this morning when Robert Tyler came to announce that three families had run away in the night, Richard threw up his hands in fury and chastised Robert for letting it happen. It seemed that a stranger had come to Meonbridge, a bailiff or steward from some distant manor, seeking workers to replace those lost in the mortality. And presumably those three families had thought his offer of land and higher wages worth abandoning all they knew.

Philip did nothing to calm his father's anger but, rather, exacerbated it by declaring that the protesting cottars were knaves who deserved to be kicked off the manor, and the runaways not worth their consideration. When he voiced this opinion at dinner, Margaret could not help but speak out.

'But you need your tenants, Philip,' she said. 'All of them. Those three tenants were all good workers, not idle or dishonest. And this talk of getting rid of cottars makes no sense.'

Philip glowered at her. 'I did not ask for your opinion, Mother,' he said. 'I am steward of this manor, and will manage its tenants as I see fit.'

Margaret blushed, humiliated by her rashness at speaking her mind to a son she knew largely disregarded her opinions, and ashamed that he should address her so insolently. But there was no-one to hear his insolence or see her blush but her husband and daughter, and neither of them would recognise either the insult or her reaction to it.

Philip's attitude towards his mother was a little less dismissive these days than it had been when he was a child. Then he would ignore her commands and generally run wild, often joining up with the village boys to hunt and get into mischief. Now at least he would sometimes talk to her, ask her opinions on domestic or social matters, as if he had an interest in such things. But he would not seek, or listen to, her views on any matters of importance, and expected her, and indeed his sister, to keep silent whenever he and his father discussed manor affairs. She knew that Richard did not fully share his son's attitude on the irrelevance of women's views, but he never contradicted him when Philip admonished his mother, perhaps regarding the insolence as a welcome sign of authority in his heir.

Nonetheless, when Richard addressed her directly, Margaret was still bold enough to express her opinions to him, even in Philip's presence.

'Philip's right, Margaret,' said Richard. 'We don't want tenants who make trouble. Perhaps better to get rid of them and bring in new ones.'

'But where from, husband?' said Margaret.

Richard huffed. 'I'm sure we can find workers elsewhere. We'll send Master Tyler off to do the same job at other manors that that fellow did here.'

Margaret knew that her next comment would not go down well but it had to be said. 'But that fellow offered them higher wages to lure them away. And land. If you would consider giving more to strangers, why not give it to the men you know?'

Philip exploded. 'Mother, I have already told you that we do not want your views on these matters.' he said, his voice raised, but Richard sought to calm him.

'No, no, Philip,' he said. 'I did address my remark to your mother, so she is entitled to make reply.'

Philip glowered, then, raising his goblet to his lips to take a long draught of wine, thumped it down again on the table.

'Even if we don't agree with her opinion,' continued Richard, smiling at his son in what Margaret took to be a gesture of reconciliation.

Margaret felt humiliated for a second time. It seemed as if Richard was playing with her, allowing her to speak her mind, but disregarding what she said. Yet still she felt driven to continue.

'Surely it is against the king's ordinance to poach tenants from your neighbours?' she said.

'Indeed it is, and also to pay higher wages,' said Richard. 'Yet you, madam, want me to pay our tenants more.'

'Only to encourage them to stay,' she said, though she could see that calling on the law was not helping her argument.

'How can I pay them more when the price of grain is falling?' said Richard.

'But if the tenants leave the manor in search of higher wages elsewhere, you'll not have enough labourers to harvest the grain.'

Philip could contain himself no longer. 'Do you imagine, Mother, that we have not considered this?' he said, his voice barely under control.

Richard raised his hand to quieten him. 'You're right, Margaret, it is a conundrum.'

'A conundrum that *we* will resolve,' said Philip, and got to his feet. 'Shall we go now, Father?'

Richard nodded and rose heavily from his chair. 'Yes, let us go about our business. And you go about yours, my dear,' he added, but gently and with one of his old familiar smiles.

After her demeaning dinner confrontation, Margaret was glad that Alice was due to visit that afternoon, for she felt sorely in need of the solace that a conversation with her friend might bring. However, since she had last spoken to Alice, the relatively quiet rumblings of revolt in Meonbridge had exploded into crisis, with the three tenant families breaking their bonds to the manor. When Alice arrived, she was in a state of some agitation. News travelled fast in Meonbridge and by now the night-time flight of the runaway families was being talked of everywhere, at the mill and at the well, at every chance meeting between neighbours, even after prayers in church.

But perhaps Alice imagined that the news might not have reached the inner chambers of the manor, for she seemed impatient to talk as soon as she had greeted Margaret and the lady had dismissed her maid.

'Have you heard, Margaret, that three families have left the village?'

'I have,' said Margaret. 'And they were good people, all of them. I would they had not deserted us.'

'You can hardly blame them for seeking a better life.'

Margaret shook her head. 'Nor do I, though I fear that their promise of prosperity may not be fulfilled.'

'Why?'

'The law says that lords and masters must keep wages as they were before the mortality and not offer to pay more. I fear that our runaway tenants may find their new masters are not as generous, or the other tenants as welcoming, as they might hope.'

'Will Sir Richard try to get them back?'

Margaret shrugged. 'I am not sure he knows where to look for them. I have heard that that fellow came from Dorchester.'

Alice smiled grimly. 'Dorchester? I'd heard he was from Farnham. Though I don't know where either of them is.'

Margaret shook her head again. 'Nor I. Though I think both are much more than a day or two's ride, and there must be so many manors between here and there.'

Alice agreed. 'What then will Sir Richard do?'

'He won't tell me, Alice,' said Margaret, despondently, then, conscious that she was about to be indiscreet, continued. 'Richard flatters me by pretending to discuss manor affairs with me, but he does not consider that I have anything useful to say nor does he tell me of his decisions.'

'I suppose he thinks that, as lord, all the decisions are his to make.'

'Yes, he does think that.' Margaret's lips widened into a thin regretful smile. 'And it is so provoking when, for so many years when he was away, it was I who made those decisions. I am not a silly young girl with no experience of these matters.'

'How well I remember those years. Your judgements were always well-regarded among the tenants.'

Margaret smiled. 'So you have told me, dear Alice. But I am sure that Richard would not consider them "well-regarded", because he would say they favoured the tenants at the expense of the manor's coffers.'

'I'm sure that wasn't true.'

Margaret leaned forward and touched Alice's hand with her own. 'Thank you for your good opinion of me, my dear friend. But in truth I expect I may indeed have favoured the tenants over the manor. For, so long as the manor was never actually harmed, I saw no reason to make life for my tenants more difficult than it need be.'

'I dare say you've never admitted this to Sir Richard?' said Alice, a whimsical smile crossing her face.

Margaret laughed out loud. 'Indeed I have not. Richard will never understand my attitude towards our tenants. I regard them as my neighbours, but he considers them his vassals.'

Later the two women took a stroll in the enclosed herber that was Margaret's physic garden. It had always been her favourite part of the manor garden, but during the mortality, and since, it had been much neglected. The grass paths were overgrown, and although the line and shape of the little clipped hedges that divided the beds could still be seen, and the thymes, sages and lavenders were a blaze of purples, pinks and blues, the plants were all leggy and tangled and badly in need of trimming.

Margaret sighed. 'Oh, Alice, there's so much to be done here, but Richard will not hear of any of the manor servants spending time on it. He says they must all work in the fields, not fret about such fancies as my herber.'

'I suppose the field work's more urgent.'

'But I use the plants for healing. If they are not tended, I shall have no medicines for the sick and no poultices to treat wounds.'

'Can you tend the herbs yourself?'

Margaret nodded. 'I shall have to, though I was wont to put my trust in Mistress Kemp, who knew more about physic and healing plants than I ever will.'

'Yes, Sybil is a great loss to Meonbridge.'

'I do miss her, Alice, even though she was in a way the cause of my daughter-in-law's death.'

'Poor Isabella.'

'Foolish Isabella,' said Margaret, raising her eyes to the heavens. 'Oh, she was a stupid girl, Alice. She told her maid that she thought Philip's eyes were straying because her belly had become so distorted with her growing baby. The maid, a simple wretch of a girl I should never have allowed to be a manor servant, told her that Mistress Kemp could give her a love potion, which she could slip into Philip's wine. Isabella of course believed her. And she chose to ignore Richard's rule that no-one was to leave the manor and go into the village. She slipped out without anyone noticing, and soon after she returned she fell ill and died within a few days.'

'Yet no-one else in the manor was afflicted?'

'Well, a number of our servants died, those who had gone to their homes to visit their sick relatives. Once we stopped them leaving the manor, no-one else became ill–'

Margaret suddenly stopped and bent down to pluck a few stems of honeysuckle and brought them to her nose. She breathed in their scent, then sighed.

'Except of course for me.'

'You?' said Alice, in astonishment. 'I didn't know.'

Margaret smiled. 'I have not let it be known in the village. I insisted that I alone nursed Isabella. I did not permit Philip or any of the servants to come near her. I developed the signs a day or two after Isabella died. Richard was terrified that I too would die. I became quite ill, and again insisted that no-one attend me. I assumed I would not survive, but after a few days the boils burst and gradually I recovered. I do not understand why I was spared.'

'I thank the Holy Mother that you were,' said Alice, taking Margaret's hand and gently squeezing it in a gesture of affection. 'Meonbridge needs you, Margaret.'

'I am not sure I can be of any help to Meonbridge. If Richard and Philip refuse to listen to my advice, I fear that the cottars will defy them even more fiercely than now. Am I right, Alice?'

Alice nodded. 'I believe you are. John is finding it hard to persuade the labourers to work on the manor without more pay. And the tenants don't want to work on the manor land, but on their own. If only you could make Sir Richard and Sir Philip understand their point of view, Margaret?'

Margaret shook her head. 'I've tried, Alice, but they will not listen. Philip in particular refuses to listen to anything I have to say. He will do as he thinks fit.'

Just beyond the physic garden was a small orchard with, at its centre, a circular tunnel arbour thickly planted with vines and white roses. The women continued their walk, and Margaret inspected the developing apples, pears and medlars.

'The fruit looks well,' said Alice.

'It does, though the trees need some attention.'

'And can you do that yourself too?'

Margaret shook her head. 'I do not know what to do. Our gardener, old John Greenfinger, was one of the first of the manor servants to die. I hope I shall find another who has his skills.'

'Or you'll have to learn them yourself, Margaret,' said Alice, a slight twinkle in her eye.

Margaret laughed. 'You are right, there is much to learn. Perhaps I should spend my time learning these new skills and leave the manor to its masters.' Though Margaret did not believe for one moment that this was really what she should, or would, do.

Shortly, they came to the arbour, and, as the hot July sun now rode high in the sky, they stepped gratefully into the coolness of the tunnel. Half way round the circle of the arbour they came to a hidden archway that led into the fragrant, flowery interior of another little enclosed herber. More roses were growing tall and leggy in the centre of the garden but were laden with sweet-smelling blooms of yellow and white and deepest red.

Margaret sighed again. 'More work.'

'But it's delightful as it is, Margaret,' said Alice. 'What does it matter if it's a little untidy? I agree that the physic garden and orchard need your attention, but surely this can wait?'

Margaret was about to reply when she heard a small voice calling, 'Mother, is that you?' and, as they rounded the central thicket of roses, they saw Johanna sitting alone on the turf seat that nestled under an arching trellis overwhelmed with honeysuckle. She had a small book on her lap and a faraway look on her face that suggested she had not been reading but wandering down the pathways of her thoughts.

'Johanna, all alone?' she said, trying to make light of her daughter's solitariness.

'Yes, Mother, you know I prefer it,' said Johanna, a sulky frown briefly crossing her face.

Margaret ignored the retort. 'Johanna, you have not seen Alice for some months. Come, tell her about Courtenay Castle, and all you saw there—'

Johanna pouted. 'I am sure that Mistress atte Wode would not be at all interested, Mother,' she said, then turned to Alice. 'I would think you have far more pressing matters to concern you?'

Margaret was embarrassed by Johanna's dismissal of her request, for it seemed like impertinence: an ill-mannered daughter as well as an insolent son. But Alice either did not notice the girl's disrespect towards her mother or chose to ignore it.

'Lady de Bohun has told me that the mortality passed by the castle,' said Alice. 'How blessed the de Courtenays must have thought themselves.'

'Indeed, Mistress atte Wode, we knew nothing of the mortality until afterwards from reports from outside the castle.'

'I'm sure Lady de Bohun's most thankful to have you home again. To know that her daughter is safe.'

Margaret did not miss the insinuation in Alice's words. She looked at Johanna and saw that she too had noticed it, for her face paled and she appeared to falter before replying.

'Yes, Mistress atte Wode, and I am glad to be home.' Johanna hesitated again, then said, in a hushed voice, 'Have you received any news of Agnes?'

Margaret felt her own face flush, and she could read the same sense of disquiet in the face of her daughter.

Alice, however, looked composed. 'No, Lady Johanna, we've no news of Agnes. I must hope that she found a place of safety, as you did, and still lives and thrives somewhere. I pray daily to Our Lady for her return.'

A tear leaked from Johanna's eye and she turned her face away.

12

The mill was always a good place for hearing gossip about the neighbours – who was courting whom, which husbands were beating their wives (and which wives beating their husbands), what news the latest tinker or pedlar had brought. The talk could be scurrilous, scandalous and often hilarious. Thomas the miller himself had once been a jolly fellow, and both he and Joan, his wife, had been eager to exchange banter with their customers, for they were a happy couple with a large brood of children and, with the lord's assertion that all the village's grain was to be milled only by Thomas and no-one else, the future of the mill and their family had seemed assured.

But during the months of the mortality, the conversation had been anything but amusing, the news, exchanged in horrified whispers and with fearful faces, only about who else had died and in what terrible agony. No pedlars or tinkers came to Meonbridge for months, and the only news of the world outside the village came from Master Tyler, who ventured out once or twice, and the priest, Master Hugo Garret, who had come recently to the village. And the news that both men brought was dire, of appalling slaughter, even worse than in Meonbridge. So, while the mortality ravaged the village, the women who occasionally gathered at the mill were not a merry band full of humorous tales of village life, but a gloomy group of individuals, keeping their distance from each other and going about their daily business without much hope of a future.

The Millers became a forlorn little family. Joan no longer came to the mill to help her husband, but stayed in their cottage, a desolate sloven who barely managed her household tasks and neglected her baby, Maud. Thomas no longer exchanged even a smile with his customers, let alone any witty banter, but carried out his work mechanically, doing only what he must to keep the mill going, while his brother Henry bore the brunt of the work.

But now the mortality really had left Meonbridge, and it seemed there was a future after all for those who'd not been taken, the mood of the women who came to the mill for their grain to be ground was undoubtedly lighter, even though there was still much to worry about.

It was quite late in the morning when Eleanor arrived, as her priority was always to her flocks and she'd gone up to Riverdown at first light. As she approached the mill, she could see several women gathered together around the door in a noisy huddle, their voices raised in animated conversation. As she got closer, one of the women, Susanna Bigge, looked round and smiled.

'Good day to you, Mistress Titherige.' Eleanor knew Susanna a little, although she was a cottar. She was only a year or two older than Eleanor but looked a lot more, for her hair was already greying, her long face thin and drawn.

Eleanor returned the greeting, and nodded also to Ann Webb and Alys Ward.

'How is Master Thomas today?' she said quietly. 'Has his humour lightened at all?'

Susanna shook her head. 'No, mistress, sadly not. He's as miserable as ever, poor soul. He were quite rude to us all just now. And I fear Joan's almost out of her wits with despair.'

'They've much to be sad about.'

Alys snorted. 'No more so than other folk. We've all lost little ones.' She sniffed and wiped the back of her grubby hand across the creased, weather-worn skin of her cheek. Eleanor wondered if Alys, a hard-bitten old woman whose long life had been one of almost constant poverty and suffering, ever wept for her lost grandchildren.

Susanna agreed. 'That's true, Alys. But to lose six children almost all at once, that's surely beyond normal suffering?'

'And to think your child's not been taken, only to have him die in an accident,' said Ann.

Alys snorted again, and shook her head. 'Thomas Miller shouldn't've let the boy enter the mill. It's no place for children.'

'But he's suffered hard for his carelessness, Alys,' said Susanna.

'Mebbe,' said Alys, her scorn apparently unrelenting. 'But what else do the Millers have to complain of? They've all this,' and she waved her hand in a gesture encompassing all the mill buildings, 'and a pledge that all the manor's grain must be ground here. They've no trouble making money. Unlike some others.'

Alys's bitterness, thought Eleanor, was clouding her compassion, though in truth Alys had always been rather heartless, resentful of those who had more than her. Her dead son Edward had been the same, always complaining about his bad lot in life. Yet Ralph, her elder son, was very different, hard-working and practical. John told Eleanor that, although Bart had spoken up first in court, it was Ralph who had the strongest opinions about injustice against the cottars, and who was agitating for higher wages for all. And since the mortality had carried off his wife and baby son, Ralph cared little about what punishment Sir Richard might impose on him for raising a rebellion.

At that moment, Thomas's brother Henry appeared at the door with three sacks of flour. 'Your flour, mistresses.' He set the sacks on the ground at their feet. 'You mustn't mind my brother Thomas,' he said, with a thin smile of apology. 'He don't mean to be rude, but he's not himself these days.'

'That's not to be surprised at, Master Henry,' said Susanna. 'Master Thomas has suffered grievously.'

'No more than the rest of us—' started Alys, but Susanna flapped at her angrily and Ann whispered to her to hush up.

Henry seemed not to have heard Alys and answered Susanna, his mouth puckering into a mournful grimace. 'Indeed he has. The loss of little Peter, the light of his life, were more 'n he could bear. And as for Joan, my sister-in-law, well, she's a lost soul, I fear. I'd bid you visit her, mistresses. Try to bring her back to us.'

. . .

The next day Eleanor arranged to go with Susanna Bigge to visit Joan Miller. Susanna had been a close friend of Joan's but she'd wistfully admitted to Eleanor that since the mortality she'd let her friendship slide. Eleanor was sympathetic, thinking guiltily of Matilda. But neglecting friendship seemed excusable enough when your husband and children had been cruelly torn from you all on the same day.

One evening in late February, Francis Bigge had come home from the fields, where he'd been part of a hedge-mending gang led by the reeve. It had been a cold, raw day, with biting winds blowing across the fields from the east and, as Francis burst through the door into their cottage, he was moaning and coughing, and declared he needed his bed. He refused the hot pottage Susanna offered him and shakily climbed the ladder to the straw-filled loft where they all slept. At first the children, already up in the loft, thought it funny Pa was coming to bed so early and crawled over to him as he lay groaning on his pallet. Young Francie climbed onto his father's chest and tweaked his beard, and Tilly, giggling, started to poke and tickle him. Francis was a sweet-natured mountain of a man who adored his children, so when he roared at his son and batted him away like a fly from his chest, the boy screamed with fear and shock, and his sister scrabbled away in terror, and the two of them huddled together in the corner of the loft whimpering. Susanna climbed the ladder to see what the commotion was about, and was shocked to find her strong husband curled up on their pallet sweating, retching and crying out in pain.

'Fran, what's up wi' you?' she said. Already many people in Meonbridge had died from the mortality, including several of her neighbours. But surely a strong man like Francis wouldn't succumb? Though, even as she thought it, she knew well enough that strength seemed no protection against the mortality, which struck at random, at the weak and the strong, rich and poor, old and young.

Francis rolled over to look her in the eyes, as she stood with her head just level with the floor of the loft. 'Susy,' he whispered hoarsely, 'Take the children away from here. Keep them safe.'

Susanna shook her head. 'But what about you?'

'I reckon I'm done for,' he groaned, then, as a fit of coughing rose in his throat and droplets of blood escaped from between his lips, he rolled himself away from Susanna and buried his face in the straw to gasp and heave. 'Go!' he cried between fits, and Susanna called to the children to come down quickly, and they'd go to her parents' until Pa was better.

But Francis did not get better, and the children showed the same symptoms as their father the very next day. Two days later all three, father and children, were dead, though neither Susanna herself nor her parents got sick.

'I don't understand,' said Susanna to Eleanor, 'why God'd take a good man like my Fran, and our innocent children, and yet spare sinners like me, and my parents, whose lives I know well enough've been far short of honest.'

Eleanor wondered briefly what sins Susanna could have committed. 'No-one understands. Why did my father die, and my sweet little brothers?'

'But if the mortality is God's punishment for our sins,' said Susanna, her eyes wide with confusion, 'why don't He take the sinners?'

Eleanor had listened closely to Master Aelwyn when he spoke in church about the reasons for the mortality and how people could avoid catching it. But although she believed the priest was doing his best to explain the inexplicable, somehow none of it made sense to her. It was obvious to anyone the mortality did not choose the sinner or the innocent but simply struck at random. No-one knew how it spread, for although several members of a family might catch it, not everyone did.

Eleanor shook her head. 'I don't know, Susanna. But perhaps all we can do now is lead guiltless lives, and pray for the souls of our loved ones?'

'And help those who've been most sorely afflicted,' said Susanna, and they agreed that trying to help Joan Miller recover her soul should be the first of such deeds.

Eleanor knew Alice atte Wode often looked in on her neighbour Joan Miller, but she'd told Eleanor that Joan had now rejected her help and even refused to speak to Master Hugo, who'd been trying to help her find comfort in prayer. It seemed unlikely she or Susanna could succeed where Alice and the priest had not, but Susanna, feeling guilty at her neglect of her friend, urged Eleanor to help her. But even her stout heart failed when they saw the state of the Millers' cottage, and the state of Joan.

Pushing open the heavy wooden door, Eleanor stepped into the gloom of the cottage and the smell of damp air and rank, sodden straw filled her nostrils. Susanna came in beside her and wrinkled up her nose.

'This straw needs sweeping out,' she said. 'It stinks.'

Eleanor nodded, and opened the wooden shutter to let in some light and air. 'But it's quite tidy.'

'Perhaps Joan does nothing to make it untidy,' said Susanna, moving around the room and peering into corners. 'But it's so quiet, Eleanor.' Then whispered fearfully, 'Where's Joan, d'you think, and why's the baby not making a noise?'

She went over to the door of the back room, and put her ear against the rough wood.

'Perhaps they're in here? But I'm afraid to look.'

'She can't be dead,' said Eleanor, trying to feel brave, 'for Henry'd surely know.' She opened the low door and the two women peered into the pitch dark of the inner room, waiting for their eyes to become accustomed to the gloom.

They could see Joan, curled up like a child, lying on her straw pallet and covered by a filthy blanket.

'I wonder if Master Miller shares this bed with his wife?' said Susanna in a low whisper.

Eleanor shook her head. 'No, Mistress atte Wode told me Thomas sleeps at the mill, and hardly comes home at all.'

'So he's just abandoned Joan?'

'Perhaps he cannot bear what has become of her.'

'But it's a husband's duty to look after his wife.'

Eleanor shrugged. 'You're right, but it seems Thomas has lost the strength to do his duty.'

Shortly a low whimper came from a dark corner of the room and Susanna darted across and threw herself onto her knees. 'Oh, my poor little sweet one,' she cried, and gently lifted the tiny bundle that was Maud up from the pile of sodden straw that served for her cot. She carried the child over to Eleanor and they stepped into the relative light of the other room to see her better. They were shocked by what they saw: Maud was a dangerously delicate bag of bones, with a blotchy face and red-rimmed empty eyes. Susanna and Eleanor exchanged expressions of horror: the child seemed barely alive, indeed barely human, with her unseeing eyes and intermittent whimpers that seemed to be little more than the grunts of a wild creature.

'It seems as if Master Henry's not realised how much Joan's neglecting Maud,' said Eleanor.

'Perhaps he thought a mother could never neglect her baby?' said Susanna. 'Thomas, too.'

'Alice said Thomas has ignored the baby ever since Peter's death. She thinks he can't bear to love another child in case she dies too.'

'But she *will* die. Look at her, the poor mite. How could they abandon her so cruelly?'

Susanna, still clasping the baby to her, went back into the room where Joan lay still. Eleanor stood by the door, horrified at the wretchedness of this little family.

Susanna knelt by Joan and touched her arm. 'Joannie? Can you hear me?'

Joan stirred and lifted her head very slightly to face the source of the voice. 'Who's there?' she said, in a low growl.

'It's me, Joannie. Susy Bigge. Your friend.' Susanna felt for Joan's hand underneath the filthy blanket and took it in hers. The hand was cold and clammy, but she squeezed it in what she hoped Joan would realise was an act of affection. But Joan didn't, for straight away she wrenched her hand from Susanna's grasp, and feebly pushed at Susanna, who lost her balance and fell back into the rank straw.

'Leave me alone,' said Joan, 'whoever you are.'

'But it's me, Joan – Susy. I want to help you,' she said, kneeling back up again.

'I don't need your help, not yours, nor anyone else's.'

'But the baby, Joan. What about Maud?'

'What about her?' repeated Joan.

'She's starving to death, Joan. Surely you don't want her to die?'

Joan did not answer.

'Joan? Maud'll die.'

Joan grunted. 'Then that'll be an end to it.'

Susanna turned to throw a despairing look at Eleanor, who

shrugged: she'd no idea how to help Joan drag herself from such depths of desolation. She'd always imagined that motherhood meant a woman would do anything for her child, anything to keep it from harm, let alone from death. Yet she'd heard stories of mothers – and fathers – abandoning their plague-afflicted children, leaving them to die alone, for fear of sickening themselves, which seemed a scarcely believable act of cruelty. Yet here was Joan – and Thomas – having lost six children, with what was perhaps their last chance of a surviving child, throwing up that chance. How could they do that? She couldn't understand it. But then she'd never been a mother, never experienced the pain of losing a child, let alone six, so perhaps she was in no position to pass judgement.

She gave Susanna an encouraging smile, hoping to urge her to try again. Susanna nodded, then lifted the edge of the blanket and gently placed the silent Maud next to her mother's breast.

'Joan,' she whispered. 'Your baby needs you.'

Joan lifted her arm and made a movement as if she were going to sweep Maud off the pallet but Susanna caught her hand deftly in mid-sweep and gently but firmly brought it down and placed it on the back of the baby's frail little body. Maud whimpered, and Joan let out a long, gasping sob.

'I can't,' she said. 'I want an end to it all.'

13

Alice was in her garden, pulling some vegetables for the evening's pottage. It had been a damp, drizzly day again, but the sun had broken through at last and she was taking the opportunity to do a little weeding. During the terrible months of the mortality, Alice had not ceased sowing and planting her potager, always believing, almost despite the evidence, that some would survive the horror and need the food that she was growing. She'd placed her faith in the Holy Mother, and despite the pain of losing Stephen and Geoffrey, and of Agnes's disappearance, she considered her own survival and that of John and Matthew to be at least partly a result of her fervent prayers.

She prayed daily for the souls of her dead husband and son. Some of her neighbours paid Master Hugo to pray for their departed, and she knew that a friar, who came to Meonbridge soon after the mortality moved on, offered his services to those who could afford it. But Alice found it no hardship to go herself to Saint Peter's twice a day and kneel before the statue of the Virgin, light two candles and pray that Stephen's and Geoffrey's souls would soon leave Purgatory and be judged fit for Paradise, as surely they both must be.

Alice prayed also in her garden, for it seemed a fitting place for prayer. While her hands were digging and hoeing in the good earth of her potager, her thoughts were far away with the souls of her loved ones. So she was startled when John suddenly leapt over the gate from the croft beyond and landed heavily beside her. She let out a cry of surprise and shock, and looked up to see her son grinning.

'Sorry, Ma, did I startle you?' he said.

'Yes, you did. Why couldn't you just walk through the gate?'

John laughed. 'Sorry, Ma, I needed to work off some of my bad humour.'

Alice hauled herself to her feet and picked up her basket of onions and cabbage.

'Take my spade and hoe, will you, son, and put them in the hut.'

John picked up the tools, and together they walked towards the cottage.

'And why're you in a bad humour?' asked Alice.

'Because of the endless arguments about the runaway families and the so-called rebel tenants.'

'Who's arguing?'

'Robert Tyler and Sir Philip. And then, when I met them in the fields, they got me involved,' he added wearily.

As they neared the door of the cottage, John stopped at the small wooden tool shed to drop off the spade and hoe, then joined his mother indoors. Alice was bustling about beginning to prepare the evening meal.

'What're they saying?' she said, as she chopped the onions and cabbage.

John poured a pot of ale and sat down heavily on one of the three-legged stools. He sighed.

'Needless to say, Philip and Robert don't agree on what to do about the rebels. Robert thinks they should be punished, and Philip thinks they should be got rid of.'

'But, surely, the manor must keep all the labour it can?'

'That's what I think, but Philip says, if the rebels stay, they'll just spread unrest.'

'But Robert thinks they should stay?'

'Made to stay and punished for their rebellion,' said John, grimacing.

'And what'll they do about the runaways?'

107

'Nothing. Sir Richard's said it's not worth trying to find them. They've no idea where they've gone—'

'Farnham or Dorchester, I've heard,' said Alice, 'wherever they are.'

John shrugged. 'I'm sure they're too far away to go searching.'

'Surely Philip should've stopped that foreign steward persuading them to leave?'

John nodded. 'You'd think so, but he and the bailiff admit they didn't realise what was going on. They claim they didn't have the time to find out what the stranger was doing here.'

'I wonder if Philip's confessed that to his father.'

John laughed grimly. 'I doubt it. I've heard Sir Richard's in a rage with him and Robert for being so useless.'

Alice stirred the pottage, thinking about her conversation earlier with Margaret. 'So what d'you think'll happen now?'

'Philip's plan is to go and get labourers from somewhere else—'

'But that's against the law.'

'I don't think Philip cares much about the law. As long as he gets what he wants, he'll just do it.'

He was frowning.

'You look troubled,' said his mother.

John nodded. 'I am a bit. It'll be me who has to work with whatever strangers he brings in. But I'm more troubled about Robert's plans to punish the rebels. If he gets tough with them, they'll just refuse to work at all. And that'll do none of us any good.'

'Would Sir Richard agree with Robert getting tough?'

John shrugged again. 'I think he just wants enough tenants to work his land. He won't question how his bailiff does it.'

'What d'you think Robert will do?' said Alice, with a rising sense of alarm.

John's face mirrored her fear. 'I dread to think. The bailiff's in constant black humour these days. He never was a merry fellow, but I can't remember when I last saw a smile crack his miserable face. Of course he may just bring the rebels to court and fine them for refusing to work, but I fear he might have some more persuasive punishment in mind.'

'What?' said Alice, troubled by John's words.

John shrugged. 'I dunno. I just reckon Master Tyler'll find a way to make it plain who's in charge in Meonbridge.'

Alice served the meal and they ate it in silence. She could see John was troubled by the turn of events, and not confident that any of those in charge would handle the situation well.

'I saw Lady de Bohun again today,' she said at length and, as always, John frowned at his mother's continued defiance of his wishes. 'Her view's that Sir Richard should encourage the rebels to stay on the manor by paying them more and offering them land at a low rent. She's always believed in taking care of her tenants rather than fighting them.'

Despite his irritation with her, John grinned weakly. 'If only Lady de Bohun was running the manor now. She seems to have a better idea of how to deal with the tenants – a hundred times better than her husband or son. She's right about what Richard should do. Offering just a little more money – even if it's against the law – and the chance to prosper with a bit of land, would surely persuade many to stay loyal to the manor?'

Alice wanted to tell John about meeting Johanna, but it seemed he'd had enough of talking, for he bade his mother goodnight soon after they'd finished their meal. She was worried about her son; despite encouraging him to accept the office, she now regretted he'd been elected reeve. The job was not easy in normal times – she knew that well enough from when Stephen was reeve – but now, with the struggle to find enough labourers to do the work, and some of those labourers refusing to work, or spending their working hours arguing and protesting, the task was perhaps too difficult for a boy of John's age.

John had said Robert Tyler never smiled these days, but he was hardly more cheerful himself, except perhaps when he was with Eleanor. Alice hoped with all her heart that John had found his future wife, but she knew it would be many months before he'd consider asking Eleanor to marry him. He had too many concerns weighing him down to think of setting up home with a new wife. His duties as reeve were chief of these concerns, and the daily effort of farming their own holding, although Alice did help to shoulder this burden, for she was still fit and strong enough to do much of the work herself, and she'd managed to find two or three cottars willing to help in the fields. But the worry, mostly unspoken, that nagged away at both of them, never quite forgotten, was the disappearance of Agnes.

Alice often thought the key to finding out what had happened to her daughter might lie with Johanna, as the two girls had been so close, and when she saw Johanna again today, her suspicion was confirmed. After all these months, the girl was still distraught, yet deeply reticent about her childhood friend. Alice felt sure that she was hiding something.

Alice couldn't decide whether to tell John about talking to Johanna. She worried that his eagerness to find out what had happened to his sister might make him incautious. Of course she wanted to know herself what more Johanna might have to say, but she was certain Johanna would not be bullied into divulging whatever it was she knew. In the end Alice felt she couldn't keep the meeting from him, and mentioned it casually, as if to play down its importance. But John, as she'd feared he might, leapt upon the news and was impatient to go and question Johanna himself. Alice groaned to herself, wishing after all she'd kept her counsel, and strongly urged him against arranging such an encounter, in case it deepened Johanna's reticence rather than drawing her out. But she knew her urging was fruitless, for he was headstrong and determined and would do whatever he wanted to do.

A few days later, as Alice approached the village green, on her way to the bakehouse, she heard the strident voice of Bart Coupar ringing out loud across the village. She could see a small group of cottars gathered together under the great oak tree that dominated the green, and Bart was in their midst, standing tall above them. Alice thought how much more fluent Bart had become since he'd made his first incoherent complaint against his masters at the court. She'd heard him several times since then, holding forth on the greed of the gentry and the suffering of the labourers: he no longer needed Ralph Ward to speak for him, except perhaps when he'd drunk too much ale. Although Ralph did still argue for higher wages, he was more interested in obtaining some of the vacant land, believing that a surer way for him to prosper.

But Bart did not seem interested in becoming a landholder, despite Emma's enthusiasm for the idea. Instead, his hostility against the manor was hardening, his condemnation of Sir Richard and his bailiff becoming more bitter. Alice listened for a while, standing a little apart from the group.

'They don't listen to us,' said Bart. 'They think they can pay us no heed – cast us off. D'they care about our friends, forced to leave their homes just to earn enough to feed their little ones? They don't.'

The group cheered in agreement, punching their fists in the air in a sign of solidarity with their departed fellow labourers.

Alice sighed. She couldn't see how this kind of talk would help the cottars' cause, and Bart's increasing venom would do him no good. Suddenly she looked up, to see Gilbert Fletcher skulking on the edge of the green, largely hidden by the huge bole of the ancient oak. He was watching. Bart's voice carried well and she was sure that Master Fletcher could hear his words. He would be reporting back to his father-in-law.

When John returned from the fields late in the evening, tired and depressed, his spirits seemed lifted when he discovered Eleanor was visiting Alice, eager to discuss what she'd heard about the cottars' continuing defiance.

'Roger says the talk at Mistress Rolfe's is that Sir Philip wants to rid the manor of any tenants who continue to defy his authority and bring in new tenants from other manors.'

'But that's against the law,' said Alice.

'Yes, of course, but, as Roger says, if that steward from Farnham or Dorchester, or wherever he was from, can steal our tenants, perhaps Sir Philip can go and steal someone else's.'

Alice shook her head. 'That doesn't seem right to me. Margaret says, and I'm sure she's right, that it's best to keep the tenants they have, persuade them to stay, not let them go.'

Eleanor was about to agree when John burst through the door.

'Gossiping, eh?' he said, smirking.

Eleanor flushed, but his mother retorted tetchily that they were not gossiping but talking, and she'd thank him not to be so insolent.

John gave her a sheepish grin and sloped off to the adjoining room to remove his coat and boots. When he returned, Alice ladled some pottage into a bowl and bade him eat. He spooned the lumpy broth hungrily into his mouth and took a great bite from a hunk of the coarse dark bread that Alice had bought at the bakehouse. After a few urgent mouthfuls, he stopped and waved his spoon in the air.

'As soon as I've finished this,' he said, grinning mischievously, 'I'll tell you about my encounter with Lady Johanna.'

Alice was alarmed by the mischievous grin: she'd hoped he would take her advice and not try to see Johanna, but clearly he'd ignored her. Alice exchanged a look of apprehension with Eleanor, in whom she'd confided her fears about John's likely headstrong behaviour. Eleanor said she was sure John only had his sister's best interests at heart, though she agreed that bullying any of the de Bohuns was unlikely to produce a satisfactory answer.

The two women tried to remain phlegmatic as John, having finished his meal, poured himself more ale and bade them listen to his story.

'I knew it'd be no good trying to arrange a meeting,' he said. 'She'd likely not agree to see me.'

Alice pursed her lips. 'Likely not.'

'So, after I'd been to the manor workshops, where I needed to have a word with Tom Carter,' John continued, 'I made my way round the back of the manor to the garden and found Lady Johanna sitting in the arbour beyond the physic garden, just like you told me, Ma.'

Alice winced, wishing she hadn't told him quite so much.

John told them that Johanna had jumped up when she saw him approaching her, dropping her book on the ground in her haste. She'd cried out, saying she'd call for help if he didn't go away immediately and leave her alone. John tried to calm her, promising that all he wanted was to ask her what she knew about Agnes. At first, she'd continued in her agitation and demanding that he leave, and he in turn continued trying to placate her, and eventually she did calm down and stopped threatening to have him arrested.

'So what did she tell you?' asked Alice.

John pulled a rueful smile. 'Not much, really, after all the fuss. I asked her why she thought Agnes disappeared, and she said perhaps Agnes was in love with Philip and couldn't bear it when he married Isabella. I said that'd be a feeble reason to run away, and my sister was more sensible than that, but Johanna just shrugged and said Agnes was headstrong.'

'And...?' said Alice, as John paused.

'Nothing,' said John, sheepishly. 'She didn't say anything else. I was just wondering whether Agnes really was so pig-headed that she'd take it into her head to run away for such a stupid reason, when Johanna muttered some excuse and ran from the garden. I thought I'd better not chase after her.'

'So she didn't say anything really,' said Eleanor, looking deflated. 'Just that Agnes might possibly have been in love with Philip.'

John shrugged. 'It sounded as if she didn't know anything. But I think she knew more than she was saying, just as Ma did.'

Alice smiled thinly. 'If Lady Johanna has more to tell, she's clearly not going to give it up easily.'

John nodded. 'You're right, Ma. But maybe Lady Johanna isn't the one I need to talk to after all.'

Alice and Eleanor both looked up in alarm. 'Who, then?' said Eleanor.

'Sir Philip, of course. He must know whether or not Agnes was in love with him–'

With one voice, the two women cried out 'You can't!' and Alice continued, 'It's quite possible he'd no idea Agnes was in love with him. He might think you're accusing him and have you arrested. No, John, you mustn't speak to Philip about this, especially now he's lost his wife and child.'

'I thought, Ma,' said John, rather petulantly, 'you wanted to find out what's happened to Agnes as much as I do.'

Alice sighed. 'Of course I do, son, but I think we have to be very careful where the de Bohuns are concerned.'

'Maybe,' said John. 'But if we're too careful, we'll never get an answer.'

113

14

AUGUST 1349

On the Friday after Lammas, the tenants and freemen of Meonbridge gathered together in the great hall of the manor. Some of the rebellious tenants were to be brought before the court. There were more of them now: not only the cottars demanding higher wages, but some villeins were refusing to do their week-work for the manor, claiming their own fields needed all their time. John was worried about the court. He thought it would show he was failing in his duty to whip the tenants into line. He didn't think he'd actually be accused of failing, but it looked bad for him that so many villeins were not turning up to work and so many cottars spent most of their time grumbling. The strain of being in the middle of the two opposing factions – the rebels and the manor – was beginning to tell, and Eleanor worried about the effect it was having on him.

John said the court had been called in order to persuade the dissenters to abandon their mutiny. Eleanor feared the persuasion would not be gentle counsel so much as some form of violent coercion, and it seemed the tensions between the tenants and the manor were taking an even more disquieting turn.

'The bailiff,' said John, 'will make it plain that all tenants owe their living to the manor and are obliged to do its bidding. If he needs to punish their disobedience, he will.' He grimaced, and drew his hand across his throat in a grim gesture.

This time the court was not so quiet: conversation reverberated around the hall like the buzzing of a swarm of hornets, as, back and forth, tenants voiced their opinions about low wages and excessive workloads. When Robert Tyler entered the hall, Philip de Bohun was with him, together with John, and George le Clerke. As the four men came forward to start the proceedings, the noise barely lessened, and Eleanor felt nervous about the implied lack of respect.

Sir Philip sat in his father's chair and the bailiff raised his hand for quiet, but the chatter still did not cease. Robert shouted for silence, his voice echoing around the stone walls of the lofty hall. The shout was answered first by some shuffling of feet and a few coughs and muttered complaints, but finally the room fell silent.

Robert Tyler nodded to the constable, Geoffrey Dyer, who stood tall and dignified as he made the court announcement:

'Oyez! Let all who have business and owe service to the lord of Meonbridge draw near. This court of the manor of Meonbridge is in session, the Friday after Lammastide, in the twenty-third year of our sovereign Edward the Third, Sir Philip de Bohun, steward of this manor, presiding. Be silent for the bailiff, Master Robert Tyler.'

Then Robert Tyler, ostentatious in his richly decorated black tunic, addressed Sir Philip. 'My lord steward, this court has been called for the special purpose of dealing with the dissent that is being perpetrated against Sir Richard de Bohun, lord of Meonbridge.'

Philip nodded but said nothing, waving his hand in a gesture that indicated Robert should proceed.

John was standing to one side of the bailiff. Eleanor looked across at him: creases furrowed his brow and beads of sweat stood out on his face. A few moments later, Robert turned to him and said 'Master Reeve, please make your presentments,' and John, looking sick at heart, stepped forward.

'My lord steward,' he said, stammering a little with unease, 'I declare that John Hylyer refused to carry out one week-work, and Adam Wragge refused two week-works, and Nicholas Cook refused four week-works. All have also refused to carry out their boon-works for the manor.'

'Are Master Hylyer, Master Wragge and Master Cook present in this court?' said the constable, at Robert's prompting, and the three men pushed their way through the crowd towards the bailiff, calling out 'Aye, here' as they came forward.

'Well,' said the bailiff, as they stood before him, 'what do you say to the charges?'

Nicholas Cook scratched his head for a moment and then said, 'Aye, Master Tyler, I admit t' the charges.'

And after a few moments John Hylyer and Adam Wragge nodded and agreed they were also guilty of refusing to give the work to the manor that their tenancy required of them. Eleanor thought they might have protested their reasons for refusing to work: they were all virgaters, men of some substance in Meonbridge, but they seemed to be crumbling already under the bailiff's stony glare.

Alice, standing at Eleanor's side, clicked her tongue and shook her head. 'I know well enough why they've refused to do their week-works,' she whispered to Eleanor, 'but it's been so hard on poor John.'

Eleanor nodded. 'Indeed, Mistress atte Wode. He's been so fearful he'll be held responsible for their dissent.'

'Pray God he won't be.'

'What says the court?' said the bailiff, and, although there was a low rumbling of comment in the hall, there were no dissenting voices among the jurors. He announced the fines each man was to pay. Philip looked pleased with the size of the fines, but the three accused men all looked a little pale, for they were much higher, Eleanor guessed, than was usual for such offences. This was, no doubt, Master Tyler's way of making it plain who was in control in Meonbridge.

Next Robert called forward three cottars: Ralph Ward and two other men. They too pushed their way to the front, accompanied by so many shouts of support from their neighbours that Eleanor wondered if the court would find in their favour rather than the manor's.

At Robert's signal, John addressed Philip again. 'My lord steward, I declare that William Mannering and William Cole have each refused to work for twelve days, and on three days, being paid for their services, have complained and argued against their masters instead of working. I declare that Ralph Ward has refused to work for twenty days, and on five days, being paid for his services, has complained and argued against his masters instead of working.'

Philip's face creased into a deep frown and he glared at the men before him, but still said nothing.

'William Mannering, William Cole and Ralph Ward, what say you to these charges?' said the bailiff.

Eleanor could see the two Williams were red in the face, perhaps wishing they'd not after all joined in with the rebellion among their fellow cottars. But Ralph looked more defiant, as if he was preparing to refute the bailiff's accusations. None of the men, though, replied.

'Well?' said the bailiff. 'Do I take your silence for assent?'

Master Mannering and Master Cole continued in silence but nodded their heads, but Ralph seemed to be working himself up to speak, for suddenly he lifted his head and straightened his back.

'Sir,' he said, 'if I've complained instead of working, 'tis because I had good reason.'

The bailiff looked black but Ralph seemed undeterred. 'Master Tyler, times have changed. Up till a year past there weren't enough land for every family to have a decent croft, and there were too many folk to do what work was needed. The result was poverty and starvation. But now there's more land than folk to farm it and too few folk to do the work that's needed...'

Master Tyler raised his hand, as if to stop Ralph speaking, but the cottar ignored the gesture and continued.

'Sir, you know well enough the manor needs tenants for its land, and labourers to work its fields. Without them, the manor'll surely not prosper–'

A buzz of consensus flew about the hall, with 'Aye' and ''e's right there' on many lips.

'Already three of our neighbours've been driven from the village–'

'Hardly driven,' said Robert, with a sneering guffaw.

'*Driven*,' continued Ralph, resolutely, 'to find a decent wage–'

'And breaking their lawful bond.'

'Sir,' said Ralph, addressing himself now to Philip, 'I'd not break my bond with the manor of my birth. I would stay. I'd fain increase my modest croft and work hard for Meonbridge's prosperity. But I and all my fellow cottars deserve a fair wage for each having to do the work of three men.'

Philip shifted in his seat but did not speak. He looked up at his bailiff for an answer.

Eleanor was astonished at how well Ralph had spoken: more like a learned lawyer than a lowly labourer.

Perhaps Master Tyler was also impressed, for he nodded curtly and allowed a thin smile briefly to broaden his lips, as if he accepted Ralph's appeal. But his face resumed its dark and gloomy expression as he spoke. 'A fine speech, Master Ward. But you have said enough, I warrant. Surely the manor would *not* prosper if it defied the king's ordinance and paid the higher wages you demand?'

Ralph opened his mouth to speak again but this time Philip himself held up his hand in a clear signal that he was to remain silent. Ralph frowned but did as the steward bid.

The bailiff turned to address the jury.

'You know well enough that all these men enjoy the benefit of the tenancy of a croft and a cottage. Without the patronage of the manor, they would have no homes for their families.' He paused. 'What the manor gives, it can also take away.'

Murmurs of disquiet rumbled at the implied threat, but Sir Philip just nodded, looking both solemn and, Eleanor thought, rather bored. She wondered if the young knight felt ill at ease in these rustic surroundings, or was perhaps indifferent to the affairs of his tenants and eager to be back on the field of battle.

Master Tyler asked the court for its view of the defendants' guilt. There was much grumbling and whispering, but no man spoke up in their defence, or sought to refute the accusations. So the bailiff consulted Philip and they agreed to fine the two Williams twelve pence each and Ralph Ward two shillings, and they were all bound over to keep the peace. Gasps hissed around the room when the fines were announced, and Eleanor looked over at John to see astonishment cross his face. Clearly these fines were heavy, intended as a strong inducement to desist from further dissent. The two Williams looked deeply shaken, but, as all three men turned to rejoin their neighbours, Ralph, his face dark with anger, looked not shaken but defiant, and as he passed Bart Coupar, who'd now been called forward to face the steward, he shot him a sullen grin of solidarity.

Bart Coupar now stood before the steward, swaying from foot to foot.

'He looks nervous,' whispered Eleanor to Alice.

Alice shook her head. 'He may be nervous, but I'd say he's more likely had too much ale. Poor Emma's been so anxious about what the court'll decide, but she says Bart seems not to care what happens.'

When the bailiff turned to Sir Philip to present the charge against Bartholomew Coupar, silence descended again on the assembled villagers. Everyone knew the charge would be more serious than that against Ralph Ward.

'My lord steward,' said Robert Tyler, 'I assert that Bartholomew Coupar has refused to work since Pentecost and has incited many others to do the same. He has made rabble-rousing speeches in public places, stirring up mutiny against the manor amongst his neighbours.'

Philip sat up straight in his grand chair and leaned forward towards Bart, who was swaying unsteadily just in front of him. It looked as if he was going to speak, for the first time today, and Eleanor sensed a collective intake of breath as everyone waited to hear what the steward would say. She could see Philip's cold eyes staring hard, with something between contempt and fury, at the man who had for weeks been insulting his father, the lord of Meonbridge. Bart appeared to be affected by his gaze, for the swaying ceased and he stood still, if not entirely upright, waiting to hear the steward's words.

When Philip spoke, his voice was low but his words were clear and clipped, teetering on the brink of rage.

'Well, Master Coupar, what say you to these grave charges? Surely you will not deny them?'

Bart shuffled his feet and coughed, started to speak but was immediately interrupted.

'My view,' continued Philip, 'is that if a Meonbridge tenant is no longer satisfied with the terms of his tenancy, he should leave the manor—'

A shared gasp fizzed around the room, and the bailiff, looking alarmed, cleared his throat.

'Sir—' he began, but Philip held up his hand.

'Fear not, master bailiff,' he said, a thin smile on his lips. 'That may be my view, but I know well enough that it is not for me to try to break the bonds of tenancy. But Master Coupar must understand that his home and livelihood are his because the manor bestows them upon him. It is not for him to refuse to fulfil his covenant. But if he does refuse, then surely he forfeits his right to the covenant?'

Eleanor could hear some murmurs of agreement with this view. Although many of Bart's neighbours had some sympathy with his cause, and that of the other dissenters in court today, in the past few days she'd overheard more than one conversation that took a harder line. Many said that, by refusing to work, or spending time complaining rather than working, the dissenters were making it more difficult for others still willing to work, and that the time for protest was over and they should all just get back to work.

'So what do you say, Master Coupar?' said Philip, glowering at him. 'Do you want to keep your croft and your means of making a living?'

Bart shuffled again, and made reply so quietly that Eleanor could not hear it.

'Master Coupar,' said Philip, 'your neighbours did not hear your answer.'

'Aye, sir,' said Bart, a little more loudly. 'I said "aye".'

'So you will cease your refusal to work?' said Philip. 'And your rabble-rousing?'

But to this Bart did not answer.

'Well?' said Master Tyler, impatiently. 'Your answer, Master Coupar.'

But Bart did not speak again, and Alice let out a quiet groan.

'Oh, Bart Coupar,' she said in an undertone, 'for mercy's sake, give an answer.'

Eleanor sensed her distress and touched her arm. 'I think Bart's intending to defy the court,' she whispered.

'Then he'll be punished for it,' said Alice, 'and so will Emma and their children.'

'Surely not?'

Alice turned a bleak face to Eleanor. 'If they lose their croft?'

Would the court really do that? Eleanor again looked up and across at John. His face was as bleak as his mother's. Philip and Robert had turned away from the court and were deep in conversation. When they faced the court again, Robert held up his hand for silence, and then addressed the court.

'What says the court to this indictment?'

After Bart's sentence had been declared, the court was quickly wound up, and the crowd spilled out of the great hall, to follow a march led at high speed by Robert Tyler down through the village towards the green. Close behind the bailiff was Bart himself, held fast by his arms on either side by Thomas Rolfe and Martin Foreman. Large and strong as he was, Bart had become a limp scarecrow, and the bailiff's two henchmen were dragging him, his feet scraping on the cobbles, urging him with shouts to move faster. It had started to rain again, and the road was slippery with mud.

Eleanor and Alice joined the march but, as Alice passed her cottage, she ran inside to find Emma and warn her that her husband had been sentenced to three days in the stocks. But Emma was already coming to the door, drawn by what sounded like the rowdy hue and cry following a burglary or assault, and she soon realised by the look on Alice's face that Bart was at the centre of the mêlée.

'He's for the stocks,' said Alice, and Emma let out a cry.

'Is that all?'

'A large fine.'

'No more?'

Alice shook her head, and Emma brought her hands to her face and closed her eyes, and tears of relief leaked from under her eyelids. 'We've not lost our croft?' she whispered.

'No, he was spared that. Though I think Sir Philip would've done it if he'd had his wish.'

Emma gave a deep sigh. 'Thank God Sir Philip stayed his hand.'

'Thank God indeed,' said Alice. 'But will you come to the green now?'

Emma shook her head. 'Why'd I want to watch that useless clout bringing shame on me and my children? No, you go, mistress. Go for me, if you will, and tell me how he is.'

Alice nodded and clasped Emma briefly to her. Then she ran from the cottage and down the road to the green, where Bart Coupar was already being manhandled into the stocks that stood to one side of the muddy sward. As she approached, Alice could see Thomas Rolfe and Martin Foreman were forcing Bart's legs and arms through the holes in the contraption, then Thomas slammed down the top board and chained it fast shut. Bart was not submitting willingly to his punishment, but even he could not resist the combined strengths of the bailiff's enthusiastic henchmen.

When Bart was firmly locked in, Thomas Rolfe bent down and pulled off the prisoner's boots, and a cry of 'Shame!' went up from the crowd. Then the bailiff held up his hand for quiet.

'Bartholomew Coupar, you have been sentenced to abide in the stocks for three days and three nights, with only bread and water to sustain you.'

If Bart had been drunk earlier in court, now he looked quite sober, and shocked to find himself so uncomfortably confined. Eleanor could hardly remember the last time she'd seen someone in the stocks. Perhaps Philip and Master Tyler hoped this public humiliation would deter others from following Bart's rebellious example. But if they'd thought his neighbours would enjoy his humiliation, they were wrong. After Master Tyler and his henchmen had left, the crowd began to disperse but a number stayed behind, not to taunt the trapped man or pelt him with rotten vegetables, but to offer him their support. Eleanor watched as one after the other, cottars and villeins alike, knelt down by Bart's side and spoke quietly to him, patting him on the shoulder.

'John's right about Bart,' said Alice to Eleanor. 'Despite being what Emma calls an idle clout, he's well-liked in the village.'

Eleanor nodded. 'Everyone seems to want to take his part.'

The two women turned to go home but, as they did, they saw Emma running down the road, one small child bouncing uncomfortably on her hip, the other being dragged along in her wake, both wailing. When she arrived at the green she was out of breath, and looked distressed.

'Is anything amiss, Emma?' said Alice, looking concerned.

Emma, trying to catch her breath, shook her head.

'Nay, mistress. But I couldn't leave my Bart to sit here alone, could I?'

Eleanor and Alice exchanged a knowing smile.

'An' I brought him a pie and some ale–'

'But you can't give them to him, Emma,' said Alice, 'The court has sentenced him to bread and water for three days.'

Emma gasped. 'My Bart can't live on bread and water!'

'He'll have to, Emma,' said Alice, patting her arm. 'It'll do him no harm, and you mustn't break the court's order.'

Emma started to weep, and sank to her knees, clutching her two children to her breast. 'Oh, poor Pa,' she said, and the children wailed with her.

'Emma's not so unfeeling towards her idle clout after all,' said Eleanor, grinning.

Alice sighed. 'No, she loves him, despite his faults.'

Most of the villagers had moved away now, but a small group of women still stood under the great oak in the middle of the green, talking in low tones and now and then taking sidelong glances at Emma and her children, huddled together, weeping, on the muddy grass several yards away from Bart. The women's grubby children were playing a noisy game of tag, splashing through the deep rain-filled ruts in the road, oblivious to both the mud splattering their legs and tunics and, for a while, the man sitting glumly in the stocks on the edge of the green. But then the children seemed to tire of their game and, looking around for something else to do, their eyes alighted on Bart.

He was sitting silently, hunched in what looked an uncomfortable position with his head resting awkwardly on the top board, his eyes closed, and although he looked up and cast an occasional glance at his weeping family he didn't call out to them. Eleanor deduced that his stupor was the result of his rough and ignominious treatment, though it did seem curious to see a man so commonly loud and garrulous now so readily reduced to silence.

The children, whispering and giggling, crept towards the silent man. Eleanor saw them and had time to wonder briefly what they were going to do, but not to warn the children off, for suddenly, as if on a signal, they all bent down and picked up a clod of muddy grass and hurled it at Bart. Most clods fell short or wide of the mark, but at least three struck Bart on his head, leaving claggy lumps of earth in his hair and wet mud dripping down his face. The clod missiles had the effect the children were almost certainly hoping for, for Bart immediately lifted his head and roared in protest. They squealed in delight and ran off, and their mothers, realising what they'd done, chased after them with strident scolding, and one or two caught their children and boxed them roughly round the ears.

At the same time, Emma leapt to her feet and ran over to Bart, hurling curses at the children and their mothers for their wickedness. She threw herself to her knees by her husband and, taking off her thin cloak, she tenderly wiped the mud from Bart's face and head. Then she put her arms gently around his neck and wept into his shoulder, and he wept too. Alice went over and scooped up the two Coupar children, Beatrix and Amice, still sitting where their mother had left them, wailing. Alice clasped the children to her, rocking back and forth, and murmured what Eleanor assumed were words of comfort.

Before long the other women dispersed, dragging their mischievous children behind them. Alice passed Emma's children to Eleanor, while she went over and gently prised Emma away from Bart. Emma resisted. 'No, mistress, no, I can't leave my Bart,' she sobbed.

'You must, Emma,' said Alice firmly. 'You have your children to care for.'

Emma sniffed back her tears and shook her head. 'I can't leave him.'

'But you must,' said Alice, 'for now.'

Emma seemed to wrestle with herself for a few moments, then she pulled away from Alice's embrace and knelt down again in front of the stocks. She took Bart's head in her hands and kissed his forehead. Then she took her cloak again and wiped the tears from his face, and kissed him firmly on the lips. 'I must go now, my love. But I'll be back tomorrow.'

Bart nodded and gave her a wan smile. 'I'll be fine. You take care o' the little ones.'

Emma called to the children. 'Come and give Pa a kiss goodnight,'

124

she said, and they obediently went over and planted kisses on their father's cheeks.

'Why's Pa not coming home with us, Mam?' said Beatrix, but Emma had no answer and, with tears still leaking from her red-rimmed eyes, merely put a finger to her lips.

15

A lice had a mind to gather some brambles to make a pudding and she knew just the place to find them. Strictly, all the woodlands in Meonbridge belonged to the manor, and villagers were not permitted to take anything from them, whether it was venison or woodcock, wood for the fire or to make furniture, or any of the fruits and fungi that could be found there. But years ago, when he was first appointed reeve, Stephen was granted the right to collect firewood and fruits from the patch of woodland immediately opposite his croft, and he built a little bridge across the river from the grove of willows that bordered the river bank at the far end of his land. Though normally honest and law-abiding, Stephen occasionally crossed the bridge to trap rabbits and game birds for the pot, as well as collect the wood and fruits. Alice did not really approve of this, worried he might be caught and hanged for poaching. Even reeves were not above the law, and Sir Richard was strict about the preservation of his privileges. But Stephen dismissed Alice's fears, telling her that the part of the wood he used was not visited by anyone else, not even the woodward, and indeed whenever Alice went to the wood herself to gather kindling or pick brambles she never saw another person there. Over the years Alice became very familiar with the trees and bushes in "their" wood, and she knew exactly where to find the best brambles, as well as a good source of hazelnuts, and, in autumn, where she'd the best chance of locating a few fungi to add savour to her pottage.

After dinner John told her he was going back to the manor fields to prepare for the harvest planned for next week, and he didn't need his brother Matthew, as it was manor business. If Alice thought it odd that John couldn't take his brother with him just because it was "manor business", she didn't say so. She was beginning to learn not to question John's decisions, to treat him as the man of authority he now undoubtedly was. She didn't need Matthew either, and told him he could go and play with his friends for the afternoon. Matthew grinned broadly: it wasn't often nowadays he was let off work for a whole afternoon, and he skipped off happily down to the green where he knew he'd find at least a few other boys wanting to play tag or go for a spot of fishing.

It was a warm day, and sunny, for once in this cool, damp summer. Alice would have liked to keep her hair uncovered, free to flutter in the light breeze. But, despite her inclination, and despite the fact she was unlikely to meet anyone on her journey through her own croft and into the unfrequented woodland, she nevertheless felt obliged, by custom and habit, to put on her wimple. She told herself it would at least prevent her hair from getting tangled in the bramble bushes. Her headdress fixed, Alice picked up her willow basket and set off across the yard at the back of the cottage, through her potager, then between the apple and pear trees in the small orchard that led down to the bank of willows and the river. She always thought of Stephen when she walked among the fruit trees, for he'd planted them when they first moved to this house nearly twenty years ago, soon after John was born. He'd nurtured them and tended them carefully for all those years, providing them with such large crops of apples and pears they were able to sell some at the market. It came as yet another shock to Alice after Stephen's death when she realised she didn't know how to look after the trees and was afraid they might die under her neglect. She needed help, just as Margaret did with her physic garden, but it was hard to find someone these days with the necessary skills.

Alice soon reached the stand of willows at the far end of the croft and, pushing her way through the thickly congested branches, she stepped carefully onto the narrow wooden bridge and edged her way across it. The river beneath her was flowing fast, swollen by the rain that seemed to have fallen incessantly nearly all year. Stepping off on to the other bank, Alice made her way into the wood. The thick scrub bordering the river soon gave way to densely growing trees: there was no proper track but Alice knew the trees well and could easily find her way to the place where the most abundant brambles grew. She was happy here in the wood, feeling close to Stephen, treading in the places he'd once trodden, remembering the man she'd loved.

Alice soon filled her basket with a good crop of plump, dark brambleberries, but she wasn't ready to go home yet. Matthew would be happy to stay out playing until supper, and she didn't expect John home until late. It was true there was work she could be doing in their fields, but she thought she deserved an afternoon to herself and she intended to enjoy it. For Alice, enjoying herself usually meant companionship and gossip, but today, with the rare warmth of the sun filtering through the high canopy of trees and the tranquillity of the birdsong that Stephen, in his few moments of spare time, enjoyed so much, she took a fancy to walk a little further. She walked in the direction of the mill and the manor. After a while Alice heard the thunder of the river water rushing through the mill wheel, which meant she was not far from the boundary of the manor's private grounds, when she would have to turn back. As she approached the boundary, the crowded trees began to thin out a little and she could see in the distance the high walls and towers built up on the hill that gave the manor its dominating position above the village, impressive with its many glass windows glinting in the sunshine.

As she gazed at the scene, Alice realised she could hear men's voices quite close by, raised voices, as if the men were arguing. Slightly apprehensive, she crept forward to where the voices came from, keeping herself well-hidden behind the trees. She had to stop herself crying out when she saw who the men were, John and Philip de Bohun, and they did indeed seem to be arguing, for both had angry faces and were gesticulating vigorously with their hands. Alice was shocked to see John and Philip alone together in such a secluded place, for it might mean that John had ignored her advice that he shouldn't speak to Philip about Agnes. Of course they might just be discussing manor business, but why here? John had said he was going to the manor fields but they were far away from here. Alice was not accustomed to eavesdropping on other people's conversations, but she felt she had to stay and listen to what John was saying to Philip. Her heart pounding, she wedged herself between two tree trunks to give herself a firm foothold, and watched.

Just at that moment, Philip threw up his hands in a gesture of despair and sat down heavily on a nearby fallen tree trunk, holding his head in his hands. He said nothing more. John stood by for a while looking perplexed and at length crouched down in front of Philip.

'So are you going to carry on claiming you're innocent, or d'you have more to tell?'

Alice put her hand to her mouth, shocked at John's insolence, but also apprehensive that she was about to hear something, something terrible perhaps, about her missing daughter. But if Philip noticed John's disrespect he did not react to it. He didn't immediately lift his head, but rocked slightly back and forth like a morose child. Alice thought it a very undignified stance for a noble knight; how very different from when he'd been presiding at the manor court. But after a while, he took his hands from his head and looked up, his expression sombre. He nodded his head slightly and said, 'You know I have, John.'

Alice stifled a gasp: was Philip going to tell John what had happened to Agnes? But he didn't say any more immediately, and John shortly got up and paced around, scowling and muttering to himself. Then he came back and stood in front of Philip.

'Well?' he said, rather brusquely. 'What d'you have to tell me?'

At length Philip looked up. 'I'll help you find her, John.'

Alice could hardly believe her ears. Did he *know* that Agnes was not already dead?

'And why'd you go to that trouble for a peasant girl that meant nothing to you?' said John.

Philip sighed heavily. 'She didn't mean nothing to me, John. I've already told you that I thought of her as a sister. When I came home from the war and saw her again, I remembered how pretty she'd been as a little girl. And how Johanna and Agnes and I had played together as children—'

'But...?'

'She was no longer a little girl. In fact, she'd grown into the loveliest maiden in Meonbridge. But she was my sister.'

'So you didn't touch her?'

Philip shook his head. 'No,' he said slowly. 'Though Agnes didn't make it very easy—'

John rounded on him. 'Are you blaming my sister?'

'No, no, not at all,' said Philip, holding his hands up in supplication. 'But she did look at me sometimes with those beautiful eyes of hers.'

Alice felt a little sick, fearing the worst.

'So you seduced her,' said John, his face dark with indignation.

Philip went a little pink, but shook his head again vigorously.

'No, John, I didn't. We met a few times alone, that was all. We talked, I read to her.' As he said this, Philip turned his face away from John, though Alice could see it clearly. It was quite flushed.

Alice had to strain her ears to hear what Philip said next. 'It was wrong to do even that. Agnes might've thought I'd marry her, though that could never be—'

'But you didn't stop meeting her?' said John.

'I couldn't. I couldn't bear to give her up.'

'Until you were forced to.'

Philip nodded. 'Once the divine Isabella arrived, I hardly saw Agnes again, except in Johanna's company.' His voice sounded bitter.

'So why did Agnes disappear?' said John. 'You can't think she ran away because she couldn't bear to see you married to Isabella? My sister'd not be so faint-hearted.'

Philip's face was still turned away from John when he replied. 'I agree, but perhaps love made her reckless—'

John snorted derisively. 'I don't believe you. My sister was wilful and obstinate, but she'd not be so "reckless", as you put it, that she'd put herself in such danger.'

Alice was aghast at John's continuing insolence towards his lord's heir. In her agitation, she slipped from her perch, lost her footing and stepped on a twig, cracking it loudly. She went cold with fear. But at that moment Philip evidently decided he was no longer willing to take such disrespect from one of his tenants, even if he was the reeve, and rounded angrily on John.

'Master atte Wode, you should remember that you're still one of my father's serfs,' he said, shouting, 'and I'll not tolerate such impertinence.'

In the heated exchange that immediately followed, Alice made her escape, her heart beating wildly.

Back home, Alice was wracked with apprehension about how the encounter between John and Philip had ended. Her relief at Philip's promise to help John find Agnes was greatly tempered by her suspicion that Philip hadn't told John the full story – just like Johanna. When John came home that evening, she kept her counsel with difficulty, hoping John would say something. But he didn't, and she was left feeling anxious, not knowing whether he and Philip had parted in anger or accord.

Days passed and John didn't mention his meeting with Philip. The atte Wodes had always been very frank with each other, and it troubled Alice that John's silence on this matter meant he had a reason to keep it secret. She wondered whether he might have told Eleanor about it and decided to go and ask her.

Eleanor couldn't allay Alice's fears; indeed, she made them rather worse. Alice was embarrassed to admit to Eleanor that she'd deliberately eavesdropped on John's conversation with Philip, but she justified it to herself as a twist of fate that she'd stumbled upon them. Alice thought, quite rightly as it turned out, that Eleanor wouldn't disapprove of her staying to listen. But when Alice asked her if John had mentioned his meeting, Eleanor shook her head.

'In fact, he said he agreed with us that it wasn't a good idea to talk to Philip about Agnes, so I assumed he wouldn't try to meet him.'

'So maybe it really was a chance encounter?'

Eleanor pulled a wry smile. 'We might think that, I suppose, but, as you've said, it was a strange place for them to be, when they should both have been miles away in the manor fields. They could hardly have just bumped into each other where neither of them had a reason to be.'

Alice nodded glumly. 'So John's hiding it from us. But why? Because he knows we'd disapprove?'

Eleanor shrugged. 'Surely it's just that.'

'I only heard part of their conversation. They were arguing when I first stumbled upon them. Then they calmed down a bit, and Philip said he'd help find Agnes. But when I made my escape, Philip had become really angry with John for being so insolent.'

'So they might not have parted friends?'

Alice's face creased into a worried frown. 'I fear they might not. John's normally so even-tempered, but Agnes's disappearance made him very angry. He believed someone was to blame and that it was up to him to find out who it was, and punish him. When the mortality came, he was frustrated he couldn't go outside the village. His vexation's been simmering away ever since. I've been afraid that if he talked to Philip about Agnes he'd just explode and do something reckless.'

'Which is what he seems to have done. And, worse, he's keeping it a secret. So perhaps he knows he's done something foolish, and won't admit it?'

Alice was even more worried after her talk to Eleanor. John's continuing secretiveness increased her fear that his meeting with Philip had turned out badly. But she had to continue to bite her tongue and wait for him to tell her about it. Right now it was probably the last thing on his mind, with the harvest almost ready to be gathered in. He'd be busy finding enough workers to help in the manor fields, when most people only wanted to bring in their own crops. John thought the harvest would be poor, with low yields of grains and pulses. The fields had been so badly neglected in the spring, when so many people were either dying of the mortality, or thinking the end of the world was come. What's more, there'd been wet weather for most of the growing year, and especially heavy rain in recent weeks, making it difficult for the crops to ripen properly. As soon as the rain stopped and the crops were judged to be reasonably ready to cut, everyone had to get out into the fields, to ensure that every last usable grain and bean was gathered before they had a chance to rot. The harvest was planned to start in a few days, and John and Robert would try to rope in every man, woman and child in Meonbridge to help. Alice hoped even those labourers who'd been agitating for higher wages would be persuaded to put aside their grievances for a few days and join in. For now that the end of the world had not come after all, ensuring reasonable stocks of food for the next year was in everybody's interest.

The day chosen for the start of the manor harvest dawned dry and clear; rain had not fallen for a few days. John bounced out of his bed well before first light, his face beaming with relief.

'It's gonna be fine, Ma,' he said. Alice poured him a cup of weak ale and put a hunk of dry bread on the table. He grabbed the cup and gulped down the lukewarm beer, but waved away the bread.

'I can't stop, Ma. I must start my rounds to make sure that all who can turn up.'

Sir Richard had promised a good dinner and plenty of ale for all who came: indeed, what he promised today was better than he'd ever provided for previous harvests, as if even the lord recognised his tenants would need a little extra persuasion to turn out for him this time. But John thought this would be the last year that villeins would postpone their own harvest in order to help on the manor's demesne.

'In future,' he said to Alice, 'folk'll negotiate the terms of their tenancies to avoid giving week-work or boon-work to the manor.'

'How?' said Alice.

'They'll simply pay a bigger fee for the tenancy.'

'But will Sir Richard allow that?'

John pulled a wry smile. 'I don't think he'll have any choice. And anyway it'll give him more money to pay the cottars to do the labouring, so perhaps everyone'll win.'

Alice shook her head. 'I'm not sure he'll give in to change so easily.'

'I agree, he won't. But in time he'll have to.'

Alice had risen just before John and now woke up Matthew, for he too would have to join her today in the manor fields.

Despite the early hour, Alice could sense warmth in the air, and she opened the wooden shutter at the window to let in a little of the fresh morning breeze. Looking out of the window, although it was still not fully light, she was surprised, and relieved, to see a stream of villagers already tramping past her house towards the manor fields, carrying their scythes and sickles. Perhaps John would not find it so hard to persuade people to come to the harvest. Though Alice knew well enough, from her years of experience of Meonbridge harvests, that the manor fields were huge and needed a lot of workers to gather in all the crops. With half of the inhabitants of Meonbridge dead, even if every single person in the village came to the fields today, it might still not be possible to bring in the full harvest.

Matthew was in a whiny mood. 'Do I have to come, Mam?' he said, picking listlessly with a grubby fingernail at his lump of bread.

Alice tried not to be cross. 'Matthew atte Wode, you're ten years old and quite big enough to do your share in the fields.'

Matthew pulled a face.

'And it's no good you scowling like that. You know everyone has to go to the harvest, especially now so many of our neighbours have died. We all have to work together to make sure we've enough to eat for the next year. And that includes all you children.'

Matthew still didn't look convinced. 'But I'd rather go and fish.'

'I daresay you would, but today you've no choice. It's the fields for you, my lad.'

The boy got up from the table and threw himself face down on his pallet in the corner of the room. Alice was not quick to anger, but knowing the strain that John was under made her impatient with Matthew and she strode over and hauled him to his feet by his tunic. He kicked out in retaliation and caught her sharply on the ankle with his boot, which made her gasp with pain. She was later sorry to recall that she too retaliated and, letting go of his tunic, clipped him smartly around the ear. Matthew was not accustomed to being struck by his mother and wailed his protest, but she took no notice. She quickly dowsed the fire, then bundled the boy and herself out of the door to join the stream of workers heading for the fields.

16

Eleanor could have spent the day as usual up at Riverdown with Walter and her sheep. It was Walter's opinion that he'd never get any better than he was now, though Eleanor was resolutely optimistic about his future, saying time would surely heal. He couldn't walk without pain, nor without the help of a crutch, and she could tell from his eyes that he thought she was humouring him. But she was determined not to give in to pessimism about her shepherd: she needed him, and his skills, if she was to fulfil her ambition and build her flock into one of the largest and best in Hampshire.

But, today, she decided to leave Walter in charge of the sheep so she could join her fellow villagers in bringing in the manor harvest. Although she was a freewoman and under no obligation, she wanted to show solidarity with her neighbours, and also hoped she might see John. She hadn't talked to him for nearly two weeks, the day of Bart's confinement in the stocks, and she'd not seen him at all since Alice overheard his angry exchange with Philip de Bohun a week ago. Eleanor sensed he was avoiding her. She assumed he didn't want to talk about his meeting with Philip, that perhaps he wanted to keep it a secret. For the same reason, Eleanor knew he was spending very little time at home, and his previously lengthy conversations with Alice about the problems of the manor were now brief. According to Alice, he'd been quiet, even morose, ever since his meeting with Philip, but when she asked if anything was wrong he dismissed it as nothing, or just the strains of work. Eleanor hoped to catch John in a quiet moment today, and perhaps encourage him to open his heart to her again.

Eleanor had never been involved in a harvest before: she'd not even helped in the family fields, for in the days before the mortality, when plenty of cottars were available for hire, her father Edward could always find enough labour to do the work. So today she had a lot to learn.

When she arrived at the field, Eleanor found herself among a group of people awaiting instructions from the bailiff. Robert, John and the hayward, Martin Foreman, were organising everyone into teams but she was disappointed to see that John was way over the other side of the field. When it was her turn to be allocated a job, she asked if she could go and work with Alice.

'I've no experience in harvest work, Master Tyler,' she said, 'and I'd feel more comfortable working with someone I know.'

The bailiff's face creased into an irritated frown. But Eleanor smiled sweetly and it seemed even Master Tyler could not resist a maiden's smile, and the frown changed into an ingratiating smirk.

'Well, Mistress Titherige,' he said. 'I suppose I must thank you for joining us here today, when you're under no obligation to come. You can work with Mistress atte Wode.' He pointed out where Eleanor could find her.

When she reached Alice, Eleanor saw she was about to start cutting the wheat with her sickle.

'I thought cutting was a man's job,' she said, 'and women did the gathering and binding.'

Alice nodded. 'Yes, usually, but you need four cutters to one binder in a team and there aren't enough men to do the cutting. I'm skilled enough with a sickle, so Master Tyler bid me do some cutting.'

'He said I could work with you,' said Eleanor.

Alice smiled. 'Good. Though you may not like it, Eleanor. It's back-breaking work, bending down all day.'

Eleanor grimaced. 'Oh, I'm young and strong, so I expect I'll manage. What do I have to do?'

'Follow behind me and the other cutters, and gather the stalks together into a sheaf, then bind it with one of these,' and she held out a rope made from straw. 'Then stand the sheaf upright and carry on to the next one.'

Eleanor nodded, but Alice smiled grimly. 'By dinner time, you'll be ready for your bed, but then you've got to keep going until sundown.'

Eleanor knew Alice was teasing her but, even so, she was already wondering if her sense of duty had been misplaced, and if, by the end of the day, she'd wish she had stayed with her sheep.

When at last the cry went up to stop for dinner, Eleanor felt it had been days she'd been bent double. Alice was right: this was certainly back-aching work. Eleanor eased herself upright and stretched her arms high up into the air then, putting her hands on her hips, rocked her body back and forth to ease the stiffness in her back. She took her straw hat from her head and wiped her face with the edge of her shawl; her long reddish hair, which she'd pinned up into a coil around her head, was damp, and perspiration was sticking her chemise uncomfortably to her skin. But when she looked back over the long, wide area of wheat that she and Alice, and the others in their team, had cut and sheafed over the past few hours, she felt quite gratified. This was the first hard physical labour she'd ever undertaken, but the experience satisfied her: she felt she understood just a little of what working life was like for villeins and cottars such as Alice and Emma Coupar.

'Shall we go and take our share of the lord's feast?' said Alice, wiping her glistening face on her sleeve but smiling broadly. 'John said Sir Richard's putting on a good dinner today.'

Eleanor was certainly looking forward to a good long drink, for the day was warm and, despite the frequent small cups of weak ale handed round throughout the morning, her mouth was parched from the effort of her labours and the dust that rose constantly from the grain as she bundled the stalks together. The two women trudged across the field to where the food was laid out on huge trestles: a loaf apiece, great hunks of cheese, and even slices of roast meat, as well as enough barrels of ale to slake the thirst of a multitude.

'Sir Richard's done us proud today,' said Alice. 'It's strange he's so generous at feasts and boon-works, yet can't be more open-handed in the paying of wages to hard-pressed cottars.'

Eleanor nodded in agreement, but she was distracted, looking for John.

Alice smiled at her. 'It's been many days since you've seen him.'

Eleanor blushed. 'I'm sure he's avoiding me, afraid I might ask why he's been acting so strangely.'

'He doesn't want to tell either of us about his meeting with Philip, does he?'

Eleanor shook her head. 'I suppose not. But does that mean he's hiding something? I wish I knew. If I see him, I'm going to ask.'

Alice frowned. 'Is that wise?'

'Probably not. But I can't bear to continue with this between us.'

John didn't come to see his mother or Eleanor during the break for dinner, and Eleanor thought her chance of talking to him today was lost.

During the afternoon, when the sun was hot in a cloudless sky and many people were finding it hard to continue working, Martin Foreman blew on his horn as a signal that work should stop so everyone could rest a while. Eleanor and Alice made for a welcome patch of shade cast by a stand of huge oaks bordering the field where they'd been working. A boy brought them some more ale, which they drank gratefully, then they lay down in the cool long grass that surrounded the roots of the ancient trees. Alice soon dropped off to sleep, snoring gently. Eleanor closed her eyes for a while, listening to Alice's snoring and the humming of the insects in the grass. After a while, she became aware of a shadow obscuring the rays of sunshine that gave a bright fringe to their shady retreat. She opened her eyes to see John standing in front of her, a dark shape with the brightness of the sun behind him.

'Mistress Titherige,' he said.

She sat up. 'So formal, John?'

'I'm sorry. I didn't mean to be.' He crouched down beside her. 'How are you enjoying your first harvest?'

She laughed. 'I'm not sure "enjoy" is the right word. It's much harder than I'd imagined. But it's pleasing to see what we've done.'

John nodded. 'Hard work can be satisfying, but perhaps not if you depend on it for your livelihood.'

Eleanor winced.

'Especially,' John went on, glumly, 'when you don't get enough money for your efforts.'

Eleanor nodded feebly and looked away, vexed by his quarrelsome tone.

'Is the harvest looking good?' she said, trying to lighten the conversation.

John shrugged. 'There's a lot less wheat in the ground than last year, what with the lost months in the spring, and the foul weather. Even so, with so few folk to do the work, we may not gather it all in.'

He paused, but Eleanor couldn't think of anything to say.

'And of course most folk just want to get back to their own harvests,' continued John. 'This weather likely won't last long, and we don't want to miss out on getting our own crops in the dry.'

John had not smiled once while he'd been talking to her; he looked, just as Alice said, morose and melancholy. Eleanor wanted so much to help him out of his unhappy mood.

'John,' she said, suddenly deciding to be bold. 'You seem much downhearted. Is anything amiss?'

John looked away. 'Why should there be?' he said, staring across the fields into the distance.

Eleanor shrugged. 'I don't know. I just wondered if something's happened to distress you?'

He turned to her, frowning. 'What sort of something?'

'Oh, I don't know,' she said again. 'A meeting, perhaps?' She knew she was treading on dangerous ground.

John's expression changed from puzzlement to irritation. 'What d'you know?'

Eleanor glanced at Alice, still sleeping soundly, and decided to tell John about his mother's ill-timed stumbling upon his conversation with Philip. As John listened, she could see his temper rising.

'So my mother spied on me?' he said, resentfully.

Eleanor had feared he'd think that. 'No, John, of course she didn't. It was chance she came upon you.'

'She didn't have to stay to listen.'

Eleanor blushed for Alice's sake, but held her ground. 'That's true. But can you wonder that she did? You were talking about *Agnes*! And your mother's been so afraid you'd risk an encounter with Sir Philip that might lead to your arrest. You did just what she'd prayed you wouldn't, and what indeed you *said* you wouldn't.'

John sprang to his feet in fury. 'And it's my affair, Mistress Titherige,' he said, shouting. 'My affair, and no-one else's.'

John's raised voice awoke his mother. Alice sat up slowly, rubbing her eyes. 'What's all the fuss?' she said.

Eleanor felt tearful. Raising this matter with John was a mistake.

John loomed over his mother. 'I hear you spied on me, Ma.' Alice looked at Eleanor for confirmation that she'd told him, and Eleanor nodded unhappily.

Alice in her turn flushed slightly, but shook her head vehemently. 'No, John, not "spied". When I stumbled across you and Sir Philip, I was concerned. Can you really blame me for that?'

'Yes, Ma, I can. You're an interfering old crone.'

Eleanor could hardly believe her ears, and Alice looked stunned.

'John, how can you speak to your mother so disrespectfully?' she said, her voice shaking. 'You know she only has your best interests at heart. As do I–'

'I'll speak to my mother as I see fit,' said John, through clenched teeth.

Eleanor steeled herself. 'In which case, Master atte Wode, please consider our friendship at an end. Not only have you insulted your mother, but you've deceived her, and betrayed her trust.' She wanted to cry but forced herself to hold back the tears.

Eleanor had never seen John's face turn so dark; it was more like the rancorous face of Master Tyler in one of his blackest moods. 'So be it,' he said, thrusting his hands violently into the air. 'I'll not have women meddling in my affairs.' He turned on his heel and marched away at speed towards the other end of the field.

Eleanor finally broke down and wept. 'Oh, Alice, what have I done?'

Alice put her arm round Eleanor's shaking shoulder and drew her towards her. 'I don't recognise my gentle son in that rude man. I imagine there was more to that conversation with Philip than I know of. And whatever it was, it's clearly worrying John.'

Eleanor nodded her head, resting against Alice's breast. This was the first time she'd had a mother's comfort for a long while, and she was grateful for Alice's affection. But if she no longer had the hope of John as a husband, then Alice would never be her mother, and her tears flowed more freely at this unhappy thought.

Alice stroked Eleanor's head. 'Don't despair. I'm sure John loves you, and his bad humour'll not last for ever.'

Eleanor looked up 'D'you really believe that?'

'Yes, my dear. I don't know how this matter'll be resolved, but it will be. You'll just have to be patient – and so will I.'

As the day dwindled, the sun began to lose its heat and the stubbly manor fields were strewn with hundreds of wheat sheaves. Towards the far side of the field, where the harvest began hours ago at dawn, Eleanor could see workers were beginning to collect up the sheaves and load them on to a cart.

'I thought they left the sheaves out for several days to dry?' she said to Alice.

Alice nodded. 'They do, but perhaps Master Tyler's worried the weather'll break again suddenly, and won't risk the wheat getting wet while we're harvesting the other crops.'

At that moment, the hayward sounded his horn and they could see him beckoning to them all to go across and help collect up the sheaves.

'We'd better go and help,' said Alice, tucking her sickle into her belt, and the two women trudged across the acres of cut stubble to where they'd begun work this morning, and started hefting sheaves on to the waiting cart. As the workers loaded sheaves, the carter moved the cart forward until the stack of sheaves was as high as it could safely be. Then it was tied down with ropes, and the carter geed up his horse and drove carefully away and out of the field towards the huge manor barns, where the sheaves would be unloaded and laid out to dry ready for threshing in a few weeks. As the carter left, another cart came forward ready to be loaded, to be followed by others as the workers moved across the fields.

Eleanor could carry only one sheaf at a time; the men, and even some of the other women, could carry two, but she was weary, and not accustomed to such heavy work. She hefted her sheaf onto the cart then, stretching her back to ease the aching, stopped briefly to gaze across the fields towards the manor. The sun was getting lower in the sky, its rays slanting across the fields of stubble and casting a golden glow, which glinted on the glass in the manor windows. Despite her fatigue, she reflected that it all looked rather lovely but, looking around and quickly realising that no-one else was admiring the view, she bent down again and heaved the next sheaf onto her back.

With the lowering sun, the light was also beginning to fade. By the time the final cart trundled into position to be loaded with the last of the sheaves, it was almost dusk. The stack on this final cart turned out a lot higher than any of the others, and it was clearly going to be difficult to tie the stack down to prevent it swaying. Bart Coupar and Ralph Ward were in the final carting team, and the hayward told the two of them to climb the stack, catch the ropes tossed up to them and then throw them down the other side. Both men scrambled nimbly up the ladders, caught each of the heavy ropes and threw them over to the ground, where others tied them to the toggles on the sides of the cart. Ralph then climbed down again using the ladder, but Bart didn't: it was well-known that his practice was to descend using one of the ropes for support. He stood fearlessly on top of the stack, his friends and neighbours cheering him on. Then he bent down and grasped one of the ropes and almost hurled himself over the edge of the stack.

Eleanor was listening in wonder as Alice explained how Bart would now walk down the side of the stack like a fly strolling on a wall, when suddenly there was a whoosh and a whistle as one end of the rope came free from its toggle and flew up into the air as Bart put his weight on it. The whistle was followed by a scream and a sickening crump as Bart landed heavily on the ground. Alice and Eleanor ran over to where he'd fallen: in the gloom it was difficult to see him clearly, but it was obvious from the awkward angle of his legs and his frantic cries that he was seriously hurt.

Suddenly John was there, taking charge.

'Don't move him,' he said. 'Ralph, run for Simon Hogge, and, William, go to the manor and tell Sir Philip.'

He knelt by Bart's side, shaking his head. 'Oh, Bart Coupar, why d'you always have to play the fool?' Then he looked up and around the group of workers, standing silent and aghast. 'Where's Emma?' he said. 'Does anyone know?'

Alice spoke. 'I think she went home a while back, to put the children to bed. I'll go and fetch her, shall I?'

John nodded curtly. 'Make haste, Mother.'

Alice glanced at Eleanor, then, touching her on the arm, whispered to her to stay. 'I'll be as quick as I can,' she said aloud.

Eleanor leaned against the side of the cart, her fatigue intensified by the horror of Bart's fall. She felt helpless. Very few in the village would know what to do. Simon Hogge, the butcher and former surgeon to Sir Richard, was the best they had, though Walter's aunt Cecily knew a lot about herbal remedies and was skilled at treating common ailments. But she couldn't mend broken bones – Simon could do that, but even his skills were soon exhausted.

It was Lady de Bohun who arrived first; neither Sir Richard nor Philip was with her. Someone brought a torch as she knelt by John's side. Bart had stopped screaming and fallen into a faint.

'Is Master Coupar alive?' she whispered, and John nodded. 'And what do you think of his condition, Master atte Wode?'

John shook his head. 'I don't know, my lady, but I reckon he's bad. Look at how his legs are twisted. Maybe Simon can help him, but it doesn't look good.'

Shortly Simon Hogge arrived on horseback and, leaping from the horse before it had come to a stop, he ran to Bart's side. 'Bring the torch closer,' he said, then ran his hands over Bart's body, spending a long time feeling the bones of his legs and lower body. Then he looked up and shook his head. 'It's not good,' he said, addressing Lady de Bohun. 'Both legs are broken. And of course his back may be broken too, though I can't tell with him lying in this position.'

'Should we move him?' said Lady de Bohun, looking very anxious.

Simon nodded. 'We'll have to, my lady. I can't set his bones here, for I need more light.'

'Then we'll take him to the manor,' she said, getting up. 'I will help you tend him, Master Hogge.'

Simon nodded and gave a grim smile. 'Very good, my lady, but I'm not hopeful Bart'll survive this. He's a heavy man, and it was a long way to fall.' He turned to John. 'Can you organise a stretcher, master reeve?'

It took an agonisingly long time for the stretcher to be found, for the poles and blanket had to be fetched, then made into a structure strong enough to bear Bart Coupar's considerable weight. Heaving him on to it risked injuring him further, but it was clear there was no alternative. Distressingly, Bart awoke from his faint as six men lifted him as carefully as they could and placed him on the stretcher, and his heart-rending screams rang out across the fields. Eleanor suddenly felt faint at the awfulness of what had happened, and, holding onto the cart for support, she carefully lowered herself to the ground to stop herself from falling over. She saw John turn his head towards her as she did so and stare briefly, but he didn't smile at her or come over. She didn't blame him, for Bart needed his attention more than she did. He quickly turned away again and followed the stretcher, along with Simon Hogge and Lady de Bohun, in the direction of the manor.

After they had gone, Susanna Bigge came over to Eleanor and crouched down by her side. 'Are you feeling unwell, Mistress Eleanor?' she said, anxiously, but Eleanor shook her head.

'No, I'm fine, Susanna. This horrible accident, after such a long and tiring day, has quite upset me, but I'll recover.' She had tears in her eyes. 'Though I fear Bart Coupar might not.'

Ralph Ward had not gone with his friend Bart. Eleanor noticed he was looking closely at the cart and the ropes, in particular where the rope Bart had swung from had been attached. It was clear he'd overheard Eleanor's remark for he came over.

'That weren't no accident, mistress,' he said. 'Someone meant Bart to fall.'

Eleanor looked up, shocked. 'Whatever d'you mean, Master Ward?'

'What I say, mistress. It weren't mishap caused Bart to fall and break his back. It were done on purpose.'

'But who'd do such a thing, Ralph?' said Susanna.

Ralph shook his head. 'I dunno, Mistress Bigge.'

A small group of men and women had gathered around, listening. 'Who tied the rope?' said William Cole. 'Does anyone know?'

Everyone denied having seen who it was, but then young Harry Mannering stepped forward. 'I saw who did it.'

'Who, Harry?' said Ralph, gently.

Harry looked a bit scared. 'What'll happen if I tell?'

'You'll not get into any trouble, Harry,' said Ralph. 'But if you tell us, it might help Bart Coupar. And he needs all the help we can give him.'

Harry continued to hesitate for a while, but then his father, William, pushed through the crowd and crouched down by the boy. He whispered something in his ear, and patted him encouragingly on the shoulder.

'It were Master Rolfe,' said Harry at length, and a buzz of disgruntlement ran round the group. Ralph nodded his head slowly, pursing his lips in anger, and went over to where the rope had been tied. Suddenly he banged the side of the cart with his hand.

'God's Eyes!' he shouted. 'There's nothing to show it.'

'What you thinking, Ralph?' said William Mannering, going over to him.

'That Master Rolfe knew very well that Bart'd play his fool trick of jumping down the stack,' said Ralph. 'So he tied the rope loosely to ensure that Bart would fall.'

'But why'd he do that, Master Ward?' said Eleanor, mystified.

But Ralph didn't have time to answer before the strident voice of Robert Tyler intruded. 'What's going on here? Haven't you all got homes to go to?' He looked around from face to face, but no-one spoke.

Eleanor thought the bailiff might be expecting some sort of explanation. 'We were discussing how the accident might've happened, Master Tyler,' she said.

'There's nothing to discuss, Mistress Titherige,' said Robert, brusquely. 'As I understand it, Bart Coupar performed his usual foolhardy trick of leaping off the stack. The rope must've simply given way under his weight.'

145

There were rumblings of disquiet, but he continued. 'An unfortunate accident, that's all. Nothing more to be said.'

Ralph looked as if he was going to argue, but he made do with a brief riposte. 'Mebbe there's nothing more to be said tonight, bailiff,' he said, glaring at Robert, 'but it's not the end of it.' And he turned and marched away into the darkness.

17

Margaret had had a long and distressing night. The stretcher party had barely set the litter down in the small room behind the manor hall that she used as a sick hay, when Emma Coupar burst into the room, with Alice close behind her, and flew to Bart's side, wailing and sobbing. Alice exchanged glances with Margaret, shaking her head, and it was clear that Alice thought this might be the final straw for Emma. Emma threw herself down by Bart's side and, flinging her arm across his chest, buried her face into the crook of his shoulder and wept into the blanket. It was some time before Alice could prise her away, as Simon Hogge paced anxiously, wanting to get on with trying to set Bart's legs. But at length Emma allowed Alice to help her up and lead her away, promising to come back with her at first light.

Simon was glad Bart was out cold when he came to set his broken legs, for they were awkward breaks and the setting would be a long and difficult process. When he had finished, exhausted and filthy with sweat and dried blood, he was almost falling over with fatigue, and Margaret led him to a chair and covered him with a blanket.

'Rest for a while, Master Hogge,' she said. 'Get a little sleep. Then you can wash and I will have someone bring you breakfast.'

Simon smiled gratefully. 'Thank you, my lady. I'll just sit here until I feel a little stronger, but then I must go home – dawn is breaking and I must be about my business.'

But Margaret shook her head. 'No, no, Simon, that can wait till you are properly rested. You have a rare skill in Meonbridge. We need you, and you must not overburden yourself.'

'You're kind, Lady de Bohun, but I fear that Bart Coupar's injuries may be beyond my skills. I reckon it's more than his legs that's broken...'

'You mean his back?'

Simon shrugged. 'More like he's bleeding inside. And I can do nothing for such injuries.'

Simon left the manor soon after dawn, leaving Margaret alone with the still insensible Bart. She thought that a little later she would send a servant to fetch Cecily Nash to help her nurse him. Margaret knew much about healing wounds and reducing fevers, but Cecily knew even more than Sybil Kemp about the healing power of herbs. Cecily was the oldest woman in the village: her back was bent and her eyes were cloudy, but her mind was as alert as a fox's. It was she who had taught Sybil, but so well that her pupil soon usurped her position as the village healer. If Cecily resented being supplanted, she had never shown it, but now Sybil was dead, she felt too old to take her place again and told Margaret that she would have to find another pupil. Margaret had wondered if she should place herself under Cecily's tutelage, though she fancied Richard would consider such an idea beneath her.

It was still barely light when Alice returned with Emma, calmer now, but anxious to know what Lady de Bohun thought of Bart's condition. Margaret dearly wished to give Emma good news, but Simon's concerns rang in her ears.

'As you can see, Master Hogge has set his legs good and straight,' she said, trying to sound positive. 'And hopefully time will heal.'

Margaret could see Alice looking at her hard, trying perhaps to discern the truth in her expression. Margaret averted her eyes.

'So will my Bart live, m'lady?' whispered Emma, kneeling by his side and taking one of his hands in hers. 'And if he does, will 'e be crippled?'

She looked up at Margaret, her face streaked with tears. She looked drained, and her eyes were red and swollen as if she had been crying all night long. Margaret felt her heart go out to this poor young woman, who worked so hard to feed her family, and so much loved this feckless man, despite his idle ways. Emma deserved a better husband than Bart.

'It's too early to say, Emma,' she said. 'Master Hogge does not know if Bart has other injuries. We just have to be patient and let time, and God, give us our answer.'

Emma nodded, and lay her head down on Bart's chest. She stroked his beard and whispered to him, though it was clear enough he could not hear her.

Alice drew Margaret away. 'Will you tell me the truth, Margaret?' she said. 'Will Bart survive?'

Margaret shook her head. 'Dear Alice, I really do not know. Master Hogge believes Bart may be injured inside, and he says that, if he is, he cannot help him.'

'So he might die?'

'Yes, he might. But if we keep him still, and comfortable, perhaps we have some cause for hope.'

Margaret gestured to Alice that they should walk outside, and leave Emma alone for a while with her husband. The two women walked out into the fresh morning air. The sun was just beginning to climb into the sky, and it seemed the weather was set fair for another long day's harvesting. Men and women were again making their way to the fields, though today, Margaret thought, they would be harvesting their own grain rather than the manor's.

Neither woman spoke for a while, then Alice said, 'But what do we hope for, Margaret?' She paused before continuing. 'Simply that Bart lives?'

Margaret knew what Alice was thinking. 'Even if he has no other injuries, with two broken legs he may never be able to walk or work again—'

'Which'll make life even harder for Emma.'

'I agree, but we must not hope that he does not live, Alice,' said Margaret, appalled that they should even be thinking it. 'That is against God's law.'

Alice smiled grimly. 'Yes, of course it is.'

They took a turn about the courtyard, then back into the hall, and through the arras to the sick room. 'I wonder what Emma wants?' said Alice quietly, looking at her lying by Bart's side, her arm encircling his shaggy head. 'Bart's not a good husband to her, but she loves him dearly.'

'God will decide,' said Margaret.

Later that afternoon, Richard returned from a visit to London. He had been away for a few days, and was tired from his travelling. But he was in an affable mood, regaling Margaret with tales of whom he had met and what he had seen on his journey. She was enjoying his company; it was a pleasant interlude after her long dismal day sitting at Bart's side and wondering what would become of him. She and Richard were laughing together, a rare occurrence in recent times, when the door to the solar banged open and Philip burst into the room. He marched over to his parents, scowling.

'Are you aware, Father,' he said, without even the courtesy of offering him a greeting, 'that your wife is giving shelter to a rebel? One of those insolent wretches who's been stirring up trouble against you–'

Richard stopped laughing, and a frown creased his brow. 'Giving shelter?' he repeated. 'What do you mean, "shelter"?'

Philip smirked. 'So she hasn't told you,' he said. 'I'm not surprised.'

Richard turned to Margaret. 'Told me what, madam?' His genial tone had vanished.

Margaret looked at her son and sighed: why did he think it such a wickedness simply to care for an injured man?

'Bartholomew Coupar had a terrible accident in our fields yesterday,' she said, 'and I brought him here so he could be cared for. That is all.'

'That is all?' said Philip, raising his voice. 'That is ALL? Mother, what are you thinking of? Bart Coupar has been stirring up bitterness against the manor for weeks. He served three days in the stocks for his transgressions, and now you are giving succour to the wretched oaf.'

Richard raised his hand to halt the flow of Philip's fury.

'Why did you bring him here, Margaret?' he said gently. 'Why could he not be taken home?'

'Because his cottage is a long way from our fields, Richard,' said Margaret. 'It was much closer to come here, and Master Hogge could come quickly and we could find enough lamps so he could set Bart's broken bones.'

Richard shook his head. 'I understand your motive, Margaret, but I agree with Philip that your decision was ill-advised.'

'But Bart Coupar is one of our tenants, Richard. We have a responsibility towards him–'

'And he has a responsibility towards us, Mother,' said Philip, 'which he has chosen to ignore.'

'I could hardly let him lie out in the field.'

'No, but you could've had him taken to his own cottage. His own wife should be tending to him, Mother, not you. I suggest, Father, that he is moved there at first light tomorrow morning.'

Margaret was horrified. 'Richard, please do not do that. Bart may die if he is moved again so soon.'

Richard seemed troubled by this prospect, and paced around the room for a while, apparently considering the arguments. At length he returned to where Margaret and Philip were standing, somewhat hostilely, at a distance from each other, not speaking, waiting for his decision.

'My dear Margaret,' he said, gently, 'I do understand your reasons for bringing this man here, but I agree with Philip that it is not fitting for you to tend him, when he has abused us – and therefore you – so insolently and with such rancour.'

Philip smirked again, presumably sensing victory.

'So you are willing to risk Bart Coupar's death and have him moved?' said Margaret.

Richard nodded. 'That is my decision,' he said.

Margaret was fearful of what the outcome of moving Bart might be. Alice had told her earlier that the rumblings among the villagers were getting louder, for Ralph was going around telling people that he thought Bart's fall was not an accident, but that someone had tried to kill, or at least, maim him. As she and Richard got ready for bed,

Margaret took the opportunity of their being alone, and out of Philip's hearing, to tell Richard what Alice had said.

To her dismay, Richard just laughed. 'It's a ridiculous idea. Bart Coupar has always been a fool and a show-off. From what I hear he caused the accident himself with his foolhardy antics.'

'But if the people suspect—' protested Margaret, but Richard held up his hand for her to be silent.

'Enough, Margaret. I'm tired and I need sleep. I may be willing to discuss it again in the morning, but not now.'

To her surprise, he came over to her, ran his fingers through her hair and gave her a gentle kiss on her lips. She did not resist, despite her anger, and allowed him to caress her body through her night chemise. Then he lifted her chemise to her waist and lightly stroked her skin, and for a while she felt sick at the thought that she would have to submit to his love-making, when that was the last thing she wanted to do. But then he stopped and let the hem of her chemise fall again. He shook his head, smiling at her, and gave her another kiss.

'Not tonight,' he said. 'Sleep.'

And Margaret breathed a silent sigh of relief.

Richard was in an unusually good humour when he awoke next morning, after a long and restful night's sleep, and Margaret thought it worth the risk of raising again the dangers of moving Bart. They were at breakfast in the hall when Simon Hogge arrived to see his patient.

'Master Hogge,' she said, 'I am so pleased you have come. We will go to see Master Coupar in a moment. But first, perhaps you would confirm a matter that I have been discussing with Sir Richard?'

Richard clearly caught the connotation of her apparently innocent question, and his genial temper at once slid away. Simon seemed to notice the rapid change in his lord's mood and a look of wary unease crossed his face.

'I have been telling Sir Richard how important it is that Bart is not moved,' she said, 'which is why he needs to stay here in our sick room.'

Simon nodded, appearing after all to sense no peril in her statement. 'Indeed, Lady de Bohun,' he said, 'you're quite right. Bart must be kept still to give his body a chance to recover.'

Richard made an angry show of clearing his throat, but Margaret ignored his warning and turned to him. 'So, Richard, we were quite right to think that Bart should remain here in the manor.'

Richard scowled. 'But you know very well, madam, that that was not my opinion, but yours alone.'

'But Master Hogge—' said Margaret.

'Master Hogge,' interrupted Richard, 'has, I am sure, given us his honest opinion, but he is not, madam, aware of the unacceptable circumstance we find ourselves in.'

Simon looked uncomfortable, and Margaret realised it would be unjust of her to oblige him to take her part and defy the will of his lord: she could not force Master Hogge to choose between them. It was Richard who had to choose: to accept the advice of his trusted surgeon or follow the prejudiced wishes of his son. She looked at Richard and could see that, despite his bad temper, he was struggling with the decision he had to make.

But Richard did not change his mind and, later that morning, Simon Hogge was obliged to supervise the manor servants in shifting Bart to his cottage. Richard did not allow Margaret to accompany them but, just before they left, she took Simon aside and bade him ask Cecily Nash to help Emma look after her husband. Simon agreed and was bold enough to take Margaret's hand.

'My lady, you've done your best for Bart Coupar. Don't blame yourself if it goes ill for him.'

It was Cecily Nash who brought Margaret the news that Bart had died. As Cecily shuffled slowly into the chamber, leaning heavily on her stick, Margaret was struck by how old she looked this morning. Her wrinkled face was grey and her grubby wimple was awry, allowing wisps of white hair to escape all around her head. She bade the old woman sit down in her chair, and when Cecily had gratefully eased herself onto the soft velvet cushions, she turned her face up towards Margaret. There were tear-stains on her cheeks.

'Oh, m'lady,' she said, her voice still strong despite her frail appearance, 'poor Bart woke from his sleep soon after he got home, and Emma was so relieved she could hardly stop from crying out with joy. Of course it were clear he were in constant pain, but my remedies did seem to ease his agony. And for a couple of days he seemed to be getting a little better, and we dared hope he might recover.' Cecily paused and her eyes filled with tears. 'But early this morning, when none of us was by his side, he left this world.' Then she whispered, 'Without a priest to hear his confession, nor even commend his soul to God.'

'So he died without the sacraments,' said Margaret, shocked, though she knew that very many who had died of the mortality had done so alone and unshriven.

Cecily nodded, looking distraught. 'Oh, m'lady, I do fear for Bart's immortal soul, going on its journey so unprepared.'

Margaret was struggling to remain composed, for the thought of dying without a priest to conduct you on the last steps of your Earthly journey was as terrifying to her as it was to Cecily.

'Do you know why he died, Mistress Nash?' said Margaret.

Cecily shook her head. 'No, m'lady. As y'know, Master Hogge thought he might've had injuries we couldn't see. If he did, then not my skills, nor even those of Master Hogge, could've saved him.'

'Oh, Cecily,' said Margaret, 'if only he had not been moved.'

But Cecily shook her head again. 'It might've made no difference, my lady. You mustn't grieve for what only might've been.'

Margaret smiled weakly at Cecily. Of course she was right: it was impossible to know whether Bart had ever had a chance of surviving his fall. But she feared that the villagers would nevertheless blame her, or Richard, for his death, and Cecily, unbidden, confirmed her fears.

'I must tell you, m'lady,' she went on, 'that the news of Bart's death's flew round the village like wildfire, and already the villagers're up in arms about it. I think they'll wait till the funeral's over, but I fear, m'lady, then there'll be trouble.'

Margaret nodded glumly. 'I have heard that Ralph Ward is convincing people Bart's fall was not an accident. Now Bart is dead, I would be surprised if he did not claim that it was murder.'

Later Margaret told Richard what Cecily had said.

'I think you should try and find out what really happened, Richard,' she said. 'If it was truly an accident, you need to convince the villagers that it was; and if not, then you have to find the culprit.'

Richard did not argue with her. She sensed that he was troubled by Bart's death, and perhaps not now entirely sure of the truth of what had happened. He summoned the bailiff so he could hear again his explanation of the circumstances of the accident, and, at Margaret's request, he agreed to see Robert without Philip being present.

Robert Tyler was cool and calm, making it quite clear that in his view the accident was just that, the result of Bart's tomfoolery. But if Richard had previously also held this view, he was now at least prepared to acknowledge his wife's contention that Ralph would have little reason to stir up trouble unless he thought he had good cause.

'So why would Ralph stir up false rumours?' said Richard.

An expression of contempt crossed Robert's face. 'Ralph Ward is as much a troublemaker as Bart Coupar was.'

Margaret, choosing to keep up her bold defiance, interrupted him.

'But, master bailiff, Ralph wants to become a landed tenant, so why would he make trouble and endanger his future if he did not believe the story to be true?'

Robert dismissed the notion that Ralph could possibly act with any foresight then, still adopting a tone of derisive mockery, questioned what evidence Ralph had for his assertions.

Richard looked thoughtful. 'Who was in charge of the stacking?' he said at length, but Robert was evasive, as if he either did not know or did not want to say.

'I saw Martin Foreman, the hayward, there,' said Margaret, after a few moments' silence. 'Was he not supervising the work?'

'It might've been Martin, my lady,' said Robert, looking vague, 'though I can't be sure.'

'Perhaps you should talk to Master Foreman, husband,' said Margaret, 'to find out what he knows?'

Robert's expression changed, Margaret thought, to one of slight alarm. 'I'm sure that won't be necessary, m'lord. Bart Coupar fell off the stack through his own foolhardiness, nothing more.'

'You seem to have no regrets about the accident, Master Tyler,' said Margaret, and Richard glared at her for her effrontery. But Robert did seem to falter for a few seconds before responding.

'Of course it's unfortunate the man has died, leaving his wife and two children,' he said. He paused, then added, 'But Emma Coupar's a good worker and a good mother, and she'll soon make some other man a good wife.'

Margaret was shocked at his coldness, but held her tongue this time. Richard seemed not to notice that the bailiff's remark ignored any possibility that Emma might have loved her husband and, apparently deciding to accept Robert's opinion, he thanked him for his time and dismissed him.

When they were alone again, much later that evening, to Margaret's astonishment, Richard confessed that he was troubled by the whole affair.

'Something's not right,' he said. 'I know Bart was a fool at times, but Ralph Ward is not a fool, and if he believes there's reason for suspicion, then I am inclined to think that I should listen to him.'

Margaret struggled to keep her delight under control. 'So what do you plan to do?'

Richard looked solemn. 'I think I should investigate further. I'll do it myself, though, without involving Master Tyler, or any of the other manor officials. What do you think of that, my lady?'

Margaret smiled. 'I think it is a splendid idea, my lord,' she said and, steeling herself for what would follow, put her arms around his waist and kissed him.

18

Alice wondered if Emma Coupar would be able to endure Bart's funeral. After the mortality Emma had found herself alone, without her parents or any siblings, fending for herself and her two youngest children, with a feckless husband whose main purpose in life seemed to be to work as little, and drink as much, as possible. Anyone might have thought Emma would collapse without the support of her family, and that she'd consider Bart a burden, encumbering her ability to make a living for their family. But the fact was, despite Bart's obvious failings as a husband, her heart never truly hardened against him. She'd fallen in love with him when he first wooed her and, though her love had been sorely tested time and again, it had never died.

But Alice knew now Emma really did feel alone. She had many friends and neighbours, but that was hardly the same as having a husband. Alice had already heard talk in the village about whom Emma might marry, for widows often remarried swiftly, especially if they were young and strong, but she thought it would be a long while before Emma would entertain any suitors hoping to take Bart's place.

The day of the funeral was bright and clear. The sun shone on Bart's official departure from the world, and for that Alice was grateful, for rainy weather made the procession along the muddy road to the church a miserable trek, and a congregation whose wet clothes steamed and dripped on to the church floor detracted from the solemnity of the soul's journey into the next life. Not that she thought Bart's journey would be to a sunny paradise; indeed she was fearful that his time in Purgatory would be long.

Alice went down to Emma's cottage early. She planned to walk with her behind the cart carrying Bart's shrouded body to the church, and support her if she felt weak. Emma was trying to be brave, so she could comfort her children, who were too small to understand why their Pa had been lying for two days cold and stiff on his pallet in the loft. She told Alice that, when her neighbours came yesterday to sew Bart into his shroud, she thought she might faint at the horror of seeing that strong, handsome body sealed inside such a loathsome wrapping. And today, try as she might, she seemed unable to stop herself crumpling frequently into sobs, reminded of Bart at every turn as she moved about the tiny cottage she'd shared with him for ten years.

When the carter arrived with a couple of strong men to lift Bart's body onto the cart, Alice called the children over and told Beatrix to take her mother's hand, while she picked up little Amice and supported her on her hip. Then she held out her other hand to Emma.

'Here, take my arm,' she said, 'I'll help you.' Emma gave a weak smile of gratitude and, grasping Alice's arm, held her head high as they followed the cart's slow passage up through the lower end of the village and across the green towards Saint Peter's church. As they passed by, from every cottage and house came men, women and children, who took their place in the slow silent procession. All Alice could hear was the rumbling of the cart's wheels, the trudging of feet, and the occasional muffled sob, but not a word was exchanged between any of the mourners.

When the procession arrived at the church, Bart's corpse was lifted out of the cart and put onto a bier, draped with a black covering and carried into the church, followed by what seemed to be the whole village. Alice went with Emma and her children to stand at the front, close to where the bier was lying on a table, and where Master Hugo Garret was waiting for the last of the mourners to push their way into the nave and stand silent and expectant. Alice was disappointed to see that none of the de Bohuns were in the church, not even Margaret, but Robert Tyler was standing in the de Bohuns' accustomed place, looking unusually ill at ease.

If Alice had hoped Master Hugo would give Emma cause for comfort in his sermon, she was wrong. The priest seemed to regard Bart's accident as an act of God, a punishment for what, he said, was the breakdown of the old order.

'God has ordained,' he said, 'that the world is divided into three estates: the rulers, the prayers and the labourers. In this world each man knows his place and obeys God's Commandments. But now, the common people are questioning the customs and precedents of centuries.'

There was some shuffling in the congregation and, glaring, the priest paused before continuing.

'Do you not remember that, only months ago, God sent a terrible mortality to punish mankind for its sins? We in Meonbridge suffered grievously. Almost half of all our families and neighbours died in the most horrible agony.'

He paused again, for the dreadful memory of those days to be recalled.

'And yet,' he cried, 'and yet, instead of humbly accepting the lesson that our loving God had given us – the lesson that He hoped would turn us from our selfish, sinful ways – people are seeking to overthrow the old order that God ordained for our comfort and well-being. Labourers are rising up against their masters, arguing against the age-old precedents. The sins of avarice and arrogance are gnawing at their hearts.'

The uneasy shuffling among the congregation grew, and there was much nervous coughing and clearing of throats. Then Master Hugo made his most terrifying pronouncement.

'These sins,' he said, raising his arm up and pointing to the high vault of the church's nave, 'are drawing God's wrath down upon us again.' And he swept his arm dramatically down and over the congregation before him, pointing his quivering finger accusingly, and the nave resounded with an eruption of groans and gasps of dread.

'Today, we have before us the corpse of one who has rebelled against his masters. One who has questioned God's authority over the world. Tomorrow,' he said, in a voice filled with doom, 'be warned, my children, that tomorrow, if we do not mend our ways, God may send the mortality back to Meonbridge, to teach us another lesson.'

Emma collapsed in a half-faint by Alice's side, undoubtedly now convinced that the soul of her beloved Bart would spend time without end in Purgatory for the sins he had committed. Alice bent down to pull her to her feet and Ralph Ward, standing close by, came over and put his arm around Emma's waist to help her stand. The service came abruptly to an end, as Master Hugo asked peremptorily for God's mercy on Bart's soul, then swept down through the nave towards the church door, the congregation pressing back to allow him to pass. Several men rushed forward to help carry the sinner's corpse and, bearing the bier aloft, they sombrely followed the priest out of the church.

There was no room for Bart in the churchyard, so the procession had to trail down to the new graveyard that Stephen had ordered to be dug when the mortality had spawned more corpses than the churchyard could hold. Alice remembered when Stephen himself, and their son Geoffrey, were lowered into the cold ground of the new cemetery back in March: it was a day she could hardly bear to recall, the day she lost both her beloved husband and the gentle son who, like his master, Master Aelwyn, refused to abandon the dying to their fate without the chance of confession and the sacraments, and paid the price for his compassion. It was not hard for her to understand how Emma must now feel, watching the shrouded body of the man she loved being dropped into the damp dark earth. Except that there was perhaps a difference: Alice had no doubt that Stephen and Geoffrey would spend only a short time in Purgatory, for God would surely know of their goodness and soon elevate them to Paradise. But if Emma already feared that Bart's idle life and rebellious behaviour meant his hapless soul would suffer in the afterlife, Master Hugo's words must have given her cause for unmitigated terror. When Alice glanced across at Emma's face, she could see written on it a dread that might never be wiped away.

· · ·

All the ale-houses were full that afternoon. There were three of them, all situated close together along one side of the village green. Mistress Rolfe's was always the most popular, but with almost the whole village wanting to drink to Bart's life, even her sizeable establishment could not cope. But, as it was summer, and a fine day, the revellers spilled out of the ale-houses and onto the green. They played games and told each other uproarious tales, and later, as many of the women drifted away to put their children to bed, and the men left behind became more and more drunk, they argued and jostled, and got into fights.

Alice recalled with a grim smile how, once Bart was in the ground and the sexton already shovelling the earth back into the grave, Master Hugo had addressed the crowd of mourners, urging them not to go drinking and revelling, but go to their fields and continue with their harvest. But it was pointless for the priest to attempt to curb the excesses of a wake, and especially this, Bart Coupar's wake. Many times in the past Master Aelwyn himself had preached on the sinfulness of these occasions, when drinking led to excesses of other kinds, but no-one took much notice of him, loved and respected as he was, so they were even less likely to obey Master Hugo, who had still failed to win approval, let alone affection, from his flock.

Yet, as she sat on the green with her neighbours, keeping an eye on the intermittently weeping Emma, Alice noticed how people did seem to have been affected by the priest's sermon. There was fear in many people's eyes, and fear too in their talk, for they talked of death, and they told stories of sinners who'd come to a bad end. She wondered if they hoped their stories would act as charms to ward off evil spirits.

But alongside the fear, she could see anger too. Ralph Ward, seemingly not at all alarmed by the priest's sermon, and also completely sober, was moving among his neighbours, quietly reiterating his opinion about Bart's so-called accident. And, as he passed among them, their faces darkened again with the anger that had been rumbling around the village since the day Bart fell off the stack.

By and by Ralph came to sit by Emma. He took her hand gently and held it between his. She looked up at him, her face blotched and streaked. She sniffed and wiped her sleeve across her cheeks.

'Oh, Ralph, what'll I do without my Bart?'

Ralph shook his head. 'I dunno, Em,' he said, and seemed unable to say any more.

'How d'you really think he died? Were it really just him playing the fool, like Master Tyler says?'

Ralph shook his head again. 'I don't believe it. Of course Bart were an idiot at times,' and he shot Emma a rueful grin, 'but, this time, it just weren't like that. The rope came free, you see, as if it hadn't been tied properly.'

'That don't mean it were planned,' said Emma, and Alice wondered if she'd perhaps prefer to believe it was an accident, rather than someone wanting her beloved husband dead.

'You may be right, Em,' said Ralph. 'I've my suspicions, but I'm not sure, so I can't go accusing anyone. But I mean to find the truth. Someone knows what happened...'

As the afternoon declined towards evening, people began to disperse back to their homes, leaving a few small groups of cottars and villeins, still drinking and arguing about the likely cause of Bart's fall and the so-called rebellion of the tenants against their masters. Eleanor invited Alice and Emma to go for supper at the forge cottage, which was just behind the church, close to the village green.

Emma was barely speaking, locked inside herself with her grief, and she ate little.

'I'm going to take Emma and the children home with me,' Alice said to Eleanor. 'I don't think she'll manage on her own.'

Eleanor nodded. 'That's kind of you, Alice. But how d'you think John'll like having guests?'

Alice shrugged. 'He may not like it, but Emma needs our help. But she's brave and I'm sure once she's got over the first shock of losing Bart, she'll get her strength back soon enough.'

Later in the evening, Emma and the children, exhausted from the stress of the day, went to sleep, curled up together on a pallet in the corner of the room where Roger sometimes slept. Alice and Eleanor sat at the door of the cottage, talking quietly together. They couldn't see the green from where they sat, but all during the evening they could hear the sound of drunken voices, sometimes laughing and cheering, sometimes shouting and swearing. Suddenly they were aware that the voices were much louder, the shouting accompanied by the sound of running feet, and it seemed to be coming rapidly towards them.

Seconds later a gang of yelling men was charging down the short lane that led down from the green and alongside Saint Peter's, towards the forge. The men ran past the door of the cottage, then darted through a little gate opposite that gave access to the churchyard; they were going in the direction of the parsonage. Alice sprang to her feet in alarm; were they going to attack Master Hugo?

No more than a few seconds later, another group of men came running down the lane. Among them was John, who stopped by his mother and Eleanor.

'Did they go into the churchyard, Ma?' said John.

'Yes, son,' said Alice, 'but where are they going? What are they doing?'

But John didn't stop to answer, but ran off with the others through the churchyard gate, calling back, 'Cottars. Going for the bailiff.'

Baffled, Alice shook her head at Eleanor. 'What did he mean "going for the bailiff"? Going to fetch the bailiff?'

'No,' said Eleanor, looking anxious. 'I think he meant the men were going to attack the bailiff.'

Alice gasped and then the two women had a single thought and, straight away, lifting the hems of their skirts, ran across the lane to the gate and followed the two groups through the churchyard. They ran on through the priest's croft to the gate that Robert Tyler had constructed in the hedge between the parsonage land and his own. They shortly found themselves at the rear of the Tylers' house, where a group of cottars was yelling for the bailiff to come out. John and his companions were trying to calm the rioters down.

Alice ran up to Henry Miller, standing on the edge of the group. 'What's going on, Master Miller?' she said.

'Oh, Mistress atte Wode, what an uproar. Those fool cottars got themselves so drunk they talked themselves into believing the bailiff's behind Bart Coupar's accident.'

'So they've come to accuse him?' said Alice.

'Yes, mistress. Or rather to attack him. But it's madness.'

Alice nodded. 'The bailiff'll deal harshly with them.'

Henry ran off to join John and the others.

A few moments later came the sound of shattering glass: someone had thrown a stone through one of Robert Tyler's precious windows. A drunken cheer went up from the cottars, and Alice ran over to Eleanor and grabbed her hand.

'Let's get away from here,' she said, but Eleanor resisted.

'No, Alice, look,' she said, pointing to where John, together with Simon Hogge, Henry Miller and a few others, were hurling themselves in amongst the rioters and trying to pull them back from the affray. At that moment the cottars turned on them and began to fight, punching and kicking. 'They'll get hurt!' she cried. 'Oh, Alice, John'll get hurt.'

As she said it, John fell to the ground, and Alice saw that the cottar closest to him, presumably the one who'd attacked him, had a knife in his hand. Eleanor screamed when she saw John fall, but Alice wouldn't let her run to him. Then Simon Hogge saw John was down and ran over and helped him to his feet. He pulled a rag from the pouch he had at his waist and tied it tightly around John's arm, then he spoke to John and pointed out where his mother and Eleanor were watching, anxious for his safety. John turned to the women, and nodded grimly, which Alice assumed was intended to imply he was not badly hurt. She'd have welcomed a smile, but tried not to let her heart grieve for what he would not give.

Despite the broken window, the rioters did not gain entry to Robert Tyler's house. One of Robert's servants had come to the window to shout and curse at the cottars, but the men held back from openly attacking him. Then someone shouted that they should burn the house down, and there was a good deal of cheering and cursing, but no-one started a fire and gradually the riot subsided, as if the gang had lost their courage, and after a while they retreated, leaving John and his comrades relieved no serious havoc had been done.

Alice and Eleanor walked back to the village green. News of the riot had spread rapidly throughout the village, as such news always did, and a number of cottar women hurried to the green, anxious to find out if their men were involved. Alice saw Ralph Ward was amidst the women, evidently trying to calm their fears. The women were angry with him for inciting their men to think they could take the law into their own hands, but Ralph was objecting.

'I didn't tell them to riot,' he said, 'and I certainly didn't tell them to go an' attack the bailiff. That's madness, for they've no proof at all that Master Tyler were responsible for Bart's fall. They might suspect it, but that's not the same.'

The women continued to blame him for leading the protest, and Ralph looked crest-fallen at the turn of events.

'I just want to try 'n' find out the truth about Bart. If you think I incited your men to riot, mistresses, then I beg your pardon.'

John and Simon reached the green at that moment. 'That could've led to serious trouble,' said John angrily to Ralph. 'You shouldn't go inciting rebellion when so much ale's been drunk.'

Ralph's face flushed with indignation, but moments later his expression softened into resignation and he nodded. 'I can see that, Master atte Wode, but it weren't my intention to cause a riot. I don't want anyone to get hurt. Not even Master Tyler,' he added, and grinned.

Then he scanned the groups of people standing around: John, Simon and Henry, dishevelled and bloodied from the fight, and the cottar women, their eyes narrowed with antagonism and their arms crossed firmly over their chests. Ralph's expression changed again to one of dogged determination. 'But I'm set on getting justice for Bart, an' I'm not going to give up the fight 'til I find the truth.'

19

SEPTEMBER 1349

Margaret had persuaded her daughter Johanna to accompany her on a stroll in the manor's gardens. At length they came to the circular arbour in the centre of the orchard, and slipped into the hidden herber where Margaret knew they would be undisturbed. She bade Johanna sit on the turf seat nestling under the honeysuckle-covered trellis, and sat down next to her. Johanna looked wary, as well she might, for it was Margaret's intention to try and find out the reason for her daughter's evident melancholy.

Margaret wasn't quite sure when Johanna's deep despondency had begun. She had certainly been very withdrawn in the weeks before last Christmas. It seemed then that she and Agnes atte Wode had had a falling out, for Agnes had stopped visiting though Johanna refused to say why. Johanna became so morose that Richard lost patience with her and decided to send her away to the de Courtenays, to provide some distraction, as he put it. But when she returned and found that Agnes had disappeared from Meonbridge the day after Christmas, her gloom deepened and had not lifted since. Margaret generally saw little of her daughter, who spent most of her time alone, apparently reading and, Margaret thought, praying, and was adept at avoiding her mother's questions. But today Johanna had agreed to the walk, and Margaret wondered if at last she had something to tell her.

But Johanna did not initiate any conversation. As they walked, they exchanged pleasantries and small talk about the unusually clement weather and the flowers in the garden, but once they sat down, Johanna became silent again, her head bowed over the small book of hours that she carried everywhere with her. Margaret had no option but to ask her the question. She leaned forward and placed a hand gently on her daughter's arm. Johanna did not flinch or pull away but raised her face to her mother's gaze, as if in expectation.

'My dear,' said Margaret, 'you must know how much I fret about you. For so many months you have been shut up inside yourself, not smiling or laughing, not even talking to anyone.'

'I have no-one to talk to,' said Johanna, petulantly. 'I have no friends, since Agnes went—'

'But before she went, indeed before *you* went away, you stopped seeing Agnes. And you refused to spend any time with Isabella.'

Johanna scoffed. 'Isabella. That silly vain girl could be no friend to me.' But then a flash of guilt crossed her face and she added quietly, 'Though of course I'd fain she'd not died so horribly.' Margaret nodded sadly, though it was true she too had found Philip's young wife foolish and proud, and regretted Richard's choice of bride for their son.

'And then when I came home,' continued Johanna, becoming a little agitated, 'I discovered that Agnes had vanished months before and no-one had told me.'

'It was difficult to get any messages sent during the mortality,' said Margaret, knowing that in truth she had not tried, for Richard had insisted that Johanna was not told. 'You know that.'

Johanna shrugged. 'I suppose so. But you cannot be surprised at how shocked I was when I found my dearest friend had gone, and no-one knew where she was.'

Margaret smiled gently. 'So you did care about Agnes after all?'

Johanna looked dismayed. 'Of course I did. How can you think otherwise, Mother?'

'Then why did you stop seeing her?'

But at this Johanna's face closed up again and she looked away. 'I cannot tell you, Mother.'

'Cannot, or will not?'

'Cannot,' said Johanna, and opened her book again.

Mother and daughter sat in silence for a while. Margaret knew it was futile attempting to press Johanna to say more; she could not be persuaded to say what she did not want to. Johanna turned the pages of her book but Margaret sensed that she was not reading them. Margaret got up and took a turn about the rose garden: the bushes were tall and unkempt but they were full of flower and she put her nose to one bloom after another to breathe in their sweet musky scent. After a time, she returned to the seat and, as she did so, Johanna looked up.

'Mother,' she said abruptly, 'I want to go to the priory as a novice.'

Margaret was aghast and could not conceal it. 'You want to become a nun? But what about the marriage your father is arranging for you?'

Johanna shook her head. 'I don't want to marry, Mother.'

'But it is not for you to decide, Johanna,' said Margaret, though her heart was already aching with the knowledge that Richard would probably force his daughter to marry against her wishes. 'Your father has planned a good match for you.'

To her dismay, Johanna began to weep; not just one or two drops but a flood of tears. Margaret moved closer and put her arm around her daughter's shoulders, but this time Johanna did pull away, and tried to wipe away the tears cascading down her cheeks. 'But I don't want it. I don't want to marry any man.'

'Then what do you want?' said Margaret, though of course she already knew the answer.

'I want to become a bride of Christ,' said Johanna, and clasped her prayer book to her heart.

Though it would undoubtedly make him angry, Margaret knew that she would have to tell Richard about Johanna's newly expressed desire to lock herself away in a nunnery. She did not want to tell him, but she thought it better to warn him now rather than have him find out when he was about to present her to a suitor. Johanna's passionate declaration filled Margaret with profound dismay: for if the girl was so desperate to renounce the world when she had all the excitement of life still ahead of her, then the root of her melancholy must be dreadful indeed.

Margaret hoped that Richard might be alone, but when she got back to their chamber in the solar she found him talking to Philip, a discussion that was causing both men to raise their voices and throw their hands in the air. Fretful as she already was from the unhappy conversation with her daughter, Margaret decided at once that she would ignore the men and retreat to the far end of the room to sit quietly with a piece of embroidery. But she found it hard to concentrate on her stitching, for her curiosity kept her ears alert to the heated exchange seething only yards away.

It seemed that, despite Richard's intention to investigate Bart's accident in secret, it had somehow reached Philip's ears that his father had questioned Martin Foreman and Thomas Rolfe. Philip was annoyed because he thought that, as steward of the manor, he should have been involved in both the plan to investigate and the questioning of the tenants. Richard said that he thought it best to talk to the men privately without making too much of it, so as not to arouse undue disquiet amongst the tenants. But Philip was scathing: he thought his father generally made too many concessions to the manor's servants.

'What did Martin say about Bart's accident?' said Philip.

Margaret looked across to see Richard's expression: she knew the interrogations had yielded no information and Richard was frustrated by his lack of progress. His face made his irritation clear, and he was undoubtedly humiliated at having to admit this to his son.

'Nothing,' he said. 'He was as vague as Robert about events, and gave no more information about who was there, or who tied the ropes.'

'You sound surprised, Father. But I daresay none of them'll admit to what they know.'

'I told Martin,' Richard continued, 'that I'd heard it was Thomas Rolfe who tied the ropes from which Bart fell, but he just said that he didn't know.'

'And what did Thomas say?'

'Oh, Thomas Rolfe didn't dissemble at all,' said Richard, guffawing despite his ill temper. 'He stoutly denied being anywhere near the cart, claiming he was elsewhere the whole evening.'

'You made no progress then?' said Philip, and Margaret could see that he was looking rather self-satisfied at his father's failure.

'Well, I did also speak to William Mannering and his son Harry, and one or two others who I'd been told were working by the cart. But it seemed no-one other than young Harry was prepared to say that Thomas Rolfe was there.'

'I'm surprised the bailiff hasn't suggested you try a little persuasion to get the truth out of these churls.'

'Persuasion?' said Richard, looking briefly confused. 'You mean...?' But then he shook his head. 'Oh, no, I don't think it should come to that.' And Margaret was relieved to hear him say it.

'Robert might think differently,' said Philip. And Margaret silently agreed that these days Master Tyler did seem to have a fondness for using various degrees of force to get his way.

But Richard shook his head again. 'No, he doesn't. Or if he does, he hasn't said so. In fact he's suggested I should give up the investigation entirely.'

'Has he indeed,' said Philip, smirking. 'Well, Father, in that I would agree with Master Tyler. I don't know why you're troubling yourself to find out what happened. What does it matter?'

At this Margaret was unable to contain herself. She jumped up and came over to the two men.

'How can you be so insensitive, Philip?' she said. 'The village is up in arms over Bart's death and if they believe it wasn't an accident they'll likely blame us for it.'

Philip threw his mother a scowl. 'Why should we care what the tenants think?' he said, addressing his father.

Richard sighed. 'Because they'll refuse to work for us.'

Margaret was pleased her husband at least seemed to be gradually realising the truth of their situation. But Philip, apparently, did not.

'How can they possibly imagine you are responsible for Bart's death, Father?' he said. 'It's absurd. It's much more likely to have been the bailiff–' He suddenly stopped short, but then continued, 'After all, didn't the rabble go and attack Robert Tyler's house last week?'

Richard nodded. 'But they didn't attack Robert himself. Perhaps even they thought better of it, without any proof he was to blame.'

Philip scoffed. 'Since when did cottars need proof before they start a fight? You know my view, Father, we should get rid of the lot of them.'

Richard sighed again. 'Yes, yes, in principle perhaps I agree with you, Philip, but it's not practical. We need them to work our fields.'

'I thought we'd agreed to bring in labourers from elsewhere.'

'We did, but to work *alongside* our present labourers, not replace them,' said Richard, looking rather exasperated. 'And why hasn't Robert yet found us any new workers?'

'I doubt he's been looking. After all, he's been concentrating on the harvest. He could hardly be away at such an important time.'

'That's true. But not for you. Why haven't you been looking?'

'I have been.'

Richard looked surprised. 'You haven't told me about it.'

'No, but I have a plan, though I'd fain not tell you about it now.'

Richard seemed sceptical and Philip looked irritated by his father's apparent lack of confidence in him.

'You made me your steward, Father,' he said, 'so now you need to trust me to do my job.'

Even if he had wanted to, Richard had no time to reassure his son of his confidence in him, for at that moment a servant came hurrying into the chamber, to announce, in red-faced agitation, that a great rabble was gathered at the manor gate, in the courtyard, and they were looking angry.

'Master Ward's there too,' he said. 'He's asking to talk to you, m'lord.'

Philip immediately protested. 'Don't demean yourself, Father, by agreeing to speak to that knave. You do know it was Ward who incited the rioters to attack the bailiff's house?'

Margaret knew that was not true. 'No, no. Alice atte Wode told me that Ralph did *not* incite that riot, Philip.'

Philip sneered. 'You think, Mother, we should trust the word of a tenant, and a woman at that?'

But, to Margaret's surprise, Richard intervened. 'No, Philip, you're misjudging Mistress atte Wode. She is entirely trustworthy, as is her son, the reeve, who I hear led a group of men to try and quell the riot, and got injured for his pains.'

Philip looked unconvinced and said nothing in response, so Richard continued, 'I think I should give Master Ward a chance to explain himself—'

Philip threw his hands in the air. 'You're wrong, Father. He should be thrown off the manor.'

Richard looked affronted by his son's criticism of his judgement but did not retaliate. Instead he shook his head and, calling the red-faced servant forward, instructed him to fetch Ralph, at which Philip let out a snarl of fury and swept out of the room.

Richard did not permit tenants to enter his private chamber, so he told the servant Ralph was to await him in the great hall. Then, bidding Margaret follow him, he descended the stairs and, sweeping aside the arras, strode into the hall. He stepped up on to the dais and sat down majestically in the grand chair from which court judgements were delivered. Margaret stood by his side. Ralph was ushered forward by the servant. Margaret noticed that Ralph's demeanour was unusually respectful; she wondered if he had been alarmed into deference by the anger and violence that his preaching had unleashed. She did not doubt that his opinions remained unchanged, but perhaps he thought he would be more successful with Richard if he was conciliatory rather than belligerent. If he did think that, he was right: Richard did not respond well to being bullied, even if he did it himself.

'Well, Master Ward?' said Richard, his face stern and unsmiling. 'You wished to speak to me.'

Ralph nodded. 'Yes, m'lord. To ask you to look into Bart's accident, to find out what happened—'

Richard raised his hand. 'You do not have to ask, Master Ward, for it is already being done.'

Ralph looked surprised and grateful at the same time. But Richard shook his head as if to dampen Ralph's gratitude.

'But I regret to say I have made little progress with my enquiries. It seems Thomas Rolfe might be at the root of it—'

'Yes,' said Ralph, interrupting. 'That's what young Harry Mannering said, sir—'

'Yet everyone denies knowing if Thomas tied the ropes,' continued Richard, 'and Thomas himself denies being there at all.'

'But that's ridiculous, sir,' said Ralph, his deference somewhat slipping. 'Thomas was definitely there—'

'But even if he was, Master Ward,' said Richard, 'unless we have some evidence that he actually tied the rope, we can hardly bring the man before the court.'

Ralph looked exasperated, and Richard was already becoming bored with the whole matter, despite his initial eagerness to discover the truth. 'Well?' he said. 'What else do you want me to do?'

Ralph shook his head. 'I dunno, sir. Will you give me leave to ask some questions?'

'Very well, but I will not indict a man without evidence, Master Ward.' Margaret suppressed a gasp of surprise: Richard was rarely so unprejudiced and even-handed.

'I understand, sir.'

'And now what of this other matter,' said Richard, brusquely. 'Your rioters at the gate. What do they want?'

'You know what they want, lord,' said Ralph, quickly recovering his former assertiveness. 'The cottars want more money for their labour and the villeins to be released from their bonds.'

'But it's against the law for me to pay more money,' said Richard, tetchily. 'And how will I manage the manor if I have no bondsmen to tend my fields?'

Ralph shuffled his feet and looked embarrassed. 'As I see it, sir, if you release the villeins from their week-works but demand higher rents, you'll get more money to pay the cottars. An' if you pay the cottars more they'll want to work for you.'

'And how do you suggest I get around the law?' said Richard in a sarcastic tone.

Ralph shrugged and did not answer for a while, but at length he said, rather quietly, 'You have to do what's best for the manor, m'lord.'

But this seemed to antagonise Richard. 'How dare you tell me what to do,' he said, voice raised and nostrils flaring, and Margaret sighed.

But Ralph appeared to ignore Richard's sudden burst of temper. 'So what'll you do, lord?'

'I will think about it,' growled Richard.

'Don't think too long, lord, or the crowd at your gate'll get nasty.'

Margaret thought his tone insolent but Richard seemed to accept the warning. He nodded.

'Call them off now, Master Ward. Persuade them to go back to work and tell them I will reflect on their demands.'

Ralph shuffled his feet and did not immediately respond to Richard's command. Richard obviously noticed his tenant seemed dissatisfied, for he flared again.

'Do not forget, Master Ward,' he said, his voice low but teetering on the edge of rage, 'that I am the lord of Meonbridge, and I will decide what to do with my tenants.

It seemed that Ralph did manage to persuade the crowd, for by the end of the afternoon the courtyard was quiet again.

But Richard was no less agitated than he had been earlier. The rioters' dispersal gave him only a short breathing space in which to decide what to do to return his manor to a place of labour and community. Margaret had noticed how Richard was becoming increasingly unable to make decisions: he might believe he was in command of any situation but in truth he was pulled this way and that by the opinions of others. In the past few days, she had realised that he was taking her more and more into his confidence. His customary advisers, his steward and his bailiff, were apparently proving troublesome counsellors, for one advised breaking the manorial bonds of recalcitrant tenants and the other favoured beating them into submission, neither of which, perhaps, Richard thought would provide a solution.

Richard was a fighting man, used to dealing out injury and death on the battlefield, and there had been many occasions in the past when he had taken a strong line with tenants who shirked their duties or caused dissension among their neighbours. But, now, he told Margaret, it made no sense either to drive away their tenants or to punish them, when the manor would clearly collapse without their labour.

'It is only you, dear wife,' he said, when they were alone again that evening, 'who seems to understand the tenants.'

Margaret was astonished that he seemed to be coming round to her point of view.

But Richard looked troubled. 'But why is it, do you think, that both Philip and Robert think I should not try to find out how Bart Coupar died?'

Margaret shook her head. 'I do not know, husband. Or rather, I think that Philip really cares so little for our tenants that he truly believes it is of no importance how they lose their lives. Though, I think he does not understand the consequences of such an opinion.'

Richard nodded glumly as she continued. 'I doubt Master Tyler thinks the same. But perhaps he is concerned that an inquiry will reveal some negligence in his duty?'

Richard looked up. 'An oversight, you mean?'

She nodded. 'Perhaps. I daresay even Master Tyler overlooks a responsibility from time to time.'

Richard looked relieved. 'Yes, yes. That must be it.'

Robert Tyler invariably took his dinner at the manor table, whether Richard ate in the hall or in the solar with his wife. Robert often brought Gilbert Fletcher with him, and occasionally also one or both of his daughters. Richard decided that today they would have their dinner in the hall, as he wanted the opportunity to observe his bailiff. When he and Margaret entered the hall and took their places at the long table, Robert rose and bowed deeply to his lord and lady, and everyone else already at the table rose too and made their obeisance.

Gilbert Fletcher was seated next to his father-in-law, with his wife Matilda on his other side. Margaret smiled to the girl as she made her curtsey, and Matilda returned the smile weakly before sitting down again and bowing her head to gaze gloomily at the tablecloth. Margaret thought how strained Matilda looked, her pretty young face pale and pinched. She noticed too how unkindly Gilbert seemed to regard his new wife, for he either deliberately turned his back on her as he addressed her father, or scowled on the few occasions he spoke to her. It was little wonder that the girl looked so alone and miserable.

Robert and Gilbert were deep in conversation with Philip. As so often, the conversation seemed ill tempered, though Margaret could not hear what they were saying. From time to time Philip looked directly at Gilbert, and Margaret wondered at what she fancied was hatred in his eyes. She also pondered on the change that had been wrought in her son's relationship with Robert Tyler, a relationship that had started when Philip was a boy.

At five years old, and with his father away in France, Philip ignored his mother's commands, running unchecked among the village lads. Margaret could not control her son, and out of desperation had appointed Robert Tyler, at that time the manor clerk, to be Philip's tutor and mentor. Robert was one of the few bondsmen who could read and write, thanks to an ambitious father who had recognised his son's ability and petitioned Sir Thomas, Richard's father, to permit the boy to receive lessons from the priest. Robert learned well but it seemed that he was not planning to train for the clergy: his ambitions lay in the direction of acquiring land and status, and he decided that a career of service to his lord was the path to achieving his desires. When the old clerk died, he put himself forward for the post despite his youth, and Richard, the new lord and still young himself, was much taken with the robust energy of his educated bondsman. When Lady de Bohun later asked him also to take responsibility for her wayward son, Robert was delighted, perhaps seeing it as another step closer to the prominence in manor society that he craved.

Robert Tyler was not only robust and energetic but tough and strong-willed, and he tolerated no argument or disobedience from his young charge. Margaret was astonished to discover that Philip did not resist Master Tyler's restraints, but seemed almost to revel in them, not apparently realising the man was in fact his servant. When Richard returned home, he was so impressed with the education of his son that he allowed him to remain another year under Robert's tutelage before finally sending him away.

Margaret now believed that, over the ensuing two years, Robert Tyler calculatingly fostered a close relationship with his lord, with the result that, before Richard departed yet again to serve the king, he had appointed Robert as his bailiff. At the time, Margaret was not sure if she was pleased or not with the appointment: it was true that the old bailiff was ageing and rather deaf, but she was somewhat nervous of Master Tyler's strength of character. But of course Richard did not consult her about the appointment, even though it would be she who had to work with the new bailiff. She felt that Robert's appointment was Richard's attempt to ensure the manor was run the way he wanted it. And it was true that, in the following few years, she did find that she had less influence on how tenants were treated, though Robert was canny enough never to overtly undermine her authority.

Thus Robert Tyler's influence in Meonbridge grew. But he continued to speak with affection of the boy, first sent away at eight to be a page, who years later went to France to fight alongside his master, the Baron de Fougère. And, in his turn, Philip, in the many letters he wrote to his mother over his years of exile from home, referred often to his former tutor as a man whom he regarded as a friend.

But Margaret had noticed that, since Philip had returned from France, and especially since he had been appointed steward, a new tension had developed between him and Robert. Any discussions that she observed between them seemed businesslike but strained, as if the two men were vying with each other for supremacy. And yet, of course, Philip was the heir to the manor and Robert, for all his power as bailiff, was still a bondsman, so that there could be no doubt who really held the superior position. So why did the strain in their former friendship worry her?

For the past few months Robert had been particularly stern and gloomy. He seemed a very different man from the one Margaret had known fifteen years ago. He had always been ambitious but he never sought to conceal it, and if he was strong-willed and tough, he was also, or so it had seemed, sincere and straightforward. But now she felt afraid because it appeared that Robert was no longer being entirely honest with Richard, or indeed with Philip, about his dealings on the manor or off it. She had begun to wonder whether the bailiff's interests were always completely focused on the manor or his own advancement.

After dinner, Margaret was anxious to tell Richard about her fears.

'Perhaps Philip's plan for getting more labour is in fact a plot with Robert?' she said.

Richard seemed unconcerned. 'What if it is? As long as they get us some labourers who want to work, I care not how they do it.'

'Do you really mean that, Richard? I am concerned that Robert Tyler has become a dangerous, wily man. Philip may be a fine knight but he has little experience of running a manor...'

'Which is precisely why I made him steward, to give him that experience. And Robert is a good adviser for him.'

Margaret shook her head. 'I am really not sure you are right about Master Tyler. Not now. He's changed.'

But Richard dismissed her fears. 'My dear Margaret, you are seeing danger where it does not exist.' He came over to her, put his broad arm around her shoulder and squeezed her to him. 'Forget about it.' He kissed her firmly on her mouth.

'And now,' he said, his eyes twinkling, 'I am away to ask the wily Tyler to help me decide what to do about those wretched rioters.'

20

Alice dreaded going to church these days, for it no longer provided the consolation she'd come to expect. No more than two weeks after Bart's funeral and Master Hugo's terrifying sermon, the priest apparently now found he had another excuse to rail against his flock. The fear he'd whipped up among his congregation with his dire warnings of doom yet to come had ensured the church was full for the main Sunday mass. This morning his face was grim as he brandished the parchment clutched in his bony hand.

'This,' he declared, waving the parchment, 'is a letter written to his bishops by the king himself.'

He paused for the eminence of the letter's author to sink in.

'It is a letter of the utmost gravity,' he continued, 'in which our noble king Edward, God bless him and save him, speaks to each and every one of you.' Glaring down at them from his high pulpit, he swept his outstretched hand, with its menacing pointing finger, over the silent, cowed assembly, shuffling uneasily in the nave.

'Our gracious king Edward writes from his noble, aching, heart,' Master Hugo said, holding a hand over his own heart and adopting an expression of profound compassion, 'when he bewails the continuing sinfulness and pride of those whom God, in His gracious wisdom, has spared the agony of the foul mortality. Our sovereign king speaks of his deep distress that so many of his subjects are recklessly displaying their ingratitude for God's compassion, by refusing to heed His judgements and His lessons, which in His loving kindness He gave to the world, in order to turn them away from their wickedness.' He drew the back of his hand across his eyes, as if wiping away emotion.

Then he lowered his voice to a doom-laden threnody. 'The king is filled with dread that a much greater calamity will soon befall us, unless God can be pacified by the people's urgent and earnest entreaty for His mercy. The king urges every one of us to penance and to prayer.'

Raising his voice again, he drove home the king's message. 'Through penance and through prayer,' he repeated, 'it is the king's fervent hope that his people will drive out the spiritual wickedness from their hearts, and that, as the people drive out their sins, so the foul malignancy of the air will also be driven out and the mortality banished from our land for ever.'

He paused once more before, yet again, sweeping his pointed finger back and forth over the glum faces of his flock. 'Not one of you here can ignore the pleading of our gracious sovereign. Renounce your sinful ways! Do penance for your sins! Pray fervently for forgiveness and deliverance!'

The congregation shuffled out of the church in morose silence. But once out of the hearing of the priest, they gathered together in little groups on the green and whispered their disquiet to each other. It was true that they were frightened by Master Hugo's words and those of the king, yet many were resentful that *all* were being accused of wickedness. Most people believed themselves God-fearing and humble: they cared for their families and their neighbours, worked hard on their farms, gave the lord his dues, and prayed for the souls of the departed. But some said perhaps all the agitation of the labourers against the manor *was* a sin, as Master Hugo said, and maybe did threaten the safety of the village.

Ralph Ward was standing close by Alice's group when someone called out to him.

'Hey, Ralph,' said the man, chortling now the shock of the sermon had somewhat faded. 'Did y'see the 'ard way priest stared at ye when he were saying how sinful w'all were?'

Ralph chortled too, though he didn't really look amused. 'Aye,' he said. ''Tis true enough he blames me for all the agitation. But I ask ye, neighbour, can it really be a sin to ask for a decent wage, and for time to farm your own land? Can it?'

Alice hadn't seen Eleanor for more than a week when the girl knocked on her door early in the evening. John was not yet home from his work, so when Eleanor stood at the threshold, looking enquiringly around the room, Alice guessed she was nervous about seeing John again since she'd told him their friendship was at an end.

'When will he be home?' said Eleanor.

Alice shrugged. 'Soon, perhaps?'

Eleanor frowned. 'Maybe I shouldn't stay, then?'

'Of course you should,' said Alice, taking her hand and pulling her gently into the room.

Alice carried on preparing the evening meal. 'Have you come to say something in particular?' she said, as Eleanor paced around looking agitated. 'Is it about John?'

Eleanor stopped pacing and sat down on a stool. 'No, not at all. It's about Matty Tyler, or rather Fletcher.'

After Matilda's wedding, Alice had told Eleanor of her apprehension for her friend's future. But now it was Eleanor's turn to tell Alice of her own unease, for Eleanor had discovered how difficult it was to see Matilda. She'd tried to call on her several times, but each time Gilbert, or one of his servants, had refused to let her in.

'I think Gilbert's given orders for me not to be admitted. But why would he do that, Alice?'

Alice shook her head. 'Have you asked Margery about her sister?'

Eleanor nodded. 'I saw her at the mill the other day, so I asked her then. But she was evasive and told me she hardly saw Matty herself now that she was married.'

'How surprising,' said Alice.

'Yes, I thought it very strange. Why wouldn't Margery see her sister, married or not?'

'Why indeed?'

'I wondered, Alice,' said Eleanor, 'if you could somehow get in to see her, to check that she's all right? You do still visit new brides, don't you? I thought maybe that could be a reason for you calling?'

Alice nodded. 'I could certainly try. Though it might be best to go when no-one else is in the house except Matilda, so I'll have to be a little wily.' She grinned. 'Leave it with me.'

Young Matthew atte Wode spent a few happy mornings sitting on the bank of the little stream that ran close by the Fletchers' house. He often fished there: he was allowed to as long as he only caught the little fish, leaving the larger ones for the manor table. So no-one would think it unusual to see him sitting there with his rod and line dangling in the water. All the same he kept himself well hidden in the thick reeds that grew along the bank, just in case that nasty Master Fletcher spotted him. Because Matthew wasn't really there to fish: his mother had given him an errand, to keep an eye on the Fletchers' house and let her know as soon as both the master and his servants left the house.

But it wasn't until the third morning's fishing that Matthew ran home as fast as he could to tell Alice that everyone had left the house except Mistress Fletcher. At once Alice ran down to the house and knocked loudly on the door. No-one came to answer for such a long time that Alice wondered if Matilda had gone out as well. But then she heard a scrabbling behind the heavy oak door, as the latch was lifted and the door slowly opened a short distance. A face peered cautiously around the edge of the door: it was Matilda.

'What d'you want?' she said, her voice a barely audible rasp. Her face was very pale and blotchy, her eyes wide and unblinking.

Alice smiled warmly. 'Mistress Fletcher,' she said, and was sure she noticed Matilda flinch a little. 'I thought it'd be neighbourly to call on you, to offer help, should you need it.'

When Stephen was reeve, Alice took it upon herself to help him by supporting the tenants' wives and families, especially when the women were pregnant or had very young children, or when new brides had no mother or married sister to advise them. She never interfered, just offered help, which some accepted and some refused.

Matilda opened the door a little more when she saw who it was, but she bit her lip. 'I can't let anyone into the house,' she said, yet Alice was sure her sad eyes showed she wanted company.

'How long'll everyone be out?' she asked.

Matilda shrugged. 'My husband's the whole morning, but the servants'll likely be back soon.'

Alice smiled again. 'Well, let's just talk a short while. I'll be on my way as soon as Nathan and Hawisa return. I've known them both for years. They'll not think it strange I'm here.'

Matilda seemed to battle with herself for a few moments, but at length opened the door wide enough for Alice to enter. She led her upstairs to the solar, to a small chamber that appeared to be separate from the room she shared with her husband, for it contained no bed but just two chairs and a small coffer. Matilda invited Alice to sit down, and she herself perched tensely on the edge of the other chair.

Matilda at first said little in response to Alice's gentle questions. But the awkward conversation soon became yet more disjointed when Matilda rose suddenly from her chair to run into her little garderobe, where she was unmistakably retching. To begin with, Alice tactfully ignored it when Matilda returned dishevelled and pale but, after the third time, she felt she could hardly continue without asking after the girl's health, and Matilda, trembling, was at last ready to pour out her melancholy.

'It's foolish of me to try to hide it from you, Mistress atte Wode,' she said, in a whisper. 'It's obvious enough that I'm with child.' Tears leaked from her eyes. 'By that vile man,' she added, through her teeth.

'Your husband?'

She nodded. 'Husband,' she repeated, spitting out the word. 'Or the odious snake my father forced me to marry.'

Alice was hardly surprised to hear Matilda give voice to her loathing of Gilbert Fletcher, having witnessed her unhappy wedding. 'You don't like him?'

Matilda threw her head back. 'Don't like him? I hate him. And he hates me too. He only married me so he could ally himself with our family. He doesn't care for me at all.'

'I suppose your father thought it a good match?'

But Matilda shook her head, and the tears flowed more abundantly.

'Oh yes, a good match for him – a chance for him to be freed from his shame. Gilbert Fletcher wanted the alliance so much he was prepared to take a bride who'd already–' She coloured suddenly as she spoke. Then she got clumsily to her feet again and rushed to the garderobe to heave and weep.

After a while, as Matilda did not return, Alice got up and went into the tiny chamber, where she found the girl crumpled on the floor with her head over a basin half full of vomit. Alice knelt down by her side and drew her thick dark hair back from her face. Matilda sat up shakily and leant back against Alice, nestling her face against her breast.

'You've been with child before?' asked Alice quietly

Matilda nodded. 'In March.'

'But not Gilbert's?' said Alice, and Matilda shook her head.

'And the baby?'

'Lost.'

Alice wondered exactly what she meant, but decided not to ask; it was common enough for a child to die in the womb.

Matilda wept softly for a while before speaking again. 'My father hates me too. So angry when he found out. Made me marry Gilbert to punish me for my sin. He reviles all sinners, Alice. Says we'll burn in Hell.'

Alice held the girl tight, to comfort her, and thought she'd made a poor job so far of giving her help. But perhaps, now Matilda had opened her heart, she'd be more willing to accept help – if she was allowed to.

'Why were you afraid to open the door to me, Matilda?' asked Alice.

'Gilbert,' said the girl. 'He doesn't want me to talk to anyone.'

'Why not?'

'Lest I say what I've just said to you, Alice,' she said, looking up at her with a thin smile. But the smile faded almost immediately. 'And if he finds out, he'll beat me.'

Suddenly Matilda started up in a fright as from downstairs came the sound of the front door scraping open and baskets and bundles being dropped to the floor. 'They're back,' she cried.

Alice gently extracted herself from Matilda's leaning body. 'You stay here, and I'll go down and talk to them.'

Nathan and Hawisa were bustling about putting away the supplies they'd bought. When Alice appeared at the foot of the stairs, they looked up aghast and were, for a few moments, speechless.

Nathan eventually found his voice. 'What you doing here, Mistress atte Wode?' Anger and fear were jostling for position on his face.

'Just visiting Mistress Fletcher,' said Alice, smiling. 'You know I visit new brides.'

'Oh, Alice,' said Hawisa, wringing her hands. 'You must go. You shouldn't have come at all—'

'Why not?' said Alice, feigning innocence.

'Because the Master won't like it,' said Nathan.

Hawisa became agitated. 'You really must go, Alice. If Master Fletcher finds out you were here, he'll beat us—'

'And the mistress,' added Nathan, glumly.

'Why?' said Alice.

'We don't know,' said Hawisa, casting a sideways glance at Nathan. 'He just don't want the mistress to talk to anyone.'

'So is she captive here?'

Nathan turned away, but Hawisa nodded, looking scared. 'Please go, Alice, or we'll surely get into trouble.'

Alice could see she had no choice, though she was deeply anxious about Matilda. She quickly went to bid farewell to her.

She took Matilda's hand. 'I promise I'll try to return,' she said. 'Somehow...'

Matilda nodded but withdrew her hand and, turning, ran back into the garderobe.

Later in the afternoon, Alice went down to the forge to tell Eleanor what she'd found out about Matilda. Eleanor was distraught at her news, and anxious they should help her friend.

But Alice shook her head. 'I'm not sure we can, or at least I don't know how to.'

'Do you truly believe she's imprisoned in her own house?' Eleanor's eyes were wide with dismay.

'Well, not all the time, for Margaret has told me that sometimes Matilda goes with her father and husband for dinner at the manor.'

'But there I suppose she'd be unlikely to say anything she shouldn't.'

Alice nodded. 'Margaret said when Matilda last went to the manor, two weeks ago, she was melancholy and hardly spoke at all. She's as concerned for Matilda's well-being as we are.'

As they were talking, the women realised they could hear a great commotion coming from the village green. They ran to the top of the narrow lane that led from the forge to the green, where they found Master Hugo Garret standing at the church door haranguing a group of cottars who'd gathered in a drunken confrontation. The priest was repeating his sermon about the growing pride and avarice of the common people and the mortal dangers of upsetting the social order. The cottars seemed no more sympathetic to the priest's dire words of warning now than they had been on the day of Bart's funeral. Indeed his preaching was aggravating their angry mood and they were looking manifestly hostile.

But then, above the ranting of the priest and the drunken clamour of the dissenting cottars, came the roar of an even angrier man, as Robert Tyler cut a swathe through the crowd, yelling at them to make way. Followed by his usual henchmen, he forced his way to the front, and stood a short distance from Master Hugo. The priest looked affronted as the bailiff gestured to him to stand aside. A larger crowd began to gather, as Robert Tyler took on the role of preacher.

'It's not fitting that custom and precedent should be overturned,' he said. 'The old order must be maintained, because,' and he paused for effect, just as Master Hugo did in church, 'that is what God Himself has ordained, and we are not at liberty to question God's holy Commandments.'

There was a rumbling of dissent, but Master Tyler would not be deflected from his purpose, raising his voice above the protests. 'If we try to change the established order that God has laid down for us, He will surely send the vile mortality upon us once again, to punish us for our unceasing sin.'

Then he glared at the faces of the defiant cottars. 'Disperse,' he shouted. 'Go home, and go about your work. There's much to be done, and no time for all this idleness.'

The bailiff looked determined and his henchmen stepped forward, brandishing their heavy staffs. Most of the cottars slunk away grumbling, seemingly not, after all, prepared to come to blows. But three young men, perhaps more drunken than the others from an afternoon of ale, were spoiling for a fight, and put up some resistance to the bailiff's men. It was a foolish act of defiance, for they didn't have the strength for such a fight and were quickly arrested on the bailiff's orders by the constable, Geoffrey Dyer. As the three boys, struggling and shouting, were dragged off to the manor cells, Ralph Ward suddenly appeared on the green.

'Master Tyler,' he said, striding towards him at speed, 'on what authority are you arresting these boys?'

The bailiff scowled at him. 'The highest authority,' he said simply, and marched off, following the prisoners and his henchmen, up the main road through the village towards the manor.

Ralph looked up to see Alice and Eleanor standing nearby. 'What d'you think he meant by "the highest authority"? Sir Richard?'

'Perhaps,' said Alice, though she suspected Robert had in fact meant God.

Ralph looked downcast. 'So our noble lord has no intention of giving us justice,' he said, sounding bitter. 'What am I to do, Mistress atte Wode? Why can't our masters see what must be done? I don't understand it.'

Alice shrugged, for she didn't understand it either.

21

It was a clear, dry morning, still quite warm for the end of September. Although it was barely light, Eleanor bounced out of bed and threw open the shutters, already determined to go early to the mill. Her sheep were now demanding constant attention as she and Walter prepared them for breeding next month, and in the few months that had passed since Eleanor had realised she was solely responsible for her own future, she had resolutely established a routine of managing her domestic tasks early and late in the day, to give herself as much time as possible to spend with her shepherd up at Riverdown. And it was working well. It was true that she was tired, for she had little time for sleep, but she was sustained by the excitement that she, and Walter, felt daily as the flock seemed to prosper and grow ever healthier. The possibility of expanding her flock into one of the best in Hampshire did not seem unattainable, and Eleanor's delight in that prospect so uplifted her spirits she was even able to put her estrangement from John atte Wode to the back of her mind. He had made no effort to heal the rift between them, so she thought perhaps he had lost interest in her. If that was so, she was saddened that Alice would never be her mother-in-law, but decided not to let it trouble her. Indeed, she found that she was content enough to give all her attention to her sheep and, after all, she and Walter did work very well together.

As Eleanor approached the end of her lane, she saw Susanna Bigge walking briskly along the main road through the village, up from the cottars' cottages. Eleanor waited for Susanna to reach her and they walked the rest of the way together, talking about Joan Miller.

'Henry's asked me to look in on Joan every day,' said Susanna, 'to see if she's looking after the baby all right.'

'And is she?'

Susanna shook her head. 'Not really. Every day I take little Maud home for a while to make sure she's clean and nourished. Poor Joannie hardly seems to notice she's gone.'

'And what of Thomas?'

Susanna shrugged. 'Henry says Thomas still spends his days in the mill, but he's really a danger to himself and everyone else. For he don't give proper attention to what he's doing. Henry's asked the bailiff if he can take over the mill himself, and Master Tyler's agreed. It'll be made legal at the next court.'

Eleanor smiled. 'Are you seeing much of Henry Miller these days, Susy?'

Susanna blushed. 'What if I am? He's a good man.'

'I don't doubt it.' Eleanor patted her friend's arm affectionately.

The two women were laughing merrily together as they approached the Millers' cottage on the edge of the mill's messuage, but their merriment promptly faded when they saw the two Miller brothers rushing to and fro in panic. Susanna ran over to Henry and grabbed his arm.

'What's up, Harry?' she said, and his face crumpled in distress.

'It's Joan,' he said, tears spurting from his eyes. 'Joan and the baby, they're gone.'

'Gone where?'

Henry shook his head in despair. 'We don't know. They're not in the cottage.'

'How long've they been gone, Master Miller?' said Eleanor, coming over.

Henry shook his head. 'Could be all night,' he said, despondently. 'For Tom spent the night on the mill floor in a drunken stupor.'

'Oh, Harry,' said Susanna, reaching out to touch his arm again, 'perhaps they've not gone far. Elly and me'll help you look.' She looked across at Eleanor, who nodded and dropped her bag of grain on the ground. 'Where've you looked?'

'In all the buildings. And Tom's been down the village.'

Susanna looked desolately at Eleanor. 'You and Tom carry on looking here, Harry, and we'll look all round the croft.' She took Eleanor's hand and drew her away behind the mill buildings towards the river. 'I can't think why they haven't looked down here.'

Eleanor felt sick with dread. 'Perhaps they couldn't bear to?' and Susanna nodded bleakly.

It wasn't long before their worst fears were confirmed. No more than a few yards from the place Henry claimed he and his brother had already searched, they found Joan. The river was still swollen from the months of rain, and the race that fed the mill wheel was a torrent. The two women stood together by the wheel, not able to hear or speak above the deafening roar of the pounding water, both dreading to look down beneath the paddles. Each gripped the other's hand and steeled herself to look, and there was Joan, with her dull brown shift and her pale matted hair, at the bottom of the race, tucked under the wheel. It was difficult to see her in the low light of the early morning, but there was no doubt it was Joan.

Susanna gasped and burst into tears, and Eleanor, trying to be brave, threw an arm around her shoulder. 'Susy, we must go and tell Henry.'

Susanna nodded. 'Let me.' She clasped Eleanor briefly then ran back to the mill.

Moments later, a great cry went up and it was clear Susanna had told Henry the terrible news. Shortly they, and Thomas, came running down to where Eleanor still stood, staring down into the rushing water. Thomas howled and threw himself down on the bank of the race, thrusting his arms into the water as if he could reach Joan from there, and his brother tried to pull him away, telling him it was too late.

Then suddenly Susanna let out a cry. 'Where's Maud? Oh, in Heaven's name, where's the baby?'

Now it was Henry's turn to throw himself down and search the surging waters for another, tiny, body. 'I can't see her. I can't see her, Tom!'

But Thomas was rocking back and forth on the grassy bank, his arms over his head, whimpering, and couldn't hear his brother.

'Maybe she's not in the water?' said Eleanor. 'Susy?' She beckoned to Susanna to follow her.

They ran alongside the race up to where years ago it had been diverted off from the river. The river itself was wide and deep, and the race was scarcely any smaller, easily large enough to drown a person. Eleanor knew Joan was not the first to die in the race, for she remembered, years ago when she was a child, one cold winter's evening, a poor benighted tinker had fallen off the bridge just below the manor and plunged into the icy waters. His body was carried down river and along the race and discovered, like Joan's, come to rest in the deep water beneath the paddles of the mill wheel.

The women continued along the bank of the river in the direction of the manor, walking slowly, hoping to see signs of where Joan might have slipped, and signs of the baby.

Just below the bridge was a particularly broad and deep section of the river, and its banks were thickly covered with reeds, rushes and willows.

'Oh, Elly,' said Susanna, 'If Joannie fell in here, the water's flowing so strong, she'd not've had the strength to get out again.'

Even if she'd wanted to, thought Eleanor, but kept her thoughts to herself. They picked their way carefully through the dense, dark vegetation, and Eleanor wished the sun would rise and bring better light to their search. But it was not long before Susanna found a patch of reeds that had been flattened into the bog at the edge of the bank.

'Here, Elly,' she called, and Eleanor came over and agreed it did look as if someone might have slipped into the water there. Only moments later, Eleanor came across a filthy wimple snagged on the branches of a squat willow, and Susanna said it did look very like one Joan had worn.

'Let's keep looking,' said Eleanor. 'Maud might be here.'

It was exhausting, stumbling through the gnarled trunks of an impenetrable grove of willows, but there were now unmistakable signs that someone had been here.

They were together when they found her. When they did, Eleanor felt sick when she realised it was pure chance they'd not passed her by. For baby Maud was making no sound, and was wrapped in a blanket so grimy it blended into the undergrowth, almost hidden from sight.

Susanna began to shake. 'Oh Elly, I'm so afraid of what'll we find when we open the blanket. For poor little Maud's not been baptised–'

Eleanor gasped. 'Why not?'

Susanna's face crumpled. 'The poor little mite were only two days old when Peter had his accident, then Joan lost her wits, and Thomas too were going mad with grief, an' it were all forgotten. So now if she's died...' Her lip began to tremble.

'We have to know, Susy.'

Susanna nodded, then knelt down and reached out with quivering fingers. Gently plucking at the frayed edge of the clammy woollen covering concealing the baby's face, she eased it away and peered inside the bundle. What she saw made her gasp and rock back on her heels. For Maud was lying quite still, her eyes wide open, red-rimmed and empty, as they were when they first found her in Joan's cottage two months ago, thin and distressed, lying on a pile of sodden straw. Since then, Maud had recovered a little, responding to Susanna's daily ministrations: she was no longer a bag of bones, and quite often smiled and might even gurgle if she was tickled.

'Is she alive?' whispered Eleanor. And clearly a sudden dread gripped Susanna's heart, as she leaned forward again and reached out with her hand to stroke Maud's face.

But then Susanna nodded and whimpered with relief. 'Cold, but alive.' She reached in between the trunks of the willow, lifted out the bundle and clasped the child tight to her breast.

'Oh, my precious,' she whispered.

When they returned to the mill house, Thomas was still sitting distractedly on the bank, and Henry was shouting instructions to the two young cottars who worked in the mill. They were standing by the sluice boards that controlled the flow of the river into the mill race, waiting for Henry's signal to close the boards and try to slow the surging water. As he saw the two women approach, Henry ran to meet them and threw his arms around Susanna and the baby, weeping with relief.

'Oh, Blessed Saint Anthony,' he cried, 'thank you for bringing our little lost lamb back to us.'

Then he turned to his brother. 'Tom? D'you see that Mistress Bigge has found our little Maud? She's not drowned after all.'

But Thomas didn't get up, or even acknowledge his brother, but continued rocking back and forth. It seemed to Eleanor that he'd finally lost his wits.

Henry bade Susanna take Maud to the cottage to feed and warm her, but Eleanor stayed by the mill, wondering if she should go and fetch anyone else to help.

'D'you want me to do anything, Master Miller? D'you want Master Hugo or the bailiff?'

But Henry shook his head. 'No, Mistress Titherige, thank ye. I'd fain do this myself. An' you needn't stay if you'd rather not.'

Eleanor shook her head. 'I'll stay.' There was nothing she could do to help and she hardly wanted to watch Henry pull his dead sister-in-law out of the race, but she somehow felt she couldn't leave.

Then Henry had another thought. 'What you could do, mistress, is tell any folk who come I'll not be milling this morning.'

She nodded. 'Yes, I'll do that. Should I say why?'

Henry hesitated. 'I'd fain these grim tidings didn't spread round the village.' But then he sighed deeply. 'But I can't ask you to tell a lie, mistress, and in truth it'll be out soon enough.'

The sun was rising now behind the woodland that stretched away on the other side of the river, and the sky brightened quickly, bringing the promise of a fine day. The sky didn't know, thought Eleanor, that today it should be in mourning. Not wanting to sit on the grass, still wet with dew, she pulled herself up onto the back of a cart standing empty in the yard, and watched as Henry waited for the level of the water in the mill race to lower sufficiently for him to climb down under the wheel. It took a while.

No-one came with bags of grain, and she was relieved. But then suddenly someone tapped her on the shoulder and, starting with surprise, she turned to find Alice standing there, looking concerned.

'I could hear shouting,' she said. 'Is something amiss?'

Eleanor nodded. 'It's Joan.' She felt tears oozing from her eyes.

'In the mill race?'

'Oh, Alice, poor Joan. She was so unhappy.'

Alice looked slightly alarmed. 'Eleanor, are you saying she drowned herself?' and Eleanor realised that she was and that she shouldn't be.

'I suppose I am. For she left baby Maud safe on the bank.'

Alice shook her head. 'She might just've slipped into the water. She was so weak the water'd easily have taken her.'

Eleanor nodded.

'Nonetheless,' said Alice, 'I'm sure it's best for the Millers if it's believed Joan suffered a mishap.' Eleanor looked up at Alice's face, which had an oddly resolute expression. 'It's mischance enough that Joan's drowned, and that Maud has lost her mother. The Millers don't deserve any worse to befall them. D'you understand me, Elly?'

Eleanor nodded again. But she felt frightened by what Alice said. Suicide was a sin: she knew those who took their own lives couldn't be buried in the churchyard; and she'd heard in some places their sinful bodies were mutilated before they were buried, to ward away the Devil. Such a fate for Joan was unthinkable, and she understood why Alice was insisting that Joan must be assumed to have drowned by accident. And of course, thought Eleanor to herself, it wasn't certain Joan jumped into the river intentionally and, even if she did, she did at least save baby Maud, and surely that would absolve her.

She looked across to where Henry had now climbed down into the mill race, and was pulling at Joan's body. Shortly, Henry had the body in his arms and was hauling it and himself out of the water. Alice walked down to speak to him, but Eleanor didn't want to go any closer, so couldn't hear what she was saying. But she could see Henry nodding and thanking Alice. Alice walked back up to Eleanor and confirmed that Henry agreed it was best if they considered Joan's death a dreadful accident.

'We'll never know what really happened,' said Alice, 'but perhaps we should take comfort from knowing God's now freed Joan from her pain?'

Henry Miller half-carried his brother Thomas into the church, and propped him up against a pillar where he drooped, dishevelled and silent, seemingly unaware why he was there. Susanna and Eleanor stood together, Susanna cradling a sleeping Maud. Eleanor noticed how Susanna kept looking across at Henry, standing upright and dignified alongside his desolate brother. Henry was not a handsome man: pale-skinned and mousy-haired, but with a kind face that Eleanor knew mirrored well his disposition. He was a good man, and it seemed Susanna thought so too.

The sound of shuffling feet and grunting came from the back of the church, and the assembly of villagers edged apart to let the coffin-bearers through to the front, where Master Hugo was waiting, gaunt and stern-faced. Eleanor wondered if he'd be more compassionate towards Joan than he'd been to Bart Coupar a month ago: but as Joan's coffin was lowered in front of him, he glared at it with an expression of such repugnance that Eleanor feared he might not be.

Susanna had told her that Henry, apparently encouraged by Alice's words, went to see Sir Richard to tell him Joan's death was an accident. For, as soon as the news of her drowning was out, rumours spread rapidly that she'd thrown herself in, her despair at the loss of her children inspired by the Devil. So Henry was nervous that Sir Richard might've already heard the rumours and decided Joan's body couldn't be buried without being put on trial.

But Richard had smiled sympathetically and patted Henry's arm. 'Fear not, Master Miller, I've heard the rumours right enough, but I pay them no heed. Mistress Miller was sick at heart but not sinful. The riverbank can be a treacherous place for the unwary. Bury your sister-in-law, Master Miller. You have my blessing on it.'

Henry was astonished, Susanna said, that the lord could be so compassionate, what with all the disagreement going on between him and the labourers.

Eleanor smiled. 'Perhaps Sir Richard's not as unfeeling as we all imagine?'

'Unlike Master Hugo,' said Susanna, grimly. 'Harry's sure he believes Joan did drown herself, for he looked so heartless at Harry when he went to arrange the funeral.'

But, if Master Hugo did believe Joan a sinner and not fit for consecrated ground, he didn't say so. Perhaps Sir Richard had instructed him in what to say. The funeral service was quick and simple, and the priest spoke a few, almost kind, words over Joan's coffin before leading the congregation out to the churchyard. There, despite the notion that the churchyard had been filled to bursting, a space was found for Joan, right next to the graves of her dead children. And indeed, little Peter's body, so recently buried in the new cemetery, had been lifted and brought to lie here with his mother. Who'd ordered this act of compassion no-one knew, but it was one that brought tears to the eyes of many of those standing silently by, as first Joan's plain wooden casket, then Peter's, were lowered into the ground.

Eleanor had so much work to do that she'd asked Susanna Bigge to help her for a while by making Roger's dinner at the forge and tending to the croft garden at the Titherige house. But as Eleanor still had little money, Susanna agreed to work for a share of the dinner she cooked and of the crops she harvested from the garden. Since their discovery of the drowned Joan and still living Maud, Eleanor and Susanna had become close, their friendship forged by the bond of their shared ordeal.

Only a few days after Joan's funeral, the two women were sitting together in a sheltered spot in Eleanor's garden, enjoying the last of the warming rays of the October sun that had made these past few autumn days so agreeable. Susanna was cradling Maud in her arms, for Henry had asked her to look after the child, so he could give his full attention to the mill. It was obvious Susanna adored her, the child she'd worked so hard to keep alive and in the end snatched from death's chilly grasp. But Maud was still not baptised, and Susanna continued to fret for her safety, fearful that if she died unbaptised she might spend her eternity in Purgatory and never be saved.

'But why has it still not been done?' asked Eleanor, perplexed.

Susanna shrugged. 'Harry's had so much to do, and poor Tom's completely out of his wits and'll discuss nothing.' But then she brightened. 'But Harry's decided it will be done, and it's all arranged, for the day after tomorrow.'

She sat a while, cooing into Maud's sleeping face, then the brightness on her face bloomed into a smile, and she looked up. 'And summat else is arranged too.'

Eleanor could guess what it was and, grinning broadly, put her arm around her friend and squeezed her affectionately. 'He's asked you to marry him?'

Susanna nodded, but then her smile faded a little. 'Oh, Elly, d'you think I'm wicked to marry him when I don't love him?'

'Does he know you don't?'

Susanna pursed her lips. 'I think so.'

'Surely most people don't marry for love?' said Eleanor. 'When you're young, your parents find you the husband they want for you, and when you're older, you marry to get a Pa for your fatherless children, or a man to manage your lands. Isn't that the normal way of things?'

Susanna shrugged. 'Maybe. I suppose I weren't really in love with Fran when I married him, for he were my Pa's choice.' Tears came to her eyes. 'Though I loved him so much at the end.' She turned away and wiped the sleeve of her tunic across her cheeks.

Eleanor touched her arm and Susanna looked up at her.

'So you're right, Elly. Lots of people marry without love. But I've no children and no land, so I've no *need* of a husband—'

'But you have, Susy,' said Eleanor. 'You're still young. Young enough to have more children.'

'I've Maud to care for. An' when I marry Henry, I'll have his little son too.'

'But they're not *your* children. Surely you'd like to have another of your own?'

'I would. And Harry'd make a good father, don't you think?'

Eleanor smiled and patted Susanna's hand. 'He'll make a good father and a good husband, Susy, and marrying a good kind man must surely be better than being alone?'

22

OCTOBER 1349

Alice was standing at the top of the green, where she had a good view of both the approaching bride and groom and the church porch. It saddened her that, once more, she was waiting here for a bride that was not her lovely Agnes. She sighed, then gave herself a little shake. For this was not a day for melancholy, but rejoicing. The couple's friends and neighbours were gathering, flocking onto the village green to see them arrive, clapping and cheering as they walked up the rise from the cottars' cottages where Henry had gone to collect his bride.

Susanna Bigge was not the comeliest of women: she was thin and ungainly, her face long and hollow-cheeked. But today she looked handsome in a fine green wool tunic and surcoat that Alice recognised as belonging to Eleanor, and her face was glowing as she walked across the green towards Saint Peter's, one arm through that of her husband-to-be, and the other clutching baby Maud. In his turn, Henry Miller seemed to have allowed the burdens that had afflicted his own and his brother's families these past months to lift and he too looked full of good spirits.

Suddenly, Alice felt a hand gently clasp her arm and found Eleanor standing beside her, smiling broadly. Alice had spent little time with Eleanor since that unhappy harvest day when John accused them both of interfering in his affairs. At first Eleanor was quite melancholy about her estrangement from John, but today it seemed her sorrow had eased.

'How are you, Eleanor?' said Alice. 'I hardly see you these days.'

'I'm in high spirits today, Alice,' she said, her face bright, 'to see my dear friend Susy getting wed again. She and Harry'll make such a happy pair, don't you think?'

'I'm sure they will,' said Alice, amused at Eleanor's excitement. Moments later Susanna and Henry stopped in front of them. Maud, wrapped in a clean woollen blanket, was sleeping soundly.

'Will you hold her for me, Elly?' said Susanna, holding out the bundle.

'Of course I'll hold my godchild,' said Eleanor, nodding happily, and took the baby and hugged her to her breast.

Henry bowed his head politely. 'I thank ye, Mistress Titherige, for agreeing to stand for my little niece.'

'You know I'm very happy to, Henry,' said Eleanor, then shooed them away. 'But go, both of you, Master Hugo's waiting for you. And God bless you both!' She looked down at the sleeping baby, her face wistful and pensive.

Alice couldn't help but ask again. 'And what of yourself, Eleanor?'

Eleanor looked up, her face clearing again. 'I'm fine, Alice, truly. I'm so busy with my fields and the sheep I hardly have time to think about...' She faltered, then, looking relieved, placed a finger on her lips. 'Master Hugo's about to start.'

The church was full for the sanctification of the marriage and the baptism of baby Maud: it seemed the whole village had turned out to share this moment of joy after the long months of misery. Even Sir Richard and Lady de Bohun had come. But John had stayed away. Eleanor seemed not to notice his absence for, when Alice mentioned it, Eleanor merely shrugged.

'I hear he and Sir Philip are seen together a good deal these days,' she said, then gave a mischievous little smile. 'Perhaps hunting's more to their taste than weddings?'

Alice was quite taken aback for, although John spent little time at home, she'd not heard he was passing his days with the steward. She felt troubled by Eleanor's news, partly at the thought that John was in Philip's company at all, but mostly because he seemed to be keeping it from her. Why would it be necessary for a reeve, who answered to the bailiff, to have more than an occasional meeting with the higher authority of the steward, unless they had some personal business? It occurred to her she was making too much of this, but she couldn't help but wonder what the two men might be doing – not hunting, for Eleanor's remark was surely in jest, unless they were hunting for Agnes? She allowed herself to be comforted with the thought they might have mended their quarrel, if quarrel it was, and gone off together in search of her daughter. It was a happy notion, but one she didn't hold too close to her heart. She had to be patient.

It was one of those balmy October days when the sun shone warm and its rays filtered low through the turning leaves to give a contented glow to those who bathed in its light. It was the sort of weather that brought out the best in people; that made them feel good about life, if only for a short time.

After his wedding to Susanna Bigge, Henry Miller threw a party. Despite the horror of the last few weeks, and the much more long-drawn-out misery of the Miller family's lives, Henry was so delighted with his new wife that he wanted to share his pleasure with his friends and neighbours. The ale flowed in the ale-houses, and, at Henry's bidding, many of the women brought food for all to share. The grass on the village green was still dry enough for everyone to sit around in cheerful groups, drinking and feasting, telling tales and laughing, while the autumn sun shone cordially down and the crisping leaves of the green's great oak glowed gold and russet.

After a while, the lilt of music drifted across the green, rising above the buzz of conversation and laughter. Alice looked up to see her near neighbour Alan Fuller taking centre stage under the great oak tree, his fiddle under his chin, playing a merry tune. She was struck by the happy expression on Alan's face, the first time perhaps he'd smiled for nine months, for his wife and daughter were among the first to succumb to the mortality and since then he'd struggled to care for his baby son. Alan was among the better-off tenants, but land and money were no recompense for losing those you loved. But today the marriage of two neighbours, who'd themselves both been bereaved, was bringing renewed joy and the possibility of hope and recovery for all.

Before long Alan was joined by Nick Cook with his pipe, and William Cole banging on his tambour. Then Adam Wragge jumped up and went over to whisper in Alan's ear. Alan nodded and shortly struck up the tune of a well-known ballad, which Adam, with his fine lusty voice, sang out loud and clear, and soon everyone was joining in the chorus, the atmosphere remarkable for its cheerfulness and ease.

Alice was sitting with young Matthew and with Eleanor, who still had charge of baby Maud. John had not returned, which Alice thought a pity, for the merriment of the occasion might have brought *him* some much-needed cheer. But John's absence didn't prevent Alice from enjoying herself. She felt almost giddy with the merry-making and high spirits.

But then Adam chose a bawdy song, whose words were clearly meant for Henry and Susanna, who blushed happily and hid her face in her wimple. Alice was amused to see Eleanor too was embarrassed by Adam's lusty singing, and although she tried to share Alice's rather guilty delight in it, her laughter was reticent and her cheeks crimson.

After several more songs, Henry Miller leapt energetically to his feet and grabbed Susanna's hand to pull her up too. 'Time for a dance, wife,' he said but Susanna demurred.

'I can't dance, Harry,' she cried, 'truly, I can't.'

But Henry wouldn't be denied and gently pulled the still protesting Susanna to a clearing on the green, where they skipped and whirled to the rhythm of the music, and soon his blushing bride was laughing for the fun of the dance. It wasn't long before impromptu couples jumped up and joined in: Ralph held out both hands to Emma and she took them, smiling; Eleanor's step-brother Roger went over to Alysoun

Green and shyly asked her to dance. Then, shortly, Adam Wragge bowed solemnly to Eleanor, who flushed bright crimson all over again.

'Mistress Titherige,' he said, 'are ye up for a turn on the green?'

Eleanor looked enquiringly at Alice.

Alice smiled. 'Go on, Elly, enjoy yourself. Matt'll look after the baby.'

Alice sat watching the dancers, thinking wistfully that she was now too old to be asked to dance, and realising how much she missed Stephen, who would've taken her in his arms and danced with her until she was dizzy. As she sat musing, she noticed Master Hugo stalk up from the parsonage and hover on the edge of the green, in front of the church porch, glaring at the merriment, contempt and disapproval on his grey gaunt face. Alice smiled to herself. She almost felt sorry for the gloomy, cold-hearted priest. Master Aelwyn had hardly encouraged merry-making or dancing, but he'd accepted them as natural pastimes for hard-working folk. But the new priest seemed intent on making his flock fearful, thinking only of the salvation of their immortal souls and not at all of their earthly lives. But God-fearing as Alice and most of her neighbours were, it was clear to everyone that, if the mortality was God's instrument of punishment, His wrath had fallen on all alike, the melancholy and the merry, the pious and the profane.

Master Hugo loomed for a while, perhaps wondering if he should wade in and stop the wickedness. But, if he was, he evidently decided that today was not the day to antagonise his parishioners and, shaking his head and muttering to himself, he retreated to his parsonage perhaps to pray for Meonbridge's collective endangered soul.

As she watched the priest withdraw from his flock, Alice became aware of someone standing at her shoulder, casting a shadow across her. She looked round to find Edmund le Bowyer smiling down at her, his almost white hair picked out as a shining halo by the sunlight.

'Mistress atte Wode,' he said, bowing low, 'would ye care to dance?'

Alice smiled back up at him. Yes, of course, at her age she should expect to be asked only by an elderly, gammy-legged soldier. Yet Edmund's deep-lined but sunny face beamed so expectantly, she felt she could hardly refuse. She nodded and graciously held out her hand to him and, with a vigour surprising in a man of his age, he pulled her to her feet. Then he boldly put an arm around her waist and guided her towards the other dancers, and though she thought him overly forward, Alice did not resist.

The merry-making continued late into the evening and it was quite dark when Alice and Eleanor said good night to their neighbours and strolled homewards arm in arm.

Alice gave a little laugh. 'Adam Wragge's a fine man Elly, but a little old for you, don't you think?'

Eleanor was indignant. 'I only danced with him!'

'*All* the time,' said Alice, smirking in the dark.

'Well, you danced with that ancient Edmund le Bowyer, but I daresay you're not planning on marrying him either.'

Alice laughed out loud. 'You're right about that. But I'm old and have no need of another husband. Whereas you're young and surely don't want to be alone.'

Eleanor was quiet for a few moments before replying. 'Don't I?'

Late in the afternoon the following day, Alice decided to call on Emma Coupar, taking with her a basket of onions, parsnips and leeks she'd picked from her garden. Emma's croft had little space for vegetable growing and Alice always had more than she needed. She often sold excess crops at the spontaneous markets held on the village green every week or so, but she always kept some back for Emma and her children.

Alice walked briskly down the hill towards the cottar cottages. Several of the cottages she passed, once the homes of both villeins and cottars, were still empty. Many belonged to families from which only children had survived the mortality and had been taken in by relatives or neighbours, or to an individual who'd been left alone and could no longer face living on their own. The crofts, large and small, were overgrown with weeds, the buildings in poor repair. If these crofts were left abandoned throughout the winter, they'd undoubtedly begin to rot.

In one of the cottages, Alice knew, lived Thomas Miller. He'd exchanged the mill cottage for his brother Henry's croft in the centre of the village, while Henry and his new wife moved to be closer to the mill. Alice saw Thomas pottering about the garden of the cottage, but the weeds were almost as high as he was, cutting them undoubtedly a task too daunting for such a broken man to tackle. It seemed unlikely he'd ever make much of the garden, and would continue to be a burden on his brother.

In the distance Alice could see someone on the roof of Emma's house and, as she drew closer, she found it was Ralph Ward, making some repairs to the thatch. He was working from a somewhat precarious looking position, with one foot perched on the top rung of a flimsy ladder, the other leg swinging free. Emma, looking anxious, stood at the bottom of the ladder, both hands grasping it tight.

'I see you don't need me here,' said Alice. 'Shall I just leave the vegetables, Emma?'

Emma shook her head. 'Oh, no, mistress, don't go. Master Ward's almost finished.'

So Alice went into the cottage and put her basket on the table. Then, taking a stool, she went to sit by the door, to enjoy the last rays of the lowering sunshine and watch Emma's children playing at spinning tops in the dusty road. It wasn't long before the girls tired of their game and, spotting Alice dozing in the sun, ran to her and shaking her arm, excitedly demanded a story. Amice climbed on to her lap and Beatrix sat close by on the door step, as Alice told them one of the very small stock of tales she'd learned at her own mother's knee. As Amice snuggled close to her breast, Alice curled an arm around the little girl and gave her a hug. The child turned her huge deep blue eyes, so reminiscent of Bart's, up to Alice's face and smiled. Alice dropped a kiss on her fair, curly head and felt wistful for the grandchildren she longed to hold. But, with Agnes gone and John seemingly unwilling to see Eleanor's point of view, Alice thought she'd have to wait a very long time.

A short while later Ralph descended the ladder and Emma, looking relieved, came indoors. Alice brought the children in and sat with them while Emma bustled about putting cups on the table and a small dish of sweetmeats that she'd made. Suddenly Ralph appeared at the door.

'I've taken the ladder back, Mistress Coupar,' he said. 'I'll be off now.'

Emma spun round, almost in alarm. 'No, Master Ward, you can't go without having a pot of ale.'

He smiled. 'I wouldn't say no, mistress. It's thirsty work up on your roof.'

As he came into the cottage, the two little girls, whispering together, giggled, and Emma's eyes threw them a sharp reprimand. If Ralph noticed, he didn't show it but sat down on the stool Emma indicated. As Emma went to fetch the jug of ale from her tiny storeroom, Ralph's eyes followed her. For the first time Alice noticed how pretty Emma had become. She'd been a pretty girl, with her fair straight hair and green eyes, and she'd been quite in demand among the village lads until Bart made her his wife. But since her marriage, worry, motherhood, and hard work had rather sullied her good looks and, for a while after Bart's death, her sallow complexion became even more sickly-looking. But Alice realised that, despite Emma's continuing worries, for the past few weeks she'd seemed much brighter, her face less drawn. When Ralph spoke, she smiled and tilted her head almost coyly as she listened to him.

Emma poured the ale and offered one of her honey sweetmeats, and Alice asked Ralph if he'd had any luck finding out the truth about Bart's death. But Ralph shook his head dolefully.

'No, Mistress atte Wode, no luck at all. Folk either really didn't see what happened or they're not telling. I reckon some are hiding what they know but I don't have the clout to force them to tell the truth.'

He became glum, but Emma leaned across and put her hand on his arm.

'I reckon you ought just try and get justice for the cottars,' she said. 'Forget about Bart's accident, Ralph. He'd understand you've done your best.'

'Perhaps Sir Richard'll yet find out what happened?' said Alice, but Ralph shook his head.

'I don't think so, mistress. He's had no better luck than me at getting folk to talk.'

Alice frowned. 'I still don't understand why anyone'd want to kill Bart. It makes no sense to me.'

As Alice was leaving Emma's house, she met Eleanor and Susanna coming down from Riverdown. Both women looked weary. They all walked together back into the village, and soon found Alice's son John and Henry Miller, sitting on a bench outside Mistress Rolfe's alehouse, supping ale together and deep in conversation. Despite her fatigue, Susanna's eyes lit up at the sight of Henry and she went over to give him a kiss. Delighted to see his new wife, Henry jumped up, saying it was time to go home, and the pair went off with their arms around each other's waists.

Eleanor inclined her head at John. 'Master atte Wode,' she said, her face impassive.

John, rocking a little, nodded back. 'Mistress Titherige,' he said, his voice slurred.

To Alice's unspoken exasperation, neither seemed inclined to say more to each other and, moments later, Eleanor touched Alice's arm in a gesture of affection. I must make Roger's supper,' she said, and hurried off towards the forge.

'I think you should come home, son,' said Alice and, nodding, John heaved himself to his feet.

'Why does she ignore me, Ma?' he said, his voice cracking.

'Because you accused her of interfering in your affairs.'

He rounded on her aggressively. 'I won't have women interfering—'

'Then you must accept a woman like Eleanor'll take it badly. She's making a life for herself now. She doesn't need a husband.'

John snorted. 'All women need husbands.'

'What makes you think that, son? Eleanor Titherige has property and the wit to make her own living. She grows stronger every day.'

'Women need to be bedded,' said John, belligerently, but Alice ignored his hostility and just smiled.

'You might think that, but I warrant many women can live well enough without it.'

. . .

They ate a very silent supper. Young Matthew was mystified by his brother's continuing glumness. He wanted John to play football with him after supper, but John refused and, rising so abruptly from his stool that it fell over with a bang, he threw on a surcoat and crashed through the croft door, mumbling about doing some digging.

Matthew burst into tears. 'What's up with John, Mam?' he said.

Alice put her arm round him and he didn't resist. 'He's got a lot on his mind.'

'It's Mistress Titherige, isn't it?' said the boy, and Alice was astonished.

She smiled at him. 'And what makes you think that?' she said, but he just shrugged. 'Don't worry, he'll come round in the end. You just have to be patient.'

Matthew pulled a face then, wiping his tears away on his grubby sleeve, stomped off to play alone in the road. Alice thought it best to leave him to sulk and followed John into the garden.

She found him not digging but leaning on his spade, gazing into the distance towards the woodland on the other side of the river. It was beginning to get dark, and he clearly didn't see or hear her approaching, for he started and lost his grip on the spade.

When he realised who it was, he looked relieved. 'You gave me quite a fright, Ma. My thoughts were far away.'

'Where were they?'

He shrugged. 'Oh, I don't know. Just not here.'

'Is it losing Eleanor making you so melancholy?'

'What else could it be?'

Alice shook her head, hoping he might suggest something. As so often recently, Alice was apprehensive about interfering in John's affairs. If he didn't want to tell her, she thought she really shouldn't ask. But it grieved her he was so downhearted, and she didn't know if he could share his worries with anyone else. She decided to take a risk.

'I've heard you've been away with Sir Philip.'

He said nothing and looked away.

'Is it a secret?' she said.

He continued silent for a few more moments, then shook his head. 'It's getting dark. Let's go back indoors.' And he gently took her elbow.

Inside the house Alice lit a candle, and raked at the fire to rekindle it. She shivered: the evenings were becoming chilly now October was advancing. John poured himself a pot of ale and, pulling a stool close to the hearth, sat down.

Alice drew up another stool. 'Are you going to tell me?'

John nodded slowly and seemed to be working out what to say. At length he said, 'I didn't want to raise your hopes, Ma.'

'About Agnes?'

He nodded. 'Sir Philip and me've had a few goes at trying to track her down.'

Alice suppressed a gasp. Despite what she'd overheard of the conversation in the wood, she was nonetheless astonished to hear that Philip really was helping to look for Agnes. She wondered why he was taking the trouble.

John appeared not to have noticed her surprise. 'We haven't had much luck so far,' he continued, 'but yesterday we heard she might've gone to Oxford. We're going to follow it up next week.'

'Why not now?'

John snorted derisively. 'Sir Philip's got other things to do, Ma, apart from looking for one of his lost villeins. He's apparently doing a deal with some labouring men.'

'Poaching them from another manor?' said Alice, disapproving.

John shook his head. 'From Winchester. Freemen. He says they're willing to move for some land.'

'And higher wages?'

John grimaced. 'I don't think so. Mebbe just the land. We've plenty to spare.'

'But they're not farming folk?'

John grimaced again. 'No, but it's labourers we need, Ma, as much as farmers.'

'Why can't Philip give the land to our own cottars?'

'Most of them don't want it. They just want more money. But the Winchester men are content to work for a fair wage and the chance of some land. Philip thinks it's a good deal.'

'And do you?'

John shrugged. 'Mebbe. But it'll be me who has to whip them into line. And only time'll tell if they fit in.'

23

Margaret was trying to remember if she had ever been as difficult a daughter as Johanna. She thought it unlikely, for her parents had been intolerant of dissent from any of their children. She supposed that she had been fortunate in her parents' choice of suitor for her, for she knew she wanted to marry Richard at their first meeting, and did not have to be persuaded. But Johanna was baulking before she had even met her suitor, and Margaret was finding her efforts to encourage her daughter both tiresome and tiring.

When she had eventually found a suitable moment to tell Richard the news of their daughter's fervent desire to enter a nunnery, he did, as she anticipated, explode with fury and frustration.

'What's the matter with the girl?' he said, storming up and down their chamber. 'No daughter of mine is going to become a "bride of Christ".' He let out an explosive snort of derision.

'Maybe she has a vocation?' said Margaret, evenly, scarcely believing it likely, though Johanna's declaration had been very passionate.

'Pah!' said Richard. 'Don't talk nonsense, Margaret. In any case, Johanna's virgin fancies are of no consequence. I've had enough of her gloomy faces and melancholy silences. She's seventeen and it's high time she made a good marriage. What she needs is bedding.'

Margaret recoiled at the notion that Richard wanted to push his daughter into some man's bed just so he could be rid of her ill humour, but she tried to conceal her feelings. 'I don't disagree she should be married, Richard—'

'Then make her see sense, madam! You're her mother. And you're also my wife, and it's your duty to support my wishes.'

Margaret sighed. 'But she doesn't listen to me, Richard.'

He rounded on her. 'Then you'll have to make her listen to you.' He laughed harshly. 'She'll not enjoy it if I have to do it.' He swept from the chamber with a dismissive gesture.

Margaret had twice before met the man that Richard had in mind for Johanna. Sir Giles Fitzpeyne had been a comrade-in-arms of Richard's, ever since they were young squires together in the service of the same lord. He won great acclaim on the battlefield for his prowess with the sword and his fearless bravado, and had been hugely rewarded with lands and riches that made him far wealthier than Richard. Unusually, perhaps, he was also a gentle man, and cultured. In principle, he was a good prospective husband for Johanna. However, Margaret was certain that, when Johanna met Sir Giles, she would want to flee. For, although she already knew he was almost as old as her own father, she was not aware that his knightly activities on the battlefields of France had left him with one or two disfigurements. Of course Richard was well aware that his friend's appearance was hardly a magnet for a young woman's desire, but this was the man he was determined his daughter would marry and he forbade Margaret to mention his less attractive characteristics.

Richard arranged for Sir Giles to visit Meonbridge to meet his prospective bride, and Margaret had been battling for days to convince Johanna to show him respect and courtesy, or incur the violent wrath of her father. Johanna tearfully protested and argued, declaring again and again that she did not want to marry anyone and that she would run away, but, with Sir Giles arriving today, Margaret had finally got her to agree at least to be polite. Of course mere courtesy would not be enough; Richard would expect much more, but in Margaret's view the battle with her daughter would have to be fought just one skirmish at a time.

. . .

When Sir Giles Fitzpeyne arrived at Meonbridge manor, it was in a style calculated to impress any normal young gentlewoman, for he came clad in magnificently embroidered scarlet velvet, and astride a huge black destrier, perhaps the very same horse that became almost as renowned as Sir Giles himself for courage on the battlefield. With him came an enormous covered wagon filled, Margaret supposed, with whatever a knight required for a few days away from home, and gifts for his future bride. Alongside rode a dozen squires and followers all dressed in red and mounted on fine-looking horses. Margaret was not easily impressed, but when she looked through the window of the chamber that overlooked the manor's courtyard, she could not help but exclaim in admiration, and called Johanna to come and look. Johanna sidled over, indifference clouding her face, but as she looked down on the vision in red, even she could not stifle a gasp.

'Doesn't he look magnificent, Johanna?' said Margaret, beaming enthusiastically.

Johanna nodded though said nothing.

Margaret sighed. 'You will treat him with courtesy, won't you?' She went to stand in front of her daughter and looked her in the eye. 'Won't you, Johanna?'

Johanna nodded again. 'I'll not disgrace you, Mother.' She twisted her mouth into an almost mischievous grin, but Margaret wasn't fooled. Whatever courtesy her daughter afforded Sir Giles, she would be giving it under sufferance.

Johanna came face-to-face with her suitor for the first time at the grand banquet her father had arranged in his honour. Margaret stood with Johanna just behind the arras that screened the foot of the solar staircase from the great manor hall. She could see Richard was in a jovial mood, talking loudly and enthusiastically with his old comrade, who in his turn appeared ebullient, his face animated by the conversation. The room was alive with the banter of friends who had not seen each other for months. Richard was determined to make this a magnificent occasion, both to impress Giles with his hospitality and to drive home its importance to Johanna, and invited friends and acquaintances from many miles around. This was the first proper banquet that the de Bohuns had held since Philip's marriage to Isabella nearly a year ago, and Margaret was delighted at the prospect of having the chance to chat with some of her own long-missed acquaintances. Johanna, on the other hand, seemed anything but excited, for she was trembling at Margaret's side.

'Are you cold?' said Margaret, being deliberately obtuse.

Johanna pulled a face. 'Hardly, Mother. I can feel the heat of the hall fire from here.'

'Then why are you shaking?' She knew well enough, for Johanna had always disliked large gatherings of people with whom she was expected to make polite conversation. And, on this occasion, she would not even be able to retreat to a quiet corner after she had done her duty, but would be the centre of attention, a role that she would loathe. But Margaret was surprised by Johanna's answer.

'I'm about to meet my prospective husband,' said Johanna, lightly. 'Surely it's fitting I should be a little nervous?' She turned to her mother and smiled.

But again Margaret was not fooled by her daughter's attempt at brightness; it was a façade. She did wonder why Johanna had apparently decided to comply with her parents', or rather her father's, wishes, and relinquish her stubbornness, but she had no time to muse upon the matter, for Richard caught her eye and gestured to her that Johanna should make her entrance. Then, raising his voice, he called out for silence.

'May I present to you, Sir Giles, and to this illustrious company, my daughter, the Lady Johanna.' He held out his hand towards her, beckoning her to come forward.

For all her bravado, Johanna faltered. 'Oh, Holy Mother, give me courage,' she whispered.

Margaret pressed her hand against the girl's back and gently pushed her forward and, as Johanna entered the hall, her eyes lowered modestly to the floor, Margaret walked by her side beaming with pleasure. The whole company applauded as Margaret led Johanna towards Sir Giles, to whom the girl dropped a low curtsey, still not lifting her eyes.

Sir Giles reached down to take Johanna's hand and raised her gently to her feet. 'Beautiful,' he whispered, and bringing his lips down to her hand, kissed it lightly.

Then, turning to his old friend, he said, 'Your daughter is a great beauty, Richard. You are to be congratulated.' Margaret suppressed a giggle, thinking it a ridiculous notion that *Richard* deserved any praise for Johanna's appearance. But then a crueller thought came unbidden. For the idea of Johanna being a great beauty was itself absurd, for, like Margaret herself, Johanna was not beautiful at all, but quite plain, with her thin light brown hair and pale, almost colourless, eyes. Yet she had a neat figure and made the best of herself by dressing in the most flattering of colours. She did look almost radiant in her new bright blue cotehardie, embroidered with a thousand tiny silver stars, which was cut low at the neck and tight around her waist and hips to show off her shape, its sleeves fastened tight about her arms with buttons, in the latest fashion.

'Johanna will accompany you to the table, Giles,' said Richard, taking his daughter's hand and placing it firmly on the knight's arm. Then he held out his hand to Margaret and drew her to his side and together they led their guests in a procession towards the laden tables set out along three sides of the great hall.

The banquet and entertainments, at Richard's insistence more lavish even than those for Philip's wedding feast, lasted for hours, and it was with relief that Margaret at length took her leave of the company and retreated to the solar, with Johanna and a few of her closer women acquaintances. As always, Richard would remain in the hall until dawn, drinking and carousing with his cronies, and she was glad to leave them to their pleasure. The women took the opportunity of their husbands' absence for some merry gossip for another hour or so and then they too withdrew to their allotted chambers around the manor, leaving Margaret alone with her daughter.

'I'll go to bed too, Mother,' said Johanna, going towards the door, but Margaret moved quickly to cut off her retreat.

'No, Johanna, stay a while,' she said, keeping her tone light. 'I want to hear what you thought of Sir Giles.'

Johanna visibly shuddered. 'Do I have to, Mother?'

'Your father will ask me, and I must give him an answer.'

Johanna turned away, sighing, and went to sit down again on a stool by the hearth. Margaret fetched her heavy blue cloak and brought another for Johanna, then, wrapping the warm woollen mantle around herself, she sat in her great oak chair and faced her daughter.

'Well?' she said, and, when Johanna remained silent, 'You must have something to say about him? Sir Giles is witty and merry, is he not?'

Johanna nodded feebly, her eyes fixed on her lap. 'Sir Giles does indeed know much about music and poetry. He is more learned and refined than I expected.'

'You did seem to be in most earnest conversation.'

'Yes, he was easy to talk to.'

'And he made you smile. I saw you.'

Johanna looked up. 'As you say, Mother, Sir Giles is a witty man.'

'But throughout your conversation, even when you were smiling, you did not look at him,' said Margaret, trying hard to mask her exasperation.

Johanna did not answer immediately, but when she did her voice was shaking. 'I did look at him, Mother. I looked at him just once, and I couldn't bear to do so again.'

Margaret was aghast. 'Johanna, what a dreadful thing to say.'

Johanna shrugged. 'You wanted to know what I thought of him, Mother. And what I thought was that he is ugly and deformed.'

Margaret was shocked that her daughter could speak so bluntly about such a gentle, noble man, but of course she knew all along that Johanna was bound to recoil against his physical imperfections. In truth, Sir Giles was neither ugly nor deformed. Margaret had first met him when he was young, when he had been as handsome and vigorous as her husband, but his fighting had given him many scars including a long livid sword slash extending from eyebrow to chin. Margaret could look at Giles' face without distaste, considering the wound a mark of honour, but it hardly surprised her that a young girl, whose model of a perfect knight was perhaps her handsome, and so far unscathed, brother, would not share her view.

But it was not only the scar on his face that caused Johanna's revulsion, for war had also deprived Sir Giles of most of his right arm, and the idea of sharing a bed with an incomplete man clearly filled her with horror.

'How could I lie with such a man,' she cried, weeping at the prospect.

Margaret sent a quick silent prayer to Saint Anne to give her a mother's strength to help her daughter make the right decision, though in truth she did not know what the right decision should be. If Johanna dreamed of a suitor, and it was by no means certain that she ever did, the vision would surely not be a hoary old soldier like Sir Giles Fitzpeyne. Indeed Giles would not be Margaret's own choice for her daughter if a younger suitor with the same qualifications of wealth and nobility could be found. But if Margaret were honest with herself, she was pleading Giles' case simply to prevent Johanna from taking the veil.

'But he's rich, with a fine castle—'

'In *Shropshire*,' said Johanna. 'It's so far away from here.' She was trembling, and Margaret remembered how she felt when her marriage to Richard meant she had to leave her home in Cheshire. Even younger than Johanna, she had found it terrifying to travel so far from her parents, but she was at least excited by her marriage to the handsome lord of Meonbridge. Now her mother's heart wanted to tell her daughter she did not have to go so far away from her home, but her wife's head made it clear she had to pursue her husband's wishes.

'You've already found him gentle and cultured,' she said, knowing how important books and music were to her daughter.

'Yes, I know,' said Johanna, quietly, 'but it's not enough.'

'I'm sure he'd make you a good husband.'

'But I don't want to marry *any* man, Mother. I want to go to the priory.'

Margaret's heart ached for her daughter's wretchedness. How cruel it was for parents to force unwanted marriages on their children. It was the way things were done, but just because it was customary did not mean it was kind. She leaned forward and took her daughter's hands and held them, stroking their backs with her thumbs. She looked up into the girl's face, streaked with tears, her eyes red, and sighed deeply. Johanna's face crumpled, as the tears flowed again, and her voice was husky as she pleaded for her freedom.

'Don't make me marry him, Mother, please.'

. . .

215

Margaret lay awake listening to Richard's snoring, wondering whether she had the courage to suggest that he send Giles away. She played out the scene in her mind and the vision of Richard's wrath made her doubt her bravery.

He had come upstairs to their chamber just as she was finally dozing off, and all thoughts of sleep were then banished as he heaved himself clumsily into the bed beside her and straight away slid his hand along her thigh and rammed his rough lips against her tender ones. She almost gagged on the vile tang of his winey breath, but tried to remember him as he was, and allowed him to enter her briefly before he rolled off her and fell noisily asleep.

Unable to find sleep, Margaret slipped quietly from the bed and wrapped her woollen cloak about her. The fire in the hearth was all but out and the huge chamber, with its damp stone walls and floors, was chilly. She could hear rain beating on the glass beyond the shutters and a draught was seeping through a crack in the window frame. She poked at the dying embers and, when a small tongue of fire leapt from one corner of the great bed of ash and charcoal, she hurried to add a small log in the hope that it would catch. Then she lit another candle and sat down in her chair and, recalling Johanna sitting on the stool opposite her, relived their unhappy conversation.

She had not been sitting long when there was a loud knock on the chamber door and Alexander, the seneschal, entered in high agitation. He was surprised to find his mistress up but seemed unwilling to tell her what he had come to say.

'Can I wake his lordship, my lady?' he said. 'I've grievous news.'

'He has only recently come to bed,' said Margaret. 'Can you not tell me?'

Alexander, normally a dignified and resolute man, shuffled from foot to foot. 'I'd fain tell Sir Richard himself, my lady. Truly I would.'

Even in the gloom of the candlelight, she could see his face looked pale and drawn. 'What's wrong, Alexander? Why can you not tell me?' She was horrified to see tears break from his eyes.

'Please, my lady. Let me wake his lordship.'

She nodded and he went over to the bed and gently shook Richard by the shoulder. His master snorted and rolled over but did not wake.

'You'll have to shake him harder than that,' said Margaret. 'Sir Richard sleeps very deeply.'

Alexander looked up to acknowledge Margaret's advice and, clearly anxious to speak urgently to his master, shook him vigorously with both hands and called out his name.

Richard surfaced abruptly with a roar of displeasure. 'Who dares disturb my sleep?'

Alexander's drawn face crumpled into fear, and Margaret was bemused that he should seem so cowed before a master whose storms and tempests he had witnessed and brushed aside for twenty years. She found herself suddenly anxious, fearful of news that Alexander thought fitting only for Richard's ears yet he was nonetheless afraid to tell him.

'It's Alexander, my lord. Can you rise, sir? I've grim news—'

'What news? Tell me!'

Alexander bent down and whispered something in Richard's ear, at which Richard hauled himself awkwardly to his feet, his dishevelled braies slipping to mid-thigh. 'Very well,' he said, grabbing his cloak from the end of the bed to cover his nakedness. He turned to his wife. 'Manor affairs, Margaret.' Then, turning back to Alexander, he gestured that they should go.

It was clear to Margaret that she was being excluded, and she had a notion it was not "manor affairs" at all. 'Why can I not hear the news?' she said again.

Alexander turned and looked at her bleakly, but Richard came across to her, wide awake now and almost affable, and gave her a brief kiss. 'Nothing to concern you, Margaret, I'm sure. I'll be back shortly and we can have breakfast, eh?' His mouth stretched into a smile, but she sensed that he was hiding something. She decided not to press him, wanting to maintain his affability in case, when he returned, she had summoned up the courage to mount a defence of Johanna's plea.

Margaret heard the two men run down the stairs from the solar to the great hall, and went to the top of the staircase thinking perhaps she would be able to hear something of what was being said. She could not make out any of the conversation, but only moments later she heard Richard let out a roar of such anguish that it caused a painful constriction in her heart. Ignoring the indignity of being clad only in her night chemise, she ran pell-mell down the narrow staircase to the hall, desperate to know what it was that had caused her husband such distress. As she appeared at the arras, Alexander ran swiftly forward to try to prevent her coming any further but she put out her arm to hold him off and shook her head at him.

'No, Alexander, I must know what is going on.'

Moments later, she wished she did not know.

In the middle of the hall, Richard was on the floor, prostrate across the almost naked body of a man, which was lying, somewhat twisted, on a crude stretcher that appeared to be made from tree branches and cloaks. Margaret's heart constricted again, and she felt faint. There was no man except one over whose body Richard would prostrate himself in grief. She did not want to acknowledge what she knew must be true, but she had no choice. Fighting her faintness, she held out a hand towards Alexander for support, and he helped her to take the few steps forward and to kneel down by the side of her husband and her son.

An hour later, Margaret and Richard were sitting alone in their chamber, trying to come to terms with the murder of their heir, and to give each other comfort. In disbelief and incomprehension, they repeated to each other over and over the few details they had been given of what was known of Philip's death. He had been found by a travelling pedlar a few miles from Meonbridge, lying among some trees just off the road from Winchester. He was almost naked, wearing only his braies, robbed of his clothes and his money, and apparently also his horse. He was badly beaten, and had a stab wound to his back. Alexander speculated that he must have been attacked by brigands, and for a while this seemed the most likely explanation, though such attacks had been rare around Meonbridge for many years.

'I must go and tell Johanna,' said Margaret after a while, realising that, despite all the uproar, her daughter had not come to investigate. She rose from her chair, and feeling faint again, staggered and had to grasp the chair for support.

'Shall I go?' said Richard, looking up, but she shook her head.

'No, I have to,' said Margaret, dreading it, knowing this might be the worst of all conversations she would ever have with Johanna.

Richard got up and came to her. He put his arms around her and clasped her to his chest. She felt his chest heave with a great sob, and could not stem the flow of her own tears.

'I will summon Robert,' he said. 'He must track those brigands down.'

She nodded, then pulled away. 'I must go to Johanna.'

As Margaret left her chamber, loud wails of lament rose up from the hall below as the news of Philip's murder spread around the manor, and squires, servants and villagers gathered to whisper to each other the dreadful details and join the mourning. Margaret found Johanna in her chamber, at the far end of the main solar, on her knees at her prie-dieu, eyes closed and praying fervently to the Holy Virgin.

Normally Margaret would not disturb her daughter at prayer, but on this occasion she thought she could not wait.

'Johanna?' she said softly, standing just inside the door so as not to intrude too far on her solitude. Johanna either did not hear her or chose not to, for she did not answer, and Margaret had to address her more loudly. Johanna looked up, irritation etched upon her face.

'Mother? You can see I am at prayer. Can I not be left in peace?'

Despite her grief, Margaret was rattled by her daughter's unknowing selfishness, but she tried to maintain an even tone.

'No, Johanna, not now. Can you not hear the uproar going on below?'

Johanna rose to her feet and came over. 'Of course I can, Mother, I am not deaf.'

'Did you not wonder what it was about?'

Johanna laughed scornfully. 'I assumed it was Father and Sir Giles engaged in some riotous knightly game. Of little interest to me.'

Margaret bristled involuntarily. 'If it were a game, I would agree it would not interest you.' Then she laid her hands on her daughter's shoulders and made her look into her face. 'But it is no game.'

When Margaret left Johanna, she wondered whether the girl should be left alone, for the news of her brother's murder caused such a severe reaction she thought Johanna might drop dead from shock and grief. She tried to give her comfort but Johanna would accept none. She sobbed and flailed about the room. Margaret stayed with her for more than an hour but then Johanna asked her to go, to leave her to grieve alone. But, as she left the room, Margaret heard Johanna fasten the lock on her door, and she felt fearful for her daughter's safety.

When she returned to her own chamber, Margaret found that Robert Tyler had responded to Richard's summons and was telling him what he knew.

'Sir Philip was seen going out of the village some days ago with John atte Wode.'

'I thought Philip had gone alone to discuss a deal with some labourers,' said Richard.

Robert shook his head. 'No, sir. He was definitely with John atte Wode.' Then Margaret thought she saw a change in Robert's expression as he continued 'Perhaps Master atte Wode lured him away on some pretext, intending to kill him?'

Richard looked bemused. 'Why would he do that?'

Robert shrugged his shoulders. 'I don't know, Sir Richard. But I do know Sir Philip and the reeve have been seen arguing, so perhaps there was some enmity between them?'

Richard paced up and down for a while. 'So you don't believe brigands murdered my son?'

Robert shook his head. 'No, m'lord, I don't.'

Richard paced some more before coming to stand next to Margaret, resting his hand upon her shoulder. 'Then you must arrest John atte Wode, Master Tyler, and we'll see what he has to say in his defence.'

Margaret did not believe that John atte Wode killed her son. Despite her love for Philip and her grief at his death, she had suffered frequent humiliation as a result of his harsh tongue, and she thought he might have enemies who would wish him dead. But it seemed unlikely that John atte Wode, of all men, would be one of them, even if they had argued. Margaret had always thought that Johanna knew more about her brother, and about what had happened in the months leading up to last Christmas, than she was prepared to admit. She left the girl alone to grieve for a few hours, then later in the morning she went again to Johanna's room and persuaded her to open her door.

Still torn in shreds from her grief, Johanna at first refused to answer Margaret's questions. But then a light seemed to dawn in her mind and her trembling lips straightened into a thin, hard line. 'John atte Wode trespassed into the bower three months ago,' she said. 'He came to ask me about Agnes.'

Margaret was shocked that John, whom she thought considerate and respectful, would do anything so intrusive.

'He threatened me,' said Johanna, looking away.

'Why?'

'He said I must know something.'

'And do you?'

Johanna kept her head turned away. 'No.'

Margaret was confused where this was leading. 'Do you have any idea why John atte Wode would want to murder your brother?'

'Perhaps he thought Philip responsible for Agnes's disappearance and wanted revenge?'

'Why would he think that? You must have told him something.'

Johanna shrugged and refused to say more. Margaret went over and, taking her daughter's shoulders, looked her in the face, but Johanna's expression told her nothing, except that she was closed to any further discussion.

24

John had come home very late last night. Alice had been in bed some hours and was dozing, when she heard the door of the house being heaved open and the sound of someone moving clumsily around in the dark. She got up, lit a candle and, opening the door from the storeroom where she slept, peered into the hall.

'John, is that you?' she said, scarcely imagining it could be anyone else.

The feeble flame of another candle hovered in the dark, then moved slowly towards her, and behind it in the gloom was her son, smiling weakly at her.

'Yes, Ma, it's me. Did you think you had robbers?'

She gave a little laugh of relief. 'Not really. Are you well, son?'

But, as her eyes became accustomed to the dim light, she could see John's clothes were more than usually rumpled and he seemed to be unsteady on his feet. He slumped into the chair by the cold hearth and, leaning forward, put his head into his hands.

Then he looked up and sighed. 'Well enough, Ma, but near falling down with lack of sleep. And my arse's gone dead from sitting so long on that palfrey.'

He'd been away four days and, though he'd not said so, Alice assumed he'd been to Oxford with Sir Philip to follow Agnes's trail.

She was anxious to hear his news but she decided not to press him until he'd rested.

But she could not resist a quick enquiry. 'Was your journey worthwhile?'

'Oh, poor Ma, you must be dying for news. But I don't have much to tell.' He heaved himself to his feet and came to put his arm round her shoulder. He pulled her close, something he'd not done for months. 'I'm sorry, Ma, but I don't have the news you want.'

Alice couldn't stop a great sigh of disappointment, and John hugged her again.

'But I'll tell you what I do know in the morning. I'm too tired now.' He dropped a kiss on the top of her head, and shambled off to climb the ladder to the loft, where Alice thought he must've flopped down on to the straw pallet without removing his boots, for almost instantly he was snoring.

As Alice turned towards her own bed, a little voice called out sleepily.

'Mam, what's going on?'

She went and crouched down by the pallet in the corner of the hall where Matthew slept. 'John's home. That's all.'

'Has he found Agnes?' said the boy, and Alice was once again startled by his awareness.

'What makes you think he were looking for her?'

'I hear things,' said Matthew, yawned, then rolled over to face the wall. Alice pulled the blanket up around his neck and patted his shoulder.

'I'm sure you do,' she said, mostly to herself.

Alice awoke again before dawn. She thought at once of what John might have to tell her and felt a little tightness in her chest. Of course she knew he'd not found Agnes, but she harboured a small hope he might at least have discovered where she'd gone, or perhaps got a little closer to where she was, or to where she'd ended her days. Alice stifled a sob at this last possibility. She didn't want to think it at all, but she knew she must prepare herself in case John suspected that his sister was no longer alive.

In spite of going to bed so late, John was also up at dawn as usual, seemingly refreshed from his sleep and ready for a day in the manor fields, sowing winter wheat and barley. Although he was in a hurry to get off to work, having been so long absent from his duties, he kept his promise of telling Alice what he'd learned on his journey with Sir Philip. Matthew, delighted to have his brother home again, despite him being so gruff and bad-tempered lately, sat close to him at the table while they ate their breakfast, eager, as always, to hear what John had to say.

'We went to Oxford as we'd planned,' said John, 'following something we heard on our last trip. Agnes did go with the mummers, as we'd thought, and they travelled together until Oxford. Someone told us the mummers knew about the mortality and were going north to try to escape it.'

'And did Oxford escape the mortality?' said Alice, hopefully.

But John shook his head gloomily. 'It seems it was even worse than here, but arrived later.'

Alice's hope changed to fear. 'So Agnes might've been there when it arrived?'

'Maybe. We heard she got taken on as a servant at a merchant's house...'

John paused to chew on his bread and take a few gulps of ale.

'...but, when the mortality came, the merchant took his family away to the country.'

'And Agnes?'

John shrugged. 'I suppose the merchant would've moved his whole household, servants and all.'

'Did you find out where to?' said Alice.

But John had to disappoint her. 'We asked around, but no-one knew.' He paused again, then looked rather bleakly at his mother. 'No-one seemed to know if he and his family had survived or not.'

Alice brought her hands up to her face to mask a sob, and she wiped the tears escaping from her eyes with the tips of her fingers. 'So Agnes may be lost,' she said in a whisper.

John reached out and touched her arm. 'She may be, Ma. But I won't give up. We had to come home so Sir Philip could complete his deal with the Winchester labourers, but he said we'd go back to Oxford soon.'

Alice nodded. 'He doesn't think the trail's gone cold, then?'

'No, Ma, he doesn't. We'll keep looking, I promise you.'

Alice looked into John's face. 'Tell me, son, are you and Sir Philip on good terms now?'

He smiled at her and took her hand. 'Ma, when you stumbled across us in the wood, I know you saw us arguing. I was angry with him, and he with me. But we mended our differences because we both want to find Agnes.'

'But why does Sir Philip want to find her?' said Alice, puzzled.

John shrugged. 'He says he thought of her as a sister.'

'And you believe him?'

He shrugged again, then straightened his shoulders. 'I've decided to, Ma, if it's the only way I can have his help.'

Alice smiled. She didn't trust Philip, though she didn't know why. But John was determined to find Agnes and, even if he too mistrusted Philip, he wasn't going to let his doubts get in the way of his resolve.

'Did Sir Philip complete his deal with the labourers?' she said.

John pursed his lips. 'I don't know. He wanted to stop off in Newbury to meet someone, one of his old comrades in arms, he said, so I left him there yesterday morning and came home alone. It's probably all arranged by now. The men'll be turning up in the next couple of days.'

At midday, John burst through the door of the cottage, hot from his labours and ravenously hungry. Alice had cooked a hearty meal for her son, so delighted was she that he seemed to have returned to his old self. His journey to look for Agnes, and perhaps also his pact with Philip, had apparently given him renewed energy and optimism, and his melancholy and petulance of the past few weeks had melted away. He even seemed to have forgotten about his estrangement from Eleanor, which Alice considered a great pity, but knowing Eleanor hadn't yet taken up with any other man, she told herself that perhaps all was not permanently lost.

John's innate ebullience was even helping him to deal with the difficulty he still had encouraging his fellow villeins to undertake their week-work for the manor, and persuading the cottars to knuckle down to their labours.

'I told some of those lazy cottars,' he said, his eyes twinkling, 'that soon Sir Philip's new labourers'll be here, and then they might find themselves out of work.'

'Though they won't, will they, because there's so much work to be done?' said Alice.

John laughed. 'No, but it was good to see the look on their faces.'

Mother and son were laughing, for the first time in many weeks, when there was a loud bang on the door.

'Who can that be, making such a noise?' said Alice, getting to her feet. Opening the door, she was surprised to find the constable, Geoffrey Dyer, standing on the threshold, together with Thomas Rolfe and three other men. The constable bowed briefly to Alice.

'Mistress atte Wode. Is your son John at home?'

Alice said he was, and opened the door wide to let the constable enter. He gestured to the other men to remain where they were, and stepped into the room. John rose from the table and came forward to greet him.

'Master Dyer, is something amiss? Some cottars in trouble?'

Geoffrey Dyer looked grave and shook his head. 'No, master reeve, it's not cottars.' He looked uncomfortable and shuffled his feet uneasily. 'It's you I've come for, John, to take you into custody, at the order of Sir Richard—'

Alice gasped. 'Whatever for, Master Dyer? Why would Sir Richard order John's arrest?'

John looked confused. 'Me? I don't understand.'

'You haven't heard, then?' said the constable.

'I've been out in the fields since just after dawn,' said John. 'Heard what?'

'That Sir Philip de Bohun's been murdered, God rest his soul,' said the constable, crossing himself.

Alice let out a cry, and John's eyes almost started from his head. 'But I was with him only yesterday,' he said, then sank back onto his stool, his face drained of colour. 'When?'

The constable shook his head. 'Who knows? Yesterday evening, perhaps? The body'd not lain out in the open for more than a few hours. He was found this morning by the pedlar, Kit Chapman, on his way into the village.'

'But I left him safe and well yesterday morning–'

'So you may say, master reeve,' said the constable. 'Perhaps you were the last person to see him alive?'

'No, Master Dyer,' said Alice. 'That person was whoever killed Sir Philip. And that was not my son.'

'How can you be so sure, Mistress atte Wode?' said the constable. 'When did he arrive home from his travels?' He fixed Alice with a stare.

She hesitated for a few moments. 'Yesterday evening, Master Dyer... early, I think...' But then she flushed and it was clear the constable thought she was prevaricating.

John stood up. 'Ma doesn't know when I got home, master constable, because it was late in the evening and she was asleep. I left Sir Philip in Newbury in the morning, after we'd travelled from Oxford together. He said he'd some fellow to meet, so I came home alone and didn't see Sir Philip again. And that's the truth.'

At that moment Thomas Rolfe burst into the room, scowling. 'I think we've heard enough, Master Dyer. Our orders from the bailiff are to arrest John atte Wode for the murder of Sir Philip de Bohun. And his orders came direct from Sir Richard. It's not your job, constable, to question the prisoner but to deliver him to the manor gaol.'

It was Geoffrey Dyer's turn to flush, and he threw a black look at Thomas Rolfe, but said nothing. Instead he turned back to John. 'I'm sorry, Master atte Wode, I've no choice but to take you in. You can explain yourself to Sir Richard.'

John protested his innocence once more, but Thomas and one of the other men stepped forward, grabbed his arms roughly and tied them behind his back with a thick rope. Alice stood aghast at the sight of her son being manhandled through the door of their cottage. Geoffrey Dyer turned to her and sighed.

'I'm sorry, Alice,' he said. 'I'll do what I can.' Then he followed the others up the road towards the manor. Alice went out on to the road to watch them go, and was horrified to see a small crowd of her neighbours watching too.

. . .

Alice ran back indoors, determined to go to the manor to plead for John. She took off her apron and put on her clean wimple, and wrapped Stephen's best cloak around her.

'Can I come with ye, Mam?' said Matthew, his eyes wide with fright at what he'd just seen.

'No, son, I'm sorry,' she said. 'I must go alone. You stay and look after the fire.'

She put her arms round him and hugged him close. He sniffed loudly, fighting back tears.

'Don't be afraid, Matt,' she said. 'It must all be a mistake. I'm sure Sir Richard'll understand when I explain.'

Matthew nodded his head against her breast and sniffed again. 'All right, Mam. I'll wait here for you and John to come back.'

Alice took his face in her hands and smiled down at him; she didn't feel at all confident she'd be bringing John home with her. She kissed the boy on top of his head, hugged him again and hurried from the house.

When Alice arrived at the manor, the gatekeeper looked at her suspiciously, as if he'd never seen her before, and she felt unexpectedly apprehensive about her likely reception by the de Bohuns. It occurred to her that, if they believed John had truly murdered Philip, they might not be willing to speak to her at all.

'Master gatekeeper,' she said, 'you know who I am. Will you not let me in?'

The man was old and grizzled, with poor eyesight, but was diligent in his efforts to protect his master and mistress from vagabonds and riffraff. He snorted derisively.

'I know ye well enough, Mistress atte Wode. Your John's been arrested for the vile murder of our gracious knight, God rest his blessed soul.'

'But John didn't kill Philip—' said Alice, but the gatekeeper snorted again.

'You're gonna say that, ain't ye?' he said, sniffing noisily, then wiping the sleeve of his filthy tunic across his leaking nose.

Alice blinked. So was John already assumed to be guilty? And was she somehow guilty too, simply because she was his mother? She was astonished that the atte Wodes' respectability might have tumbled so quickly into dishonour. But surely Margaret wouldn't believe John could commit so foul an act as murder? Alice's heart quaked at the startling possibility that her friend might not want to see her.

The gatekeeper, clearly relishing his power to control who came and went through the manor's gate, continued to thwart Alice's entry for a while longer, but eventually allowed her to pass as far as the gatehouse and sent a runner to fetch one of Lady de Bohun's servants. It was Margaret's maid Agatha who came.

'Sir Richard says her ladyship don't want to see you, Mistress atte Wode,' she said, 'for she's dying of grief.'

'I realise how distraught Lady de Bohun must be,' said Alice. 'But please, Agatha, go and beg her to speak to me for just a few moments, for the sake of our long friendship.'

Agatha wavered but at length agreed. It was so long before she returned, Alice wondered if Richard was protecting Margaret and had forbidden the maid to come back. But eventually Alice saw the girl hurrying towards the gatehouse.

'Sir Richard's gone out,' she said, a little breathless. 'And Lady de Bohun says she'll see you for just a little while.'

Alice followed Agatha through the maze of courtyards and corridors up to Margaret's private chamber. Agatha knocked gently on the door and entered the room, and Alice stepped in behind her, feeling tense.

Margaret rose as Alice came forward, though she didn't hold out her hand in greeting. She made no attempt to hide the grief etched on her face; indeed Alice had never seen Margaret look so dishevelled and distressed, for her wimple was awry, her hair escaping from all sides, and her nose and eyes were red from weeping.

'Leave us, Agatha,' said Margaret. 'I'll call you when Mistress atte Wode is ready to go.'

Agatha nodded and left the room and Margaret gestured to Alice

her Eleanor was still up in the pasture. Alice wasn't sure she had the strength to walk all the way up to Riverdown, but her need for Eleanor's common sense and good judgment was great. But by the time she'd struggled up the steep uphill path and reached the top of the downland, she was exhausted and weepy. Eleanor ran to meet her as Alice's stumbling figure appeared over the crest of the hill, and she caught her as she collapsed into her arms.

'Alice, whatever's the matter?' she cried, helping her to her feet and half-carrying her to Walter's cottage. Walter had already reached the cottage and was readying a stool and pouring a cup of ale. For a while Alice was too tired to speak, but she could see her silence was making Eleanor fretful and fought to calm herself so she could tell her story.

'You won't have heard what's happened?' she said.

Eleanor shook her head. 'No, what?'

Alice let it all out in a rush. 'Sir Philip's been murdered, and the bailiff says John and Philip were seen arguing, and John's been arrested and is in the manor gaol.'

Eleanor sat down suddenly by Alice's side, her eyes wide with shock. 'It's been so peaceful here since I came up at dawn, I can hardly believe there's been such horror down in the village.'

Alice's agitation subsided a little and she related the whole story, of John's arrest and her unhappy visit to the manor. 'I'm afraid for John, for Master Tyler seems so certain that he's guilty and Sir Richard trusts his bailiff's opinion.'

'But John can't have killed Sir Philip,' said Eleanor. 'Even if they had a serious disagreement, John'd never try and resolve it by violence.'

Alice looked relieved. 'You do believe that, don't you, Elly?'

'Of course I do. John's spoken some harsh words, but it's a ridiculous notion he would even threaten Philip, still less kill him.'

'I'm sure Lady de Bohun believes John can't be guilty, and would listen to us. But Sir Richard seems so intent on keeping me from her, I may not be able to speak to her again.'

'Then I must find a way of speaking to her,' said Eleanor. 'Surely Sir Richard'll not stop me from seeing her?'

Alice felt revived simply for having someone to share her worries and she walked back down the hill with much more energy than when she had climbed it, as she and Eleanor discussed how to break through

Sir Richard's barricade. When they reached the point where the track down from Riverdown joined the road, they saw a straggling group of working people emerge from behind the trees that edged the road to Nether Brooking, men, women and children, with a single dilapidated horse-drawn wagon loaded high with bits of furniture, sacks and boxes. Alice whispered to Eleanor that they might be Sir Philip's Winchester labourers, then gave them a friendly greeting.

'Are we near Meonbridge, mistress?' asked one of the men, a tall young man with a rather refined face that seemed ill-suited to a labourer. Alice said they would be there within moments.

'I'm glad to hear that,' said the man, 'for we're tired from our journey.'

'Where are you from?' asked Eleanor, and the answer was not a surprise.

'From Winchester. We've come at the bidding of the steward of Meonbridge, Sir Philip de Bohun. He's offered us land in return for our labour. D'ye happen to know where we'll find him?'

Alice and Eleanor exchanged looks and it was clear one of them would have to tell this unlucky band about the demise of their patron. Alice tacitly accepted the task.

'Master...?' she began.

'Nicholas Ashdown, mistress,' said the man, who clearly spoke for the group.

'Master Ashdown, I'm afraid I've grave news of Sir Philip. He's dead, God rest his soul. Killed by brigands on the road, we believe.'

Cries of horror burst forth from the group, and Nicholas Ashdown crossed himself and uttered a curse against the brigands. 'But, mistress, we spoke to Sir Philip, God rest his soul, only yesterday morning, when he told us he were ready for us to come. When was he murdered?'

'We don't know. Perhaps last night.'

The other men then cursed and the women moaned, and all demanded to know what they were to do, now they'd left their homes and come all this way.

Alice shrugged. 'I'm truly sorry for your trouble, but I can't help you. You'll have to speak to the bailiff. Let's go together to Mistress Rolfe's ale-house, and you can wait there while we send a lad to find him.'

It was hardly surprising that the labourers were disgruntled at their predicament, but Alice didn't feel she could take responsibility for them. She found a group of boys playing on the green and, calling them over, offered a farthing to the one who could be trusted to go and find Master Tyler and bring him to Mistress Rolfe's. She chose Harry Mannering for the task.

'Harry's a good lad,' she said to Nicholas. 'We can rely on him to keep looking till he's found the bailiff.'

Nicholas Ashdown thanked her, but when he asked if she'd stay until the bailiff arrived, Alice shook her head, saying she and Eleanor needed to get home, for they were already late and would be missed.

'In truth,' she said, as she and Eleanor headed off towards the forge, 'I'm so anxious for us to talk about how we're going to get Sir Richard to listen to us, I had to leave those poor folk to shift for themselves.'

As Alice and Eleanor crossed the green, they saw, in the middle, close by the great central oak tree, a huddle of people jostling and laughing. As they came closer, Alice could see that the huddle was surrounding a pedlar selling his wares, the same pedlar, she assumed, whom had found Philip's body.

As they approached the edge of the crowd, a voice suddenly cried out.

'Here's Mistress atte Wode.' It was Ann Webb, and she pointed at Alice.

Alice was surprised, almost offended, to be accosted so bluntly.

'Who wants me?' she said.

'Master Chapman here,' said Ann, beckoning to Alice to come closer. 'He were asking if we knew you.'

'Why?' said Alice, and pushed her way to the front of the crowd. 'What d'you want with me, Master Chapman?'

The pedlar looked up, grimy and toothless, and smiled. ''Cause I've summat for ye, mistress.'

'What on earth d'you mean?' said Alice, irritated and anxious to get away.

The pedlar fished around inside his grubby satchel and pulled out an object that he kept hidden inside his closed fist. Then, with a sense of drama, he held out his fist towards her and slowly uncurled his fingers. Alice looked. Lying on his filthy, deeply lined palm was a circular copper brooch. Her heart missed a beat. It was unremarkable; it could've been any brooch, but she knew it wasn't.

'Where did you get that?' she whispered, hardly daring to believe what she was seeing.

'Young wench gave it me,' he said, 'and made me promise to give it ye.'

'What wench?' said Alice. 'Where?'

'Ah, fine comely wench she were,' said the pedlar, 'with long yellow curls and a smile as pretty as a mermaid's.'

Alice felt faint.

'It were in Chipping Norton I met her,' continued the pedlar, 'and she asked if I ever came this way.'

Alice smiled as she thought how typical it would be of Agnes to trust her precious brooch to a pedlar: it must be hers. She fumbled in her purse for some coins and, placing them on the pedlar's open palm, picked up the brooch with trembling fingers.

'How long ago did you meet the girl?'

The pedlar thought for a moment. 'Not much more 'n a month.'

Alice gulped and tears ran down her cheeks. She felt Eleanor put an arm round her shoulder.

'Oh, Alice,' she whispered, 'she's alive.'

Alice nodded. 'Well, she was a month ago.' Then she turned back to the pedlar.

'Thank you, master pedlar, for bringing me news of my daughter,' she said. 'God bless you.'

25

E leanor was watching the first light of dawn seep through the shutters, thinking about the promise she'd made to Alice, to try and see John today, and somehow arrange a meeting with Lady de Bohun. She wished now she'd not made such a promise, for she was apprehensive about persuading Sir Richard's gaoler to let her see John, and she couldn't imagine what to say to Lady de Bohun. She lay in the gradually receding darkness worrying about the day ahead, when she became aware of the sound of urgent rapping on the outer door. She climbed quickly out of bed and, wrapping a cloak around her shoulders, ran downstairs. Somewhat nervous, she opened the door only a little, but was astonished to find Matilda Fletcher standing outside, dressed only in her night chemise, her uncombed hair wild about her head.

'Matty, what are you doing here at this hour?' said Eleanor.

Matilda was shaking, and her eyes flickered over towards her own house and back again. 'I crept out of the house. I had to come and see you, Elly, to tell you what I know.' Her voice was a whisper.

Eleanor opened the door wider to let Matilda in. 'What is that, Matty?'

'That Philip's been murdered and John atte Wode's been arrested–'

'Yes, I know–'

'But John *didn't* kill Philip, Elly, because I know very well who did!'

Eleanor's hand flew to her mouth, but then she felt afraid. 'Won't Gilbert be angry, when he finds you gone?'

Matilda shook her head, and scowled. 'He's snoring like a pig, dead drunk. He won't wake up for an hour yet, and I don't care if he does. As God's my witness, Elly, I've got to tell you what I know.'

Eleanor led Matilda into the hall, and, gesturing to her to sit down, started to rekindle the fire.

'Don't worry about that, Elly,' said Matilda. 'I don't have much time.' Eleanor nodded and instead hurried over to one of the great oak coffers that stood at the side of the room to find another cloak for her friend, then came and sat down next to her.

'I hardly know where to begin,' said Matilda.

She told Eleanor that last night her father came back with Gilbert, and Thomas Rolfe was with them. It was very late. It seemed they'd been drinking heavily at Ellen Rolfe's, for they were quite unguarded in their talk. Matilda heard her father ask Gilbert where she and the servants were, and Gilbert told him the servants had gone home and she was locked in her room and out of hearing. Gilbert always assumed, she said, that sound didn't travel up through the heavy timber floors of his substantial house, but he didn't realise that, in the floor of Matilda's chamber right above the hall, there were some holes, hidden beneath a small carpet.

Eleanor laughed at this, and her mirth broke Matilda's gloom, so she too smiled broadly.

'Silly, isn't it? But that mischievous beetle has been my salvation, for I've heard many things my husband and father would certainly not have wanted me to hear. And now I can tell you.'

She shivered and pulled Eleanor's cloak tight around her.

'Shall I do the fire after all?' said Eleanor, but Matilda shook her head.

'No, don't, Elly,' she said again. 'I'll be fine. I just need to talk. Though it's hard to tell...'

She hesitated then breathed deeply. 'I'll tell you what happened a few weeks ago.'

Eleanor was startled to hear that Matilda had overheard Robert and Gilbert plotting to get rid of Sir Philip.

'Why would they want to do that?' said Eleanor, her eyes wide.

Matilda grimaced. 'To have their revenge on Philip for getting me with child,' she said, and Eleanor caught her breath at both what Matilda said and the bitterness with which she said it.

'But where's the baby?' she said.

'Lost,' said Matilda promptly, but then seemed to reconsider. 'No, not lost at all, but removed. From me. By Alys Ward.' Tears filled her eyes. 'My father made her do it.'

Eleanor gasped yet again at this shocking revelation. 'But, Matty, that's a sin!'

'*Another* sin,' said Matilda bleakly. And all at once Eleanor realised how innocent she was herself, for in truth she knew about sin only from what she'd heard in sermons. It was true John atte Wode had awoken feelings in her she'd not experienced before. And, although she knew some of her friends had gone into the fields with boys, she never had, and she now thought her lack of knowledge made her still a child.

But Matilda, it seemed, had sinned enough for both of them.

'Did Philip force you then, Matty?' said Eleanor quietly.

Matilda shook her head, and managed a weak smile. 'Not really. You must agree he is – was – a fine-looking man? At dinner up at the manor, he'd look at me across the table with those piercing blue eyes of his.'

'When was this?'

Matilda frowned. 'Oh, I know what you're going to think. It was March. Isabella's baby was growing and she was getting fat. Philip's eyes were wandering, and they wandered my way.'

'Oh, Matty!' said Eleanor, unable to help herself, though she realised at once how insufferably priggish she sounded.

Matilda pulled a face. 'I know, Elly, but I couldn't resist him. We took a tumble together, well, several tumbles. But I quickened straight away.' She grimaced. 'My ill fortune, eh?'

Eleanor wasn't sure if it was ill fortune or the penalty for her sin, but she was soon chastened for her pompous notion when Matilda said her father swore that she and Philip would spend their eternities in Purgatory.

'How did your father find out?'

Matilda scowled. 'My beloved sister found me in the garderobe. It must have been her who told him.'

Eleanor had never much liked Margery, who always seemed somewhat mean-spirited, and envious of her prettier younger sister.

'He decided to punish me,' Matilda continued, wiping away the tears still squeezing from her eyelids, 'by forcing me to marry Gilbert Fletcher.'

'And did Gilbert know about Philip and the baby?'

Matilda gave a bitter laugh. 'Oh, yes, he knew. But he wanted to get his disgusting bony hands on me, and most of all he wanted to ally himself with my father, so he was willing enough to take me as his wife even though I was soiled goods.'

She began to rock back and forth, and Eleanor, thinking she'd pressed her too far, went and put her arm around Matilda's shoulder. Matilda stilled her rocking and leaned her head against Eleanor's shoulder, sobbing quietly.

'But he's taken advantage of my shame ever since,' she went on. 'He beats me... and worse...' She sniffed. 'And I'm with child again.'

'I know,' said Eleanor, miserably recalling Alice telling her of Matilda's melancholy, and regretting that she'd done nothing to try and help her friend.

'I hate him,' said Matilda fiercely, 'and I hate the baby.'

'You mustn't hate an innocent child,' said Eleanor, though it was hardly for her to tell Matilda what to feel.

Matilda nestled her head against the crook of Eleanor's shoulder as she continued with her story, how her husband and father vowed they'd punish Philip for his sins against them by getting rid of him, making it look as if he'd been attacked by brigands.

'So they killed him for revenge?'

Matilda nodded. 'And for hatred. My father's mad with hatred. But also mad with fear of losing his power and rank. When Sir Richard made Philip steward, my father felt his influence was diminished. He was affronted by Sir Richard's decision and resentful of Philip's position. And he was also afraid that Philip's plan to bring in free labourers from Winchester would weaken his authority yet more.'

All this was news to Eleanor. She'd never imagined Robert Tyler, the most powerful man in Meonbridge apart from Sir Richard himself, would feel anything but in complete control.

'Did you know his mother was a cottar, Elly?' said Matilda.

Eleanor gasped. 'I'd no idea.'

Matilda sighed. 'He's so afraid to lose all he's gained, you see.' She sounded almost sympathetic.

So Matilda's long story came back to the events of yesterday evening, as she described how the three men continued drinking, their talk growing louder, as they became exhilarated by what they'd done.

'And what had they done?' said Eleanor.

'Well, it was actually what Thomas Rolfe had done. The evening before last he waylaid Philip in the wood, pretending to be a highwayman, beaten him and robbed him of his money and clothes, then stabbed him to death, leaving him just in his braies.'

Suddenly there was a hammering on the door, and Eleanor extricated herself from Matilda and ran to see who it was. Hawisa was on the threshold, hopping agitatedly from foot to foot. She called out to Matilda.

'Oh, mistress, come home quick!'

Matilda got to her feet in alarm. 'How d'you know I was here, Hawisa?'

'I heard you leave the house. But, mistress, master's awake and shouting for you. I sent Nathan up to stall 'im, but you must come home quickly now!'

Matilda threw a look of fear and despair at Eleanor. 'Remember what I've told you, Elly. You won't keep it to yourself?'

As Eleanor suddenly understood what Matilda was expecting of her, she felt sick with panic, but shook her head. 'I won't, Matty,' she said, 'I understand.' She ran to Matilda and hugged her before Hawisa grabbed her mistress's hand and dragged her away. Eleanor shut the door, then went and sank onto her father's favourite three-legged stool, her elbows on the table in front of her, her hands covering her face. She felt afraid, for Matilda and for herself. Though she knew that, for Matilda's sake, and for John's and Alice's, she must be brave. Matilda's story could not remain within the walls of this house.

. . .

Only a short while later, Eleanor was knocking on Alice's door. It was Matthew who opened it, bleary-eyed and mostly still asleep. He didn't speak but simply let her in.

'Where's your mam, Matthew?' said Eleanor, and he pointed to the cross-passage door that led to the croft garden at the back of the house.

'Feeding the hens,' he mumbled, then drifted back to his pallet to lie down again.

Eleanor rushed out into the garden, down to where Alice kept her flock. As she approached, Alice looked up in surprise.

'You're early,' she said, a welcoming smile on her face, but the smile faded as she saw Eleanor's agitation.

'What's amiss, Elly?'

Eleanor threw up her arms in bewilderment and anxiety. 'Oh, Alice, you won't believe what I've to tell you. Can you come indoors?'

Alice nodded. 'Go in, and I'll be there in a few moments.'

In the cottage, Eleanor busied herself with tending to Alice's fire, but she felt agitated and scared and was longing to share Matilda's distressing story and get Alice's advice on what to do.

When Alice returned with a basket of eggs, she made her sit down and calm herself, but Eleanor found it impossible not to just blurt out the whole account, so anxious was she to unburden herself of the awful news.

When Eleanor finished telling the story, Alice seemed not to know whether to be shocked or relieved.

'I should just be horrified,' she said.

'But I suppose you're also relieved to know John didn't kill Philip?' said Eleanor.

Alice nodded slowly. 'Yes, of course. But will Sir Richard believe Matilda's story? Or will he just think it's the ravings of an abused, resentful wife?'

Eleanor was shocked that Alice could be so harsh about Matilda, but Alice denied she was being unkind.

'Of course I'm sorry for Matilda's plight,' she said. 'She's been brutally treated. But Sir Richard trusts his bailiff, who'll surely deny his daughter's story. How then will Sir Richard regard poor Matilda?'

Eleanor was quiet for a while. 'You may be right, but if I take the story to Lady de Bohun, perhaps she will listen?' she said at last.

Alice agreed. 'I'm certain Margaret doesn't trust Robert Tyler, even if Sir Richard does. She's already said how unhappy Matilda looked when she dined at the manor, so she might be very willing to listen to her story. And, if she listens, she might then be able to persuade Sir Richard to free John.'

Eleanor's heart went out to Alice, so wise and brave despite her distress. For Eleanor herself, she didn't know what to think about John. She thought him simply a good man, who she was certain could never commit a murder. She realised his release from gaol might be in her power to arrange. She was afraid of going to the manor but, if she could steel herself, it was not only John she might save but Matilda too.

Eleanor agreed with Alice that she'd go to see Lady de Bohun before dinner. She chided herself for what she knew was procrastination, but she wanted to compose herself for what she thought would be a very difficult conversation by going for a walk up to Riverdown and letting the wind blow through her hair.

By the time Eleanor left her house, folk were bustling about, taking grain to the mill and flour to the baker, fetching water from the well, and buying food or exchanging goods at the market on the green. The news of Philip's murder was on everyone's eager lips and several people waylaid her, asking what she knew or what she thought. But she just smiled grimly, saying she was too busy to gossip, and strode on briskly towards the cottars' district, then on to Riverdown. The track up the hill towards the down was open and exposed to the weather, which today was blustery, and Eleanor struggled to keep her cloak from billowing out. But she enjoyed the sensation of her hair being blown about by the swirling gusts, and she often thought how much she'd miss it if she married and no longer had a maiden's freedom to wear her hair uncovered.

At the top of the track, quite close to where it opened out on to the pasture, the trail cut through a small but dense copse of young beeches. The trees were swaying in the breeze, and their leaves, brown now and crisp, but still clinging to the branches, rustled and crackled around her ears. Eleanor hurried forward, eager to reach the down where the ordinariness of her shepherd would calm her. As she hurried, from the corner of her eye she sensed movement among the trees, yet when she turned to look, she saw nothing.

But then she heard a scuffle behind her, and all of a sudden her head was enveloped in a great cloth, a cloak perhaps, and it was being pulled tight about her face, and she was struggling to breathe. Eleanor, terrified by what had come at her so violently, tried to cry out, but her mouth was sealed by the pressing fabric. Her attacker grunted as he threw her to the ground upon her back. Eleanor screamed in her head as he lifted her skirt and flung it up towards her waist, exposing her naked thighs. Understanding with horror what the man was about to do, she summoned all her strength and flailed her arms around, striking him so hard across the head that he lost his grip on her for long enough for her to get to her feet and rip the suffocating cloak from her face.

She gasped when she saw her attacker. 'Master Fletcher!' she cried. 'Why...?'

His nose was bleeding from the blow, and he was trying to staunch the flow. 'You know well enough, mistress,' he said, bitterly. 'You might think you're going to spread my bitch-wife's lies around the village, but you're not.'

He lunged at her and pushed her to the ground again, his hands around her neck. Eleanor now realised neither rape nor a beating was Gilbert's plan, and she mustered her strength again in order to defend herself. As he leaned over her, trying to bear down on her neck, she brought a knee up sharply and caught him so hard between his legs that his hands flew from her throat as he fell back in pain. But he wasn't giving up and grabbed at her yet again, though this time Eleanor had the presence of mind to shout for help. She knew Walter was not far away, which Gilbert probably didn't realise, and she screamed at the top of her voice, just before Gilbert fixed his bony fingers around her neck again and began to squeeze the life out of her. She continued to struggle against him, willing Walter to have heard her.

Then suddenly the shepherd was there, falling heavily upon Gilbert's back, thrashing and punching him with a force she found hard to believe, yet Gilbert took the blows and held his grip fast upon her neck. But then he let out a blood-curdling yell as Walter plunged the points of his sheep shears into the back of Gilbert's thigh, ramming them deep into the flesh. Eleanor heard the grind of the shears meeting the bone and Gilbert at last let go of her neck and rolled over in agony. Walter, despite his own injured leg, kicked at Gilbert's wounded thigh. Gilbert howled in pain, but somehow struggled to his feet and waddled off into the trees.

'Shall I go after him, mistress?' said Walter, ready to run, but Eleanor shook her head.

'Let him go,' she said, her voice hoarse. 'His actions clearly implicate him in Philip's murder. I'll go and see Lady de Bohun this afternoon, as I'd planned.' Then she smiled thinly. 'And now I've even more to tell her.'

They watched as Gilbert staggered back down the hill, trailing his leg, the wound left by the shears bleeding profusely.

'I wonder if he'll go back to his house?' said Walter, running his fingers through his hair. 'You'd best be careful when you go home.'

Eleanor nodded. Then, as the moment of drama passed, she realised he was shaking, the colour drained from his face. She gestured to him to sit down and he almost collapsed onto the ground, throwing aside his bloodied shears. He went very quiet, sitting with his head held between his hands, still glistening red with Gilbert's blood.

Eleanor sat down too, and thus they remained for a time, not speaking. She looked across at Walter, and saw a different man from her lowly shepherd.

'You saved my life,' she said at length.

Walter looked up and smiled weakly, his trembling gradually easing. 'Yes, mistress, I did, as you once saved mine.'

'I was near to death if you'd not come,' said Eleanor, smiling back. 'As once was I.'

She reached out and touched Walter's arm. 'You were very brave.'

But he shook his head. 'I couldn't let that scoundrel hurt you.' Then he leaned forward and, gently taking Eleanor's hand, clasped it between his own.

2 6

Richard was staring out of the window of their chamber, at the long, broad panorama of the manor's estate. He stood for a while, looking, then moved to another window, which gave a view out across the village. Then he turned to his wife, who was sitting on the bed, still in her night chemise, exhausted from another night-long sleepless vigil and disinclined to greet the day.

'No-one's working in the fields,' he said at length. 'They should be sowing winter wheat.' The tone of his voice was melancholy more than angry.

Margaret looked up at her husband. His face was grey and drawn. She thought he also had slept little.

'Perhaps the villeins have laid down their tools as a mark of respect to Philip?' she said, though she thought it unlikely they would have done any such thing.

Richard came and sat next to her. He took her hand and, lifting it his lips, kissed it lightly. 'Perhaps you are right, my dear,' he said, and forced a thin smile.

Hours later, Margaret had not left her chamber. Richard had gone out without bothering with breakfast, not saying where he was going, though Alexander later answered her enquiry by saying he had ordered his mount and ridden alone out of the manor gate towards the forest. Alexander also ventured to tell her that Sir Richard had given him strict orders that she was to receive no visitors today. Margaret resented Richard's protection of her; she understood he wanted to save her from distress and was touched by his solicitude, but she felt like a captive. She wanted to talk, but Richard had retreated into his own counsel. She forced herself to dress, then sat in front of her mirror to brush her hair. The woman looking back at her had aged since yesterday: her face, like Richard's, was ashen and pinched, and she felt too weary to do more than wind her greying hair into a knot and tuck it inside a silver snood.

Margaret had deepened Richard's melancholy, and her own, with her decision to broach the issue of Johanna's determination to take the veil. It was hardly the time to discuss the loss of a second child when they were still reeling from the loss of the first. But she felt she could no longer avoid the conversation.

Richard did not understand why his daughter would want to lock herself away, as he put it, and give up the chance of making a good marriage.

'She will surely make a most devout nun,' said Margaret, trying to sound optimistic, 'and make a great success of it, perhaps even becoming prioress?'

But Richard was entirely unconvinced of the virtue of Johanna's choice, and although he could, of course, simply have refused to allow it, he seemed too debilitated by the chaos that was still going on around him to put up much of a fight.

Margaret too, despite her decision to take her daughter's part, was deeply saddened by Johanna's longing to leave the world, and them, for a life of seclusion and solitude. It seemed such a waste, but of course Johanna did not see it that way.

Richard returned for an early dinner, which they ate alone in a gloomy silence. After he had picked at his food for a while and drunk several cups of wine, Richard rose and again went over to the window. Suddenly his mood changed to anger, as he declared that still no-one had appeared in the fields. Then he marched over to the door to throw it open and shout for Alexander, demanding he find out what was going on. It was not long before Alexander returned to the chamber, his face plainly wearing the apprehension with which he was about to relate his news.

'Your lordship,' he said. 'I'd fain not tell you what I've learned—'

Richard threw his hands in the air and demanded to be told.

'No-one's working, sir, because they're angry that their reeve has been arrested,' said Alexander. 'And without Master atte Wode, there's no-one to organise the work.'

Richard let out an explosive roar. 'Why isn't the bailiff organising it?'

Alexander shrugged. 'Master Tyler's nowhere to be found, m'lord.'

Richard rolled his eyes and demanded that Alexander find the bailiff and send him here. The seneschal bowed deeply and withdrew.

Richard paced the floor, and Margaret wearily rose to her feet and went over to try to calm him.

'I can understand the villeins and cottars might want to defend John,' she said. 'In truth, Richard, I'm doubtful that he, of all men, could have murdered Philip.'

But her words were not what her husband wished to hear, and he exploded once again.

'Are you denying Robert's testimony?'

She nodded. 'John's guilt is merely Master Tyler's opinion. It is not a fact.'

Richard looked up at her and narrowed his eyes.

'As you know, Richard,' she went on, 'I do not trust Master Tyler...'

Richard stared at her, as if he had heard this from her for the first time. But he continued to say nothing.

'Perhaps when Alexander finds the bailiff,' she went on, 'you'd better ask him what's happening on the manor, and why he seems to be losing his authority.'

Richard was unprepared to wait for Alexander to return with Robert Tyler. After pacing up and down the chamber for a while, he uttered a few curses and left the room, ostensibly to go in search of his errant, and perhaps erring, bailiff. Moments later Agatha entered the room to say that Mistress Titherige was at the manor gate asking to see her ladyship. Margaret felt childishly pleased to have a visitor whom neither Richard nor Alexander could forbid entry, but nonetheless she told Agatha to bring Eleanor to her private garden so they could talk without fear of discovery.

When Eleanor approached with Agatha, Margaret dismissed her maid and led Eleanor to a seat in the physic garden.

'What is it you have to tell me?' said Margaret.

Eleanor shook her head slowly. 'Oh, my lady, I hardly believe it myself, but what happened to me a short while ago has convinced me it must be true.' She spoke quietly, her voice hoarse.

'What happened?'

For reply, Eleanor drew back her hood, which she had been holding close around her head, pulling it away from her neck to reveal a livid bruise on either side of her throat.

Margaret gasped. 'My dear, how did you get those?'

Eleanor looked directly into Margaret's face. 'Gilbert Fletcher tried to kill me.'

Margaret's eyes opened wider. 'Why would he do that?'

'To stop me talking to you, or to anyone. For what I'm about to tell you, my lady, I got from Gilbert's wife Matilda. She was a close friend of mine, and she used to be so lively and gay. I've been so worried to see how much she's faded since she married Master Fletcher.'

Margaret nodded. 'Yes, I have noticed too how unhappy she looks. Thinner and drawn, and, as you say, quite changed from the spirited girl she used to be.'

'I think Gilbert beats her...' said Eleanor, then stopped. 'But let me tell you Matilda's story, Lady de Bohun, as she bade me do.'

As the story unfolded, Margaret was shocked, but in truth not now surprised, to hear that Robert Tyler had plotted to kill Philip, and got his henchman Thomas Rolfe to do the deed.

'But why?' she said. 'Why would Robert want to kill the man he had so loved as a boy?' Despite her growing distrust of Robert, Margaret had not imagined he could have turned against her son so viciously.

Eleanor bit her lip. 'I think the reasons may be complicated. And I hesitate to tell you these things, my lady, when I know you'll find them so distressing.'

But Margaret put out a hand and laid it on Eleanor's arm. 'Go ahead, my dear. The greatest pain has passed. Now, I just want to know the truth.' She smiled encouragingly at Eleanor, who gave a weak smile in return.

'Matilda said that, at first, it was because Master Tyler resented Sir Philip being made steward and usurping some of his authority. Then more recently he thought that Philip's plan to bring in labourers from Winchester would undermine his influence even more.'

She paused, and Margaret could see dread in Eleanor's eyes. 'Go on.'

Eleanor swallowed a gulp. 'But the real reason,' she said, her voice hushed, 'was his hatred of Sir Philip for getting Matilda with child—'

Margaret gasped. 'With child? So the child she is carrying is Philip's?'

Eleanor shook her head. 'Sadly not. That child is Gilbert's. Philip's child was...' she hesitated, '...taken.'

Margaret's eyes grew wider still with horror. 'Taken? By whom?'

Eleanor hesitated again and looked up at Margaret with solemn eyes. 'I cannot say, my lady.'

Margaret saw that Eleanor was reluctant to accuse a village woman, whoever she was, and did not press her. 'How long had Matilda carried Philip's child?' she said instead.

'She thought about two months,' said Eleanor, and Margaret nodded.

The two women sat in silence for a few moments, Margaret folding her hand over Eleanor's and squeezing it gently.

'So Robert wanted revenge against Philip for getting his daughter with child?' she said at length.

'It seems so,' said Eleanor, 'then he forced Matilda to marry Gilbert, perhaps knowing, and not caring, that he would mistreat her. It seems unspeakably cruel.'

Margaret looked away into the distance, across the garden and the manor fields towards a dense patch of woodland on the horizon. Tears came to her eyes and she was not ashamed to acknowledge them and wipe them away.

'Eleanor, I have known Robert Tyler for twenty years. He was always ambitious but a good man, and so helpful to me when Richard was away. It seems that somehow he has become corrupted by the power that he gained.'

'And also filled with hatred and revenge. I wonder when that began?'

'Perhaps when Philip returned? The boy he had raised and tutored went away and came back, not just a man, but a knight who had won honours on the battlefield. Richard made Philip steward to give him a role on the manor. I am sure he gave no thought to what Robert's view of it might be. It would not have occurred to him to think that Robert would object.'

They sat quietly again, both watching the sun begin to drop behind the distant woodland. Then Margaret let out a deep sigh.

'Eleanor,' she said, 'did Matilda tell you how Philip was killed and how he was found?'

Eleanor gulped. 'Yes,' she whispered, 'but I'd fain not tell you, my lady, for it will surely break your heart to hear it.'

Margaret nodded. 'It will but, if what Matilda said accords with what I know, I'll be the more convinced of her story's truth.'

So when Eleanor told her that Philip had apparently been beaten and stabbed, and stripped of his clothes, Margaret could not stop herself from weeping as the image of the broken, dishonoured body of her son lay once more before her eyes.

'Yes, that is what we know,' she whispered.

Eleanor seemed to think for a moment. 'I suppose Matilda could've heard that from her father?'

'She could have, but I'm not convinced that Matilda would invent the whole story, Eleanor. She is a most unhappy girl, perhaps seeking revenge herself against her husband and her father, but I don't believe she's capable of thinking up that plot.'

'I agree, my lady. Matilda's old self might've done, but her spirit's broken. Alice has said the same. I'm sure Matilda does want revenge, but only by revealing the truth. Perhaps it's spirit enough to denounce your husband and father?'

Margaret nodded. She regarded Eleanor for a moment: a young woman whose comfortable upbringing would have led her to imagine a future of ease and wealth, but who was having to make a life for herself, to determine her own future. And now she was taking up the cudgel for her friend, risking her own life to see justice done. How could she do other than support the girl's efforts?

'So it's clear John atte Wode is not guilty,' she said. 'You must be relieved about that, my dear?' A slight twinkle gleamed in her eyes.

But, to her surprise, Eleanor shook her head. 'Of course I'm glad to be reassured that Master atte Wode's not a murderer, though I never thought he could be. But...' she looked away as she hesitated, '...he and I are estranged, Lady de Bohun.'

Margaret was shocked. 'Oh, my dear, but I thought...'

'I know,' said Eleanor, and a bleakness crossed her face. 'But John became very withdrawn and ill tempered. Alice thought it was because of his disagreement with Sir Philip about what happened to Agnes.'

Margaret nodded. 'Yes, she told me. But how did you and John become estranged?'

'One day, during harvest, the day of Bart Coupar's accident, I tried to speak to John but somehow made him angry and we exchanged such harsh words I told him our friendship was at an end.' Eleanor sighed heavily. 'We haven't really spoken since.'

Margaret wondered for a few moments if what she was about to say was tactless. 'I'd been going to suggest that you might like to see him,' she said, 'but perhaps after all you'd rather not?'

Eleanor looked up, the melancholy passing from her face. 'Oh, no, my lady, I'd like to see him. He must be so miserable and worried, locked up down there.'

'He must indeed,' said Margaret, smiling. 'I'll arrange for you to visit.'

'Can I tell him Matilda's story, d'you think?' said Eleanor.

Margaret considered for a moment. 'Yes, I think so. But we should be careful, for it is Sir Richard we must convince of its truth. And I think he'll not readily accept that Robert Tyler murdered his son.'

Eleanor looked suddenly afraid but Margaret patted her hand. 'Don't worry, my dear, I'm sure we can persuade him.' And she forced a sunny smile.

Margaret suggested that, before Eleanor visited John, they should try and speak to Richard. They found him in the hall, looking distracted and restless. As the two women entered from the courtyard, they could see he was involved in a three-way conversation with Ralph Ward and another man. Margaret gestured to Eleanor that they should withdraw to one side of the hall: she wanted to overhear the conversation but not appear to be intruding.

It seemed that Ralph had come to explain why the villagers had laid down their tools. No work would be done in the manor fields, he said, until the reeve was freed, for it was obvious to anyone that an honest man like John atte Wode could never kill a man, no matter what the provocation.

'Of course the cottars're still up in arms about their wages,' he went on. 'And that's been worsened by these Winchester folk.' He gestured towards the other man, but also shot him a rueful grin.

The man removed his hat and bowed slightly, then announced himself as Nicholas Ashdown, spokesman for the group of Winchester labourers come to Meonbridge by agreement with Sir Philip de Bohun. He looked uncomfortable, nervously passing the brim of his hat through his hands.

Eleanor gave a little gasp. 'That's the man Alice and I met on the road,' she whispered.

'He doesn't look much like a labourer,' said Margaret, thinking his skin as pale and fresh as a maid's.

Eleanor nodded, a delicate blush reddening her cheek. 'No, indeed, m'lady. Alice and me thought the same.'

Nicholas continued. 'It's not our intent to take work from the Meonbridge folk, sir, but nor do we want to leave. Sir Philip said you needed more labour, promising us land and a fair wage if we agreed to come.'

Richard was standing with his back towards Margaret, so she could not see the expression on his face. But from his stance he appeared to be listening to the men, and not unsympathetically, for he was not shouting or remonstrating with them but nodding and making conciliatory noises. She held her breath in anticipation that, finally, he was understanding their points of view and was about to offer a solution to their demands. But, if he was, the moment was lost, as Robert Tyler burst into the hall like a chilly gust of late autumn wind. Richard immediately turned to hail him, so Margaret could now see his face, and she was disappointed to see he looked relieved at the arrival of his bailiff. To the obvious bewilderment of the two men who had come to seek his counsel, Richard straight away shouted to one of his squires and announced that he was going hunting.

Margaret could not believe her husband was simply going to walk out and leave the two men's problems hanging in the air. She started forward, annoyed, about to say how inappropriate it was for Richard to hunt when he had the labourers' concerns to resolve, as well as Philip's murder. But she immediately thought better of her impetuosity and held back, for the very last thing she wanted to do was antagonise her husband. As he swept from the room, Richard's face bore the look of a boy let out to play.

Margaret took Eleanor's hand and together they followed Richard out into the courtyard. They stood watching while his squire brought over his fine chestnut hunter and his falconer came out with his elegant little hawk. Richard was mounting the horse when he noticed the women watching and, gently kicking the horse's flanks, he turned and came over to where they stood.

'You disapprove, Margaret,' he said, grinning broadly. 'You think I should stay here and give in to those fellows' demands.'

Margaret chose to smile back at him. 'You are right, my lord. You should give them an answer. But it is not for me to disapprove.'

'Ha!' he said, throwing his head back in a loud guffaw. 'I can see the disapproval on your face, madam. But, no matter. I will hunt, and Master Tyler will deal with the cottars.'

Then he leaned right over and, clasping the back of her head, he pulled her towards him and kissed her hard upon her lips. Margaret involuntarily recoiled from this public display and Richard drew back, looking affronted. He kicked the horse again and made to gallop off, but she swiftly grasped the reins to stay the animal, and forced herself to smile up at him.

'Enjoy your hunting, Richard,' she said. 'I am sure Robert will carry out your wishes in the matter of the cottars.'

He nodded and smiled back. 'I warrant it,' he said, gathering the reins, then kicked yet again and was off at a gallop through the manor gates, his squire and his falconer in close pursuit.

. . .

The two women returned to the hall, where an argument appeared to be in progress. There was no one else about and Robert seemed not to have noticed that they had returned, so Margaret gestured to Eleanor that they should move out of Robert's line of sight. She was determined to witness how the bailiff handled what seemed to be developing into an awkward encounter.

'But Sir Richard seemed willing enough to honour his son's agreement,' said Nicholas, and Ralph nodded in support.

Robert's face was dark, his stance stiff. 'But I warrant he didn't actually confirm that your contract stood?' he said.

Nicholas shuffled a little from foot to foot, nodding uncomfortably, but did not reply.

'So the agreement doesn't stand,' said Robert, a note of victory in his voice, 'until Sir Richard's signed it.'

Nicholas looked troubled. 'And when'll that be, master bailiff?'

The bailiff snarled. 'Our lord has just found his son murdered. Don't you imagine he's things on his mind other than the mewlings of a bunch of labourers?'

Nicholas hung his head, looking defeated. Margaret could understand the man might find it hard to argue against a man like Robert Tyler, whose very expression these days made many a strong man quake.

But then Ralph stepped forward. 'And what about the cottars, master bailiff? We're sorry for what's happened to Sir Philip, but it don't alter the situation about their wages. And now these folk from Winchester are come, with offers of land—'

Robert interrupted. 'Which, as you just heard, Master Ward, hasn't been agreed.'

Nicholas seemed to recover his courage a little. 'So what're we supposed to do, master bailiff?'

The bailiff's mouth stretched into a sneer of contempt. 'I care not. You can please yourselves. Stay in your tents on the green until Sir Richard's ready, or go back to wherever it is you came from.'

'But there's so much to be done here, master bailiff,' said Ralph, 'we surely need all the labour we can get—'

'And we want to work—' added Nicholas.

'Though with the reeve in gaol,' continued Ralph, 'there's no-one to organise it.'

Robert turned on him. 'If you weren't such a pack of greedy, idle sluggards,' he said, his voice rising, 'you'd get on with the work with or without someone else to tell you what to do.'

Ralph looked affronted at this outburst. 'Why would we,' he said, sneering, 'if you're not willing to pay the wages?'

Robert was warming to the argument. 'You *are* paid wages,' he cried. 'Good wages–'

'But not good enough. And why didn't Sir Philip offer *us* some land, if he was prepared to offer it to strangers?' He quickly glanced at Nicholas and shrugged.

Margaret could see that Nicholas Ashdown was taken aback by this mounting dispute. He turned around, as if to disassociate himself from the argument, and noticed her looking at him. She threw him a remorseful grin but, clearly embarrassed, he looked away again, a slight flush rising on his pale skin.

Robert reacted strongly to Ralph's taunt about the land. 'Because most of you are indolent wastrels, who idle your time away at Mistress Rolfe's and wouldn't know a harrow from a plough.'

Ralph looked increasingly irritated by the bailiff's insults, and his face grew surly. Margaret knew he was a moderate God-fearing man, who commonly resisted the temptation of anger. Robert on the other hand, she mused, seemed to make little effort these days to deny the demon Wrath.

Ralph protested to the bailiff that he was being unfair in his criticism of the cottars, who were willing enough to work, even if they did enjoy the fruits of their labour when they could afford to.

But now Robert allowed his demon to get the better of him. 'And *what* fruits!' he cried. 'Not just the delights of the ale-house, eh, Master Ward?'

Ralph flushed red. 'What're you getting at, Master Tyler?' All deference had gone from his voice.

'Fornication,' said Robert, 'is what I'm getting at, Master Ward.'

Eleanor gasped by Margaret's side. 'How dare he say that,' she said, in a shocked whisper.

'As soon as any one of you finds a tasty widow's to be had, you tumble her into bed. Isn't that right, Master Ward?'

Ralph took a step towards the bailiff and raised his hand, but Nicholas lunged forward and pulled his fellow labourer back. 'No, Ralph, don't.'

Robert seemed either not to notice Ralph's increasing temper, or did not care, for he simply continued with his accusations, as if he had forgotten he was in a public place.

'You claimed Bart Coupar was your friend, and yet you think nothing of fornicating with his wife.' His voice was bitter. 'But of course her lazy wastrel of a husband was undoubtedly a lecher as well as a scoundrel, and is surely already rotting in hell as he deserves.' He paused, leaving a silence hanging in the air that neither of the other men could fill, standing as they were with mouths agape at the venom issuing forth from this pillar of the community. But then, as if he was addressing no-one but himself, Robert spoke again, shaking his head. 'Emma Coupar, and Meonbridge, are better off without him.'

Margaret was stunned. Her mind was racing, and it was clear Eleanor's was too, for the girl touched her on the arm. 'It *was* him, my lady,' she said, barely letting the words pass her lips. 'He did kill Bart Coupar!'

Margaret heard her and knew she was right, though Robert's words were hardly a confession. She did not know what she was going to do or say but instinct made her rush towards the three men. As she did so, Robert Tyler seemed to recover from his trance and saw her approaching. A look of wild panic crossed his face and, without a word, he moved swiftly towards the outer door, too fast for Margaret to intercept him. By the time she reached the door, he was marching at speed in the direction of the manor gate.

'Shall I go after him, m'lady?' said Ralph, scratching at his head.

'I think not, Master Ward,' said Margaret. 'I am sure Sir Richard will deal with Master Tyler later.' But she was as bemused as Ralph about what had just happened. 'What were his words?' she said. 'That Emma and Meonbridge were *better off* without Bart Coupar? Did he really say that?'

Ralph nodded. 'He did, m'lady, though I can scarce believe it.'

Eleanor joined them. 'Can he really have condemned himself

without realising it? For a man such as Robert Tyler that's also hard to credit.'

Moments passed as they all mused upon what they had just witnessed.

Then Margaret gave herself a little shake, breathed in deeply and took Eleanor's hand. 'Come, my dear. Let us visit Master atte Wode. I think perhaps you have even more good news to tell him.'

27

Despite her deep anxiety about John, Alice felt herself sustained by the thought that Agnes might still be alive. She'd not told young Matthew about the brooch she'd bought from the pedlar, so as not to raise the boy's hopes. But she longed to be able to tell John, to ask him if he thought the pedlar's story could be true. Alice had no idea if the place called Chipping Norton was anywhere near Oxford but, if it was, and if the merchant Agnes worked for did have his country house there, then perhaps... She had to force herself to stop musing on what might, or might not, be.

Alice had been restless all day, eagerly awaiting a visit from Eleanor, hoping to hear that she'd seen John. She stayed at home all afternoon, expecting her to come. As darkness began to fall, hardly able to concentrate on anything until she had news of John, she could do little more than cut some bread and a small piece of cheese for supper for herself and Matthew. She picked at her share distractedly, yet still there was no Eleanor. When at last there was a knock on the door, Matthew had gone to bed and Alice was dozing in the chair by the side of a dying fire. At the sound of the rap, Alice started awake, disorientated. She'd been dreaming of Agnes and John as children, when John, four years older than his sister, had been eager to protect her from the rough and tumble of village life. But in the dream Agnes appeared as a bright vision, shining like an angel. As she emerged from sleep, the vision left her in a perplexing fog, fearful that Agnes must be dead, but glad that, if she was, she must already be in Paradise. Moments later, the shining image of Agnes melted away, the fog lifted, and Alice realised that someone was knocking on the door.

'I'm sorry it's so late, Alice,' said Eleanor. 'But it's been a strange day, and so much has happened.'

Alice ushered the girl inside. 'Have you seen John?' she asked, unable to keep the anxiety from her voice.

Eleanor smiled and touched Alice's arm. 'Yes, and I've spoken to Lady de Bohun. Oh, Alice, I've so much to tell you.'

'Please tell me about John first,' said Alice, stoking the fire and lighting another candle. 'I'm so anxious to know how he is.'

'Of course you are, Alice,' said Eleanor, taking a stool as Alice sat back in her chair.

It was only then that Alice realised how hoarse Eleanor's voice was. She frowned. 'Do you have a quinsy?' she asked, but Eleanor shook her head.

'Though my throat's very sore. I'll tell you why in a moment. But first let me tell you about John.'

She explained how Lady de Bohun had taken her down to the gaol, built below the floor of the old manor keep, and ordered the gaoler to open the door and let them both in.

'Both?' said Alice, surprised.

Eleanor nodded. 'Lady de Bohun came right down into the gaol with me. She wanted to reassure herself that John wasn't suffering too badly. But once she'd seen him, she left me to speak to him alone.' Eleanor gave a croaky little laugh. 'The gaoler was quite uneasy about that, but Lady de Bohun was very stern with him.'

'And how was John?'

'Well enough. The cell was dark and damp but he'd a pallet to lie on and a blanket, and I could see he'd eaten.'

Though it seemed much longer, Alice reminded herself he'd only been in the cell a day, and he was strong enough to bear the discomfort. 'And how was his humour?'

'Angry and gloomy when I first saw him, though happier by the time I left. But, Alice, I must tell you everything I told him. For, since I left you this morning, much has changed.'

Alice was aghast when she heard how close Eleanor had come to losing her life. She was surprised how calm Eleanor seemed now about the terrifying incident.

'I can't believe he tried to strangle you,' she said.

Eleanor nodded. 'I was so afraid, Alice. At first I couldn't see who my attacker was, and thought he simply wanted to force me. That was frightening enough, but when I found it was Gilbert Fletcher, I knew what he must want.'

'But why'd he want to kill you?'

'He must've found out that Matilda came to talk to me. I expect he beat her to make her tell him what she'd said.'

'And have you seen her since then?'

Eleanor pursed her lips. 'No, I've not had a chance. I'll go first thing tomorrow—'

Then Alice had a sudden thought. 'But if Gilbert's there, he might attack you again.'

Eleanor shook her head. 'I don't think he will be there. But I'll be careful.' She gave a rueful smile and patted Alice's arm.

She then continued with her story, about meeting Lady de Bohun, and how Margaret had told her of her long-held suspicions about Robert Tyler.

'In the end she said it was plain John couldn't have murdered Philip, and she suggested I went to see him, which of course is what I'd planned to do. But first she wanted me to tell Sir Richard Matilda's story. He was in the hall, talking to Ralph Ward and the leader of that group of labourers from Winchester. He seemed to be listening attentively to their petitions, or at least that's what her ladyship thought.'

'At last,' said Alice.

'Well, yes, except that just then Robert Tyler burst into the hall and interrupted the conversation. Sir Richard looked so relieved and immediately said he was going hunting, leaving the bailiff to deal with the labourers.'

'So he wasn't really listening after all?' said Alice.

Eleanor gave a little shrug. 'Perhaps not. Lady de Bohun was furious with him, but kept her counsel so as not to vex him.'

'And how did the bailiff deal with Ralph and Master Ashdown?' Was he understanding of their demands?'

Eleanor laughed hoarsely, then, clutching at her throat, grimaced with pain. 'Oh dear, I shouldn't laugh.'

Alice smiled sympathetically. 'But was Robert's behaviour a cause for laughter?'

'No, not at all. He became quite wild, making wicked accusations against Ralph, and then against Bart Coupar.'

She told Alice everything Robert had said and Alice's eyes grew wide with disbelief. The Robert Tyler whom Eleanor was describing was a very different man from the one Alice thought she'd known. She'd always thought of him as a man of gravity and integrity, not the irrational, undignified man of Eleanor's account.

'But why'd the bailiff want to kill Bart Coupar?' said Alice.

Eleanor shook her head again. 'In truth, Alice, I don't really know, but he spoke as if he believed poor Bart had gone straight to Hell.' She shuddered. 'It was horrible. Then he suddenly panicked and ran to the door.'

'Did no-one go after him?'

'He went in such haste we were all taken by surprise, but Lady de Bohun said to let him go. There were plenty of witnesses to his behaviour, she said, not only Ralph and Nicholas and me, but Alexander, the seneschal, had come to find out what the noise was about, and Sir Richard would never doubt his word.'

'So you had all this to tell John?'

'I was there a long time. He had so many questions. But, despite what I told him, he still doubted Sir Richard would believe Robert to be guilty.'

'And you couldn't get him freed from gaol?'

'Sir Richard hadn't returned by the time I left. I went back to see her ladyship and she told me to be patient. She was sure John would be free tomorrow.'

'Tomorrow,' cried a third voice, and both women started with surprise, as Matthew crawled from his pallet in the corner of the room and came to kneel by his mother, looking up at her with half-closed eyes.

'Is John coming home tomorrow?' he said, his attempted smile collapsing into a wide yawn.

Alice laughed and ruffled his hair. 'How long've you been awake?'

The boy shrugged. 'A while.'

'So how much've you heard of Mistress Titherige's story?'

'A bit,' he said, and managed a sheepish grin.

'I expect that means most of it,' said Eleanor, looking a little troubled.

Alice nodded. 'Don't worry, he'll have forgotten most of it by the morning.'

'No, I won't,' said Matthew indignantly, then yawned again hugely.

'Bed,' said Alice firmly, getting to her feet and ushering the boy back to his pallet.

'I must go too,' said Eleanor. 'It must be nearly morning.'

Alice opened the door and looked out. It was quite bright outside, but the light came from the full moon. 'No, it's still night,' she said. 'Plenty of time for sleep. And I should think you need it after your eventful day.'

She put her arms around Eleanor and gave her a hug. 'God give you good rest,' she said, and Eleanor wrapped her cloak tightly around herself and ran the short distance to her house.

Alice doused the fire and put out one of the candles, taking the other to the little room where she had her bed. She said a prayer and lay down, covering herself in the rough blanket. She'd have liked to know how John had behaved alone with Eleanor in his cell, but she sensed no intimacy or gesture of affection had passed between them. As sleep overcame her, she told herself she simply must be patient.

Alice slept deeply for a few hours, until her inner timekeeper woke her with the coming of dawn. She rose and pottered for a while, preparing breakfast and wondering whether she'd be able to settle to anything today, or spend another day waiting and hoping.

She was in the garden, letting her hens out into the yard and scattering some grain from a basket, when she heard a yelp of excitement from Matthew. She turned to see the frame of the cottage door suddenly fill with the shape of her elder son, a broad smile beaming from his face. Alice dropped her basket and ran towards him, weeping with relief and joy. John grasped her waist, lifted her up and whirled her around.

'Tears, Ma?' he said, 'Aren't you pleased I'm home again?'

'Oh, son, of course I am,' she said, wiping her face on her apron. 'You don't know how pleased.'

'Old Ned, the gaoler, woke me at first light, and said I could go. He didn't say why.'

'Eleanor told you Margaret was sure Sir Richard'd free you once he heard the truth.'

She thought she noticed John flush a little at the mention of Eleanor's name, but he betrayed nothing in his words. 'Yes, she told me, though I scarce believed it.'

'So it must be true,' she said. 'He did listen. I wonder what'll happen now, to Robert and Gilbert Fletcher?'

John shrugged. 'Even supposing they can be found.'

She left John playing a game of knucklebones with Matthew, who, scarcely able to contain his happiness that his grumpy brother was home, insisted on sitting as close to him as he could. And John, seemingly no longer ill tempered, accepted his brother's affection and openly returned it.

'I'll go up to the fields later, Ma,' he said.

'Did Eleanor tell you all the labourers downed tools in protest against your arrest?' said Alice. John shook his head, and she wondered if perhaps Eleanor hadn't known about the protest. 'So you may find the fields empty.'

'Then I'll have to go and round folk up,' he said, grinning. 'As Sir Richard's given me my freedom, I'd best make an effort to get back to my job.' His grin bore a tinge of regret.

Alice knelt in prayer in front of the statue of the Virgin. She lit two candles for Stephen and Geoffrey and prayed as usual for their passage out of Purgatory and into Paradise, then gave thanks for Sir Richard's understanding of the truth and her son's release from captivity. She let her hood hang down around her bowed head, to give her the sense of seclusion that made prayer more personal. She continued kneeling in silence for some time, and no sound intruded into her solitude. But suddenly she looked up, hearing movement that she thought came from one of the other side chapels. Looking around, she saw Thomas and Ellen Rolfe kneeling together in the chapel of Saint Peter, just feet away from where she was. They were both sobbing.

Alice was out of their sight, hidden behind the Virgin's statue, but she remained silent and unmoving, hoping perhaps she could overhear some of their conversation and learn the reason for their distress. Brother and sister spoke quietly, but occasionally their voices were raised in despairing entreaty and, in the silence of the church, their words carried easily enough to Alice's ears.

It seemed that Thomas had become afraid for his immortal soul and had come here to confess his sins to God. Ellen was terrified that her brother's crimes would keep him out of Paradise forever. They clung together, weeping and distraught, both begging for Thomas to be forgiven.

As Alice listened to the litany of sins spouting from Thomas's mouth, she wondered if she'd somehow been given this opportunity to bring the murderer of Sir Philip, and perhaps also of Bart Coupar, to justice. It struck her also that if Thomas Rolfe was to have any chance of salvation in the next world, he had to confess his sins to a priest. Thomas and Ellen both seemed so distracted by their anguish that Alice realised she could easily fetch Master Hugo without attracting their attention.

She found Hugo in his parsonage, working on a sermon, and he listened attentively to what she had to say. His eyes seemed to light up at the prospect of confronting such a heinous sinner, and he rose immediately to go with her. As they walked, Alice briefly saw a different priest from the usual proclaimer of fire and brimstone, for he was expressing sympathy over the injustice of John's arrest and accusation, saying he knew a man like John was incapable of such a crime. When they arrived at the church, Alice saw that Ellen had gone, but the brother she'd apparently abandoned was lying prostrate on the chapel floor. Master Hugo strode to the chapel entrance and barred the way, though Thomas seemed in no mood to flee. He turned his face to the priest; he looked defeated. Nonetheless the priest went into the chapel and, closing the gate behind him, locked it. He asked Alice to find the sexton and tell him to come with a rope.

The sexton was digging a fresh grave in the new churchyard, and seemed as pleased as Master Hugo to hear Alice's news. He fetched a rope from his hut, and hurried with her back to the church, where they found Master Hugo and Thomas both on their knees, praying together, though Thomas's prayers were accompanied by much quaking and moaning. Seeing the sexton arrive, Hugo made the sign of the cross over his breast and got to his feet, then unlocked the chapel's gate. Thomas rose too, his eyes wild and distracted, and for a moment Alice thought he might try to make his escape after all, but Master Hugo took him firmly by the arm and called the sexton forward to tie Thomas's hands behind his back.

'We'll go to the manor together, shall we, Mistress atte Wode?' he said. 'I think Master Rolfe has something to tell Sir Richard, and I'm sure you'd like to hear him absolve your son from all taint of accusation.'

Alice was nervous about going to the manor, given the way she was treated only two days ago. But she need not have worried, for she was received warmly by both Margaret and Richard, though Richard made no apology for throwing her son so ignominiously into gaol. She thanked him for releasing John, but he dismissed her gratitude, though not unkindly, as of little consequence. However, in the brief conversation that followed she discovered he had still not accepted that Robert Tyler was the guilty party.

Margaret raised her eyes upwards and sighed deeply. 'I have told my husband, Alice,' she said, 'that several people witnessed Master Tyler's violent outburst yesterday, and Richard has heard Alexander himself confirm that the bailiff was acting most indiscreetly. Yet,' she sighed again, 'regardless of all that he has heard, he still resists what is accepted by so many others.'

Alice thought Sir Richard looked sheepish rather than affronted at his wife's rather indelicate tirade against him, which made her wonder if perhaps he was not far from being persuaded.

'And he maintains his stubbornness,' continued Margaret, in a tone of profound frustration, 'despite the fact that Master Tyler has not been seen since he left the manor in such unseemly haste late yesterday afternoon.'

Master Hugo arrived at the manor a little after Alice, entering the manor hall with something of a flourish, followed by his sexton who was urging on a dejected Thomas Rolfe. The priest told Sir Richard that Thomas had confessed his sins and was now prepared to tell him what he had done. He beckoned to the sexton to bring Thomas forward and, with a firm hand on Thomas's shoulder, pushed him to his knees in front of his lord.

'Well, Master Rolfe,' said Sir Richard sternly, 'what have you to say?'

Thomas Rolfe looked quite a different man from the one who'd stood up at the manor court only a few months ago to declare John an unsuitable choice for reeve. Then he'd been self-assured before Sir Richard, but now he was craven. He didn't raise his head as he spoke.

'I told the priest it were me who killed Sir Philip,' he said, so quietly it was hard to catch the words. 'And it were me who tied the rope so Bart Coupar'd fall off the stack.' Then he looked up. 'But I did both on the orders of Gilbert Fletcher, m'lord. God help me, I committed those dreadful deeds at his behest, not my own.'

Margaret and Alice exchanged looks, and Alice supposed Margaret thought as she did, surprised Thomas should name Gilbert Fletcher rather than Robert Tyler.

'And where is Master Fletcher?' asked Sir Richard, but Thomas shook his head.

'You'll recall, Richard,' said Margaret, 'that he attempted to kill Eleanor Titherige, so he has undoubtedly fled Meonbridge to avoid arrest.'

'So he is evidently the guilty man,' said Richard, looking relieved, 'along with Master Rolfe here.'

Margaret looked exasperated. 'But, as you already know, Richard,

Matilda Fletcher told Eleanor that her father was also involved in the plot.'

'But why would Robert want to kill Philip?' said Richard, clearly still resisting what everyone else could see was true. 'He loved the boy when he was a child...' And he drifted off into a brief reverie, perhaps remembering times long past. But moments later, he returned to the present.

'Send for Matilda Fletcher,' he said. 'I want to hear this story from the girl's own lips.'

Alice stepped forward to say she'd fetch Matilda, for she'd likely be nervous about coming to the manor and might need encouragement. Richard agreed and bid her return with Matilda after dinner, then gave orders for Thomas to be taken to the gaol and put in chains.

Alice was glad not to have to return to the manor immediately, for she wanted to find Eleanor, thinking she could more readily persuade Matilda to face Sir Richard. As it was near dinner time, she hoped to find her at the forge rather than up at Riverdown, and she did.

'I went up to the pasture early this morning,' said Eleanor.

'So you don't know John's been freed?' said Alice, and was pleased to see Eleanor's face break into a delighted smile.

It was now Alice's turn to tell the story of her eventful few hours, and Eleanor was relieved that at last it seemed Sir Richard was beginning to learn the truth, and even to believe it.

'But not quite yet,' said Alice. 'He wants to see Matilda, to hear the story from her own lips, as he put it. But I thought she might be more willing to go if you came with us, Elly. D'you have time?'

Eleanor nodded. 'How could I not have the time to see these dreadful crimes brought to justice?'

Together they hurried to Matilda's house.

'I hope I'm right that Gilbert hasn't come home,' said Eleanor, grimacing as they approached the door.

But when Hawisa gingerly answered their knock they were both relieved to find Gilbert indeed appeared to have fled.

'He hasn't been back since he flew out the house yesterday morning,' said Hawisa.

'D'you know where he went?' asked Eleanor, but Hawisa shook her head. So Eleanor told her how he'd followed her and tried to kill her, and showed Hawisa her bruised neck.

Hawisa gasped at the sight of it. 'He near killed the mistress, too, after she'd slipped out to see you. She's in a bad way.'

'Can I see her?' said Eleanor, alarmed. 'Sir Richard knows her story, as she wanted him to, but he said he won't truly believe it until he hears it from her.'

Hawisa pursed her lips. 'She'll not want to show her face in public, the mess it's in.

'Let me try and persuade her, Hawisa,' said Eleanor. The servant nodded, and gestured to her and Alice to follow her upstairs to the solar.

'Where's the master gone then?' she said, as they climbed the stairs.

'I don't know,' said Eleanor, 'but when my shepherd Walter saved me from Gilbert's murderous hands, he inflicted a deep wound in his leg. Gilbert staggered off, but he was bleeding badly, so he may not have got far. If his horse was close by, he might have got away. But I expect he'll not return here.'

Hawisa breathed out and uttered a brief prayer before knocking on the door of Matilda's chamber.

Eleanor and Alice exchanged looks of horror when they saw Matilda's face. It was badly bruised, with one eye black and swollen, her lips fat and purple. Eleanor went over to her friend and put a consoling arm around her. Then she laid a hand gently on Matilda's swelling belly.

'The child...?' she said.

Matilda looked up, blank-faced. 'Still kicking,' she said, her tone bitter. 'He was careful enough to avoid harming his spawn—'

Alice sat on a stool on the other side of the room, keeping her distance to allow Eleanor to comfort her friend. When Matilda seemed composed, Eleanor told her that Richard wanted to see her. It was not a surprise that Matilda at once refused on account of her appearance. Eleanor shot Alice a pessimistic grimace, but Alice pointed to her own neck and tried to nod meaningfully. Eleanor understood and told Matilda how Gilbert had tried to kill her, and showed her her bruised neck. Matilda was so shocked she broke down again into weeping. Then she suddenly groaned and clutched at her belly, and Alice started forward in alarm.

'The baby?' she said, but Matilda shook her head.

'Fear not, Mistress atte Wode,' she said and grimaced feebly. 'The baby's well. Just trying to kick its way out.' Then she changed her mind about Sir Richard.

'Perhaps the evidence of my face as well as your poor neck, Elly, will convince Sir Richard Gilbert Fletcher's the vilest of rogues.' She smiled weakly. 'Anyway, why should I care what I look like? A scorned woman.'

'You won't always be scorned, Matilda,' said Alice. 'One day some good man'll show you you're worthy of love and respect.'

Matilda tried to smile again, wincing at the pain of stretching her battered lips. 'Thank you, Mistress atte Wode. I can hardly believe that'll ever happen, but I'll try and hope it might.'

On the way to the manor, Eleanor told Matilda about her father's extraordinary behaviour. 'Have you seen him since yesterday?'

Matilda shook her head. 'Margery came to see me quite late, and she said he'd not come home.'

At the manor, it was Sir Richard's turn to be shocked by Matilda's horribly injured face. He guided her gently to one of his great chairs, and fetched a couple of cushions to ease her discomfort, while Lady de Bohun raised her eyebrows at Alice. He then drew up a simple stool next to Matilda and listened attentively to her story. Though he'd already heard the story twice before, it seemed that having it from Matilda's own lips made the difference, and when he also learned that her father seemed to be missing as well as her husband, Richard finally acknowledged what everybody else already knew, that the man he'd trusted with his manor and his family for more than twenty years was as guilty of murder as Gilbert Fletcher and Thomas Rolfe.

28

O nce it fully dawned on Matilda that both her father and her
husband were fugitives from the law, she found herself at a loss
to know how to proceed with her life. The disappearance of the two
men was perhaps only temporary, but she realised that, if they did not
return to Meonbridge or were found and brought to justice, they
would be removed from her life forever. The thought of this made her
feel most unsettled, with an uneasy relief that the misery of the last
few months might be over. Except that in her belly she still carried
"Gilbert's spawn", a child she neither wanted nor knew how she could
possibly love, given all the pain its father had inflicted upon her. All
this she poured out to Eleanor during the long night that followed Sir
Richard's pronouncement on her father. She'd asked Eleanor to go
home with her, for she said she needed the companionship of a friend.

'I'm so afraid,' she said, 'Gilbert and my father may come back, and
my misery will start again.'

'But if they come back, they'll be hanged for murder,' said Eleanor.

Matilda did not look comforted. 'They might find a way of killing
me first. That's why I'm afraid to be alone.'

Eleanor didn't say she had Hawisa to look after her, and Nathan to protect her, for she realised that what Matilda needed most was a friend to confide in. She stayed with Matilda all night and most of the following day but, by late afternoon, with Matilda's agreement, she returned to the manor to ask Lady de Bohun if she could provide sanctuary for Matilda until Robert and Gilbert either returned or were found and taken into custody. Margaret readily agreed and arranged for a room to be prepared, while Eleanor returned to Matilda's house to fetch her.

As Eleanor prepared to leave her in Lady de Bohun's care, Matilda looked both relieved and bereft. 'Visit me every day, won't you, Elly?' she said.

Sir Richard had sent a messenger to the sheriff of Hampshire requesting a visit from the county coroner to carry out a proper investigation. The coroner arrived a few days later and set up his court in the great hall at the manor. He called before him all those who had stories to tell. Alice, John, Matilda and Eleanor were among those who had to stand before him and repeat what they knew. Poor Thomas Rolfe spent hours being questioned again and again until the officer was satisfied that his confession to Philip's murder was the truth.

Eleanor noticed that no-one, including Sir Richard, seemed to think the coroner needed to know that, only a few days ago, John had been suspected of the murder. She assumed that, because Thomas had confessed and Gilbert and Robert were seemingly on the run, Sir Richard must have realised that his arrest of John was a misunderstanding best forgotten.

Early in November, a small party of travellers arrived in Meonbridge, but they came not weary from their journey and seeking rest and refreshment, but in haste and with horror on their travel-worn faces, for they'd found the body of a man in a ditch, a mile or two from the village. It was early in the morning and the green was bustling with the little market. Eleanor was walking up and down the stalls with her friend Susanna Miller, inspecting what was available to buy for her own household and for Roger. A crowd quickly gathered around the travellers, demanding answers they couldn't give. But shortly Nicholas Cook, who was minding his booth of cheeses, spoke up above the hubbub that surely the constable should be called, and he sent his young son Ben to fetch Master Dyer. Eleanor and Susanna waited until the constable came and looked on while he commandeered a few men from the crowd to go with him to retrieve the body.

As soon as the men had gone, taking one of the travellers with them to show them where the body had been found, the crowd erupted into excited conversation about whose body it might be, whether it was some stranger or perhaps even Master Tyler.

'I wonder if it's Gilbert Fletcher,' said Eleanor quietly to Susanna. She felt a lump in her throat. 'I must confess I'd be relieved to find he's dead.'

Susanna touched her arm. 'That's hardly a surprise, Elly. Why wouldn't you want him dead?'

Eleanor nodded but, despite all that Gilbert had done, she knew it was sinful to wish any man dead.

'Wait with me, Susy? I don't want to go home until I know.'

When the men returned with the body, it was Gilbert Fletcher's. The constable announced they'd found him quite close to where Sir Philip himself was murdered. Gilbert's horse was grazing nearby, one side of the saddle soaked in blood, the other streaked from where it seemed Gilbert might have fainted and fallen off, never to ride again. Master Dyer sent for Simon Hogge to examine the body, and Simon soon declared that Gilbert had bled to death, perhaps only a day or two ago.

There was much curiosity over the body, and people jostled to see the face of the man now assumed by all to be a murderer. Eleanor compelled herself to look at it too, though she was fearful of looking on the face of a man whose soul was already in Purgatory. Susanna helped her push her way to the front of the small crowd, and she linked arms with her to give her courage. Eleanor looked down at the twisted body, then, forcing her eyes up to his face, she almost gagged. For Gilbert's face was contorted into a ghastly grimace, evidence of the pain he must've suffered as the blood drained from his wound. He'd clearly attempted to stem the flow by ripping his cloak into strips and binding them tightly around his leg, but it had been no good. The wound was too deep and, without surgery, said Simon, he had stood no chance.

The constable ordered the men to take Gilbert's body to the manor, so Sir Richard could decide what to do with it. Eleanor went with them, thinking Matilda might need her support when she saw her husband's corpse. Lady de Bohun and Sir Richard together brought Matilda down to the hall, where the body was lying on its side on a pallet on the floor.

At first Matilda simply stared at the corpse, walking slowly around it. Then she looked up at Eleanor, and the spark of hatred in her eyes blazed more fiercely. She leaned over and spat into Gilbert's face, then, lifting her skirts slightly, she put out a foot and kicked the body, in the head, in the chest and in the groin. The corpse shuddered a little at each blow, as if it could still feel pain. Eleanor felt uneasy at Matilda's desecration of her husband's body but, looking around at the other onlookers, she could see no-one else was reproaching Matilda for her actions.

'I'm glad he suffered,' said Matilda. 'And I'm glad he died without being shriven, so he'll be forever in mortal sin and go straight to Hell.' She laughed, but it was a bitter laugh that quickly turned to frantic weeping, as the child evidently kicked again and she fell to her knees clutching at her belly.

Some hours later Sir Richard sent the sexton and a couple of manor servants to the cross-roads outside Meonbridge, where they buried Gilbert Fletcher's body. None but those three witnessed the burial and Sir Richard gave instructions that no sign was to be left to mark the spot. And it seemed no-one, not even Master Hugo, questioned the lord's decision or cared that Gilbert Fletcher had no proper resting place.

It was well into November before Robert Tyler reappeared in Meonbridge. Many people said he'd not left the village at all but was holed up somewhere out of sight, but Sir Richard sent out search parties to look for him both within and beyond the village and they always returned empty-handed.

It was early in the morning, and chilly, with a cold winter wind blowing across the common fields to the south of the village. Eleanor and Susanna were making their way up the track to Riverdown. A few cottars and villeins were working in the fields, mending some of the many fences that had been broken down by cattle that, unguarded, ran amok during the months of the mortality. Suddenly a cry went up and Eleanor looked back across the fields to see a man floundering along in the stream that ran along the field's edge and led back into the village. The workers were pointing towards the man and yelling, then someone, who looked like John, gave chase and others followed, raising the hue and cry as they ran. The man looked behind him and ran faster and, when he reached the rough little bridge that crossed the stream, hauled himself from the water onto the bridge and ran along the narrow track that wound its way towards the village green. Eleanor wanted to know if the man was Robert Tyler, and she and Susanna turned and ran back towards the village.

As the two young women arrived at the green, although John and the others had chased him into the village, the fugitive had proved so swift and nimble, that he'd disappeared. But the hue and cry had been heard across the village and people were coming out of their houses to see what was going on. They were gathering on the green, asking each other where the fugitive had gone. The pursuers ran around the village for a while trying to find him, but soon returned, baffled, to the green. Then a cry went up and a woman pointed to the roof of the church tower. Everyone looked up and saw Robert Tyler standing there, leaning against the parapet, his head uncovered, his long dark hair blowing wildly in the wind.

A short while later, the constable, Geoffrey Dyer, arrived, and Eleanor was surprised to see Alice with him. Master Hugo then appeared at the church door and spoke urgently to Master Dyer. Eleanor couldn't hear what was being said, but Alice joined in the conversation, becoming quite agitated with the priest. But eventually Master Hugo nodded, and both Alice and the constable followed him back into the church. Shortly afterwards came the sound of frantic chopping and splintering wood, and a few moments later Geoffrey Dyer and Alice emerged at the top of the tower.

Alice seemed to be holding firmly onto the iron cross in the centre, and her wimple was so buffeted by the wind that escaped strands of hair were blowing in her face. But then she edged past the cross towards Robert, clearly talking to him. Eleanor could not see his face, but he and Alice seemed to be having a conversation, though he did not move from the parapet wall.

The watching crowd below became restless, demanding of each other what was going on up there and, to Eleanor's horror, they started joking about what it would be like if the bailiff jumped.

But then Matilda arrived, accompanied by Sir Richard and Lady de Bohun, and, going to the foot of the tower, she stared up at her father, her face impassive, and saying nothing.

Then someone called out, "E's going to grab 'er!" and Eleanor looked up to see Robert shuffling forwards, his arms held out to Alice. The crowd let out a collective cry and, as if it were some sort of signal, Geoffrey Dyer lunged forward, thrusting himself between Alice and Robert, and Robert retreated rapidly, back towards the low parapet wall. But Alice pushed past the constable, towards Robert, crying out and with her arms outstretched. But, if she was trying to save him, she was too late, for he retreated too far and toppled backwards, falling from the tower like a cloth doll onto the stone path below, to a clamour of screams and cheers from the crowd.

Matilda did not move as her father's body hurtled to the ground and landed with a sickening crump not far from where she was standing. Eleanor was shocked, if not surprised, to see how calm and stony-faced Matilda was at the sight of his twisted body, his head smashed open by the impact, oozing blood and brains onto the path. Moments later her sister Margery was there too, screaming, and threw herself onto the body, weeping inconsolably. But there were no tears from Matilda. Eleanor wanted to go to her, but Matilda looked so cold she decided that perhaps, at this moment, she needed no-one and nothing but her own thoughts.

After a while, Alice emerged from the church, grey-faced, leaning on Geoffrey Dyer's arm. Eleanor instinctively went forward to help her, and smiled wanly at the constable, who nodded and, withdrawing his arm gently, gave Alice into Eleanor's charge. Eleanor led her round the corner of the church and down to the forge, where she sat her down in the one good chair and poured her a cup of wine.

Alice's colour did not return as she told Eleanor what had happened inside the church.

'Robert fled to the church for sanctuary,' she said, 'and Master Hugo begged him to confess his sins and obtain absolution. But Robert was too terrified to linger in the confessional, claiming his pursuers would kill him if he did not flee, and in a frenzy he ran from the priest to the church tower. He barricaded the door before Hugo could reach him.'

Alice put her hand across her mouth as she recalled what happened next. 'Master Hugo argued strongly against cornering Robert in case he took fright, but Geoffrey insisted on breaking down the tower door and following him to the top.'

Alice looked up at Eleanor, her chin trembling. 'I asked if I could go up too, for I thought I might be able to convince Robert to give himself up. Master Hugo tried hard to dissuade me, but at length Geoffrey said I should try, and he and I climbed the stair.'

'Why did you think Master Tyler would listen to you, Alice?' said Eleanor. 'When I think of his wild behaviour at the manor, it seemed he'd lost his wits.'

Alice shook her head sadly. 'I don't think he'd truly lost his wits. And I hoped that, because of what he'd once felt towards me, he might listen to me. I tried to persuade him to confess his sins, so if all else failed he'd at least gain God's grace.'

She paused, tears running down her ashen cheeks. 'For a few moments,' she went on, 'I saw understanding on Robert's face. He told me all he'd done.' She looked up. 'It was his confession, Elly. But then he took a few steps towards me. He was going to give himself up, I'm certain of it. But Geoffrey mistook Robert's intent, for he threw himself forward to protect me. Robert recoiled in fear and stepped back.' She covered her face with her hands and sobbed.

Eleanor was mystified about why Alice cared so much about this harsh, malevolent man who'd been the agent of such disorder and mayhem.

'I tried to stop him falling,' continued Alice, weeping. 'I don't understand what became of the old Robert. He wasn't always a bad man.' And Eleanor recalled Lady de Bohun saying much the same thing.

. . .

Towards the end of November, Thomas Rolfe was removed from the manor gaol and taken to Southampton where he would be tried at a session of the shire court. In the days before, Thomas's sister Ellen, who'd given up the running of her ale-house, spent every moment in her brother's dark, dank cell, trying to find comfort in the last few opportunities for his company.

When Thomas was finally bundled into the caged wagon to make the journey to Southampton, Ellen returned to her house and, it was said, locked the door. For several days, each time Eleanor passed the house, on her way to and from Riverdown, she invariably saw a group of boys throwing stones at the close-fastened shutters, or a few people standing outside the house, jeering and reviling Ellen as a murderer's sister. Eleanor felt sorry that Ellen should have to suffer for her brother's crimes, but didn't have the courage to tell the hecklers to let her alone. But days passed and at length the taunting stopped, though Ellen still didn't emerge from her house or go about the village.

Alice had evidently also noticed Ellen Rolfe's isolation for, when Eleanor saw her a few days later, Alice asked whether she thought they should interfere or leave Ellen alone.

'I suppose it's hardly our affair,' said Eleanor, 'but somehow I feel badly about her. Perhaps we should call on her together, just to be neighbourly?'

To their surprise, Ellen was grateful for their visit.

She'd once been a woman of low repute in Meonbridge, not because she sold her body to all-comers, but because her daughter's father had run off before she was born, and no other man ever considered courting Ellen after that. She made up for her humiliation by setting up as brewster, and ran her flourishing ale-house with a dispassionate toughness that made her as feared as any man. But now, without her brother, she was truly alone, and admitted she was afraid of what the future held, for her, as well as for Thomas's immortal soul.

'But I don't think Tom were afraid,' she said, her face brightening a little. 'He knew well enough that he were guilty, and there were no hope for him on this Earth. He spent his time in gaol on his knees, praying God'd see the repentance in his heart. Tom hopes he'll be found guilty soon, so he can take his first step on the road to Purgatory and then, through God's gracious mercy, to Paradise.' She paused a moment. 'Though of course he knows that might take many lifetimes...'

She talked matter-of-factly, as if Thomas's confidence that he'd eventually attain Paradise was a certainty from which she could draw comfort. Eleanor exchanged looks with Alice, and could see Alice felt as she did: Ellen was deluding herself. But she felt there was little merit, or goodwill, in trying to convince Ellen otherwise and wondered if it was time to leave.

However, Alice had a question. 'But, Mistress Rolfe,' she said, her tone compassionate, 'what I can't understand is why a prosperous, upright man like your brother would put his immortal soul in danger by committing such dreadful crimes. What can possibly have driven him to kill?'

Eleanor thought perhaps Alice had gone too far, for the tough-minded Ellen began to cry. But then she wiped her tears on her apron, and looked up, shaking her head. 'You're right, Mistress atte Wode, Tom were an honest villein, and a good husbandman. But when the bailiff, God rest his soul, first offered him some land in return for a favour—'

'What sort of favour?' said Eleanor.

Ellen shrugged. 'I don't know. It happened right after your John were made reeve, Mistress atte Wode. Tom were so aggrieved the vote didn't go his way. He said, even if his neighbours didn't want him, at least the bailiff could see his virtues. But I could see Tom were getting drawn in by that man and felt uneasy, though I didn't know why. Tom laughed it off, saying I were being foolish.' The tears flowed again. 'But I were right, weren't I?'

In the days following John's release from gaol, Eleanor found his moroseness seemed to have passed away, his old good humour and cordiality returned. He wasn't exactly courting her, but when he saw her in the village he stopped to speak and was not merely polite but warm.

One chilly day in late November, Eleanor was coming back down from Riverdown with Susanna, after a morning's work inspecting the sheep for foot rot, when they met John in the village returning home for his dinner. Despite the keen wind, they stopped and chatted for a while, exchanging pleasantries. Then John asked Eleanor if she knew about the brooch Alice had bought from the pedlar, and she said she did, wondering if this meant John had more news of Agnes.

'When Sir Philip and me went to Oxford,' he went on, 'I thought we were getting closer to Agnes. So if that pedlar really did see her in Chipping Norton...'

'Oh, he must've met her there, Master atte Wode,' said Eleanor, 'for I'm certain Agnes sent the brooch as a sign. And it's only two months ago the pedlar said he saw her.'

John nodded. 'I oughtn't let it rest,' he said, frowning. 'But I'd fain not travel all that way alone and, with Sir Philip gone, I don't know who to ask.'

He trailed off, and a cold gust of wind made them all draw their cloaks close about them.

'We'd best be on our way,' said John, 'before we freeze.' And, nodding politely to Susanna, and smiling at Eleanor, he hurried off.

Eleanor and Susanna walked briskly across the green towards the forge.

'Even though he were talking about Agnes, he were thinking about you,' said Susanna shortly, looping her arm affectionately through her friend's.

'He was not,' said Eleanor. 'He's obviously afraid to go on such a journey by himself, and was hoping I might suggest who could go with him.'

Susanna shook her head, and grinned mischievously. 'No, he were just chatting, so he could gaze into your eyes.'

Eleanor felt sick at heart. 'I do hope you're wrong, Susy, because I really don't feel that way about him any more. It's true I ended our friendship when he was so disrespectful to his mother, but he's never tried to win me round, so I've assumed he's no longer interested in me.' She pursed her lips. 'And now I'm no longer interested in him. Truly, Susy, I'm happy as I am.'

. . .

A couple of weeks later, John called at Eleanor's house. It was late afternoon and quite dark, and Eleanor was nervous of opening her door to callers. Opening it just a little way, she peered around the edge. John stood on the threshold, a broad smile on his face. Her heart sank.

'Master atte Wode,' she said, trying to keep her tone light, 'It's late for you to be calling.'

The smile became a sheepish grin. 'Indeed, Mistress Titherige, and I'm sorry, but I've something to say to you, and couldn't keep it to myself any longer.'

When John said goodnight a short while later, his smiling face had crumpled. Embarrassed by his proposal of marriage, Eleanor could say nothing other than that she'd think about it, even though she knew she probably wouldn't. But she was sorry for the deep disappointment that clouded his bright eyes. After he'd left, she sat in the dark for some time, waves of guilt as well as a sort of grief washing over her, as she wondered if she'd ever be any man's wife.

Next morning, although a chilling rain had joined the wind to make walking abroad unpleasant, Eleanor rose at first light and struggled up the track to Riverdown. There was little to do with the flock this time of year, but she wanted to see Walter.

As the rain battered against the shutters, they sat together in his tiny cottage, huddled around a feeble fire that guttered constantly from the windy blasts trespassing beneath the ill-fitting door.

'Master atte Wode's asked me to marry him,' she said.

Though the light in the cottage was dim, with just one stub of a candle, Eleanor felt sure she could see disappointment cross Walter's face. But, if he was unhappy at her news, his voice did not betray his feelings.

'John atte Wode's as good a man as any lives in Meonbridge, and all of Hampshire. You could have no finer husband, Mistress Eleanor.'

She nodded, but when she looked up she saw Walter's face was turned away from her, and he was bent over, poking at the fire.

Eleanor owed Walter a huge debt of thanks but, as she watched him tend the fire, then get up to pour her a pot of warmed ale, she wondered if she felt more for him than simple gratitude. She asked herself why she'd come here at all: was it to hear Walter say she should marry John, or to see his face when she told him the news?

'He is a good man,' she said, 'but I've not accepted him.'

Walter sat down again and wrapped his big hands around his cup of ale. When he looked at her again, Eleanor saw relief on his face, and she realised with sudden shame that she'd now given *this* man cause for hope. Having thought herself a grown woman, she now felt as witless as a maid. For long moments she sat silent, not knowing what now to say to recover the predicament she'd created. But at length it came to her what she should say, whether or not it was the truth.

'I'm not ready for marriage,' she said. 'We've the flock to build, you and I, and I need nothing else for now.'

29

DECEMBER 1349

When Richard discovered his long-trusted bailiff had apparently turned against him, he withdrew into himself again, spending long hours alone riding the estate. As he said to Margaret, he still could not believe Robert had murdered the boy he spent so many years nurturing towards manhood. And he found it harder still to accept his own action of appointing Philip as steward might have finally tipped Robert over into the madness that led to his crimes. It pained him greatly that he could no longer ask Robert what had led him to conclude that murdering Philip was the only course open to him. They had only Matilda's story as evidence of the true state of Robert's mind. He had hoped that Thomas Rolfe's trial might reveal more of the reasons for the conspiracy, but nothing more came to light than what Matilda had already said. So Richard remained dispirited and ill-at-ease.

One early morning, well before sunrise, Margaret and Richard were lying in their bed, both wide awake. Richard had hardly slept again, thought Margaret, counting up his sleepless nights. It troubled her that he also ate little and drank much, and was still not in proper charge of his affairs and the manor.

'I wonder if Mistress atte Wode would tell us what Robert said to her on the top of the church tower?' said Richard in the dark.

Margaret sighed. 'I doubt it, for Alice regards what Robert told her as his confession.'

'But it wasn't a real confession.'

'Real enough,' said Margaret. 'Surely you remember that during the mortality we were told that *in extremis* people could confess to a lay person and even to a woman–'

'But that was only during the mortality.'

Margaret sighed again. 'Alice might feel Robert's confession was made *in extremis* and is therefore sacrosanct.'

'Nonetheless,' said Richard, persisting, 'send for her to come here, so you can ask her.'

Margaret had not seen Alice for the three weeks since Robert Tyler's death, so she was eager enough to invite her, though much less willing to ask Alice to divulge what had passed between her and Robert in the final moments of his earthly life. But she agreed to send a messenger to Alice first thing after breakfast.

Richard agreed with Margaret that Matilda could continue to live at the manor until her baby was born. Margaret was concerned that Matilda's melancholy and oft-expressed loathing of her unborn baby might endanger the child's survival, and she determined to do all in her power to help Matilda welcome the new life God's grace had granted her.

When Alice was ushered into Margaret's chamber soon after dinner, Matilda was dozing in a chair alongside Lady de Bohun's, a thick cloak wrapped around her despite the warmth of the fire blazing in the hearth. Margaret rose to greet her friend, and drew her towards the window seat at the other end of the chamber, to be out of Matilda's hearing.

'Dear Alice,' she said, 'I am so glad to see you. You look a little happier than when I last saw you.' In truth, Alice's face was hardly less grey than it had been when she emerged from her horrifying encounter on the roof of the church tower, though perhaps her eyes showed the merest hint of returning brightness.

But Alice shrugged. 'Perhaps a little. But I've been quite melancholy these past weeks. Despite all he'd done, I'd so hoped Robert could gain God's grace by his confession to me.' Alice's face then crumpled. 'But since then, I've realised more and more it wasn't a true confession.'

'But Master Hugo told us that, in an emergency, confession could be made to a lay person if no priest were available,' said Margaret.

Alice nodded. 'I remember. But when Robert sought sanctuary in the church, Master Hugo begged him to confess and Robert refused.' She paused, then said miserably, 'So I'm afraid Robert did die unshriven after all.'

Margaret understood that Alice might be justified in her fear, yet she wondered why she was so concerned about this man's immortal soul. 'Did you care for him, Alice?' she said quietly.

Alice looked up at her and smiled wanly. 'I did. I loved Stephen dearly, and he was a good husband. He disliked Robert and always said he was untrustworthy, but I never told him that, when I was a girl, before Stephen came to Meonbridge, Robert Tyler and I... Well, let's say I thought he'd ask me to be his wife. But then he became more interested in his own advancement and Stephen took his place in my heart.' She sighed. 'I thought Robert such a handsome man.'

Margaret nodded. 'He was. Handsome and strong. I remember him too, when he first became Philip's tutor, then later manor bailiff. Robert was always ambitious, but I thought him an honest man.'

'We were both wrong, then, my lady,' said Alice.

Margaret shook her head. 'He changed, Alice, from an honest man into a...' She trailed off, not knowing quite what she thought Robert had become, dishonest, callous, or even wicked.

Alice shrugged and did not attempt an answer. 'But there's one other thing I should tell you about Robert Tyler,' she said at length. 'In June, he did ask me to marry him.' Margaret gasped, and Alice grinned. 'I refused him, for I'd decided to remain a widow, though, in truth, I was already afraid of him and his reputation. And yet...' She faltered.

Margaret looked her friend in the eye. 'And yet?'

Alice sighed deeply. 'I found I still had a place for him in a corner of my heart.'

Margaret placed a hand on Alice's arm. 'Dear Alice, I understand why you wanted to save his soul. You have no reason to chide yourself for it.'

They sat in silence for several moments.

Then Alice said, 'How's Mistress Fletcher?'

'Melancholy,' said Margaret, sighing, 'and not at all prepared for the confinement.'

'That's easy enough to understand,' said Alice, 'after all the misery the child's father inflicted on her.'

'Indeed, but I hope that, once the child is born, she'll feel differently.'

Alice nodded uncertainly. 'Perhaps.' Then, she gave a little gasp and clapped her hand across her mouth. 'Oh, I've just remembered, I've a message for Matilda. I must deliver it.'

The two women returned to the hearth, and Margaret touched Matilda gently on the shoulder. She awoke with a start, and quickly wiped away some tears glistening on her eyelashes. 'Oh, my lady,' she said, struggling to sit more upright, 'I was far away. Have I slept long?'

'Not long,' said Margaret, 'but deeply. You must be tired.'

Matilda sighed. 'I am.' She stared down at her swollen belly. 'How I wish this burden would be lifted.'

'It won't be long now, my dear,' said Margaret, smiling encouragingly. 'But Mistress atte Wode has something to tell you,' and she gestured to Alice to sit down by Matilda.

'What have you to say to me, Mistress?' said Matilda, plucking at her skirt.

Alice pursed her lips. 'I'd fain not remind you of the dreadful day your father died—' she began, but Matilda interrupted.

'I don't care about that day,' she said, 'nor that he died.'

Alice flinched. 'Yet, Matilda, I'm bound to fulfil the promise I made him.'

'I'm sure, Mistress atte Wode, you're under no obligation to that rogue.'

Alice visibly steeled herself against Matilda's bitterness. 'He was not always a rogue, Matilda. Lady de Bohun and I remember him as an honest man. An honest man who, for reasons we may never understand, changed into a wicked one.'

Matilda snorted. 'But I do know the reasons, Mistress atte Wode, and I suffered for them.'

Margaret could see Alice was finding this conversation difficult, but she struggled on. 'Your father implored me to ask you to forgive him for what he'd done. He begged you to pray for him.'

But it was clear Matilda was unalterably hardened against her father. 'I'll never forgive him,' she cried, 'neither for the anguish he inflicted on me, nor the terrible sins he committed. Perhaps God'll forgive him, but I cannot. And as for praying for him, I'll not spend a single penny on candles or masses. He can languish in Hell for eternity for all I care.'

Margaret could see in Alice's eyes the heartache Matilda's hostility was causing, and wished now she had not brought Alice here. She got up and called Agatha to fetch some wine and sweetmeats, hoping they might lighten the mood a little.

None of the women spoke for a long while, each seemingly content with her own thoughts, until, to Margaret's surprise, Matilda cleared her throat and turned to Alice.

'Mistress atte Wode,' she said, quietly. 'Please forgive my inexcusable discourtesy. I know you tried to help my father and, though I cannot thank you for it, I was wrong to condemn you for bringing me his message.' Alice gave her a brief but understanding smile, then Matilda turned to Margaret.

'And I apologise to you, also, Lady de Bohun, for betraying your hospitality so disrespectfully.'

Margaret leaned forward and patted her hand. 'Alice and I both understand how you have suffered, my dear. Let us put this unhappiness behind us for now.'

Agatha arrived with the wine and a tray of sweet delicacies, and Margaret guided the talk towards the Christmas festivities.

As the light began to fade beyond the windows, Alice rose from her chair, saying it was time to leave. Matilda tried to rise also, to say farewell, but as she did so grimaced and clutched at her belly.

Alice asked how the baby was, and Matilda seemed to make an effort to suppress a scowl. 'It seems healthy enough, Mistress atte Wode, given all the kicking and squirming going on inside me.'

'Matilda is to birth her child here at the manor,' said Margaret.

'But I'll not keep it,' said Matilda. 'I'll give it away to some childless couple in the village. There are plenty of those, I'm sure.'

As Margaret walked with Alice down to the hall, Alice agreed it was not for them to try to persuade Matilda to forgive her father. 'If she ever does, she'll do so in her own time,' said Margaret.

'Nor, I suppose, should we interfere in her decision about the child,' said Alice.

Margaret nodded. 'Nonetheless, I am hoping she will fall in love with the child when it is born and find she wants to keep it after all. Perhaps, Alice, we should both pray fervently to Saint Anne that Matilda is granted a mother's love for her child?'

Next day, when Margaret and Richard were eating a lonely dinner together, in their chamber, Alexander came to announce that a small deputation had come to the manor gate demanding, politely, to see Sir Richard. Richard was annoyed at the interruption of his dinner, but Margaret suggested that the men had probably come to try to resolve the problems on the manor.

'I hardly have to remind you, Richard,' she said, 'and I am sorry to have to say it at all, but, as we have no steward and no bailiff on the manor, John atte Wode is bearing all of the responsibility. You really cannot ignore the situation any longer.'

'But there are no longer any riots,' said Richard, scowling.

'Maybe not, but since those first three families left in July, many more have gone, unwilling to wait for your decision about the wages. And I've heard that even a few of those fellows from Winchester have returned home.'

Richard looked up, evidently surprised by this information.

Margaret sighed. 'I've also heard that John has been trying hard to get the labourers to work and the tenants to give their dues. But, although he commands their respect, he is struggling to make them comply. So there may not be open riots, Richard, but an undercurrent of rebellion does remain.'

He shrugged and got up to go and stare through the window, while Margaret despaired yet again that her husband had still not grasped their hopeless situation.

'Surely, Richard, we cannot afford *not* to meet the cottars' and the tenants' demands, if the manor is to survive?'

To her surprise and relief, Richard then turned back towards her and nodded. He neither objected nor expressed any doubts about what she said. 'You are right,' he said. 'I admit I've been much diverted from making a decision by everything that has happened here of late. There has been so much distraction.' He enumerated the distractions on his fingers. 'First, Philip and Robert were so strongly opposed to giving in to the rebels that I could hardly go against them. Then I had to investigate Bart Coupar's accident.'

Margaret considered these excuses rather than distractions, but held her tongue while Richard continued to list his beloved son's murder, the unmasking of the murderers, and finally the discovery that his trusted bailiff had turned against him. Of course, Margaret was not unsympathetic. All of these appalling events, coming so soon after what had seemed the greatest disaster ever to befall Meonbridge and the world, were undoubtedly enough to weaken the resolve of any man, though not, she might have once thought, that of her valiant husband.

'But now it's all over,' he concluded, 'I agree that resolution of the workers' demands can be put off no longer.' He turned to Alexander, patiently waiting for instructions, and bade him admit the deputation to the hall. Then he went over to Margaret, gave her a brief kiss and, taking her hand, helped her down the narrow solar staircase to the hall.

Shortly, Alexander returned with John atte Wode, Ralph Ward and Nicholas Ashdown, who bowed respectfully to their lord and lady and removed their hoods. Richard gestured to John to begin.

At first, John repeated much of what Margaret had just said to Richard in their chamber. 'But although, m'lord,' he added, 'it's quiet enough right now in the fields, if folk continue to leave, it'll be a desperate situation come the spring, when we need to plough and sow.'

Ralph stepped forward to say that the cottars who left had not wanted to leave their homes at all but felt they had to do their best for their families.

'But they'll likely find other lords no more willing to pay,' said Richard.

'I know that may be true, sir,' said Ralph, 'but you can't blame them for trying to make a better life.'

Nicholas seemed diffident about putting his own case, but Richard bade him say his piece. 'Some of our group are working for one or two of the wealthier tenants, sir,' he said, 'but a few have gone back to Winchester. They don't have much to go back to, but became disheartened that you wouldn't give them what your son had promised, and were afraid to face a winter here with nought to live on.'

Margaret saw Richard wince at the mention of Philip's promise, but he made no objection, and encouraged the men to say all that was on their minds.

'The villeins don't want to give up their fealty to you, Sir Richard,' said John, 'but they're angry you don't seem to understand they need to work their own lands if they are to survive.' He flushed bright red, but again Richard did not object but appeared to accept the implied reproach.

John, perhaps already sensing that Richard was listening to him at last, carried on. 'The best plan is surely to commute the villeins' week-works to money rents and use the money to pay the cottars more.'

'Which is what we've been asking for all these months,' added Ralph.

'And if you rent out the spare land at low rents to Nicholas's group and some of our cottars, then as much of the manor land as possible will be farmed,' said John, drawing to a conclusion.

When Margaret climbed into bed that evening, a wave of relief and even peace flowed over her. The turmoil and mayhem of this dreadful year seemed to be coming to an end. Richard had finally understood his responsibilities towards his manor servants, and, when the deputation left the hall, the men seemed content that their demands would now be met. Margaret was not so naïve that she thought tensions between a lord and his tenants could be resolved by a single judgement, but what happened in the hall this afternoon was surely a beginning. The rebels would cease their protests, and working life on the manor would return to a settled rhythm. It would not be forever, for she sensed much change was yet to come. But for now, it would suffice.

She turned and moved closer towards Richard. He rolled over on to his side, so that he was facing her and, placing his hand behind her shoulder, he drew her gently towards him. He kissed her lightly on her mouth.

'We've turned a corner at last, Margaret,' he said, stroking her hair.

She smiled at him. 'We have, Richard. Though you do know, don't you, that the whole world has changed.'

He nodded. 'What I have decided today has changed forever the bond between us and our tenants. I do not think I like it much, but I know we had no choice.'

Margaret kissed him. 'I am so relieved to have back my noble knight. I was fearful he had abandoned me.' She gave him a demure, almost girlish, smile.

Richard laughed. 'Your knight is returned and in fine fettle.' He brought his arm down to her waist and pulled her body close to his.

Matilda's baby was born in the middle of a particularly cold December night. But it was an easy birth and Margaret was pleased with the midwife she had chosen from among those in Meonbridge who had survived the mortality.

At first Matilda refused to look at the child, telling the midwife to take her away. But Margaret insisted that the baby be put into Matilda's arms.

'She is your flesh, Matilda. You cannot deny her her mother's love.'

Matilda protested, trying to push the swaddled bundle away, but then Margaret took the bundle herself and placed her on the bed beside her mother.

Matilda turned her head away and closed her eyes. 'I've told you, my lady, I will not keep the child.'

Margaret was frustrated at the girl's obduracy, but would not give up. 'Try to look at her, Matilda, your perfect healthy little daughter.'

And, at the word "daughter", Matilda looked back at Margaret.

'A girl?' she said, and Margaret nodded, beaming.

'Yes, Matilda, a girl.'

Matilda dropped her eyes down to the white woollen shawl that enclosed her daughter, and drew back the edge to fully reveal the little face, peaceful and serene. Matilda looked, and the baby seemed to return her gaze.

Moments passed while Matilda stared, and Margaret held her breath. Then Matilda sighed and drew the baby towards her.

Margaret, exultant but composed, announced she would find someone to take messages to Eleanor and Matilda's sister, and instructed the midwife to await her return. When she came back, her heart leapt at the sight that greeted her, for she found Matilda with the baby at her breast. Matilda looked up as she entered the room, and gave her a small smile.

Margaret sat down on the bed next to her. 'Shall I see if I can find a couple in the village to take her?' she said, matter-of-factly.

'Take her?' said Matilda. 'Of course not, she's my daughter.'

Margaret smiled broadly and nodded. 'I hoped you'd say that.' The baby slipped off the breast and fell asleep.

'You and your daughter need sleep now. I have asked Eleanor to come and sit with you. She will call me if you need anything.'

'Thank you, my lady,' said Matilda. 'I'm truly grateful for your care and solicitude, when I've been so ill tempered.'

'Ill tempered with good reason, my dear. But that time is past and you can look forward to a new year and a new life.'

Joyful as Margaret was at the birth of Matilda's baby, and at Matilda's acceptance of her new daughter, the arrival also brought her sadness. For it brought home to her, and indeed to Richard, that, with their son dead and Johanna soon lost to them as a daughter, no more de Bohun babies would be born in Meonbridge.

Richard remained furious with his daughter for making what he considered a ridiculous decision, but he conceded that the aftermath of Philip's murder and the continuing rebellion on the manor had distracted him from taking a stand against it. By the time he had sufficiently recovered his strength of will, Johanna had made arrangements to enter the priory and take her dowry with her. It would have been dishonourable to renege on the agreement.

The time for her departure to the priory was fast approaching: it was agreed that she would enter as a novice in January. Margaret was dreading the day, even though Johanna would not be far from home, for the priory was only half a day's ride away. What she feared most was that Johanna would go while antagonism still divided them, for since the dreadful day of Philip's death, and Johanna's reaction to it, at first grief-stricken and later bitter, Johanna had scarcely spoken to her mother. In the two months during which her parents grieved for their lost son, and the village was engrossed in the mystery and excitement of who had killed him and why, Johanna absented herself from it all, giving herself up to prayer, or at any rate to staying in her room. She even avoided being summoned by the coroner. And Margaret, busying herself with the concerns of other young women, Eleanor Titherige and Matilda Fletcher, realised that she appeared to have neglected her own daughter and unwittingly allowed the gulf between them to deepen.

It was unfortunate for Sir Giles Fitzpeyne that the murdered body of his bride's brother was discovered the very night after he had come to court her but, as he said to Margaret, it would be unseemly for him to stay on and attempt to plead his case with Johanna when the family was in mourning and the entire manor in turmoil. Richard permitted Margaret to tell Sir Giles that Johanna was simply too distraught to contemplate marriage, and he slipped quietly away, disappointed but resigned that she would never be his bride.

When Margaret told Johanna that Sir Giles had gone, the girl was insensitive enough to remark that she had had a fortunate escape. Margaret, shocked at her callousness, castigated her for thinking she had won her reprieve at the cost of her brother's death, at which Johanna broke down into desperate heaving sobs and demanded that her mother leave her room.

It troubled Margaret that Johanna's overwrought reaction to Philip's death was so intense, more so than one might expect. She thought the key to it all might lie in the secret she was sure Johanna was harbouring over Agnes atte Wode's disappearance. But she knew also it was quite beyond her powers to convince her daughter to reveal it and thought it likely Johanna would take the secret with her to the priory.

·　·　·

As Margaret and Richard sat together by the fire one evening in the week before Christmas, Richard spoke for them both.

'So who will inherit our estates?'

Margaret's heart ached at the disappointment and regret she heard in his tremulous voice. Yet she felt the same. Richard had a cousin in Herefordshire who would probably lay claim to Meonbridge after his death, for Richard had no closer relatives, and neither did she. It was upsetting to think that, after striving so hard to maintain the manor through the long years of famine, war and mortality, it might be passed on to someone who cared little for the place.

'Perhaps we should leave the estate to the priory?' she said, but Richard bridled.

'What does a bevy of nuns know about running an estate?'

'Many priories run large estates, Richard, as well you know. It would surely be preferable to giving it to a man you hardly know who lives in Herefordshire?'

Richard cleared his throat noisily. 'I just wanted to leave it to my son and grandsons...' he said softly, and she could see his cheeks glistening in the candlelight.

30

In the days leading up to Christmas, many of the village women spent time up at the manor, working together to deck the hall for the festivities. Last year it was left to Lady de Bohun to make all the arrangements, for the food, the decorations and the entertainment. But after such a year of shared horror, Alice thought it fitting if the shared celebration could extend to renewing the bond shared between the manor and its tenants. It was easy enough to persuade Eleanor and Susanna and many of the villein and free wives to help, though most cottar women, still smarting from the months of rebellion, were more resistant. But in the end there was a good gathering and, in the hustle and bustle of hanging up holly and mistletoe, and making garlands and swags from pine branches and ivy, a sense of excitement and anticipation grew, not only for the festivities themselves, but for the hope that the new year would bring cheer and prosperity for everyone.

Three days before Christmas, the morning dawned crisp and cold, and Alice was up early, enjoying the crunch of frost under her feet as she picked her way carefully down the path to her potager. Later she set Matthew to preparing vegetables for the pottage, ignoring his complaints that he'd rather be with the pigs, while she spent most of the morning putting the finishing touches to a new surcoat for Lady de Bohun. She was glad of the day's bright light, though it was chilly sitting next to the wide-open shutters.

A little before the time when she expected John to come bursting into the cottage, ravenous for his dinner, Alice became aware of a faint clamour of excited chatter and whoops of joy, as if a group of travelling players or an itinerant juggler was performing on the green. She wanted to go out to investigate but was more anxious to finish her work before dinner. Even when she realised the noise was getting closer, still she didn't get up to look, concentrating on a particularly delicate piece of stitching. But, moments later, the sound was so loud it was clearly right outside her house, and she was forced to move when a knock came on the door. Grumbling to herself, she set the sewing down, hauled herself painfully to her feet, and shuffled to the door. She had to pull hard on the latch to wrench open the winter-swollen door, and was caught off balance as she found herself staring at a crowd of her friends and neighbours.

They were all grinning at her and cheering, and Alice felt foolish and embarrassed being the centre of the spectacle. Then suddenly Eleanor was there, coming forward with a broad smile on her face and her hands held out, beckoning to Alice to step outside. Alice frowned but did as she was bid.

'What's going on, Elly? Why's everyone here?'

Eleanor eyes were shining. 'Because we've brought someone to see you, Alice.' And with a dramatic sweep of her hand, she pointed to where the crowd parted, shuffling back to reveal a young woman, and a man carrying a young child.

For several moments Alice didn't know who they were or why they were standing there. But then the young woman pushed back the hood of her heavy travelling cloak to reveal a halo of yellow curls, and Alice burst into tears.

Agnes ran forward to the cottage door and took her mother in her arms, and the crowd clapped and cheered again.

'Oh, Ma,' she said, 'I'm sorry I've been away so long.'

'I didn't know if you were alive or dead,' said Alice, sobbing, 'and it's been so hard to bear, not knowing why you'd gone or where you were...'

Then suddenly Matthew appeared at the croft door and, running across the room, launched himself at his sister, crowing with delight. Agnes hugged him close and laughed. 'Careful, Matt, you'll have me over.'

The man holding the baby shuffled from foot to foot on the doorstep, and gave a discreet cough. Agnes laughed again and beckoned to him to come inside.

'Ma, this is Jack Sawyer, my husband.' Jack bowed to Alice and she was charmed. He was not handsome, but tall and well made, and in his other hand he was holding a heavy-looking bag of tools. He noticed her looking at them.

'I'm a carpenter,' he said.

'And a good one, Ma,' said Agnes.

'Meonbridge needs a good carpenter,' said Alice, grinning. Then she pointed to the baby, lying quietly in the crook of Jack's other arm. 'And who's this?'

'Richard,' said Agnes.

'He's a fine boy.'

'He's a very fine boy,' said Agnes, smiling and stroking the child's cheek.

The crowd began to disperse but Eleanor lingered and Agnes gave her a brief hug.

'Thanks for all you've done for Ma, Mistress Titherige.'

Eleanor shook her head. 'We've helped each other. I'm glad to see her happy at last.' She took Agnes's hand and squeezed it.

Agnes smiled and, while Eleanor joined the rest of the crowd as they drifted away, she picked up the bundle of belongings she'd left propped up by the door and went into the house.

Alice didn't know if it was delight or relief that was swinging her between tears and laughter. Trying to maintain a grip on practicalities, she instructed Matthew to fetch more vegetables for the pottage and carved off a few more slices from the remains of the smoked ham hanging from the rafters. She bustled about for a while, adding more chunks of onion and cabbage to the pottage, as Agnes wandered dreamily about the little house, looking into the nooks and crannies she'd not seen for a year.

'When I left here I were a child, Ma,' she said.

'And you've returned a woman,' said Alice, and Agnes nodded, smiling.

Then she seemed to have a sudden thought. 'Where's Pa, and John and Geoffrey?' she said.

Alice couldn't suppress a gasp, but kept her voice steady as she answered. 'John'll be back soon for his dinner, but Pa and Geoffrey won't be coming home, Agnes. The mortality took them both in March.'

Agnes cried out and collapsed onto a stool, her face in her hands. 'Oh, Ma,' she said, tears streaming, 'how could God've taken them, of all men, when they were so honest, good and kind?'

Alice nodded. 'Both spent those dreadful days tending the sick until they fell ill too. They died within days of each other. But John and Matthew and me, we escaped, though we don't how or why. Near half the folk in Meonbridge died, so many good people and little children too. It's been a terrible year.'

Agnes was quiet for a long time, weeping softly. Jack sat quietly by, rocking the baby in his arms until the boy fell asleep. 'And what of you?' said Alice. 'Did you see anything of the mortality?'

At length Agnes lifted her face and shook her head. 'I found work as a servant with a merchant in Oxford. But as the mortality crept closer, he took his whole household, with all us servants, away to his house near Chipping Norton. We all stayed there 'til he'd heard the sickness had moved on. Master Woollacott made us pray morning, noon and night that God might spare us. The house was out-of-the-way and he forbade anyone to come or go, and no-one in the house got sick. But when Master Woollacott went back to Oxford he found hundreds had died there.'

At that moment, the door was shoved open and John fell into the room, his hood tied close about his head, declaring he was starving. It took him moments to realise his mother was not alone. But when he saw it was his sister, he roared with delight, grabbed her by the waist and whirled her around.

'God's bones, I'm glad to see you, little sister,' he cried.

297

'Careful,' said Agnes, and, lowering her voice, added, 'I'm with child.' Jack smiled proudly and Alice clapped her hands with joy.

When the pottage was ready, and everyone sat down, crowding round the little table, John was all for tucking in at once, but Alice stayed his hand on the ladle, saying she wanted to offer a prayer, to give thanks for returning their beloved Agnes to them. John looked sheepish, and Agnes's face went a little pink, but Alice made no attempt to rush her earnest prayer. When she'd finished, she smiled and invited Jack to help himself first to the pottage and bread, while she bade John pour the ale. Both Agnes and Jack wolfed down their food as ravenously as John and, as she wiped the gravy from the wooden trencher with her bread, Agnes noticed her mother was regarding her with an enquiring smile. She flushed again.

'Oh, Ma, I'm sorry. You must think Jack and me such greedy pigs, but we're that hungry. We've eaten little for two or three days now.'

Alice patted her hand and grinned. 'In that case, as a good mother, I'll have to make sure you get plenty to eat while you're here.'

She turned to John. 'Are you going back to work, son?'

He shook his head. 'Not now. With my long-lost sister here, work can wait. They can shift well enough without me.'

Alice told Agnes proudly about John's appointment. 'He's well-respected by both the tenants and Sir Richard–'

John grunted. 'Well, perhaps I am now, Ma, but it hasn't been easy.'

Alice raised her eyebrows and smiled at Agnes, who touched John on the arm. 'I'm proud of you, brother. I always knew you'd make Pa proud of you.'

Then John started to tell her how he'd gone looking for her, following the mummers' trail, and they'd got as far as Oxford before the trail went cold.

Agnes's brow wrinkled a little. 'But how did you know where to go?'

'Sir Philip came with me,' said John. 'He seemed to know where the mummers went.'

At the mention of Philip's name, Agnes flushed crimson and exchanged an anxious look with Jack. Alice saw the flush and the look, and without thinking took a sideways glance at the baby dozing peacefully on Matthew's pallet in the corner of the room, which Agnes in her turn clearly noticed. She went over to pick up the baby, cradling his sleepy head carefully in her hand. She went back to Alice and placed the child in her arms.

'Your grandson, Ma,' she said, 'as I'm sure you know.'

Alice gently raised the baby higher in her arms and smiled down at his sweet face, just as he awoke and gazed up at hers. Then she looked up and across at Agnes, trying not to let her thoughts show on her face. 'And who else's grandson is he?'

Agnes looked at Jack and he nodded. 'Sir Richard and Lady de Bohun's,' she said quietly, lowering her eyes to her lap.

'I thought so,' said Alice, lightly rocking the child in her arms.

Agnes gave a little gasp, perhaps expecting her mother to disapprove of what she'd just been told.

'I guessed,' said Alice, permitting herself a small smile. She turned to Jack. 'You're a good man to take on another's child.'

Jack shrugged. 'I love Agnes.'

Then Alice noticed that John was staring at her, and slightly shaking his head. Her smile faded. 'We haven't told you about Philip,' she said.

'What about him?' said Agnes. 'Do he and Isabella have a child?'

Alice shook her head sadly. 'Both of them are dead. Poor Isabella died in the mortality, along with her unborn child, and Philip was murdered no more than two months ago.'

'Murdered?' said Agnes, tears springing to her eyes. 'Who'd do that?'

So Alice told her everything.

Agnes was so distressed by Philip's death that Alice wondered if she had indeed been in love with him. Perhaps she still harboured some affection for the father of her little boy, despite the evidence that he seemed simply to have abandoned her?

No-one spoke for a while. Jack got up and, taking the baby from Alice, put him back on the pallet in the corner. Matthew, looking bored by the conversation, fetched a toy horse his father had carved for him when he was little and, lying down beside his nephew, put it into the baby's hands. The child straight away put the wooden animal into his mouth and gnawed at it with his gums, gurgling with delight, and his contentment brought some relief from the melancholy of the moment.

Then Agnes seemed to recall what had started the sad telling of Philip's death, and turned to her brother. 'Did you say Philip went with you to look for me?'

John nodded. 'He said he cared for you. He regretted you'd fallen in love with him, because he knew you'd be hurt when he had to marry Isabella.' His expression darkened. 'But he didn't tell me you were with child when you ran away,' he said. 'He denied that you'd been lovers.'

Agnes coloured and hung her head. 'It was our secret,' she said. 'I went away because I wanted to keep the child but didn't want to shame Philip, or Ma and Pa, by having it born here. I thought if I went away I could start a new life.'

'You must've been scared,' piped up Matthew.

Agnes looked up and gave him a weak little smile. 'Yes, Matt, I was, but excited too in a way. I made friends with the mummers and they said I could travel with them. But by the time we got to Oxford I was already tired of travelling and decided to stay and find a job. It was such good fortune I was taken on at Master Woollacott's, for he and the mistress were so kind to me, even though I was with child. Then of course I met Jack,' and she threw him a loving smile, 'so it seemed everything turned out for the best.'

'But Philip just let you go,' said John bitterly.

'Not really, brother,' said Agnes. 'He gave me money and promised he'd come and make sure I'd found somewhere to live and was thriving, but I suppose the mortality stopped him coming.'

Alice nodded. 'It stopped your father trying to find you.'

'Don't be too hard on Philip, John,' said Agnes. 'I've forgiven him.' Then she looked wistfully across at baby Richard, sucking happily on the wooden horse. 'But I do wish he'd known about his son.'

'Will you tell the de Bohuns?' asked Alice.

'D'you think I should?' said Agnes, and Alice told her Johanna was going to be a nun, so Sir Richard and Lady de Bohun believed now they'd not have any grandchildren. 'They may be pleased to find they have a grandson after all.'

'Even if he's a bastard?' said Agnes.

Alice shrugged. 'They might not mind too much.'

Alice thought it'd be kinder to warn Margaret that Agnes had returned home, and ask her if she could bring Agnes and her new husband to visit her and Sir Richard. She sent Matthew up to the manor with the message first thing in the morning and it was not long before the boy returned saying they were all to come for dinner.

After all that had passed, Agnes was nervous of seeing Lady de Bohun again, and even more so, Sir Richard. Despite her mother's assurance that the de Bohuns would welcome the discovery of a grandson, Agnes voiced all sorts of concerns.

'Suppose they think I was just one of the village floosies?'

Alice shook her head. 'They won't think that, Agnes.'

John scoffed. 'Though you must know, sis, our noble young knight took a tumble with nearly every girl in the village, so the de Bohuns are hardly going to be surprised he did with you too.' He sounded as if he was speaking in jest, but Agnes looked stricken and Alice glared at him. But, taking no notice, he blundered on. 'Baby Richard's probably not the only grandchild the de Bohuns have got in Meonbridge—'

For the first time, the expression on Jack's face changed from one of goodwill to anger. Perhaps he thought his newfound brother-in-law had gone too far and opened his mouth to make some sort of retort. But Alice, incensed by John's tactlessness, gestured to Jack to leave the retort to her.

'John atte Wode, will you hold your mischievous tongue,' she said, her voice raised to a level that shocked even John into silence. 'It may be common enough knowledge that Sir Philip had a roving eye for the maids of Meonbridge, but no other girl has ever claimed him as the father of her child.'

She pointed a quivering finger in the direction of the baby. 'Richard is the de Bohuns' *only* grandchild,' she said, with such decisiveness that John lowered his eyes and slunk away to the storeroom to busy himself with some unforeseen task.

When they first arrived at the manor, Alice took Margaret aside and told her in a low whisper intended only for her ears that Agnes would understand if she and Sir Richard didn't wish to acknowledge the baby as their grandchild. But, to Alice's horrified surprise, Margaret seemed aghast and led her even further away from the rest of the company, into the small chamber behind the solar arras, to continue their conversation in greater privacy.

'I don't understand, Alice,' she said, her eyes flashing. 'I assumed the child's parents were Agnes and her husband. Are you telling me this child is Philip's?'

Alice nodded, her face ablaze with embarrassment that she'd misjudged the warmth of Margaret's earlier welcome of the baby. 'I'm so sorry, my lady,' she said, her voice quavering, 'I'd assumed you'd realise...'

Margaret's face quickly softened and she shook her head. 'No, Alice, I did not.'

She went over to the window and gazed out at the manor's fields and forests, which stretched far into the distance but today were shrouded in a fog of rain. She stood quietly for a while, then, sighing heavily, turned back to Alice.

'Of course it would've taken little wit to work out that the child is rather too old to be the son of the charming Jack.' She smiled. 'And why else would Agnes name him "Richard"?'

She took Alice's hands in hers and held them gently. 'My dear friend, forgive me for my sharpness.'

Alice looked up at her. 'Will Sir Richard be shocked at this discovery, d'you think?' she said, now not so confident in her earlier prediction. But Margaret laughed lightly and shook her head.

'I think he will be delighted. He has been so melancholy since Johanna insisted on joining the priory, for the prospect of having *no* grandchildren means that Meonbridge and his other estates would pass to a distant cousin. Such an outcome for his guardianship of the de Bohun lands has greatly disheartened him.'

She smiled at Alice. 'I think he will welcome his namesake. The child may not be legitimate, but he is the grandson Richard has longed for and I believe he will consider him an unexpected gift from God. I have discovered, Alice, that my husband is more tender-hearted than you might expect.'

'Let's hope his heart beats tenderly when his eyes fall upon the child,' said Alice, praying silently that Margaret's judgement of her husband was correct.

The two women returned to the company just as Richard blustered into the hall, letting in a squall of wind and rain as he came through the main door. 'You called for me, madam,' he said to Margaret, somewhat alarming Alice by the testiness of his tone.

But Margaret took his arm and spoke soothingly to him. 'Yes, my dear, for it is dinner time and we have guests, as I told you before you went out.' She gave him the sunniest of smiles and his bad humour seemed to melt away.

'Ah, yes,' he said. 'Young Agnes atte Wode has returned.' He looked across at the group of people clustered together close to the warmth of the hearth. 'Where is she?'

Agnes, her face pale, stepped forward and dropped him a low curtsey.

'Ah, yes,' he said again. 'Agnes with the golden curls, the prettiest maid in Meonbridge. And the one most likely to have stolen my son's heart. And who'd be surprised at that?' He grinned mischievously.

Alice looked across at Margaret to see her mouth drop open with unbecoming astonishment, and she herself hardly knew what emotion she should allow her face to express, for it seemed Richard knew all along about his son's love for her daughter. Agnes blushed deeply as Richard took her hand and lifted her to her feet.

'And who has come with you, my dear?' he said. Agnes gestured towards Jack, who was staring at the floor, and Richard allowed her to lead him towards her husband.

'My lord, this is my husband, Jack Sawyer,' she said. 'A carpenter.'

Jack bowed his head and Richard clapped him on the shoulder. 'Good!' he said. 'Meonbridge is in sore need of a skilled carpenter.'

Jack nodded and tried to smile, and Alice thought how hard this must be for him. And she thought again how very fortunate Agnes was to have found a man like Jack, who loved her enough to bring up another man's illegitimate child as his own.

Alice saw Agnes take a deep breath before she then led Sir Richard to where Margaret's maid Agatha held baby Richard in her arms. 'And this, my lord, is my son, Richard,' she said, visibly trembling.

Margaret then came forward. 'Agnes's son. And your grandson, Richard.'

No-one present, except perhaps Lady de Bohun, might have expected the reaction of Sir Richard de Bohun to this piece of news. Margaret may have claimed he had a tender heart but as Alice had never seen it revealed before she was uncertain whether to believe it. Alice held her breath for the moments that passed before Richard responded. When he did, what she saw she thought she'd unlikely ever see again, for, with tears glittering on his eyelashes, he stretched out his arms and took the child from Agatha. The company was silent as he gently held the boy upright against his chest and peered closely at his face.

Then he heaved a great sigh. 'This *is* Philip's son,' he declared, 'and my heir.' The baby reached out a hand and pulled on his grandfather's beard. Sir Richard laughed. 'My grandson,' he said, and everyone breathed out and clapped.

He carried the child around the room, introducing him to his ancestral home, while Alice marvelled at his lack of reproach for the circumstances of his grandchild's birth. Then he returned to Agnes and Jack and placed the boy in her arms.

'Take good care of my grandson, Mistress Sawyer,' he said. 'For he is a de Bohun.'

Agnes bobbed a curtsey and murmured that the child was more precious to her than life.

Then he turned to Jack. 'You'll stay in Meonbridge,' he said. It sounded like a command rather than a request but Jack didn't hesitate to agree, so Alice thought perhaps it was his intention all along. 'I'll find you a place to live,' continued Richard, 'and the carpenter's shop is vacant, if you'd like to take it on.'

Jack bowed his acceptance, and Richard again clapped him on the shoulder, beaming.

Margaret then came over to him. 'Shall we have dinner, now, my lord? I'm sure everyone must be hungry after all this excitement.' He nodded happily and taking her arm, led her and the rest of the company towards the laden trestles at the far end of the hall.

· · ·

With all that had happened, it was not until they'd almost finished dinner that Alice realised Johanna had not joined her parents' table. She turned to Margaret and asked after her daughter.

Margaret sighed and shook her head. 'Oh, Johanna never takes her meals with us. She insists on eating in her room.'

Agnes overheard her comment. 'How is Lady Johanna? I'd like to see her, if she would, my lady.'

Margaret sighed again. 'Oh, she is well enough, Agnes. But has Alice told you she has decided to become a nun? Sir Richard is furious with her for refusing the man he chose for her, but her mind is quite made up.'

'I'm sure Lady Johanna'll prove a most devout nun,' said Agnes.

Margaret smiled wanly. 'I do hope you are right, my dear—'

At that moment, Sir Richard rose from his chair, saying he had manor affairs to attend to, and inviting Jack to accompany him. Jack looked across at his wife, who nodded and smiled encouragement. The two men threw on their cloaks and, as a squire opened the door to the courtyard to let them out, Alice saw that the rain had stopped and a little sunshine was breaking through. As Richard and Jack left, all the squires and the other men, and most of the women who had been dining, also took their leave. Lady de Bohun then called Agatha over to take the baby upstairs to her chamber, and suggested to Alice and Agnes that they all retire to the solar, where perhaps Johanna would be willing to join them.

Once in the privacy of her chamber, Lady de Bohun confided to Agnes that Johanna was making herself unhappy by harbouring a secret. 'It's about you and Philip.' Agnes looked discomfited, but Margaret asked her if she might encourage Johanna to unburden herself.

When Johanna entered her mother's chamber, she seemed unsure whether to be pleased or not to see Agnes, but came forward and took Agnes's hands in hers. Agnes then indicated the baby, asleep again, in the cradle that Margaret had ordered to be brought upstairs.

'He's Philip's son,' said Agnes, and Johanna sat down heavily, covering her face with her hands.

Agnes sat by her and said that, now everything was out in the open, she no longer had a reason to keep her secret. Johanna shook her head.

'I have *every* reason, Agnes,' she said, her face wet with tears, 'for if I reveal my secret, then I will reveal my own shame, and my guilt.'

'But, my dear,' said Margaret, 'harbouring guilt is bad for your soul. Why not unburden yourself and free it from remorse?'

For answer, Johanna got up and went to kneel at her mother's prie-dieu under the window at the far end of the chamber. With her hands tightly clasped together and her head bowed low, she whispered her prayers, occasionally sighing, and occasionally allowing a sob to shudder through her body. She knelt for a long time, and the other women sat quietly, patiently waiting for her to rejoin them. At length, she raised her head a little and, as she did so, a shaft of sunlight pierced the window and shone on to her face. Smiling, she turned her face towards the light. At the other end of the room, Agnes gasped and Margaret made the mark of the cross upon her breast, whilst Alice wondered if Johanna really had just received a sign from God.

Then Johanna got to her feet and came back to join the others. She knelt before her mother and lay her head in Margaret's lap, whilst Agnes sat next to Alice with her head bowed. Johanna told her mother how she'd arranged for Philip to make love to Agnes in her room, pretending it was she who was with Agnes.

'I knew it was a sin,' she said bleakly. 'But I did it for Philip, because he asked me to... I so wanted to please him.' She bowed her head. 'I loved him too much,' she whispered, a sob catching in her throat. 'And I'll spend my life atoning for it.'

Alice looked across at Margaret, who looked back at her with eyes filled with anguish. But she seemed unable to comfort her daughter.

Then Johanna looked up and turned to Agnes. 'It was you he loved. Only you. After Isabella died, taking their unborn child with her, Philip became such an ill-mannered, bad-tempered boor I thought he was grieving for them. But it was *your* loss that he mourned, Agnes, not theirs.'

A few days later it was Christmas, and it seemed the whole village had turned out for the festivities at the manor, for as Alice gazed around the huge hall, decked out in all its Christmas finery and with enough candles at every niche and ledge to make the great chamber as bright as day, she could think of no-one who was not there.

As she looked upon her friends and neighbours, she counted the couples come together since this time last year. Among them, Henry and Susanna Miller were already expecting a baby, Ralph Ward and Emma Coupar were celebrating their betrothal, and Roger Stronge was clearly courting Alysoun Greene. Then of course there were her beloved Agnes and her faithful Jack. And Eleanor Titherige had come to the feast on the arm of her shepherd Walter Nash.

John was sitting with his younger brother, morose and miserable.

'I reckon she'll marry that shepherd,' he said to his mother, in such a melancholy mood that Alice felt her heart constrict with grief.

'Walter'd hardly be a good match for her,' she said. 'He's only a cottar, with nothing to his name.'

But John scorned her doubts. 'He knows everything there's to know about sheep,' he said bitterly. 'And these days *sheep* are all Eleanor Titherige cares about.'

EPILOGUE

Alice stood at the mill door with Susanna Miller, enjoying the warmth of the summer sun and waiting for her bag of grain to be ground into flour. Young Tom, Susanna's stepson, was sitting in the grassy yard, in the shade of a towering oak tree, with his little cousin Maud and newborn baby brother Francis. Tom's job was to look after the babies, so that Susanna could help his father run the mill. But the boy looked both bored and bad-tempered.

'Poor Tom,' said Susanna, nodding her head towards him. 'He so wants work with his Pa in the mill.'

But Alice knew Henry Miller forbade all children from entering his flour mill, and in particular his own son, Tom, who was eight years old and would have to wait until he was at least twelve before he'd be allowed even to step inside the mill house.

'I'm sorry for the boy,' said Susanna. 'But after Peter...'

Henry Miller was as desperate as any father to protect his young family. It was a task for which Henry, and most other fathers in Meonbridge, felt remarkably inadequate. His experience of life in the past twelve months proved what he thought he already knew, that men have no power to control the forces of the world around them. The Church taught that God gave men free will, but free will meant nothing when in His wrath He sent the mortality to punish them for their sins, and allowed as many innocents to die as sinners. It was hard for a simple man to understand.

Susanna went to church every day, to light candles and pray for the souls of her first husband and children, of Henry's own dead wife and children, and his sister-in-law Joan and hers. And Susanna prayed for God's mercy on the blighted life of Henry's brother, Thomas, who, having lost his wife and six of his children, had also lost his wits.

So much loss, so much pain, so many souls to pray for release from Purgatory and entry into the final sanctuary of Paradise.

Henry no longer prayed in church. From time to time he offered a private prayer, here in the mill, asking simply for the protection of his family.

But he was no longer sure anyone was listening.

Before long, Henry appeared at the mill house door, his brown hair dusty and his red, shiny face crinkled into a broad smile.

'Your flour, Mistress atte Wode,' he said, and hefted the bag into the back of Alice's little cart. 'But can't stop to natter, mistress,' he continued, 'for I've my orders from Lady de Bohun. I've hardly time to kiss my wife with all the flour I've got to grind for the feast.' Susanna giggled and Henry planted on her cheek a light, moist and dusty kiss.

Alice smiled at them both. The mill had at last returned to a place where laughter was heard daily, where the gossip was once more of betrothals and rumours of scandal and news from abroad. She was willing to believe God was once more smiling upon Meonbridge. Nothing was certain but she, along with all her neighbours, believed their lives had, for now, settled back into a steady rhythm.

Henry grinned back happily and, whistling a merry tune, ran back upstairs to fill yet another sack of flour destined for the bread and pies of the Midsummer feast.

A MESSAGE FROM THE AUTHOR...

If you've enjoyed reading *Fortune's Wheel*, please do consider leaving a brief review on your favourite site. Reviews are of enormous help to authors, both in terms of providing feedback and in building readership. Thank you!

And, if you enjoy my writing, perhaps you'd like to join "Team Meonbridge"?

In return for your support, I will send you updates on my books and my writing, and periodically ask for your help or feedback.
As a small "thank you" for joining the team, I will send you FREE novellas featuring some of the Meonbridge characters.

If you are interested, please visit my website at www.carolynhughesauthor.com and select **JOIN THE TEAM!** to open the sign up form.

I look forward to your company!

ABOUT THE AUTHOR

CAROLYN HUGHES has lived much of her life in Hampshire. With a first degree in Classics and English, she started working life as a computer programmer, then a very new profession. But it was technical authoring that later proved her vocation, as she wrote and edited material, some fascinating, some dull, for an array of different clients, including banks, an international hotel group and medical instruments manufacturers.

She has written creatively for most of her adult life, but it was not until her children flew the nest several years ago that writing historical fiction took centre stage, alongside gaining a Master's degree in Creative Writing from Portsmouth University and a PhD from the University of Southampton.

Fortune's Wheel is the first MEONBRIDGE CHRONICLE.

You can connect with Carolyn through her website www. carolynhughesauthor.com and social media:

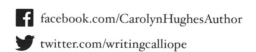

facebook.com/CarolynHughesAuthor

twitter.com/writingcalliope

ALSO BY CAROLYN HUGHES

A WOMAN'S LOT: The Second Meonbridge Chronicle

How can mere women resist the misogyny of men?

1352. In Meonbridge, a resentful peasant rages against Eleanor Titherige's efforts to build up her flock of sheep. Susanna Miller's husband, grown melancholy and ill-tempered, succumbs to idle talk that his wife's a scold. Agnes Sawyer's yearning to be a craftsman is met with scorn. And the village priest, fearful of what he considers women's "unnatural" ambitions, is determined to keep them firmly in their place.

Not all men resist women's desire for change – indeed, they want it for themselves. Yet it takes only one or two misogynists to unleash the hounds of hostility and hatred...

"I didn't so much feel as if I were reading about mediaeval England as actually experiencing it first hand." Linda's Book Bag @Lindahill50Hill

"The dialogue is very well done. I certainly felt I was right there." Chill with a Book @ChillwithaBook

"I adored this book! A highly recommended read for lovers of historical fiction." Brook Cottage Books *@BrookCottageBks*

"It's a great tribute to Carolyn's wonderful writing and her ability to recreate the era and its people that I slipped back in time quite effortlessly, and thoroughly enjoyed the experience." Being Anne @Williams13Anne

"Another fantastic piece of completely immersive historical fiction from Carolyn Hughes...I'll definitely be at the front of the queue for her next book." The Book Magnet @thebookmagnet

"...an absorbing account of the times" Historical Novel Society @histnovsoc

DE BOHUN'S DESTINY: The Third Meonbridge Chronicle

How can you uphold a lie when you know it might destroy your family?

1356. Margaret, Lady de Bohun, is horrified when her husband lies about their grandson Dickon's entitlement to inherit Meonbridge. She knows Richard lied for the best of reasons – to safeguard his family and its future – but lying is a sin. Yet she has no option but to maintain his falsehood...

Her companion, Matilda, decides that the truth about young Dickon's birth has to be told, if only to win the heart of Thorkell Boune. But she's oblivious to the danger, for Thorkell won't scruple to pursue exactly what he wants, no matter who or what gets in his way.

"This isn't a book you simply read, but an extraordinary immersive experience"
Being Anne @Williams13Anne

"In three words: Absorbing, engaging, intriguing" What Cathy Read Next
@Cathy_A_J

"A brilliantly researched, immersive and fascinating book that really brings the fourteenth century to life" Over the Rainbow Book Blog @JoannaLouisePar

"Compelling and intriguing historical fiction...it felt so real, I forgot it was fiction"
Jessica Belmont @jessicaxbelmont

"Stunning evocative writing ... a time-portal into the 14th Century" The Book
Magnet @thebookmagnet

"Rich language, a great historical vibe, strong characters, treachery and villainy, community and courage – it had everything and more." Just4mybooks @lfwrites

"Once you dip your toe into the Meonbridge Chronicles, you'll never want to leave..."
Brook Cottage Books @BrookCottagebks

Made in the USA
Coppell, TX
20 June 2021

57773997R00187